PHILLIP MARGOLIN

GONE, BUT NOT FORGOTTEN

HarperTorch
An Imprint of HarperCollinsPublishers

HARPERTORCH
An Imprint of HarperCollins*Publishers*
10 East 53rd Street
New York, New York 10022-5299

Copyright © 1993 by Phillip M. Margolin
Excerpt from *Lost Lake* copyright © 2005 by Phillip Margolin
ISBN: 0-06-073751-4

First HarperTorch paperback printing: February 2005

HarperCollins®, HarperTorch™, and ❦™ are trademarks of HarperCollins Publishers Inc.

Printed in the United States of America

Visit HarperTorch on the World Wide Web at www.harpercollins.com

10 9 8 7 6 5 4 3

Acknowledgments

A lot of people helped me transform the idea for *Gone, But Not Forgotten* into the book you are reading. Dr. William Brady and Dr. Edward Colbach answered my technical questions about medicine and psychiatry; Dr. Stanley Abrams not only reviewed my manuscript but let me borrow extensively from his paper, *The Serial Murderer*; my friend and fellow novelist Vince Kohler graciously took time from writing his most recent Eldon Larkin mystery to critique my manuscript; and my brother, Jerry, gave me his "elementary" assistance.

Once a manuscript is finished, it has to find a home. I cannot speak too highly of Jean Naggar, Teresa Cavanaugh and everyone else at the Jean V. Naggar Literary Agency. Everybody should be this lucky in their choice of an agent.

I am greatly indebted to David Gernert for the time he invested in editing *Gone, But Not Forgotten*. It is a much better book now than it was when he first read it because of his suggestions. I am also grateful to Deborah Futter for her editorial assistance and everybody at Doubleday for their support.

And, of course, there is my wife, Doreen, and my fantastic children, Daniel and Amy, who critiqued the book and provided a happy home in which to write it.

Part One

WAKE-UP CALL

Chapter One

I

"Have you reached a verdict?" Judge Alfred Neff asked the eight men and four women seated in the jury box.

A heavy-set, barrel-chested man in his mid-sixties struggled to his feet. Betsy Tannenbaum checked the chart she had drawn up two weeks ago during jury selection. This was Walter Korn, a retired welder. Betsy felt uncomfortable with Korn as the foreman. He was a member of the jury only because Betsy had run out of challenges.

The bailiff took the verdict form from Korn and handed it to the judge. Betsy's eyes followed the folded square of white paper. As the judge opened it and read the verdict to himself, she watched his face for a telltale sign, but there was none.

Betsy stole a glance at Andrea Hammermill, the plump, matronly woman sitting beside her. Andrea stared straight ahead, as subdued and resigned as she had been throughout her trial for the murder of her husband. The only time Andrea had shown any emotion was during direct examination when she explained why she shot Sidney Hammermill to death. As she told the jury about firing the revolver over and over until the dull click of hammer on steel told her there were no more bullets, her hands trembled, her body shook and she sobbed pitifully.

"Will the defendant please stand," Judge Neff said.

Andrea got to her feet unsteadily. Betsy stood with her, eyes forward.

"Omitting the caption, the verdict reads as follows: 'We the jury, being duly impaneled and sworn, do find the defendant, Andrea Marie Hammermill, not guilty . . .'"

Betsy could not hear the rest of the verdict over the din in the courtroom. Andrea collapsed on her chair, sobbing into her hands.

"It's okay," Betsy said, "it's okay." She felt tears on her cheeks as she wrapped a protective arm around Andrea's shoulders. Someone tapped Betsy on the arm. She looked up. Randy Highsmith, the prosecutor, was standing over her holding a glass of water.

"Can she use this?" he asked.

Betsy took the glass and handed it to her client. Highsmith waited a moment while Andrea regained her composure.

"Mrs. Hammermill," he said, "I want you to know that I prosecuted you because I believe you took the law into your own hands. But I also want you to know that I don't think your husband had the right to treat you the way he did. I don't care who he was. If you had come to me, instead of shooting him, I would have done my best to put him in jail. I hope you can put this behind you and go on with your life. You seem like a good person."

Betsy wanted to thank Highsmith for his kind words, but she was too choked up to speak. As Andrea's friends and supporters started to crowd around her Betsy pushed away from the throng to get some air. Over the crowd she could see Highsmith, alone, bent over his table, gathering law books and files. As the assistant district attorney started toward the door, he noticed Betsy standing on the fringe of the crowd. Now that the trial was over, the two lawyers were superfluous. Highsmith nodded. Betsy nodded back.

2

With his back arched, his sleek muscles straining and his head tipped back, Martin Darius looked like a wolf baying over fallen prey. The blonde lying beneath him tightened her legs around his waist. Darius shuddered and closed his eyes. The woman panted from exertion. Darius's face contorted, then he collapsed. His cheek fell against her breast. He heard the blonde's heart beat and smelled perspiration mingled with a telltale trace of perfume. The woman threw an arm across her face. Darius ran a lazy hand along her leg and glanced across her flat stomach at the cheap digital clock on the motel end table. It was two p.m. Darius sat up slowly and dropped his legs over the side of the bed. The woman heard the bed move and watched Darius cross the room.

"I wish you didn't have to go," she said, unable to hide her disappointment.

Darius grabbed his kit off the low-slung chest of drawers and padded toward the bathroom.

"I've got a meeting at three," he answered, without looking back.

Darius washed away the sheen of sweat he had worked up during sex, then toweled himself roughly in the narrow confines of the motel bathroom. Steam from the shower misted the mirror. He wiped the glass surface and saw a gaunt face with deep-set blue eyes. His neatly trimmed beard and mustache framed a devil's mouth that could be seductive or intimidating. Darius used a portable dryer, then combed his straight black hair and beard. When he opened the bathroom door, the blonde was still in bed. A few times, she had tried to lure him back into bed after he was showered and dressed. He guessed she was trying to exercise sexual control over him and refused to give in.

"I've decided we should stop seeing each other," Darius said casually as he buttoned his white silk shirt.

The blonde sat up in bed, a shocked expression on her normally confident, cheer-leader face. He had her attention now. She was not used to being dumped. Darius turned slightly so she would not see his smile.

"Why?" she managed as he stepped into his charcoal gray suit trousers. Darius turned to look at her so he could enjoy the play of emotions on her face.

"To your credit, you are beautiful and good in bed," he said, knotting his tie, "but you're boring."

The blonde gaped at him for a moment, then flushed with anger.

"You shit."

Darius laughed and picked up his suit jacket.

"You can't mean it," she went on, her anger passing quickly.

"I'm very serious. We're through. It was nice for a while, but I want to move on."

"And you think you can use me, then toss me away like a cigarette," she said, the anger back. "I'll tell your wife, you son-of-a-bitch. I'll call her right now."

Darius stopped smiling. The expression on his face forced the blonde back against the headboard. Darius strolled around the bed slowly, until he was standing over her. She cowered back and put her hands up. Darius watched her for a moment, the way a biologist would study a specimen on a slide. Then he grabbed her wrist and twisted her arm until she was bent forward on the bed, her forehead against the crumpled sheets.

Darius admired the curve of her body from her backside to her slender neck as she knelt in pain. He ran his free hand along her rump, then applied pressure to her wrist to make her body quiver. He liked watching her breasts sway rapidly as she jerked to attention.

"Let me make one thing very clear to you," Darius said in the same tone he might use with a recalcitrant child. "You will never call my wife, or me, ever. Do you understand?"

"Yes," the blonde gasped as he twisted her arm behind her, pushing it slowly up toward her shoulder.

"Tell me what you will never do," he commanded calmly, releasing the pressure for a moment and stroking the curve of her buttocks with his free hand.

"I won't call, Martin. I swear," she wept.

"Why won't you call my wife or bother me?" Darius asked, putting pressure on the wrist.

The blonde gasped, twitching with the pain. Darius fought back a giggle, then eased up so she could answer.

"I won't call," she repeated between sobs.

"But you haven't said why," Darius responded in a reasonable tone.

"Because you said I shouldn't. I'll do what you want. Please, Martin, don't hurt me anymore."

Darius released his hold and the woman collapsed, sobbing pitifully.

"That's a good answer. A better one would be that you won't do anything to annoy me, because I can do far worse to you than I just have. Far, far worse."

Darius knelt by her face and took out his lighter. It was solid gold, with an inscription from his wife. The bright orange flame wavered in front of the blonde's terrified eyes. Darius held it close enough for her to feel the heat.

"Far, far worse," Darius repeated. Then he closed the lighter and walked across the motel room. The blonde rolled over and lay with the white sheet tangled around her hips, leaving her slender legs and smooth back exposed. Each time she sobbed, her shoulders trembled. Martin Darius watched her in the motel mirror as he adjusted his wine-red tie. He wondered if he could convince her this was all a joke, then get her to submit to him again. The thought brought a smile to his thin lips. For a moment, he toyed with the image of the woman kneeling before him and taking him in her mouth, convinced that he wanted her back. It would be a challenge to get her on her knees after the way he had crushed her spirit. Darius was confident he could do it, but there was a meeting to attend.

"The room's paid for," he said. "You can stay as long as you want."

"Can't we talk? Please, Martin," the woman begged, sitting up and turning on the bed so that her small, sad breasts were exposed, but Darius was already closing the motel room door.

Outside, the sky looked ominous. Thick, black clouds were rolling in from the coast. Darius unlocked the door of his jet-black Ferrari and silenced the alarm. In a short while, he would do something that would increase the woman's pain. Something exquisite that would make it impossible for her to forget him. Darius smiled in anticipation, then drove off without the slightest suspicion that someone was photographing him from the corner of the motel parking lot.

• • •

Martin Darius sped across the Marquam Bridge toward downtown Portland. The heavy rain kept the pleasure boats off the Willamette River, but a rusty tanker was pushing through the storm toward the port at Swan Island. Across the river was an architectural mix of functional, gray, futuristic buildings linked by sky bridges, Michael Graves's whimsical, post-modern Portland Building, the rose-colored U.S. Bank skyscraper, and three-story historical landmarks dating back to the eighteen hundreds. Darius had made his fortune adding to Portland's skyline and rebuilding sections of the city.

Darius changed lanes just as a reporter began the lead story on the five o'clock news.

"This is Larry Prescott at the Multnomah County Courthouse speaking with Betsy Tannenbaum, the attorney for Andrea Hammermill, who has just been acquitted in the shooting death of her husband, City Commissioner Sidney Hammermill.

"Betsy, why do you think the jury voted 'not guilty'?"

"I believe it was an easy choice once the jurors understood how battering affects the mind of a woman who undergoes the frequent beatings and abuse Andrea suffered."

"You've been critical of this prosecution from the start. Do you think the case would have been handled differently if Mr. Hammermill was not a mayoral candidate?"

"The fact that Sidney Hammermill was wealthy and very active in Oregon politics may have influenced the decision to prosecute."

"Would it have made a difference if District Attorney Alan Page had assigned a woman deputy to the case?"

"It could have. A woman would have been able to evaluate the evidence more objectively than a man and might have declined prosecution."

"Betsy, this is your second acquittal in a murder case using the battered wife defense. Earlier this year, you won a million-dollar verdict against an anti-abortion group and *Time* magazine listed you as one of America's up-and-coming female trial lawyers. How are you handling your newfound fame?"

There was a moment of dead air. When Betsy answered she sounded uncomfortable.

"Believe me, Larry, I'm much too busy with my law practice and my daughter to worry about anything more pressing than my next case and tonight's dinner."

The car phone rang. Darius turned down the radio. The Ferrari purred as it pulled away from the traffic. Darius glided into the fast lane, then picked up on the third ring.

"Mr. Darius?"

"Who is this?"

Only a few people knew the number of his car phone and he did not recognize the voice.

"You don't need to know my name."

"I don't need to speak to you, either."

"Maybe not, but I thought you'd be interested in what I have to say."

"I don't know how you got this number, but my patience is wearing thin. Get to the point or I'll disconnect."

"Right. You're a businessman. I shouldn't waste your time. Still, if you hung up now, I can guarantee I'd be gone but not forgotten."

"What did you say?"

"Got your attention, huh?"

Darius took a deep, slow breath. Suddenly there were beads of perspiration on his brow and upper lip.

"Do you know Captain Ned's? It's a seafood place on Marine Drive. The bar's pretty dark. Drive there now and we'll talk."

The connection was broken. Darius lowered the phone onto its cradle. He had slowed without realizing it and there was a car on his bumper. Darius crossed two lanes of traffic and pulled onto the shoulder of the road. His heart was racing. There was a shooting pain in his temples. Darius closed his eyes and leaned back against the headrest. He willed his breathing back to normal and the pain in his temples eased.

The voice on the phone was rough and uncultured. The man would be after money, of course. Darius smiled grimly. He dealt with greedy men all the time. They were the easiest to manipulate. They always believed the person they were dealing with was as stupid and frightened as they were.

The pain in his temples was gone now and Darius was breathing easily again. In a way he was grateful to the caller. He had grown complacent, believing he was safe after all these years, but you were never safe. He would consider this a wake-up call.

3

Captain Ned's was weathered wood and rain-spattered glass jutting out over the Columbia River. The bar was as dark as the voice promised. Darius sat in a booth near the kitchen, ordered a beer and waited patiently. A young couple entered, arm in arm. He dismissed them. A tall, balding salesman in a disheveled suit sat on a stool at the bar. Most of the tables were taken by couples. Darius scanned the other booths. A heavy-set man in a trench coat smiled and stood up after Darius fixed on him.

"I was waiting to see how long it would take you," the man said as he slipped into the booth. Darius did not reply. The man shrugged and stopped smiling. It was unsettling to sit opposite Martin Darius, even if you thought you held the winning hand.

"We can be civilized about this or you can be bitchy," the man said. "It don't matter to me. In the end, you'll pay."

"What are you selling and what do you want?" Darius answered, studying the fleshy face in the dim light.

"Always the businessman, so let's get down to business. I've been to Hunter's Point. The old newspapers were full of information. There were pictures, too. I had to look hard, but it was you. I got one here, if you'd like to see," the man said, sliding his hand out of his coat pocket and pushing a photocopy of a newspaper front page across the table. Darius studied it for a moment, then slid it back.

"Ancient history, friend."

"Oh? You think so? I have friends on the force, Martin. The public don't know yet, but I do. Someone has been leaving little notes and black roses around Portland. I figure it's the same person who left 'em in Hunter's Point. What do you think?"

"I think you're a very clever man, Mr. . . . ?" Darius said, stalling for time to dope out the implications.

The man shook his head. "You don't need my name, Martin. You just have to pay me."

"How much are we talking about?"

"I thought two hundred and fifty thousand dollars would be fair. It'd cost you at least that much in attorney fees."

The man had thinning, straw-colored hair. Darius could see flesh between the strands when he bent forward. The nose had been broken. There was a gut, but the shoulders were thick and the chest heavy.

"Have you told the people who hired you about Hunter's Point?" Darius asked.

There was a brief flicker of surprise, then a flash of nicotine-stained teeth.

"That was terrific. I ain't even gonna ask how you figured it out. Tell me what you think."

"I think you and I are the only ones who know, for now."

The man did not answer.

"There is one thing I'd like to know," Darius said, eyeing him curiously. "I know what you think I've done. What I'm capable of doing. Why aren't you afraid I'll kill you?"

The man laughed.

"You're a pussy, Martin, just like the other rape-os I run into in the joint. Guys who were real tough with women and not so tough with anyone else. You know what I used to do to those guys? I made 'em my girls, Martin. I turned 'em into little queens. I'd do it to you too, if I wasn't more interested in your money."

While Darius considered this information, the man watched him with a confident smirk.

"It will take me a while to come up with that much money," Darius said. "How much time can you give me?"

"Today is Wednesday. How's Friday?"

Darius pretended to be considering the problems involved with liquidating stocks and closing accounts.

"Make it Monday. A lot of my holdings are in land. It will take me until Friday to arrange for loans and sell some stock."

The man nodded. "I heard you didn't believe in

bullshit. Good. You're doing the right thing. And, let me tell you, friend, I'm not someone to fuck with. Also, I'm not greedy. This'll be a one-shot deal."

The man stood. Then he thought of something and grinned at Darius.

"Once I'm paid, I'll be gone *and* forgotten."

The man laughed at his little joke, turned his back and left the bar. Darius watched him go. He did not find the joke, or anything else about the man, amusing.

4

A hard rain hit the windshield. Big drops, falling fast. Russ Miller switched the wiper to maximum. The cascade still obliterated his view of the road and he had to squint to catch the broken center line in the headlight beams. It was almost eight, but Vicky was used to late suppers. You put in the hours at Brand, Gates and Valcroft if you expected to get anywhere. Russ grinned as he imagined Vicky's reaction to the news. He wished he could drive faster, but a few more minutes would not make much difference.

Russ had warned Vicky he might not be home on time as soon as Frank Valcroft's secretary summoned him. At the advertising firm, it was an honor to be asked into Valcroft's corner office. Russ had been there only twice before. The deep, wine-colored carpets and dark wood reminded him of where he wanted to be. When Valcroft told him he was going to be in charge of the Darius Construction account, Russ knew he was on his way.

Russ and Vicky had been introduced to Martin Darius this summer at a party Darius hosted to celebrate the opening of his new mall. All the men who worked on the account were there, but Russ had this feeling that Darius had singled him out. An invitation to join Darius on his yacht arrived a week later. Since then, he and Vicky had been guests at two house parties. Stuart Webb, another account executive at Brand, Gates, said he felt like he was standing in a chill wind when he was with Darius, but Darius was the most dynamic human being Russ had ever met and he had a knack for making Russ feel like the most important person on Earth. Russ was certain that Martin Darius was responsible for making him the team leader of the Darius Construction account. If Russ was successful as team leader, who knew what he would be doing in the future. He might even leave Brand, Gates and go to work for the man himself.

As Russ pulled into his driveway the garage door opened automatically. The rain pounding on the garage roof sounded like the end of the world and Russ was glad to get inside the warm kitchen. There was a large, metal pot on the stove, so he knew Vicky was making pasta. The surprise would be the sauce. Russ shouted Vicky's name as he peeked under the cover of another pot. It was empty. There was a cutting board covered with vegetables, but none of them was sliced. Russ frowned. There was no fire under the large pot. He lifted the lid. It was filled with water, but the pasta was lying, uncooked, next to the pasta maker he had bought Vicky for their third anniversary.

"Vick," Russ shouted again. He loosened his tie and took off his jacket. The lights were on in the living room. Later, Russ told the police he had not called sooner because everything looked so normal. The set was on. The Judith Krantz novel Vicky was reading was open and facedown on the end table. When he realized Vicky was not home, he assumed she was over at one of the neighbors.

The first time Russ went into the bedroom, he missed the rose and the note. His back was to the bed when he stripped off his clothes and hung them in the closet. After that, he slipped into a warm-up suit and checked the cable guide to see what was on TV. When fifteen more minutes passed without Vicky, Russ went back into the bedroom to phone her best friend, who lived down the block. That was when he saw the note on the pillow on the immaculately made bed. There was a black rose lying across the plain, white paper. Written in a careful hand were the words "Gone, But Not Forgotten."

Chapter Two

As Austin Forbes, the President of the United States, walked toward United States Senator Raymond Francis Colby he passed through the rays of sunlight streaming through the high French windows of the Oval Office, creating the impression that God was spotlighting a chosen son. Had he noticed, the diminutive Chief Executive would have appreciated the vote of confidence from above. The results of his earthly polls were not nearly as complimentary.

"Good to see you, Ray," Forbes said. "You know Kelly Bendelow, don't you?"

"Kelly and I have met," Colby said, remembering the in-depth interview the President's troubleshooter had conducted just two weeks before.

Senator Colby sat in the chair the President indicated and glanced out the east windows toward the rose garden. The President sat in an old armchair that had graced his Missouri law office and followed him up the ladder of power to the Oval Office. He looked pensive.

"How's Ellen?" Forbes asked.

"She's fine."

"And are you fine? You're in good health?"

"Excellent health, Mr. President. I had a thorough

physical last month," Colby answered, knowing that the FBI would have furnished Forbes with his doctor's report.

"No personal problems. Everything's going well at home? Your finances are sound?"

"Ellen and I are celebrating our thirty-second anniversary next month."

Forbes stared hard at Colby. The good old boy vanished and the hard-nosed politician who had carried forty-eight states in the last election took his place.

"I can't afford another fiasco like this Hutchings thing," Forbes said. "I'm telling you this in confidence, Ray. She lied to me. Hutchings sat where you're sitting and lied. Then that reporter for the *Post* found out and . . ."

Forbes let the thought trail off. Everyone in the room was painfully aware of the blow that had been dealt to Forbes's prestige when the Senate voted against confirming the nomination of Mabel Hutchings.

"Is there anything in your past that can cause us problems, Ray? Anything at all? When you were c.e.o. of Marlin Steel did you ever pay a corporate bribe? Did you use marijuana at Princeton or Harvard Law? Did you knock up some girl in high school?"

Colby knew the questions were not ridiculous. The aspirations of presidential hopefuls and Supreme Court nominees had run aground on just such rocky shoals.

"There will be no surprises, Mr. President."

The silence in the Oval Office grew. Then Forbes spoke.

"You know why you're here, Ray. If I nominate you to be Chief Justice of the United States, will you accept?"

"Yes, Mr. President."

Forbes grinned. The tension in the room evaporated.

"We make the announcement tomorrow. You'll make a great Chief Justice."

"I'm indebted to you," Colby said, not trusting himself to say more. He had known the President would make the offer when he was summoned to the White House, but that did not keep him from feeling as light as a free-floating cloud.

Raymond Colby sat up as quietly as possible and shuffled his feet along the carpet until he found his slippers. Ellen Colby stirred on the other side of their king-size bed. The senator watched the moonlight play on her peaceful features. He shook his head in amazement. Only his wife could sleep the sleep of angels after what had happened today.

There was a liquor cabinet in the den of Colby's Georgetown town house. Colby fixed himself some bourbon. On the upper landing the antique grandfather clock ticked away the seconds, each movement of the ancient hands perfectly audible in the stillness.

Colby rested his glass on the fireplace mantel and picked up a framed and fading black and white photograph that had been taken the day his father argued a case before the United States Supreme Court. Howard Colby, a distinguished partner in Wall Street's most prestigious law firm, died at his desk two months after the photograph was taken. Raymond Colby may have been first at Harvard Law, c.e.o. of Marlin Steel, the governor of New York and a United States senator, but he always saw himself in relationship to his father as he had been that day on the steps of the Court, a ten-year-old boy under the protection of a wise and gruff giant whom Raymond remembered as the smartest man he had ever known.

There were fifty-three broad steps leading from the street to the entrance to the Court. Raymond had counted as he climbed them, hand in hand with his father. When they passed between the columns supporting the west portico, his father had stopped to point out "Equal Justice Under Law" engraved in the bone-white marble of the Great Hall.

"That's what they do here, Raymond. Justice. This is the court of last resort. The final place for all lawsuits in this great country."

Massive oak doors guarded the Court's chambers, but the courtroom was intimate. Behind a raised mahogany bench were nine high-backed chairs of various styles. When the justices filed to their seats, his father stood. When Howard Colby addressed the Court, Raymond was surprised to hear respect in the voice of a man who commanded the respect of others. These men in black, these wise men who towered over Howard Colby and commanded his respect, left a lasting impression. On the train ride back to New York, Raymond swore silently to sit some day upon the bench of the nation's highest court. His dream would come true when the President made his announcement at tomorrow's press conference.

The waiting had begun Friday when a White House source told him that the President had narrowed his choice to the senator and Alfred Gustafson of the Fifth Circuit Court of Appeals. This afternoon, during their meeting in the Oval Office, the President told Colby it was his membership in the Senate that made the difference. After the disastrous defeat of Mabel Hutchings, his first nominee, the President wanted a sure thing. The Senate was not going to reject one of its own, especially someone with Colby's credentials. All he need do now was pass through the nominating process unscathed.

Colby put down the photograph and picked up his

drink. It was not only the excitement of the nomination that kept him from sleep. Colby was an honest man. When he told the President that there was no scandal in his past, he was telling the truth. But there *was* something in his past. Few people knew about it. Those who did could be trusted to keep silent. Still, it concerned him that he had not been entirely candid with the man who was fulfilling his greatest dream.

Colby sipped his drink and stared at the lights of the capital. The bourbon was doing its job. His tense muscles were relaxing. He felt a bit sleepy. There was no way to change history. Even if he knew what the future would bring, he was certain he would have made no other choice. Worrying now would not change the past and the chances of his secret surfacing were very small. Within the hour the senator was sound asleep.

Chapter Three

I

The pathetic thing was that after the affairs and the lies, not to mention the divorce settlement, which left Alan Page living in the same type of shabby apartment he had lived in when he was a law student, he still loved Tina. She was what he thought about when he was not thinking about work. Going to a movie did not help, reading a book did not help, even bedding the women with whom his well-meaning friends fixed him up did not help. The women were the worst, because he always found himself comparing and they never stacked up. Alan had not been with a woman in months.

The district attorney's mood was starting to affect his staff. Last week, Randy Highsmith, his chief deputy, had taken him aside and told him to shape up, but he still found it hard to cope with bachelorhood after twelve years of what he thought was a good marriage. It was the sense of betrayal that overwhelmed him. He had never cheated on Tina or lied to her and he felt that she was the one person he could trust completely. When he found out about her secret life, it was too much. Alan doubted he would ever fully trust anyone again.

Alan pulled into the City garage and parked in the spot reserved for the Multnomah County district attorney, one of the few things Tina hadn't gotten in the divorce, he mused bitterly. He opened his umbrella and raced across the street to the courthouse. The wind blew the rain under the umbrella and almost wrenched it from his hand. He was drenched by the time he ducked inside the gray stone building.

Alan ran a hand through his damp hair while he waited for the elevator. It was almost eight. Around him, in the lobby, were young lawyers trying to look important, anxious litigants hoping for the best and dreading the worst, and a bored-looking judge or two. Alan was not in the mood for aimless social chatter. When the elevator came, he pushed six and stepped to the rear of the car.

"Chief Tobias wants you to call," the receptionist told him as soon as he entered the district attorney's office. "He said it was important."

Alan thanked her and pushed open the low gate that separated the waiting area from the rest of the offices. His private office was the first on the right along a narrow hall.

"Chief Tobias called," his secretary said.

"Winona told me."

"He sounded upset."

It was hard to imagine what could upset William Tobias. The slender police chief was as unflappable as an accountant. Alan shook out his umbrella and hung up his raincoat, then sat behind his large desk and dialed across the street to police headquarters.

"What's up?" Alan asked.

"We've got another one."

It took a moment for Alan to figure out what Tobias was talking about.

"Her name is Victoria Miller. Twenty-six. Attractive, blond. Housewife. No kids. The husband is with Brand, Gates and Valcroft, the ad agency."

"Is there a body?"

"No. She's just missing, but we know it's him."

"The same note?"

"On the bed on the pillow. 'Gone, But Not Forgotten.' And there's another black rose."

"Was there any sign of a struggle this time?"

"It's just like the others. She could have disappeared in a puff of smoke."

Both men were silent for a moment.

"The papers still don't know?"

"We're lucky there. Since there aren't any bodies, we've been handling them like missing persons cases. But I don't know how long we can keep this quiet. The three husbands aren't going to just sit around. Reiser, the lawyer, is on the phone every day, two or three times a day, and Farrar, the accountant, is threatening to go public if we don't come up with something soon."

"Do you have anything?"

"Not a thing. Forensics is stumped. We've got no unusual fibers or hairs. No fingerprints. You can buy the notepaper at any Payless. The rose is an ordinary rose. Ditto the black dye."

"What do you suggest?"

"We're doing a computer search on the m.o. and I've got Ross Barrow calling around to other police departments and the FBI."

"Are you looking into possible connections between the victims?"

"Sure. We've got lots of obvious similarities. The three women are around the same age, upper middle-class, childless, housewives with executive-type husbands. But we've got nothing connecting the victims to each other."

Tobias could have been describing Tina. Alan closed his eyes and massaged the lids.

"What about health clubs, favorite stores, reading circles? Do they use the same dentist or doctor?" Alan asked.

"We've thought of all those and a dozen more."

"Yeah, I'm sure you have. How far apart is he working?"

"It looks like one a month. We're into what? Early October? Farrar was August and Reiser was September."

"Christ. We better get something going soon. The press will eat us alive once this breaks."

"Tell me about it."

Alan sighed. "Thanks for calling. Keep me up-to-date."

"You got it."

Alan hung up and swiveled his chair so he could look out the window. Man, he was tired. Tired of the rain and this asshole with the black rose and Tina and everything else he could think of. More than anything, he wanted to be by himself on some sun-soaked beach where there were no women and no phones and the only decision he would have to make was about the strength of his suntan lotion.

2

No one ever called Elizabeth Tannenbaum stunning, but most men found her attractive. Hardly anyone called her Elizabeth, either. An "Elizabeth" was regal, cool, an eye-catching beauty. A "Betsy" was pleasant to look at, a tiny bit overweight, capable, but still fun to be with. Betsy suited her just fine.

A Betsy could also be a bit frazzled at times and that was how Betsy Tannenbaum felt when her secretary buzzed her just as she was stuffing the papers on the Morales case into her briefcase so she could work on them at home this evening, after she picked up Kathy from day care and cooked dinner and straightened the house and played with Kathy and . . .

"I can't take it, Ann. I'm late for day care."

"He says it's important."

"It's always important. Who is it?"

"He won't say."

Betsy sighed and looked at the clock. It was already four-thirty. If she got Kathy by five and rushed to the store, she would not be done cooking until six. On the other hand, if she did not keep bringing in clients she would have all day to shop. Betsy stopped pushing papers into her briefcase and picked up the phone.

"Betsy Tannenbaum."

"Thank you for taking the call. My name is Martin Darius."

Betsy caught her breath. Everyone in Portland knew who Darius was, but he did not call many of them.

"When does your staff leave?" Darius asked.

"Around five, five-fifteen. Why?"

"I need to speak to you this evening and I don't want anyone to know about it, including your secretary. Would six be convenient?"

"Actually, no. I'm sorry. Is there any way we can meet tomorrow? My schedule is pretty open then."

"How much is your normal fee, Mrs. Tannenbaum?"

"One hundred dollars an hour."

"If you'll meet me at six tonight, I'll pay you twenty-five hundred dollars for the consultation. If I decide to hire you, you will be extremely pleased by the fee."

Betsy took a deep breath. She dreaded doing it, but she was going to have to call Rick. She simply could not afford to turn down that kind of money or such a high-profile client.

"Can I put you on hold, Mr. Darius? I have another obligation and I want to see if I can get someone else to take care of it."

"I can hold."

Betsy dialed Rick Tannenbaum on the other line. He was in a meeting, but his secretary put her through.

"What is it, Betsy? I'm very busy," Rick said, making no attempt to hide his annoyance.

"I'm sorry to bother you, but I have an emergency. A client needs to meet me at six. Can you get Kathy at day care?"

"What about your mother?"

"She's playing bridge and I don't have the number at her friend's house."

"Just tell the client you'll meet him tomorrow."

"He can't. It has to be tonight."

"Damn it, Betsy, when we separated, you promised you wouldn't do this to me."

"I'm really sorry," Betsy said, as angry at herself for begging as she was at Rick for making this so difficult. "I rarely ask you to pick up Kathy, but I need you, this once. Please."

Rick was silent for a moment.

"I'll do it," he answered angrily. "When do I have to be there?"

"They close at six. I really appreciate this."

Betsy hung up quickly, before Rick could change his mind.

"Six will be fine, Mr. Darius. Do you know the address of my office?"

"Yes," Darius said, and the line went dead. Betsy put the phone down slowly and sank into her chair, wondering what business a man like Martin Darius could possibly have with her.

Betsy glanced at her watch. It was six thirty-five and Darius had not arrived. She was annoyed that he had kept her waiting after she had put herself out, but not annoyed enough to jeopardize a twenty-five-hundred-dollar fee. Besides, the wait had given her time to work on the Morales case. She decided to give Darius another half hour.

Rain spattered against the window behind her. Betsy yawned and swiveled her chair so she could look out into the night. Most of the offices in the building across the way were deserted. She could see cleaning women starting to work. By now, her own building was probably deserted, except for the night people. The silence made her a little uncomfortable. When she swiveled back, Darius was standing in the doorway. Betsy started.

"Mrs. Tannenbaum?" Darius said, as he entered the room. Betsy stood. She was almost five feet eleven, but she had to look up to Darius. He extended his hand, exposing the exquisite gold cuff links that secured his French cuffs. His hand was cold and his manner distant. Betsy did not believe in auras, but there was definitely something about the man that did not come across on television or in newspaper photos.

"I'm sorry to be so mysterious, Mrs. Tannenbaum," Darius said when they were seated.

"For twenty-five hundred dollars you can wear a mask, Mr. Darius."

Darius grinned. "I like an attorney with a sense of humor. I haven't met too many of them."

"That's because you deal with business lawyers and tax attorneys. Criminal lawyers don't last long without a sense of humor."

Darius leaned back in his chair and looked around Betsy's cluttered office. It was her first and it was small and cramped. She had made just enough money this year to think about moving to larger quarters. If she ever collected the verdict in the abortion case she would definitely move, but that case was bogged down in the appellate courts and she might never see a penny.

"I was at a charity affair for the Portland Opera the other night," Darius said. "Do you go?"

"I'm afraid not."

"Too bad. It's quite good. I had an interesting discussion with Maxine Silver. She's on the staff. A very strong-minded woman. We were discussing Greig's book. Have you read it?"

"The novel by the serial killer?" Betsy asked, puzzled by the direction the conversation was taking.

Darius nodded.

"I've seen a few reviews, but I don't have time to read anything but legal periodicals. It's not my kind of book, anyway."

"Don't judge the book by its author, Mrs. Tannenbaum. It's really a very sensitive work. A coming-of-age story. He handles the subject of his protagonist's abuse with such tenderness that you almost forget what Greig did to those children. Still, Maxine felt it shouldn't have been published, solely because Greig wrote it. Do you agree with her?"

Darius's question was strange but Betsy decided to play along.

"I'm opposed to censorship. I would not ban a book because I disapproved of the person who wrote it."

"If the publisher bowed to pressure from, say, women's groups and withdrew the book from circulation, would you represent Greig?"

"Mr. Darius . . ."

"Martin."

"Is there a point to these questions or are you just making small talk?"

"Humor me."

"I could represent Greig."

"Knowing that he's a monster?"

"I would be representing a principle, Mr. Darius. Freedom of speech. *Hamlet* would still be *Hamlet*, even if Charles Manson wrote it."

Darius laughed. "Well put." Then he took a check out of his pocket.

"Tell me what you think, after reading this," he said, placing the check on the desk between them. The check was made out to Elizabeth Tannenbaum. It was for $58,346.47. Something about the figure was familiar. Betsy frowned for a moment, then flushed when she realized the sum was her exact gross income for the previous year. Something Darius would know only if he had access to her tax returns.

"I think someone has been invading my privacy," Betsy snapped, "and I don't like it."

"Twenty-five hundred dollars of this is your fee for this evening's consultation," Darius said, ignoring Betsy's anger. "The rest is a retainer. Place it in trust and keep the interest. Someday, I may ask you to return it. I may also ask you to represent me, in which case you may charge me whatever you believe the case is worth over and above the retainer."

"I'm not certain I want to work for you, Mr. Darius."

"Why? Because I had you investigated? I don't blame you for being angry, but a man in my position can't take chances. There is only one copy of the investigative report and I'll send it to you no matter how our meeting concludes. You'll be pleased to hear what your colleagues have to say about you."

"Why don't you give this money to the firm that handles your business affairs?"

"I don't wish to discuss this matter with my business lawyers."

"Are you being investigated in connection with a crime?"

"Why don't we discuss that if it becomes necessary."

"Mr. Darius, there are a number of excellent criminal defense attorneys in Portland. Why me?"

Darius looked amused. "Let's just say that I believe you are the most qualified person to handle my case, should representation become necessary."

"I'm a little leery of taking a case on this basis."

"Don't be. You're under no obligation. Take the check, use the interest. If I do come to you and you decide you can't represent me, you can always give the money back. And, I can assure you, if I'm accused I will be innocent and you will be able to pursue my defense with a clear conscience."

Betsy studied the check. It was almost four times the largest fee she'd ever earned and Martin Darius was the type of client a sane person did not turn down.

"As long as you understand I'm under no obligation," Betsy said.

"Of course. I'll send you a retainer agreement that spells out the terms of our arrangement."

They shook hands and Betsy showed Darius out. Then she locked the door and reentered her office. When Betsy was certain Darius was gone, she gave the check a

big kiss, gave a subdued whoop and whirled around. A
Betsy was allowed to indulge in immature behavior from
time to time.

3

Betsy was in a terrific mood by the time she parked her
station wagon in her carport. It was not so much the retainer, but the fact that Martin Darius had chosen her
over all the other attorneys in Portland. Betsy was building a reputation with cases like *State* v. *Hammermill*, but
the big-money clients were still going to the big-name
criminal defense attorneys. Until this evening.

Rick Tannenbaum opened the door before Betsy
fished her key out of her purse. Her husband was slender
and an inch shorter than Betsy. His thick black hair was
styled to fall across his high forehead, and his smooth skin
and clear blue eyes made him look younger than thirty-
six. Rick had always been overly formal. Even now, when
he should be relaxing, his tie was still knotted and his suit
coat was on.

"Damn it, Betsy, it's almost eight. Where were
you?"

"My client didn't come until six-thirty. I'm sorry."

Before Rick could say anything else Kathy came
tearing down the hall. Betsy dumped her briefcase and
purse on a chair and scooped up their six-year-old daughter.

"I made a picture. You have to come see," Kathy
yelled, fighting to get down as soon as she received a hug
and kiss from her mother.

"Bring it to the kitchen," Betsy answered, lowering
Kathy to the floor and taking off her jacket. Kathy

streaked down the hall toward her bedroom with her long, blond hair flying after her.

"Please don't do this to me again, Betsy," Rick said, when Kathy was far enough away so she wouldn't hear. "I felt like a fool. I was in a meeting with Donovan and three other lawyers and I had to tell them I couldn't participate any longer because I had to pick up my daughter from day care. Something we agreed is your responsibility."

"I'm sorry, Rick. Mom wasn't available and I had to meet this client."

"I have clients too and a position to maintain in my firm. I'm trying to make partner and that's not going to happen if I get a reputation as someone who can't be relied on."

"For Christ's sake, Rick. How many times have I asked you to do this? She's your daughter, too. Donovan understands you have a child. These things happen."

Kathy rushed into the kitchen and they stopped arguing.

"This is the picture, Mom," Kathy said, thrusting forward a large piece of drawing paper. Betsy scrutinized the picture while Kathy looked up at her expectantly. She was adorable in her tiny jeans and striped, long-sleeve shirt.

"Why Kathy Tannenbaum," Betsy said, holding the picture at arm's length, "this is the most fantastic picture of an elephant I have ever seen."

"It's a cow, Mom."

"A cow with a trunk?"

"That's the tail."

"Oh. You're sure it's not an elephant?"

"Stop teasing," Kathy said seriously.

Betsy laughed and returned the picture with a hug

and kiss. "You are the greatest artist since Leonardo da Vinci. Greater even. Now let me get dinner ready."

Kathy ran back to her room. Betsy put a frying pan on the stove and took out a tomato and some lettuce for a salad.

"Who is this big client?" Rick asked.

Betsy didn't want to tell Rick, especially since Darius wanted his visit kept secret. But she felt she owed Rick the information.

"This is very confidential. Will you promise not to breathe a word if I tell you?"

"Sure."

"Martin Darius retained me, tonight," she said, breaking into a huge grin.

"Martin Darius?" Rick answered incredulously. "Why would he hire you? Parish, Marquette and Reeves handles his legal work."

"Apparently he thinks I'm also capable of representing him," Betsy answered, trying not to show how much Rick's reaction hurt her.

"You don't have a business practice."

"I don't think it's a business matter."

"Then what is it?"

"He didn't say."

"What's Darius like?"

Betsy thought about the question. What was Darius like?

"Spooky," Betsy answered just as Kathy hurtled back into the kitchen. "He likes to be mysterious and he wants you to know how powerful he is."

"What are you cooking, Mom?"

"Roast, little girl," Betsy said, picking up Kathy and nibbling her neck until she squealed. "Now, buzz off or I'll never get dinner ready."

Betsy lowered Kathy to the floor. "Do you want to

stay for dinner?" she asked Rick. He looked uncomfortable and checked his watch.

"Thanks, but I've got to get back to the office."

"All right. Thanks, again, for picking up Kathy. I do know how busy you are and I appreciate the help."

"Yeah, well . . . Sorry I jumped down your throat. It's just . . ."

"I know," Betsy said.

Rick looked like he was going to say something but went to the closet instead and got his raincoat.

"Good luck with Darius," Rick told her as he was leaving. Betsy shut the door behind him. She had heard the hint of jealousy in his voice and regretted telling Rick about her new client. She should have known better than to say anything that would let him know how well she was doing.

" 'But it takes time to make a raft, even when one is as industrious and untiring as the Tin Woodman, and when night came the work was not done. So they found a cozy place under the trees where they slept well until the morning; and Dorothy dreamed of the Emerald City, and of the good Wizard of Oz, who would soon send her back to her own home again.'

"And now," Betsy said, closing the book and laying it on Kathy's bed, "it's time for my little wizard to hit the hay."

"Can't you read one more chapter?" Kathy begged.

"No, I cannot read another chapter," Betsy said, giving Kathy a hug. "I already read you one more than you were entitled to. Enough is enough."

"You're mean, Mommy," Kathy said, with a smile Betsy could not see because her cheek was against Kathy's baby-soft hair.

"That's tough. You're stuck with the world's meanest mommy and there's nothing you can do about it." Betsy kissed Kathy's forehead, then sat up. "Now get to bed. I'll see you in the morning."

"Night, Mom."

Kathy rolled onto her side and wrestled Oliver, an oversized, stuffed skunk, into position against her chest.

"Night, hon."

Betsy closed the door of Kathy's room behind her and went into the kitchen to wash the dishes. Although she would never admit it to her feminist friends, Betsy loved washing dishes. It was perfect therapy. A lawyer's day was littered with stressful situations and insoluble problems. Washing dishes was a finite task that Betsy could do perfectly every time she tried. Instant gratification from a job well done, over and over again. And Betsy needed some instant gratification after being with Rick.

She knew why he was so angry. Rick had been a superstar in law school and Donovan, Chastain and Mills had lured him to their two-hundred-lawyer sweatshop with a large salary and glowing promises of a fast track to a partnership. The firm had worked him like a dog, constantly holding the partnership just out of reach. When he was passed over last year, just as her career was starting to take off, it had been a crushing blow to his ego. Their ten-year-old marriage had not been able to withstand the strain.

Two months ago, when Rick told her he was leaving, Betsy was stunned. She knew they had problems, but she'd never imagined that he would walk out. Betsy had searched her memory for a clue to Rick's jealousy. Had he changed or was he always so self-centered? Betsy had trouble believing that Rick's love was too fragile to withstand her success, but she was not willing to give up her career to appease his ego. Why should she? The way she saw it, it was a matter of Rick accepting her as an equal. If he couldn't do that then she could never stay married to him. If he loved her, it should not be such a hard thing to do. She was proud of his achievements. Why couldn't he be proud of hers?

Betsy poured herself a glass of milk and turned off the light. The kitchen joined the rest of the house in soothing darkness. Betsy carried her glass to the kitchen table and slumped into a chair. She took a sip and gazed sleepily out the window. Many of the houses in the neighborhood were dark. A streetlight cast a pale glow over a corner of the front yard. It was so quiet with Rick gone and Kathy asleep. No traffic sounds outside, no television on. None of the little noises people make shuffling around a house.

Betsy had handled enough divorces to know that many estranged husbands would never have done what Rick had done for her tonight. He had done it for Kathy, because he loved her. And Kathy loved Rick. The separation was very hard on their daughter. There were times, like now, when the house was quiet and Betsy was alone, that she missed Rick. She was not certain she loved him anymore, but she remembered how good it had been. Sleeping alone was the hardest thing. She missed the lovemaking, but she missed the cuddling and the pillow talk more. Sometimes she thought they might get back together. Tonight, before Rick left, she was certain that there was something he wanted to tell her. What was he about to say? And if he said he wanted her back, what would she say? After all, he was the one who had walked out on ten years of marriage, a child, their life together. They were a family and Rick's actions told her that meant nothing to him.

The night Rick walked out, alone in bed, when she

couldn't cry anymore, Betsy had rolled on her side and
stared at their wedding picture. Rick was grinning. He
had told her he had never been so happy. She had been
so filled with joy, she was afraid she could not hold all of
it. How could a feeling like that disappear?

Chapter Four

I

"Late night?" Wayne Turner's secretary asked, trying, unsuccessfully, to conceal a grin.

"It shows, huh?"

"Only to those who know how perky you usually look."

The night before, Turner, Senator Raymond Colby's administrative assistant, had gotten stinking drunk celebrating the senator's nomination to the Supreme Court. This morning he was paying for his sins, but he didn't mind. He was happy for the old gent, who had done so much for him. His only regret was that Colby had not run for President. He would have made a great one.

Turner was five feet nine and slender. He had a narrow face, high cheekbones, close-cropped, kinky black hair that was graying at the temples and brown skin a few shades darker than his tan suit. Turner weighed about what he had when he first met Colby. He hadn't lost his intensity, but the scowl that used to be a permanent feature had wilted over the years. Turner hung his jacket on a hook behind the door, lit his fourth Winston of the day and sat behind his cluttered desk. Framed in the window at his back was the shining, white dome of the Capitol.

Turner shuffled through his messages. Many were from reporters who wanted the inside scoop on Colby's nomination. Some were from a.a.s for other senators who were probably calling about Colby's crime bill. A few were from partners in prestigious Washington law firms, confirmation that Turner need not be worried about what he would do after the senator became Chief Justice. Washington power brokers were always interested in someone who had the ear of a powerful man. Turner would do all right, but he would miss working with the senator.

The last message in the stack caught Turner's eye. It was from Nancy Gordon, one of the few people whose call he would have returned yesterday afternoon if he had made it back to the office. Turner assumed she was calling about the nomination. There was a Hunter's Point, New York, number on the message slip.

"It's Wayne," he said when he heard the familiar voice at the other end. "How you doin'?"

"He's surfaced," Gordon answered without any preliminaries. It took Turner a few seconds to catch on, then he felt sick.

"Where?"

"Portland, Oregon."

"How do you know?"

She told him. When she was through, Turner asked, "What are you going to do?"

"There's a flight to Portland leaving in two hours."

"Why do you think he started again?"

"I'm surprised he held out for so long," Gordon answered.

"When did you get the letter?"

"Yesterday, around four. I just came on shift."

"You know about the senator?"

"Heard it on the news."

"Do you think there's a connection? The timing, I mean. It seems odd it would be so soon after the President made the announcement."

"There could be a connection. I don't know. And I don't want to jump to conclusions."

"Have you called Frank?" Turner asked.

"Not yet."

"Do it. Let him know."

"All right."

"Shit. This is the absolute, worst possible time for this to happen."

"You're worried about the senator?"

"Of course."

"What about the women?" Gordon asked coldly.

"Don't lay that trip on me, Nancy. You know damn well I care about the women, but Colby is my best friend. Can you keep him out of it?"

"I will if I can."

Turner was sweating. The plastic receiver was uncomfortable against his ear.

"What will you do when you find him?" he asked nervously. Gordon did not answer immediately. Turner could hear her breathing deeply.

"Nancy?"

"I'll do what I have to."

Turner knew what that was. If Nancy Gordon found the man who had haunted their dreams for the past ten years, she would kill him. The civilized side of Wayne Turner wanted to tell Gordon that she should not take the law into her own hands. But there was a primitive side of Wayne Turner that kept him from saying it, because everyone, including the senator, would be better off if the

man Homicide Detective Nancy Gordon was stalking
died.

2

The microwave buzzed. Alan Page backed into the
kitchen, keeping one eye on the television. The CBS
anchorman was talking about the date that had been set
for Raymond Colby's confirmation hearing. Colby would
give the Supreme Court a solid conservative majority and
that was good news, if you were a prosecutor.

Alan took his TV dinner out of the microwave, giving
the food the briefest of glances. He was thirty-seven, with
close-cropped black hair, a face that still bore the scars of
acne and a sense of purpose that made most people nervous. His rail-thin body suggested an interest in distance
running. In fact, Alan was thin because he had no use for
food and ate the bare minimum that would keep him going. It was worse now that he was divorced. On a good
day, breakfast was instant coffee, lunch a sandwich and
more black coffee and dinner a pizza.

A reporter was interviewing someone who knew
Colby when he was c.e.o. of Marlin Steel. Alan used the
remote to jack up the volume. From what he was hearing,
there was nothing standing in the way of Colby's confirmation as Chief Justice of the United States. The doorbell
rang just as the Colby story ended. Alan hoped it wasn't
business. There was a Bogart classic on at nine that he'd
been looking forward to all day.

The woman standing on Alan's doorstep held a briefcase over her head to shield herself from the rain. A
small, tan valise stood beside her. A taxi was waiting at

the curb, its wipers swinging back and forth and its headlight beams cutting through the torrent.

"Alan Page?"

He nodded. The woman flipped open a leather case she was clutching in her free hand and showed Alan her badge.

"Nancy Gordon. I'm a homicide detective with the Hunter's Point P.D. in Hunter's Point, New York. Can I come in?"

"Of course," he said, stepping back. Gordon signaled the taxi, then ducked inside. She held the briefcase at arm's length, shook off the water on the welcome mat, then pulled in the valise.

"Let me take your coat," Alan said. "Can I get you something to drink?"

"Hot coffee, please," Gordon answered as she handed him her raincoat.

"What's a detective from New York doing in Portland, Oregon?" Alan asked as he hung the coat in the hall closet.

"Does the phrase 'Gone, But Not Forgotten' mean anything to you, Mr. Page?"

Alan stood perfectly still for a second, then turned around. "That information hasn't been released to the public. How do you know about it?"

"I know more than you can imagine about 'Gone, But Not Forgotten,' Mr. Page. I know what the note means. I know about the black rose. I also know who took your missing women."

Alan needed a moment to think.

"Please sit down and I'll get your coffee," he told Gordon.

The apartment was small. The living room and kitchen were one space divided by a counter. Gordon chose an armchair near the television and waited patiently while Alan mixed water from a tea kettle with Folger's instant. He handed the cup to the detective, turned off the set, then sat opposite her on the couch. Gordon was tall with an athlete's body. Alan guessed she was in her mid-thirties. Her blond hair was cut short. She was attractive without working at it. The most striking thing about the detective was her utter seriousness. Her dress was severe, her eyes were cold, her mouth was sealed in a straight line and her body was rigid, like an animal prepared to defend itself.

Gordon leaned forward slightly. "Think of the most repulsive criminals, Mr. Page. Think of Bundy, Manson, Dahmer. The man leaving these notes is smarter and far more dangerous than any of them, because they're all dead or in prison. The man you're after is the man who got away."

"You know who he is?" Alan asked.

Gordon nodded. "I've been waiting for him to surface for ten years."

Gordon paused. She looked into the steam rising from her cup. Then she looked back at Alan.

"This man is cunning, Mr. Page, and he's different. He's not human, the way we think of human. I knew he wouldn't be able to control himself forever and I was right. Now he's surfaced and I can catch him, but I need your help."

"If you can clear this up, you've got all the help you want. But I'm still confused about who you are and what you're talking about."

"Of course. I'm sorry. I've been involved with this case so long, I forget other people don't know what happened. And you'll need to know it all or you won't understand. Do you have the time, Mr. Page? Can I tell you now? I don't think we can wait, even until morning. Not while he's still out there, free."

"If you're not too tired."

Gordon stared into Alan's eyes with an intensity that forced him to look away.

"I'm always tired, Mr. Page. There was a time when I couldn't sleep without pills. I'm over that, but the nightmares haven't stopped and I still don't sleep well. I won't until he's caught."

Alan did not know what to say. Gordon looked down. She drank more coffee. Then she told Alan Page about Hunter's Point.

Part Two

HUNTER'S POINT

Chapter Five

I

The sprawling, two-story colonial was in the middle of a cul-de-sac, set well back from the street. A large, well-tended lawn created a wide buffer zone between the house and those on either side. A red Ferrari was parked in the driveway in front of a three-car garage.

Nancy Gordon knew it was going to be bad as soon as she saw the stunned expressions on the faces of the neighbors, who huddled just outside the police barriers. They were shocked by the presence of police cars and a morgue wagon in the quiet confines of The Meadows, where the houses started at half a million and crime was simply not permitted. She knew it was going to be really bad when she saw the grim faces of the two homicide detectives who were talking in low tones on the lawn near the front door.

Nancy parked her Ford behind a marked car and squeezed through the sawhorses. Frank Grimsbo and Wayne Turner stopped their conversation when they saw her. She was dressed in jeans and a T-shirt. The call had come while she was sprawled in front of the TV in a ratty nightgown, sipping a cheap white wine and watching the Mets smoke the Dodgers. The clothes were the first thing she could find and the last thing she thought about.

"Newman said there's a body this time," she said excitedly.

"Two." .

"How can we be sure it's him?" Nancy asked.

"The note and the rose were on the floor near the woman," Grimsbo answered. He was a big man with a beer gut and thinning black hair who wore cheap plaid jackets and polyester slacks.

"It's him all right," said Turner, a skinny black man with close-cropped hair and a permanent scowl who was in his second year in night law school. "The first cop on the scene was smart enough to figure out what was going on. He called me right away. Michaels did the note and the crime scene before anyone else was let in."

"That was a break. Who's the second victim?"

"Melody Lake," Grimsbo answered. "She's six years old, Nancy."

"Oh, fuck." The excitement she felt at finally getting a body disappeared instantly. "Did he . . . Was there anything done to her?"

Turner shook his head. "She wasn't molested."

"And the woman?"

"Sandra Lake. The mother. Death by strangulation. She was beaten pretty badly, too, but there's no evidence of sexual activity. Course, she hasn't been autopsied."

"Do we have a witness?"

"I don't know," Grimsbo answered. "We have uniforms talking to the neighbors, but nothing yet. Husband found the bodies and called it in to 911 about eight-fifteen. He says he didn't see anyone, so the killer must have left way before the husband got home. We got a cul-de-sac here and it leads into Sparrow Lane, the only road out of the development. The husband would have seen someone coming in or out."

"Who's talked to him?"

"I did, for a few minutes," Turner answered. "And the first cops on the scene, of course. He was too bent out of shape to make any sense. You know him, Nancy."

"I do?"

"It's Peter Lake."

"The attorney?"

Grimsbo nodded. "He defended Daley."

Nancy frowned and tried to remember what she could about Peter Lake. She had not done much in the Daley investigation. All she recalled about the defense attorney were his good looks and efficient manner. She was on the stand less than a half hour.

"I better go in," Nancy said.

The entryway was huge. A small chandelier hung overhead. A sunken living room was directly in front of her. The room was spotless. She could see a small man-made lake out back through a large picture window. Strategically placed around the room, most probably by an interior decorator, were bleached oak tables with granite tops, chairs and a sofa in pastel shades and macramé wall hangings. It looked more like a showroom than a place where people lived.

A wide staircase was off to the left. A polished wood banister followed the curve of the stairs to the second floor. The posts supporting the banister were closely spaced. Through the spaces, halfway up the stairs, Nancy could see a small lump covered by a blanket. She turned away.

Lab technicians were dusting for prints, taking photographs and collecting evidence. Bruce Styles, the deputy medical examiner, was standing with his back to her in the middle of the entryway between a uniformed officer and one of his assistants.

"You finished?" Nancy asked.

The doctor nodded and stepped aside. The woman was facedown on the white shag carpet. She was wearing a white cotton dress. It looked well suited for the heat. Her feet were bare. The woman's head was turned away. Blood matted her long brown hair. Nancy guessed she had been brought down by a blow to the head, and Styles confirmed her suspicion.

"I figure she was running for the door and he got her from behind. She could have been partly conscious or completely out when he strangled her."

Nancy walked around the body so she could see the woman's face. She was sorry she looked. If the woman had been attractive, there was no way to tell now. Nancy took a couple of deep breaths.

"What about the little girl?" she asked.

"Neck broken," Styles answered. "It would have been quick and painless."

"We think she was a witness to the mother's murder," Turner said. "Probably heard her screaming and came down the steps."

"Where's the husband?" Nancy asked.

"Down the hall in the den," Turner said.

"No sense putting it off."

Peter Lake slumped in a chair. Someone had given him a glass of scotch, but the glass was still more than half full. He looked up when Nancy entered the den and she could see he had been crying. Even so, he was a striking man, tall with a trim, athletic build. Lake's styled, gold-blond hair, his pale blue eyes and sharp, clean-shaven features were what won over the women on his juries.

"Mr. Lake, do you remember me?" Nancy asked.

Lake looked confused.

"I'm a homicide detective. My name is Nancy Gordon. You cross-examined me in the Daley case."

"Of course. I'm sorry. I don't handle many criminal cases anymore."

"How are you feeling?" Nancy asked, sitting across from Lake.

"I'm numb."

"I know what you're going through . . ." Nancy started, but Lake's head jerked up.

"How could you? They're dead. My family is dead."

Lake covered his eyes with his hands and wept. His shoulders trembled.

"I do know how you feel," Nancy said softly. "A year ago my fiancé was murdered. The only good thing that came out of it was that I learned how victims really feel, and sometimes I can even help them get through the worst of it."

Lake looked up. He wiped his eyes. "I'm sorry," he said. "It's just so hard. They meant everything to me. And Melody . . . How could someone do that to a little girl? She couldn't hurt anybody. She was just a little girl."

"Mr. Lake, four women have disappeared in Hunter's Point in the past few months. A black rose and a note, identical to the ones you found, were left at each home. I know how much you're grieving, but we have to act fast. This is the first time we have actually found a victim. That could mean you surprised the killer before he had time to take your wife away. Anything you can tell us would be deeply appreciated and may help us catch this man before he kills again."

"I don't know anything. Believe me, I've thought

about it. I was working late on a case. I called to let Sandy know. I didn't see anything unusual when I drove up. Then I . . . I'm really not too clear on what I did after I . . . I know I sat down on the bottom step."

Lake paused. He breathed deeply, trying to keep from crying again. His lip trembled. He took a sip of his scotch.

"This is very hard for me, Detective. I want to help, but . . . Really, this is very hard."

Nancy stood up and placed a hand on Lake's shoulder. He began to weep again.

"I'm going to leave my card. I want you to call me if I can do anything for you. Anything. If you remember something, no matter how insignificant you may believe it to be, call me. Please."

"I will. I'll be better in the morning and I'll . . . It's just . . ."

"It's all right. Oh, one other thing. The media will be after you. They won't respect your privacy. Please don't talk to them. There are many aspects of this case we are not going to release to the public. We keep back facts to help us eliminate phony confessions and to identify the real killer. It's very important that you keep what you know to yourself."

"I won't talk to the press. I don't want to see anyone."

"Okay," Nancy said kindly. "And you're going to be all right. Not one hundred percent, and not for a long time, but you'll deal with your grief. It won't be easy. I'm still not healed, but I'm better, and you'll be better too. Remember what I said about calling. Not the police business. You know, if you just want to talk."

Lake nodded. When Nancy left the den, he was sprawled in the chair, his head back and his eyes closed.

2

Hunter's Point was a commuter suburb with a population of 110,000, a small downtown riddled with trendy boutiques and upscale restaurants, a branch of the State University, and a lot of shopping centers. There were no slums in Hunter's Point, but there were clusters of Cape Cods and garden apartments on the fringe of the downtown area that housed students and families unable to afford the high-priced developments like The Meadows, where the commuting lawyers, doctors and businessmen lived.

Police headquarters was a dull, square building on the outskirts of town. It sat in the middle of a flat, black-topped parking lot surrounded by a chain link fence. The lot was filled with police cars, unmarked vehicles and tow trucks.

The rose killer task force was housed in an old storage area in the back of the building. There were no windows, and the fluorescent lights were annoyingly bright. A watercooler was squeezed between two chest-high filing cabinets. A low wood table stood on rickety legs against a cream-colored wall. On the table sat a coffee maker, four coffee mugs, a sugar bowl and a brown plastic cup filled with several packets of artificial creamer. Four gunmetal-gray, government-issue desks were grouped in the center of the room. Bulletin boards with pictures of the victims and information about the crimes covered two walls.

Nancy Gordon hunched over her reports on the Lake murders. The flickering fluorescents were starting to give her a headache. She closed her eyes, leaned back and pinched her lids. When she opened her eyes, she was staring at the photographs of Samantha Reardon and Patricia Cross that Turner had tacked to the wall. The photos had been supplied by their husbands. Samantha on the deck of a sailboat. A tall woman, the wind blowing her flowing brown hair behind her, a smile of genuine happiness brightening her face. Pat in shorts and a halter top on a beach in Oahu, very slender, too thin, actually. Her friends said she was overly conscious of her figure. Except for Reardon, who had been a nurse, none of the women had ever held a meaningful job, and Reardon stopped working soon after her marriage. They were happy housewives living in luxury, spending their time at golf and bridge. Their idea of contributing to the community was raising money for charity at country club functions. Where were these women now? Were they dead? Had they died quickly, or slowly, in agony? How had they held up? How much of their dignity were they able to retain?

The phone rang. "Gordon," she answered.

"There's a Mr. Lake at the front desk," the receptionist said. Nancy straightened up. Less than seventy-two hours had passed since her visit to the crime scene.

"I'll be right out," Gordon said, dropping her pen on a stack of police reports.

Inside the front door of the police station was a small lobby furnished with cheap chairs upholstered in imitation leather and outfitted with chrome armrests. The lobby was separated from the rest of the building by a counter with a sliding glass window and a door with an electronic lock. Lake was seated in one of the chairs. He was dressed in a dark suit and solid maroon tie. His hair was carefully combed. The only evidence of his personal tragedy was red-rimmed eyes that suggested a lack of sleep and a lot of mourning. Nancy hit the button next to the receptionist's desk and opened the door.

"I wasn't certain you'd be here," Lake said. "I hope you don't mind my showing up without calling."

"No. Come on in. I'll find us a place to talk."

Lake followed Nancy down a hall that reminded him of a school corridor. They walked on worn green linoleum that buckled in places, past unpainted brown wood doors. Chipped flakes of green paint fell from spots on the walls. Nancy opened the door to one of the interrogation rooms and stood aside for Lake. The room was covered with white, soundproof tiles.

"Have a seat," Nancy said, motioning toward one of the plastic chairs that stood on either side of a long wooden table. "I'll grab us some coffee. How do you take yours?"

"Black," Lake answered.

When Nancy returned with two Styrofoam cups, Lake was sitting at the table with his hands in his lap.

"How are you feeling?" she asked.

"I'm very tired, and depressed. I tried going to work today, but I couldn't concentrate. I keep thinking about Melody."

Lake stopped. He took a deep breath. "Look, I'll get to the point. I can't work, and I have a feeling I'm not going to be able to work for quite a while. I sat down with the papers on a real estate closing this morning and it seemed so . . . It just didn't mean anything to me.

"I have two associates who can keep my practice going until I'm able to cope, if that ever happens. But now all I want to do is find out who killed Sandy and Melody. It's all I can think about."

"Mr. Lake, it's all I can think about too. And I'm not alone. I'm going to tell you some things. This is highly confidential. I'll need your promise to keep it confidential."

Lake nodded.

"There were four disappearances before your wife and daughter were killed. None of those women has been found. It took us a while to catch on, because there were no bodies. At first, we treated them like missing persons. But a note with 'Gone, But Not Forgotten' and a black rose was left at each crime scene, so after the second one we knew what we were dealing with. The chief has put together a task force to work on the cases. . . ."

"I'm sure you're working very hard," Lake interrupted. "I didn't mean to be critical. What I want to do is help. I want to volunteer to be part of the task force."

"That's out of the question, Mr. Lake. You aren't a police officer. It also wouldn't be advisable. You're too emotionally involved to be objective."

"Lawyers are trained to be objective. And I can add something to the investigation—the unique insight into the criminal mind that I developed as a defense attorney. Defense attorneys learn things about the way criminals think that the police never know, because we have the criminal's confidence. My clients know they can tell me anything, no matter how horrible, and I will respect their privacy. You see criminals when their false face is on. I see them the way they really are."

"Mr. Lake, police officers get a real good look at the criminal mind—too good. We see these guys on the street, in their homes. You see them cleaned up, in your office, a long way from their victims and after they've had time to rationalize what they've done and cook up a sob story or a defense. But none of that matters, because you simply cannot work on this case. As much as I appreciate the offer, my superiors wouldn't allow it."

"I know it sounds strange, but I really do think I could contribute. I'm very smart."

Nancy shook her head. "There's another good reason you shouldn't get involved in this investigation—it would mean reliving the death of your wife and daughter every day, instead of getting on with your life. We have their autopsy photos lying around, their pictures posted on the wall. Do you want that?"

"I have their pictures all over my house and office, Detective Gordon. And there isn't a minute I don't think about them."

Nancy sighed. "I know," she said, "but you have to stop thinking about them that way or it will kill you."

Lake paused. "Tell me about your fiancé," he said quietly. "How . . . how did you stop thinking about him?"

"I never did. I think about Ed all the time. Especially at night, when I'm alone. I don't want to forget him and you won't want to forget Sandy and Melody.

"Ed was a cop. A drunk shot him. He was trying to calm down a domestic dispute. It was two weeks before our wedding date. At first I felt just like you do. I couldn't work. I could barely make it out of bed. I . . . I was racked with guilt, which is ridiculous. I kept on thinking there was something I could have done, insisted he stay home that day, I don't know. I wasn't really making much sense.

"But it got better, Mr. Lake. Not all better, not even mostly better. You just get to a point where you face the fact that a lot of the pain comes from feeling sorry for yourself, for what you've lost. Then you realize that you have to start living for yourself. You have to go on and keep the memories of the good times. If you don't, then whoever killed your little girl and your wife will have won. They will have killed you too."

Nancy reached across the table and put her hand on Peter Lake's arm.

"We'll get him, Mr. Lake. You have so much to deal

with, you don't want to get involved with this too. Let us handle it. We'll get him, I promise."

Lake stood up. "Thank you, Detective Gordon."

"Nancy. Call me Nancy. And give me a call anytime you want to talk."

3

A week later, Hunter's Point Chief of Police John O'Malley entered the task force office. He was usually in shirtsleeves with his tie askew and his top button open. This morning, O'Malley wore the navy blue suit he saved for Rotary Club speeches and meetings with the city council.

The chief had the broad shoulders and thick chest of a middleweight boxer. His nose had been broken by a fleeing burglar when he worked in New York's South Bronx. His receding red hair revealed an old scar, a memento of one of many gang fights he had been in as a youth in Brooklyn. O'Malley would have stayed in New York City if a heart attack hadn't forced him to pursue police work in a less stressful environment.

Walking behind O'Malley was a huge man dressed in a tan summer-weight suit. Nancy guessed that the suit was custom-tailored, because it fit perfectly, even though the man was oddly oversized, like a serious bodybuilder.

"This is Dr. Mark Klien," O'Malley said. "He's a psychiatrist who practices in Manhattan, and an expert on serial killers. Dr. Klien was consulted in the Son of Sam case, the Atlanta child murders, Bundy. He's worked with VICAP. I met him a few years ago when I was with the NYPD and working a serial case. He was very helpful.

Dr. Klien's seen a full set of reports on these disappearances and the deaths of Melody and Sandra Lake.

"Dr. Klien," O'Malley said, pointing to each member of the task force in turn, "this is Nancy Gordon, Frank Grimsbo, Wayne Turner and Glen Michaels. They've been on this case since it started."

Dr. Klien was so massive, he filled the entrance to the office. When he stepped into the room to shake hands, someone else followed him in. O'Malley looked uncomfortable.

"Before Dr. Klien gets started, I want to explain why Mr. Lake is here. Yesterday the mayor and I met. He explained that Mr. Lake was volunteering to assist the task force in finding the killer of his wife and daughter."

Nancy Gordon and Frank Grimsbo exchanged worried glances. Wayne Turner's mouth opened and he stared at O'Malley. O'Malley flushed angrily, stared back and continued.

"The mayor feels that Mr. Lake brings a unique insight into the criminal mind, developed as a defense attorney, that will give us a fresh perspective on the case."

"I hope I'll be of use," Peter Lake said, smiling apologetically. "I know I'm not a trained policeman, so I'll try to keep out of the way."

"Dr. Klien has a busy schedule," O'Malley said, ignoring Lake. "He has to take a two-fifty shuttle back to the city, so I'm going to let him take over."

Lake took a seat behind everyone in the back of the room. Frank Grimsbo shook his head slowly. Wayne Turner folded his arms across his chest and stared accusingly at O'Malley. Nancy frowned. Only Glen Michaels, the chubby, balding criminologist O'Malley had assigned to do the forensic work for the task force, seemed uninterested in Lake. He was riveted on Mark Klien, who went to the front of the room and stood before a wall covered with victim information.

"I hope what I have to say is of some use to you," Klien said, talking without notes. "One disadvantage a small department like Hunter's Point has in these cases is its inexperience with crimes of this type. Although even larger departments are usually at a loss, since serial killers, for all the suffering they cause and all the publicity they receive, are, fortunately, rare birds. Now that the FBI has established the Violent Crime Apprehension Program in Quantico, small departments, like yours, can forward a description of your case to VICAP and learn if any similar murders have taken place in other parts of the country. VICAP uses a computer program to list violent crimes and their descriptions throughout the country and can hook you up with other police agencies where similar crimes may have occurred, so you can coordinate your investigation.

"What I want to do today is give you a profile of the serial killer in order to dispel any stereotypes you may have and list some common factors you can look for. The FBI has identified two separate categories: the disorganized asocial and the organized nonsocial. Let's discuss the latter type first. The organized nonsocial is a sexual psychopath and, like any psychopath, he is unable to empathize, to feel pity or caring for others. His victims are simply objects he uses as he wishes to serve his own perverted needs. Venting his anger is one of these needs, whether through mutilation or debasing the victim. The Boston Strangler, for example, placed his victims in a position so that the first sight anyone had of them as they entered the room was to see them with their legs spread apart. Another killer mailed the foot of his victim to her parents in order to expand the pain and misery he had already caused."

"Excuse me, Dr. Klien," Wayne Turner said. "Is it possible that our killer is leaving the notes to torment the husbands?"

"That's a good possibility. The cruelty in torturing a victim's loved ones, and thereby creating more victims, would be very attractive to a sexual psychopath, since he is unaffected by any moral code and has no sense of remorse. He is capable of any act. Preserving body parts and eating them is not unusual, and having sex with the corpse of a victim is even less rare. Lucas decapitated one of his victims and had oral sex with the head for a week until the odor became so extreme he had to dispose of it."

"Is that the type of crazy bastard we're dealing with here?" Grimsbo asked.

"Not 'crazy,' Detective. In spite of the extremes of their behavior, these people are not legally insane. They are well aware of what is morally and legally right and wrong. The terrifying thing is that they do not learn from their experiences, so neither treatment nor imprisonment is likely to alter their behavior. In fact, because of the compulsiveness associated with these sexual acts, it is most likely that they will kill again."

"What does the black rose mean?" Nancy asked.

"I don't know, but fantasy and compulsion are very much a part of these killers' actions, and the rose could be part of the killer's fantasy. Prior to the killing, they fantasize about it in great detail, planning very specifically what they will do. This increases their level of excitement or tension so that ultimately their act is one of compulsion. When the murder is completed there is a sense of relief until the tension builds up again, starting the cycle anew. Son of Sam talked of the great relief he felt after each killing, but he also demonstrated his faulty judgment when he said he did not know why his victims struggled so much, since he was only going to kill them, not rape them.

"Since fantasy is so much involved in their behavior, these killers often take a specific body part or item of clothing with them. They use it to relive the act. This heavy use of fantasy also results in the crimes being very well planned. The Hillside Strangler not only brought a weapon, he brought plastic bags to help him dispose of the bodies. This could account for the absence of forensic evidence at your crime scenes. I would guess that your killer is very knowledgeable in the area of police investigation. Am I correct that an analysis of the notes and the roses have yielded no clues, and that the crime scenes haven't turned up so much as a fiber or hair that's been of use?"

"That's pretty much true," answered Glen Michaels. "We did get a print from the Lake note, but it turned out to be the wife's. All the other notes were spotless and there was nothing unusual about the paper or the ink. So far, the lab hasn't picked up a thing we can use."

"I'm not surprised," Klien said. "There is a peculiar interest among these men with police and police work. Some of them have even been involved on the fringes of law enforcement. Bundy attended FBI lectures and Bianchi was in security work and in the police reserve. That means they may be aware of the steps they must take to avoid detection. Their interest in police work may also lie in a need to know how close the police are to catching them.

"Let's talk about the victims. Usually they're accidental, in that the killer simply drives around until he fixes on someone. Prostitutes make easy victims, because they'll get in a car or even allow themselves to be tied up. The victim is generally not from the killer's home turf and is usually a stranger, which makes apprehension much more difficult."

"Do you see that as being true in our case?" Nancy asked. "I mean, these women all fit a pattern. They're married to professionals, they don't have regular jobs, and except for Mrs. Lake they were all childless. They're also from the same town. Doesn't that show advance planning? That he's looking for a particular victim who fits into his fantasy, rather than grabbing women at random?"

"You're right. These victims don't seem to fit the usual pattern of random selection. It's pretty clear that your killer is stalking a particular type of woman in a particular area, which suggests he may live in Hunter's Point."

"What I don't understand is how he gets to them," Wayne Turner said. "We're dealing with educated women. They live in upscale neighborhoods where the residents are suspicious of strangers. Yet there's no sign of a struggle at any home but the Lakes', and, even there, the crime scene was relatively undisturbed."

Klien smiled. "You've brought us to one of the major misconceptions about serial killers, Detective Turner. In the movies they're portrayed as monsters, but in real life they fit into the community and do not look suspicious. Typically, they're bright, personable, even good-looking men. Bundy, the I-5 Bandit, the Hillside Strangler, Cortez—they're all respectable-looking men. So our killer is probably someone these women would let into their home without fear."

"Didn't you say there were two types of serial killers?" Grimsbo asked.

"Yes. There's also the disorganized asocial killer, but in this case we're not dealing with someone who fits that category. That's unfortunate, because they're easier to catch. They're psychotic loners who relate quite poorly to others and don't have the charm or ability to melt into the community. Their acts are impulsive and the weapon is usually whatever is at hand. The body is often mangled or blood-smeared and they frequently get blood all over themselves. The crime scenes can be very gruesome. They're also not mobile, like the organized nonsocials. Their homicides often take place close to their homes and they often return to the scene of the crime, not to check up on the investigation, but to further mutilate the body or relive the killing. Rarely do they penetrate the body sexually. They usually masturbate on it or in the immediate area, which can be helpful, now that we have workable DNA testing. But your boy is much too clever to be a disorganized asocial."

"Why haven't we found the bodies?" Turner asked.

"He's obviously hiding them, like the Green River Killer. Chief O'Malley tells me there's a lot of farmland and forest in this area. Someday a hiker is going to stumble on a mass grave and you'll have your bodies."

"What will they look like, Dr. Klien?" Nancy asked.

"It won't be pretty. We're dealing with a sexual sadist. If he has his victim isolated and he has time . . . You see, these men are expressing their rage toward their women victims. The mutilation and murder increases their sexual stimulation. In some instances, where the killer is usually impotent, the violence makes sex possible. The fantasy and the torture are the foreplay, Detective. The killing is the penetration. Some of these men ejaculate automatically at the moment they kill."

"Jesus," Grimsbo muttered. "And you say these guys aren't crazy."

"I said they weren't crazy, but I didn't say they were human. Personally, I see the man you're looking for as less than human. Somewhere along the way, some of the things that make us human were lost, either because of genetics or environment or . . . Well," Klien shrugged, "it really doesn't matter, does it, because he's beyond hope and must be stopped. Otherwise he'll go on and on and on, as long as there are women out there for him to feed on."

4

Nancy Gordon, Wayne Turner, Frank Grimsbo and Glen Michaels were waiting in O'Malley's office when he returned from dropping Dr. Klien at the airport.

"I sort of expected this," he said, when he saw them.

"Then please explain to us what the fuck is going on," Turner demanded.

"There's no way to sugarcoat it," O'Malley said. "I argued with the mayor and lost, period. We're stuck with Lake."

"You're shitting me," Grimsbo said.

"No, Frank, I'm not shitting you. I'm telling you the facts of political life."

"The guy's a potential suspect," Grimsbo said.

"Let's get this on the table, boys and girls, because I might be able to dump him, if it's true."

"I don't think it is, John," Nancy said. "I've met with him a few times and he's pretty broken up about losing his wife and kid."

"Yeah," Turner countered, "but he says he didn't see anyone coming from the house. Where did the killer go? There's only one road out of that development from the cul-de-sac."

"The neighbors didn't see anyone either," Nancy said.

"No one saw anyone at the scene of any of the disappearances, Wayne," said Glen Michaels.

"What I want to know is what a civilian is doing on a police investigation," Grimsbo said.

O'Malley sighed. "Lake's fixed politically. He's known as a criminal lawyer because he won that insanity defense for that fruitcake Daley. But the guy's specialty is real estate law and he's made a few million at it, some of which he has contributed to the mayor's campaign chest. He's also a major contributor to the governor and he serves on some land use planning council in Albany. The bottom line is, the governor called the mayor yesterday, who then called me to explain how Lake's experience as a criminal lawyer will be invaluable in the investigation and how lucky we are to have him on our team. The press is already on the mayor's ass for keeping the disappearances quiet until the Lake murders forced his hand. He's desperate for results and he's not going to buck a request from the governor or a major campaign contributor."

"I don't trust him," Turner said. "I had a case with Lake a few years back. We served a warrant on this guy and found a kilo of coke in his room. There was a pregnant woman at the house with no record. She swore the coke was hers and the guy was doing her a favor by letting her stay in his room while she was expecting. The defendant beat the case and the d.a. didn't even bother to indict the chick. I could never prove it, but I heard rumors that Lake paid the woman to perjure herself."

"Anyone else heard anything like that?" O'Malley asked.

Michaels shook his head. "He's cross-examined me two or three times. My impression is that he's very bright. He did an excellent job in a case involving blood-spatter evidence. Really had me going up there."

"I've heard he's a smart guy," Grimsbo said, "but I've heard those rumors about the fix too, and a few of the lawyers I know don't like Lake's ethics. He's still a suspect, even if he's a long shot, and I just don't like the idea of a citizen working on something this sensitive."

"Look, I agree with you, Frank," O'Malley said. "It stinks. But it doesn't matter. Until I can convince the mayor otherwise, Lake stays. Just try to keep him out from under our feet. Give him lots of busy work, make him read all the reports. If something comes up you don't want him to see, or there's trouble, come to me. Any questions?"

Turner muttered something about the mayor and Grimsbo shook his head in disgust. O'Malley ignored them.

"Okay, get outta here and back to work. You all heard Klien. We have to stop this psycho fast."

5

Nancy Gordon's stomach growled. She guessed it was a little after six. Her watch said it was almost seven. She had been writing reports and lost track of time. On the way out of the station, she walked by the task force office and noticed the lights were still on. Peter Lake was in shirtsleeves, his feet up on the corner of the desk. Near his elbow were a large stack of reports and a yellow pad. He was making notes as he read.

"You're not going to solve this case in one night," Nancy said quietly. Lake looked around, startled. Then he grinned sheepishly.

"I always work this hard. I'm compulsive."

Nancy walked over to Lake's desk. "What are you doing?"

"Reading about the Reardon and Escalante disappearances. I had an idea. Do you have time?"

"I was going to eat. Want to join me? Nothing special. There's an all-night coffee shop over on Oak."

Lake looked at the stack of reports and the clock.

"Sure," he said, swinging his legs off the desk and grabbing his jacket. "I didn't realize how late it was."

"I was caught up in something too. If my stomach hadn't yelled at me, I'd still be at my desk."

"You must like your work."

"Sometimes."

"How did you get into it?"

"You mean, what's a nice girl like me doing in a job like this?"

"That never occurred to me."

"That I was a nice girl?"

Lake laughed. "No. That you're not suited for police work."

Nancy checked out at the front desk and followed Lake outside. After sundown Hunter's Point was a ghost town, except for a few spots that catered to the college crowd. Nancy could see the marquee of the Hunter's Point Cinema and the neon signs outside a couple of bars. Most of the stores were shuttered for the night. The coffee shop was only a block and a half from the station. An oasis of light in a desert of darkness.

"Here we are," Nancy said, holding open the door of Chang's Cafe. There was a counter, but Nancy led Lake to a booth. Chang's wife brought them menus and water.

"The soup and the pies are good and the rest of the menu is edible. Don't look for anything resembling Chinese. Mr. Chang cooks Italian, Greek and whatever else strikes his fancy."

"You're not from Hunter's Point originally, are you?" Lake asked, after they ordered.

"How could you tell?"

"You don't have the accent. I'm a transplanted westerner myself. Let's see. I'd guess Montana."

"Idaho," Nancy said. "My parents still live there. They're farmers. My brother is a high school teacher in Boise. Me, I didn't love Idaho and I wanted to see the world. Fortunately I run a mean eight hundred meters and the U. offered the best scholarship. So I ended up in Hunter's Point."

"Not exactly Paris," Lake commented.

"Not exactly," Nancy said with a smile. "But it *was* New York, and without the scholarship there was no way I could afford college. By the time I realized New York City and Hunter's Point, New York, were worlds apart I was enjoying myself too much to care."

"And the police work?"

"My major was Criminal Justice. When I graduated, the Hunter's Point P.D. needed a woman to fill its affirmative action quota."

Nancy shrugged and looked at Lake, as if expecting a challenge.

"I bet you made detective on merit," he said.

"Damn straight," Nancy answered proudly, just as Mrs. Chang arrived with their soup.

"How did you end up here?" Nancy asked, as she waited for her minestrone to cool.

"I'm from Colorado," Lake said, smiling. "I went to Colorado State undergraduate, then I served a hitch in the Marines. There was a guy in the judge advocate's corps who went to law school here and suggested I apply. I met Sandy at the U."

Lake paused and his smile disappeared. He looked

down at his plate. The action had an unnatural quality to it, as if he suddenly realized that a smile would be inappropriate when he was discussing his dead wife. Nancy looked at Lake oddly.

"I'm sorry," he apologized. "I keep thinking about her."

"That's okay. There's nothing wrong with remembering."

"I don't like myself when I'm maudlin. I've always been a person in control. The murders have made me realize that nothing is predictable or permanent."

"If it's taken you this long to figure that out, you're lucky."

"Yeah. A successful career, a great wife and kid. They blind you to the way the world really is, don't they? Then someone takes that away from you in a second and . . . and you see . . ."

"You see how lucky you were to have what you had, while it lasted, Peter. Most people never have in their lifetime what you and I had for a little while."

Lake looked down at the tabletop.

"At the station you said you had an idea," Nancy said, to break his mood.

"It's probably just playing detective," he answered, "but something struck me when I was going through the reports. The day Gloria Escalante disappeared, a florist's truck was delivering in the area. A woman would open the door to a man delivering flowers. She would be excited and wouldn't be thinking. He could take the woman away in the back of his truck. And there's the rose. Someone who works in a florist's would have access to roses."

"Not bad, Peter," Nancy said, unable to hide her admiration. "You might make a good detective after all. The deliveryman was Henry Waters. He's got a minor record for indecent exposure and he's one of our suspects. You probably haven't gotten to Wayne's report yet. He's been doing a background check on Waters."

Lake flushed. "I guess you were way ahead of me."

"Peter, did Sandy have any connection with Evergreen Florists?"

"Is that where Waters works?"

Nancy nodded.

"I don't think so. But I can look at our receipts and the checkbook to see if she ever ordered anything from them. I'm pretty certain I never did."

Their dinner arrived and they ate in silence for a few minutes. Nancy's spaghetti was delicious, but she noted that Lake just picked at his food.

"Do you feel like talking about Sandy?" Nancy asked. "We're trying to cross-reference the activities of the victims. See if they belonged to the same clubs, subscribed to the same magazines. Anything that gives us a common denominator."

"Frank asked me to do that the night of the murder. I've been working on it. We were members of the Delmar Country Club, the Hunter's Point Athletic Club, the Racquet Club. I've got a list of our credit cards, subscriptions, everything I can think of. I'll complete it by the end of the week. Is Waters your only suspect?"

"There are others, but nothing solid. I'm talking about known sex offenders, not anyone we've linked to any of the crimes." Nancy paused. "I had an ulterior motive for asking you to eat with me. I'm going to be totally honest with you. You shouldn't be involved in this investigation. You have pull with the mayor, so you're here, but everyone on the task force resents the way you forced yourself on us."

"Including you?"

"No. But that's only because I understand what's

driving you. What you don't understand is how self-destructive your behavior is. You're obsessed with this case because you think immersing yourself in detective work will help you escape from reality. But you're stuck in the real world. Eventually you'll have to come to terms with it, and the sooner you do that the better. You've got a good practice. You can build a new life. Don't put off coming to grips with what's happened by continuing to work on the murders."

Nancy was watching Lake as she spoke. He never took his eyes off her. When she was finished speaking he leaned forward.

"Thank you for your honesty. I know my intrusion into the task force is resented and I'm glad you told me how everyone feels. I'm not worried about my practice. My associates will keep it going without me and I've made so much money that I could live nicely without it. What matters to me is catching this killer before he hurts someone else."

Lake reached across the table and covered Nancy's hand with his.

"It also matters to me that you're concerned. I appreciate that."

Lake stroked Nancy's hand as he spoke. It was a sensual touch, clearly a come-on, and Nancy was struck by the inappropriateness of his action, even if Lake was not.

"I'm concerned for you as a person who is the victim of a horrible crime," Nancy said firmly, as she slid her hand out from under Lake's. "I am also concerned that you might do something that would jeopardize our investigation. Please think about what I've said, Peter."

"I will," Lake assured her.

Nancy started to open her purse but Lake stopped her.

"Dinner's on me," he smiled.

"I always pay my own way," Nancy answered, laying the exact amount of her dinner on top of the check and putting a dollar tip under her coffee cup. She slipped out of the booth and started toward the door.

Peter placed his money next to hers and followed her outside.

"Can I give you a lift home?" he asked.

"My car's in the lot."

"Mine too. I'll walk you back."

They walked in silence until they reached the police station. The lot was dimly lit. Patches were in shadow. Nancy's car was toward the back of the station where the windows were dark.

"It could have happened someplace like this," Lake mused as they walked.

"What?"

"The women," Lake said. "Walking alone at night in a deserted parking lot. It would be so easy to approach them. Didn't Bundy do that? Wear a false cast to elicit sympathy. They would be in the killer's trunk in a minute and it would all be over for them."

Nancy felt a chill. There was no one in the lot but the two of them. They entered an unlit area. She turned her head so she could see Lake. He was watching her, thoughtfully. Nancy stopped at her car.

"That's why I wanted to walk with you," Lake continued. "No woman is safe until he's caught."

"Think about what I said, Peter."

"Good night, Nancy. I think we work well together. Thanks again for your concern."

Nancy backed her Ford out of its space and drove off. She could see Lake watching her in the rearview mirror.

6

Nancy stood in the dark and pumped iron, following the routine she and Ed had worked out. Now she was doing curls, with the maximum weight she could manage. Her forearm arced toward her shoulder, slowly, steadily, as she muscled up the right dumbbell, then the left. Sweat stained her tank top. The veins stood out on her neck.

Something was definitely wrong. Lake had been coming on to her. When Ed died, she had lost all interest in sex for months. It had hurt just to see couples walking hand in hand. But when Lake held her hand, he had stroked it, the way you would caress a lover's hand. When he said he thought they worked well together, it was definitely a proposition.

Nancy finished her curls. She lowered the weights to the floor and took a few deep breaths. It was almost six. She had been up since four-thirty, because a nightmare woke her and she couldn't get back to sleep.

Frank had considered Lake a suspect and she had disagreed. Now she was beginning to wonder. She remembered what Dr. Klien said. Lake was bright and personable. It would have been easy for him to gain the confidence of the victims. They were the type of women he met every day at his clubs, and he was the type of man the victims encountered at theirs.

The organized nonsocial was a psychopath who could not feel pity or care for others. The type of person who would have to fake emotions. Had Lake been caught off guard in the coffee shop between remembering his first meeting with Sandra Lake and making the appropriate reaction to that memory? There had been a brief moment when Lake's features had been devoid of emotion.

Klien also said that these killers were interested in

police work. Lake, an experienced criminal defense attorney, would know all about police procedure. Nancy dropped to the floor and did fifty push-ups. What was normally an easy set was difficult. She couldn't focus. Her head filled with a vision of Lake, alone in the shadows of the parking lot, waiting. How did he know about Bundy's fake cast? Dr. Klien had not mentioned it.

After the weights, she and Ed would run a six-mile loop through the neighborhood. Ed was stronger than Nancy, but she was the faster runner. On Sundays, they raced the loop. The loser cooked breakfast. The winner decided when and how they made love. Nancy could not touch the weights or run the loop for two months after the shooting.

One hundred crunches. Up, down, up, down. Her stomach tight as a drumhead. Her thoughts in the dark, in the parking lot with Lake. Should she tell Frank and Wayne? Was she just imagining it? Would her suspicions sidetrack the investigation and let the real killer escape?

It was six-fifteen. The weights were in a small room next to the bedroom. The sun was starting its ascent over the wealthy suburbs to the east. Nancy stripped off her panties and top and dropped them in the hamper. She had put on weight after Ed died. Except for a month when she was recovering from a hamstring pull in her sophomore year, it was the first time since junior high that she had not worked out regularly. The weight was off now and she could see the ridged muscles of her stomach and the cords that twisted along her legs. Hot water loosened her up. She shampooed her hair. All the time, she was thinking about Peter Lake.

Why were there no bodies found before? Why were the Lake murders different from the others? Sandra Lake had apparently been killed quickly, suddenly. Why? And why would Peter have killed her? Had she discovered something that would link him to the other murders and confronted him with the evidence? And that still left the hardest question of all, was Lake such a monster that he would kill his own daughter to cover his crimes?

As she dressed, Nancy tried to find one concrete fact that she could present to the other detectives. One piece of evidence that linked Peter to the crimes. She came up dry. For the moment, she'd have to keep her feelings to herself.

7

Frank Grimsbo ran a forearm across his forehead, staining the sleeve of his madras jacket with sweat. He was wearing a short-sleeve, white shirt and brown polyester pants, and had jerked his paisley print tie to half mast after unbuttoning his top button. The heat was killing him, and all he could think about was cold beer.

Herbert Solomon answered the door on the third ring. Wearily, Grimsbo held up his shield and identified himself.

"This is about the Lakes, right?" asked Solomon, a stocky man of medium height who sported a well-groomed beard and was dressed in loose green-and-red-checked Bermuda shorts and a yellow T-shirt.

"That's right, Mr. Solomon. My partner and I are canvassing the neighborhood."

"I already spoke to a policeman on the evening it happened."

"I know, sir. I'm a detective on the special task force that's investigating all of the killings, and I wanted to go into a little more detail with you."

"Have there been other murders? I thought these women just disappeared."

"That's right, but we're assuming the worst."

"Come on in out of the heat. Can I get you a beer, or can't you drink on duty?"

Grimsbo grinned. "A beer would be great."

"Wait in there and I'll grab one for you," Solomon said, pointing to a small front room. Grimsbo pulled his shirt away from his body as he walked toward the den. Thank God they were canvassing in The Meadows, where everyone had air-conditioning.

"I hope this is cold enough for you," Solomon said, handing Grimsbo a chilled Budweiser. Grimsbo placed the cold bottle against his forehead and closed his eyes. Then he took a sip.

"Boy, that hits the spot. I wish they could think up a way to air-condition the outside."

Solomon laughed.

"You an accountant?"

"A c.p.a."

"I figured," Grimsbo said, pointing his beer at two large bookcases filled with books about tax and accounting. A desk stood in front of the only window in the room. A computer and printer sat in the center of the desk next to a phone. The window looked out at Sparrow Lane across a wide front lawn.

"Well," Grimsbo said, after taking another swig from the bottle, "let me ask you a few questions and get out of your hair. Were you around the night Mrs. Lake and her daughter were murdered?"

Solomon stopped smiling and nodded. "Poor bastard."

"You know Peter Lake?"

"Sure. Neighbors and all. We have a home-owners committee in The Meadows. Pete and I were on it. We played doubles together in the tennis tournament. Marge —that's my wife—she and Sandy were good friends."

"Is your wife home?"

"She's at the club, playing golf. I didn't feel like it in this heat."

Grimsbo put down the beer and took a pad and pen out of his inside jacket pocket.

"About what time did you get home on the night it happened?"

"It had to be about six."

"Did you see anything unusual that night?"

"Not a thing. I was in the dining room until we finished dinner. The dining room looks out into the back yard. Then I was in the living room for a few minutes. It's in the back of the house too. After that I was in here working on the computer with the blinds drawn."

"Okay," Grimsbo said, reluctantly ready to wrap up the interview and trudge back out into the heat.

"One thing I forgot about when the officer talked to me the night of the murder. There was so much excitement and Marge was hysterical. I did see Pete come home."

"Oh, yeah? When was that?"

"I can get pretty close there. The Yankees played a day game and I caught the score on 'Headline Sports.' CNN runs the sports scores twenty after and ten to the hour. I went into the den right after the score, so figure seven twenty-two or so. I saw Pete's Ferrari when I closed the blinds."

"He was heading home?"

"Right."

"And you're certain about the time."

"Twenty after the hour, every hour. So it had to be about then, give or take a minute."

"Did you notice a florist's truck at any time that night, near The Meadows or in it?"

Solomon thought for a second. "There was a TV repairman at the Osgoods'. That's the only unusual vehicle I saw."

Grimsbo levered himself out of his seat and extended his hand. "Thanks for the beer."

Wayne Turner was leaning against the car, looking so cool in his tan suit that it pissed Grimsbo off.

"Any luck?" Turner asked, as he pushed off the car.

"Nada. Oh, Solomon, the last guy I talked to, saw Lake driving home past his house about seven-twenty. Other than that, I don't have a thing that wasn't in the uniforms' reports."

"I struck out too, but I'm not surprised. You get a development like The Meadows, you get houses with land. They're not leaning over each other. Less chance anyone will see what's going on at the neighbor's. And with heat like this, everyone's either inside with the air-conditioning on or out at their country club."

"So what do we do now?"

"Head back in."

"You get a hit on a florist truck?" Grimsbo asked, when he had the car started.

"There was a cable TV repairman at the Osgoods', but no florist."

"Yeah, I got the TV guy too. What do you think of Waters?"

"I don't think anything, Frank. You seen him?"

Grimsbo shook his head.

"Our killer's got to be high IQ, right? Waters is a zero. Skinny, pimple-faced kid. He's got this little wisp of a beard. If he's not retarded, he's not far from it.

Dropped out of school in the tenth grade. He was eighteen. Worked as a gas station attendant and a box boy at Safeway. He lost that job when he was arrested for jacking off outside the window of a sixteen-year-old neighbor girl. The girl's father beat the crap out of him."

"He sounds pretty pathetic," Grimsbo observed.

"The guy's got no life. He lives with his mother. She's in her late sixties and in poor health. I followed him for a few days. He's a robot. Every day it's the same routine. He leaves work and walks to the One Way Inn, this bar that's halfway to his house. Orders two beers, nurses 'em, doesn't say a word to anyone but the bartender. Forty-five minutes after he goes in, he leaves, walks straight home and spends the evening watching TV with his mother. I talked to his boss and his neighbors. If he's got any friends, no one knows who they are. He's held this delivery boy job with Evergreen Florists longer than any of his other jobs."

"You writing him off?"

"He's a weeny-waver. A little twisted, sure, but I don't make him for our killer. He's not smart enough to be our boy. We don't have anything with Waters."

"We don't have anything, period."

Glen Michaels walked into the task force office just as Grimsbo and Turner were finishing the reports on their interviews in The Meadows.

"Whatcha got?" Grimsbo asked. He had shucked his jacket and parked himself next to a small fan.

"Nothing at all," Michaels said. "It's like the guy was never there. I just finished all the lab work. Every print matches up to the victims, Lake or one of the neighbors. There's nothing to do a DNA test on. No unusual hairs, no fibers, no semen. This is one smart cookie, gentlemen."

"You think he knows police procedure?" Turner asked.

"I have to believe it. I've never seen so many clean crime scenes."

"Anyway," Michaels said, heading for the door, "I'm out of here. This heat is boiling my blood."

Turner turned to Grimsbo. "This perp is starting to piss me off. Nobody's that good. He leaves no prints, no hairs, no one sees him. Christ, we've got a development full of people and no one reports an unusual occurrence. No strangers lurking around, not a single odd car. How does he get in and out?"

Grimsbo didn't answer. He was frowning. He levered himself out of his chair and walked over to the cabinet where they kept the master file on the case.

"What's up?" Turner asked.

"Just something . . . Yeah, here it is."

Grimsbo pulled a report out of the file and showed it to Turner. It was the one-page report of the dispatcher who had taken the 911 call from Peter Lake.

"You see it?" Grimsbo asked.

Turner read the report a few times and shook his head.

"The time," Grimsbo said. "Lake called in the 911 at eight-fifteen."

"Yeah? So?"

"Solomon said he saw Lake driving by at seven-twenty. He was certain he'd just heard the sports scores. CNN gives them at twenty after."

"And the bodies were in the hall," Turner said, suddenly catching on.

"How long does it take to park the car, open the door? Let's give Lake the benefit of the doubt and assume Solomon is a little off. He's still gonna be inside by seven-thirty."

"Shit," Turner said softly.

"Am I right, Wayne?" Grimsbo asked.

"I don't know, Frank. If it was your wife and kid . . . I mean, you'd be in shock."

"Sure, the guy's knocked out. He said he sat down on the stairs for a while. You know, gathering himself. But for forty-five minutes? Uh-uh. Something doesn't wash. I think he spent the time cleaning up the crime scene."

"What's the motive? Jesus, Frank, you saw her face. Why would he do that to his own wife?"

"You know why. She knew something, she found something, and she made the mistake of telling Lake. Think about it, Wayne. If Lake killed them it would explain the absence of clues at the crime scene. There wouldn't be any strange cars in the neighborhood or prints that didn't match the Lakes or the neighbors."

"I don't know . . ."

"Yes you do. He killed that little girl. His own little girl."

"Christ, Frank, Lake's a successful lawyer. His wife was beautiful."

"You heard Klien. The guy we're looking for is a monster, but no one's gonna see that. He's smooth, handsome, the type of guy these women would let in their house without a second thought. It could be a successful lawyer with a beautiful wife. It could be anyone who isn't wired right and is working in some psycho world of his own where this all makes sense."

Turner paced around the room while Grimsbo waited quietly. Finally Turner sat down and picked up a picture of Melody Lake.

"We aren't going to do anything stupid, Frank. If Lake is our killer, he is one devious motherfucker. One hint that we're on to him and he'll figure a way to cover this up."

"So, what's the next step? We can't bring him in and sweat him and we know there's nothing connecting Lake to the other crime scenes."

"These women weren't picked at random. If he's the killer, they've all got to be connected to Lake somehow. We have to reinterview the husbands, go back over the reports and recheck our lists with Lake in mind. If we're right, there's going to be something there."

The two men sat silently for a moment, figuring the angles.

"None of this goes in a report," Turner said. "Lake could stumble across it when he's here."

"Right," Grimsbo answered. "I'd better take Solomon's interview with me."

"When do we tell Nancy and the chief?"

"When we have something solid. Lake's very smart and he's got political connections. If he's the one, I don't want him beating this, I want him nailed."

8

Nancy Gordon was deep in a dreamless sleep when the phone rang. She jerked up in bed, flailing for a moment, before she realized what was happening. The phone rang again before she found it in the dark.

"Detective Gordon?" the man on the phone asked.

"Speaking," Nancy said, as she tried to orient herself.

"This is Jeff Spears. I'm a patrolman. Fifteen minutes ago we received a complaint about a man sitting in a car on the corner of Bethesda and Champagne. Seems he's been parked there for three successive nights. One of the neighbors got worried.

"Anyway, Officer DeMuniz and I talked to the guy. He identified himself as Peter Lake. He claims he's working on the task force that's looking into the murders of those women. He gave me your name."

"What time is it?" Nancy asked. The last thing she wanted to do was turn on the light and scorch her eyeballs.

"One-thirty. Sorry about waking you," Spears said apologetically.

"No, that's okay," she answered as she located the digital clock and confirmed the time. "Is Lake there?"

"Right beside me."

Nancy took a deep breath. "Put him on."

Nancy heard Spears talking to someone. She swung her legs over the side of the bed, sat up and rubbed her eyes.

"Nancy?" Lake asked.

"What's going on?"

"Do you want me to explain with the officer standing here?"

"What I want is to go back to bed. Now, what's this about you sitting in a parked car in the middle of the night for three straight nights?"

"It's Waters. I was staking out his house."

"Oh, fuck. I don't believe this. You were staking him out? Like some goddamn movie? Peter, I want you at Chang's in twenty minutes."

"But . . ."

"Twenty minutes. This is too stupid for words. And put Spears back on."

Nancy heard Lake calling to the officer. She closed her eyes and turned on the bedside lamp. Then she raised her lids slowly. The light burned and her eyes watered.

"Detective Gordon?"

"Yeah. Look, Spears, he's okay. He is working on the task force. But that was heads-up work," she added, since he sounded young and eager and the compliment would mean something.

"It sounded suspicious. And, with the murders . . ."

"No, you did the right thing. But I don't want you to mention this to anyone. We don't want what we're doing getting around."

"No problem."

"Thanks for calling."

Nancy hung up. She felt awful, but she had to find out what Lake was up to.

Lake was waiting for her in a booth when Nancy arrived at Chang's. The little cafe stayed open all night for cops, truckers and an occasional college student. It was a safe place to meet. There was a cup of coffee in front of Lake. Nancy told the waitress to make it two.

"Why don't you clue me in on what you thought you were doing, Peter," Nancy said when the waitress left.

"I'm sorry if I was out of line. But I'm certain Waters is the killer. I've been tailing him for three days. Believe me, I did a great job. He has no idea he was followed."

"Peter, this isn't how things are done. You don't go running off with some half-baked idea you picked up from 'Magnum, P.I.' The task force is a team. You have to run your ideas by everyone before you make a move.

"More important, you don't know the first thing about surveillance. Look how easily you were spotted by the neighbor. If Waters saw you, and it spooked him, he might go to ground and we'd lose him forever. And, if he is the killer, you could have been in danger. Whoever killed your wife and daughter has no conscience and he has no compunction about taking a human life. Remember that."

"I guess I was foolish."

"There's no 'guess' about it."

"You're right. I apologize. I never thought about blowing the case or the danger. All I thought about was . . ."

Lake paused and looked down at the table.

"I know you want him, Peter. We all do. But if you don't do this right, you'll ruin the case."

Lake nodded thoughtfully. "You've gone out of your way to help me, Nancy, and I appreciate it. I'm finally starting to cope with losing Sandy and Melody and you're one of the reasons."

Lake smiled at her. Nancy did not return the smile. She watched Lake carefully.

"I've decided to go back to work. This little incident tonight has convinced me I'm not very valuable to the investigation. I thought I could really help, but that was ego and desperation. I'm not a cop and I was crazy to think I could do more than you're doing."

"Good. I'm glad to hear you say that. It's a healthy sign."

"That doesn't mean I'm going to abandon the case altogether. I'd like copies of all the police reports sent to my office. I still might spot something you miss or offer a different perspective. But I'll stop haunting the station house."

"I can have the reports sent, if O'Malley says it's okay. But you'll have to keep them strictly to yourself. Not even your associates should see them."

"Of course. You know, you've really taken good care

of me," Lake said, smiling again. "Do you think we could have dinner sometime? Just get together? Nothing to do with the case."

"We'll see," she said uneasily.

Lake checked his watch. "Hey, we'd better get going. We're going to be dead tired in the morning. I'm paying this time, no arguments."

Nancy slid out of the booth and said good-bye. It was late and she'd had little sleep, but she was wide-awake. There was no question about it now. With his wife dead less than three weeks, Peter Lake was coming on to her. And that wasn't the only thing bothering her. Nancy wanted to know the real reason Peter Lake was tailing Henry Waters.

9

"Dr. Escalante," Wayne Turner said to a heavy-set, dark-complected man with the sad eyes and weary air of someone who has given up hope, "I'm one of the detectives working on your wife's disappearance."

"Is Gloria dead?" Escalante asked, expecting the worst.

They were sitting in the doctor's office at the Wayside Clinic, a modern, two-story building located at the far end of the Wayside Mall. Escalante was one of several doctors, physical therapists and health care specialists who made up the staff of the clinic. His specialty was cardiology and he had privileges at Hunter's Point Hospital. Everyone spoke highly of Dr. Escalante's skills. They also thought he was one hell of a nice guy who was unfailingly cheerful. Or, at least, he had been until a month and a half ago, when he came home to his Tudor-style house in West Hunter's Point and found a note and a black rose.

"I'm afraid we have no more information about your wife. We assume she's alive, until we learn otherwise."

"Then why are you here?"

"I have a few questions that may help us with the case."

Turner read off the names of the other missing women and their spouses, including the Lakes. As he read the names, Turner placed photographs of the victims and their husbands faceup on Escalante's desk.

"Do you or your wife know any of these people in any capacity whatsoever, Doctor?" Turner asked.

Escalante studied the photographs carefully. He picked up one of them.

"This is Simon and Samantha Reardon, isn't it?"

Turner nodded.

"He's a neurosurgeon. I've seen the Reardons at a few Medical Association functions. A few years ago, he spoke at a seminar I attended. I don't recall the topic."

"That's good. Were you friendly with the Reardons?"

Escalante laughed harshly. "People with my skin color don't travel in the same social circles as the Reardons, Detective. I don't suppose you were permitted to interview the esteemed doctor at the Delmar Country Club."

Wayne nodded.

"Yeah. Well, that's the type of guy Simon Reardon is . . ."

Escalante suddenly remembered why Turner was interested in Samantha Reardon and his wife.

"I'm sorry. I should be more charitable. Simon is probably going through the same hell I am."

"Probably. Any of the others ring a bell?"

Escalante started to shake his head, then stopped.

"This one is a lawyer, isn't he?" he asked, pointing at Peter Lake's photograph.

"Yes, he is," Turner answered, trying to hide his excitement.

"It didn't hit me until now. What a coincidence."

"What's that?"

"Gloria was chosen for jury duty six months ago. She sat on one of Lake's cases. I remember because she said she was glad it wasn't a medical malpractice or she would have been excused. It didn't matter though. The lawyers settled the case halfway through, so she didn't vote on it."

"You're certain it was Peter Lake's case?"

"I met her after court. We were going to dinner. I saw him."

"Okay. That's a big help. Anyone else look familiar?" Turner asked, although, at this point, he really didn't care.

"It's Lake, Chief," Frank Grimsbo told O'Malley. "We're certain."

"Are we talking hard evidence?" O'Malley asked.

"Not yet. But there's too much circumstantial to look the other way," Wayne Turner answered.

"How do you two feel about this?" O'Malley asked Glen Michaels and Nancy Gordon.

"It makes sense," Michaels responded. "I'm going back over the evidence in all of the cases tomorrow to see if I have anything I can tie to Lake."

O'Malley turned toward Nancy. She looked grim.

"I'd reached the same conclusion for other reasons, Chief. I don't know how we can nail him, but I'm certain he's our man. I talked to Dr. Klien this morning and ran Lake's profile by him. He said it's possible. A lot of sociopaths aren't serial killers. They're successful businessmen or politicians or lawyers. Think of the advantage you have in those professions if you don't have a conscience to slow you down. In the past few days, I've been talking to people who know Lake. They all say he's charming, but none of them would turn their back on him. He's supposed to have the ethics of a shark and enough savvy to stay just this side of the line. There have been several Bar complaints, but none that was successful. A few malpractice suits. I talked to the lawyers who represented the plaintiffs. He skated on every one of them."

"There's a big difference between being a sleazy lawyer and killing six people, including your own daughter," O'Malley said. "Why would he endanger himself by getting so close to the investigation?"

"So he can see what we've got," Grimsbo said.

"I think there's more to it, Chief," Nancy said. "He's up to something."

Nancy told O'Malley about Lake's stakeout.

"That doesn't make sense," Turner said. "Waters isn't really a suspect. He just happened to be around the Escalante house the day she disappeared. There's no connection between Waters and any other victim."

"But there is a connection between Lake and every victim," Grimsbo cut in.

"Let's hear it," O'Malley said.

"Okay. We have Gloria Escalante sitting on one of his juries. He and the Reardons belong to the Delmar Country Club. Patricia Cross and Sandra Lake were in the Junior League. Anne Hazelton's husband is an attorney. He says they've been to Bar Association functions the Lakes attended."

"Some of those connections are pretty tenuous."

"What are the odds on one person being linked to all six victims?" Turner asked.

"Hunter's Point isn't that big a place."

"Chief," Nancy said, "he's been coming on to me."

"What?"

"It's sexual. He's interested. He's let me know."

Nancy recounted the way Lake acted during their two meetings at Chang's.

O'Malley frowned. "I don't know, Nancy."

"His wife died less than a month ago. It's not normal."

"You're attractive. He's trying to get over his grief. Maybe he and Mrs. Lake didn't get along that well. Did you find any of that when you talked to the neighbors?"

Grimsbo shook his head. "No gossip about the Lakes. They were a normal couple according to the people I talked to."

"Same here," Turner said.

"Doesn't that undercut your theory?"

"Dr. Klien said a serial killer can have a wife and family, or a normal relationship with a girlfriend," Nancy answered.

"Look at the Lake murders," Turner offered. "We know from one of his associates, who was working late, that Lake was at his office until shortly before seven. The neighbor sees him driving toward his house at seventy-twenty, maybe a little after. There's no 911 call until forty-five minutes later. What's he doing inside with the dead bodies? If they're dead, that is."

"We think he came in and his wife confronted him with something she'd found that connected him to the disappearances."

"But they weren't news. No one knew about them," O'Malley said.

"Oh, shit," Michaels swore.

"What?"

"The note. It was the only one with prints on it."

"So?" Grimsbo asked.

"The other notes had no fingerprints on them, but

the note next to Sandra Lake's body had her prints on it. According to the autopsy report, Sandra Lake died instantly or, at least, she was unconscious as soon as she was hit on the back of the head. When did she touch the note?"

"I still don't . . ."

"She finds the note or the rose or both. She asks Lake what they are. He knows the story will break in the paper eventually. No matter what he tells her now, she'll know he's the rose killer. So he panics, kills her and leaves the rose and the note next to the body to make us think the same person who's taken the other women also killed his wife. And that explains why only Lake's note has a print and why it's Sandra Lake's print," Michaels said. "She was holding it before she was killed."

"That also explains why no one saw any strange vehicles going in or out of The Meadows."

O'Malley leaned back in his chair. He looked troubled.

"You've got me believing this," he said. "But theories aren't proof. If it's Lake, how do we prove it with evidence that's admissible in court?"

Before anyone could answer, the door to O'Malley's office opened.

"Sorry to interrupt, Chief, but we just got a 911 that's connected to those women who disappeared. Do you have a suspect named Waters?"

"What's up?" Grimsbo asked.

"The caller said he talked with a guy named Henry Waters at the One Way Inn and Waters said he had a woman in his basement."

"Did the caller give a name?"

The officer shook his head. "Said he didn't want to get involved, but he kept thinking about the little kid who was murdered and his conscience wouldn't leave him alone."

"When did this conversation at the bar take place?" Nancy asked.

"A few days ago."

"Did Waters describe the woman or give any details?"

"Waters told him the woman had red hair."

"Patricia Cross," Turner said.

"This is Lake's doing," Nancy said. "It's too much of a coincidence."

"I'm with Nancy," Turner said. "Waters just doesn't figure."

"Can we take the chance?" Michaels asked. "With Lake, all we have is some deductive reasoning. We know Waters was around the Escalante residence near the time she disappeared and he has a sex offender record."

"I want you four out there pronto," O'Malley ordered. "I'd rather be wrong than sit here talking when we might be able to save one of those women."

Henry Waters lived in an older section of Hunter's Point. Oak trees shaded the wide streets. High hedges gave the residents privacy. Most of the homes and lawns were well kept up, but Waters's house, a corner plot, was starting to come apart. The gutters were clogged. One of the steps leading up to the shaded front porch was broken. The lawn was overgrown and full of weeds.

The sun was starting to set when Nancy Gordon followed Wayne Turner and Frank Grimsbo along the slate walk toward Henry Waters's front door. Michaels waited in the car in case he was needed to process a crime scene. Three uniformed officers were stationed behind the house in an alley that divided the large block. Two

officers preceded the detectives up the walk and positioned themselves, guns drawn but concealed, on either
side of the front door.

"We take it easy and we are polite," Turner cau-
tioned. "I want his consent or the search and seizure
issues could get sticky."

Everyone nodded. No one cracked a joke about Turner and law school, as they might have under other circumstances. Nancy looked back at the high grass in the
front yard. The house was weather-beaten. The brown
paint was chipping. A window screen was hanging by one
screw outside the front window. Nancy peeked through a
crack between a drawn shade and the windowsill. No one
was in the front room. They could hear a television playing somewhere toward the back of the house.

"He'll be less fearful if he sees a woman," Nancy
said. Grimsbo nodded and Nancy pressed the doorbell.
She wore a jacket to conceal her holster. There had been
some respite from the heat during the day, but it was still
warm. She could feel a trickle of sweat work its way down
her side.

Nancy rang the bell a second time and the volume of
the TV lowered. She saw a vague shape moving down the
hall through the semi-opaque curtain that covered the
glassed upper half of the front door. When the door
opened, Nancy pulled back the screen door and smiled.
The gangly, loose-limbed man did not smile back. He was
dressed in jeans and a stained T-shirt. His long, greasy
hair was unkempt. Waters's dull eyes fixed first on Nancy,
then on the uniformed officers. His brow furrowed, as if
he were working on a calculus problem. Nancy flashed
her badge.

"Mr. Waters, I'm Nancy Gordon, a detective with
the Hunter's Point P.D."

"I didn't do nothin'," Waters said defensively.

"I'm certain that's true," Nancy answered in a firm but friendly tone, "but we received some information we'd like to check out. Would you mind if we came in?"

"Who is it?" a frail female voice called from the rear of the house.

"That's my mom," Waters explained. "She's sick."

"I'm sorry. We'll try not to disturb her."

"Why do you have to upset her? She's sick," Waters said, his anxiety growing.

"You misunderstood me, Mr. Waters. We are *not* going to bother your mother. We only want to look around. May we do that? We won't be long."

"I ain't done nothin'," Waters repeated, his eyes shifting anxiously from Grimsbo to Turner, then to the uniformed officers. "Talk to Miss Cummings. She's my p.o. She'll tell you."

"We did talk to your probation officer and she gave you a very good report. She said you cooperated with her completely. We'd like your cooperation too. You don't want us to have to wait here while one of the officers gets a search warrant, do you?"

"Why do you have to search my house?" Waters asked angrily. The officers tensed. "Why the hell can't you leave me be? I ain't looked at that girl no more. I'm workin' steady. Miss Cummings can tell you."

"There's no need to get upset," Nancy answered calmly. "The sooner we look around, the sooner we'll be out of your hair."

Waters thought this over. "What do you want to see?" he asked.

"The basement."

"There ain't nothin' in the basement," Waters said, seeming genuinely puzzled.

"Then we won't be here long," Nancy assured him.

Waters snorted. "The basement. You can see all the

basement you want. Ain't nothin' but spiders in the basement."

Waters pointed down a dark hall that led past the stairs toward the rear of the house.

"Why don't you come with us, Mr. Waters. You can show us around."

The hall was dark, but there was a light in the kitchen. Nancy saw a sink filled with dirty dishes and the remains of two TV dinners on a Formica-topped table. The kitchen floor was stained and dirty. There was a solid wood door under the staircase next to the entrance to the kitchen. Waters opened it. Then his eyes widened and he stepped back. Nancy pushed past him. The smell was so strong it knocked her back a step.

"Stay with Mr. Waters," Nancy told the officers. She took a deep breath and flicked the switch at the head of the stairs. There was nothing unusual at the bottom of the wooden steps. Nancy held her gun with one hand and the rickety railing with the other. The smell of death grew stronger as she descended the stairs. Grimsbo and Turner followed. No one spoke.

Halfway down, Nancy crouched and scanned the basement. The only light came from a bare bulb hanging from the ceiling. She could see a furnace in one corner. Odd pieces of furniture, most with a broken look, were stashed against a wall surrounded by cartons of newspapers and old magazines. A back door opened into a concrete well at the back of the house near the alley. Most of the corner near the door was in shadow, but Nancy could make out a human foot and a pool of blood.

"Fuck," she whispered, sucking air.

Grimsbo edged past her. Nancy followed close behind. She knew nothing in the basement could hurt her, but she was having trouble catching her breath. Turner aimed a flashlight at the corner and flicked it on.

"Jesus," he managed in a strangled voice.

The naked woman was sprawled on the cold concrete, swimming in blood and surrounded by an overpowering fecal smell. She had not been "killed" or "murdered." She had been defiled and dehumanized. Nancy could see patches of charred flesh where the skin was not stained with blood or feces. The woman's intestines had burst through a gaping hole in her abdomen. They reminded Nancy of a string of bloated sausages. She turned her head aside.

"Bring Waters down here," Grimsbo bellowed. Nancy could see the tendons in his neck stretching. His eyes bulged.

"You don't lay one hand on him, Frank," Turner managed between gasps.

Nancy grabbed Grimsbo's massive forearm. "Wayne's right. I'm handling this. Back off."

A uniform hustled Waters down the steps. When Waters saw the body, he turned white and fell to his knees. He was mouthing words, but no sound came out.

Nancy closed her eyes and gathered herself. The body wasn't there. The smell wasn't in the air. She knelt next to Waters.

"Why, Henry?" she asked softly.

Waters looked at her. His face crumpled and he bleated like a wounded animal.

"Why?" Nancy repeated.

"Oh, no. Oh, no," Waters cried, holding his head in his hands. The head snapped back and forth with each denial, his long hair trailing behind.

"Then who did this? She's here, Henry. In your basement."

Waters gaped at Nancy, his mouth wide open.

"I'm going to give you your rights. You've heard them before, haven't you?" Nancy asked, but it was clear

Waters was in no condition to discuss constitutional rights. His head hung backward and he was making an inhuman baying noise.

"Take him to the station," she ordered the officer who was standing behind Waters. "If you, or anyone else, asks this man one question, you'll be scrubbing toilet bowls in public rest rooms. Is that understood? He hasn't been Mirandized. I want him in an interrogation room with a two-man guard inside and another man outside. No one, including the chief, is to talk to him. I'll call from here to brief O'Malley. And send Michaels in. Tell him to call for a full forensic team. Post a guard on the stairs. No one else comes down here unless Glen says it's okay. I don't want this crime scene fucked up."

Grimsbo and Turner had drawn closer to the body, making certain to stay outside the circle of blood that surrounded it. Grimsbo was taking short, deep breaths. Turner willed himself to look at the woman's face. It was Patricia Cross, but barely. The killer's savage attack had not been limited to the victim's body.

The young uniformed officer was also riveted on the body. That is why he was slow to react when Waters leaped up. Nancy was half-turned and saw the action from the corner of her eye. By the time she turned back, the cop was sprawled on the floor and Waters was bolting up the stairs, screaming for his mother.

The officer who was watching the cellar door heard Waters's scream. He stepped in front of the entrance to the basement, gun drawn, as Waters barreled into him.

"Don't shoot!" Nancy screamed just as the gun exploded. The officer stumbled backward, crashing into the wall opposite the cellar door. The shot plowed through Waters's heart and he tumbled down the stairs, cracking his head on the cement floor. Waters never felt the impact. He was dead by then.

10

"It was on the late news. I can't believe you caught him," Nancy Gordon heard Peter Lake say. She was alone in the task force office, writing reports. Nancy swiveled her chair. Lake stood in the doorway of the office. He wore pressed jeans and a maroon and blue rugby shirt. His styled hair was neatly combed. He looked happy and excited. There was no indication that he was thinking of Sandra or Melody Lake. No sign of grief.

"How did you crack it?" Lake asked, sitting in the chair opposite Nancy.

"An anonymous tip, Peter. Nothing fancy."

"That's terrific."

"It looks like you were right."

Lake shrugged his shoulders, stifling a smile.

"Say," Lake asked sheepishly, "you didn't tell anyone about my stakeout, did you?"

"That's our little secret."

"Thanks. I feel like a fool, going off on my own like that. You were right. If Waters caught on, he probably would have killed me."

"You must feel relieved, knowing Sandy's and Melody's killer has been caught," Nancy said, watching for a reaction.

Lake suddenly looked somber.

"It's as if an enormous weight was taken off my shoulders. Maybe now my life can go back to normal."

"You know, Peter," Nancy said casually, "there was a time when I tossed around the possibility that you might be the killer."

"Why?" Peter asked, shocked.

"You were never a serious suspect, but there were a few inconsistencies in your story."

"Like what?"

"The time, for instance. You didn't call 911 until eight-fifteen, but a neighbor saw you driving toward your house around seven-twenty. I couldn't figure out why it took you so long to call the police."

"You've got to be kidding."

Nancy shrugged.

"I was a suspect because of this time thing?"

"What were you doing for almost an hour?"

"Jesus, Nancy, I don't remember. I was in a daze. I mean, I might have blacked out for a bit."

"You never mentioned that."

Lake stared at Nancy, openmouthed.

"Am I still a suspect? Are you interrogating me?"

Nancy shook her head. "The case is closed, Peter. The chief is going to hold a press conference in the morning. There were three black roses and another one of those notes on a shelf in the basement. And, of course, there was poor Patricia Cross."

"But you don't believe it? You honestly think I could have . . . ?"

"Relax, Peter," Nancy answered, closing her eyes. "I'm real tired and not thinking straight. It's been one very long day."

"I can't relax. I mean, I really like you and I thought you liked me. It's a shock to find out you seriously thought I could do something . . . something like what was done to that woman."

Nancy opened her eyes. Lake looked distant, like he was visualizing Patricia Cross's eviscerated body. But he had not been to the crime scene or read an autopsy report. The media had not been told the condition of Patricia Cross's body.

"I said you were never a serious suspect and I meant it," Nancy lied with a forced smile. "If you were, I would have told Turner and Grimsbo about the stakeout, wouldn't I?"

"I guess."

"Well, I didn't and you can't be a suspect anymore, what with Waters dead, can you?"

Lake shook his head.

"Look," Nancy told him, "I'm really whacked out. I have one more report to write and I'm gone. Why don't you go home too, and start getting on with your life."

Lake stood. "That's good advice. I'm going to take it. And I want to thank you for everything you've done for me. I don't know how I would have gotten through this without you."

Lake stuck out his hand. Nancy stared at it for a second. Was this the hand that ripped the life out of Patricia Cross and Sandra and Melody Lake or was she crazy? Nancy shook Lake's hand. He held hers a moment longer than necessary, then released it after a brief squeeze.

"When things get back to normal for both of us, I'd like to take you to dinner," Lake said.

"Call me," Nancy answered, her stomach churning. It took every ounce of control to keep the smile on her face.

Lake left the room and Nancy stopped smiling. Waters was too good to be true. She did not believe he was responsible for the carnage in his basement. Lake had to know about the alley and the back door. With Waters at work and the mother an invalid, it would have been simple to drive behind the house without being seen, put the body in the basement and butcher it there. Lake was the anonymous caller, she was certain of it. But she had no proof. And O'Malley would soon tell the world that Henry Waters was a serial killer and the case of the missing women was closed.

Part Three

CLEAR AND CONVINCING EVIDENCE

Chapter Six

"And that's what happened, Mr. Page," Nancy Gordon said. "The case was closed. Henry Waters was officially named as the rose killer. Shortly after, Peter Lake disappeared. His house was sold. He closed his bank accounts. His associates were handed a thriving business. And Peter was never heard from again."

Page looked confused. "Maybe I'm missing something. Your case against Lake was purely circumstantial. Unless there was more evidence, I don't understand why you're so certain Peter Lake killed those women and framed Waters."

Gordon took a newspaper clipping and a photograph of a man leaving a motel room out of her briefcase and laid them side by side.

"Do you recognize this man?" she asked, pointing to the photograph. Page leaned over and picked it up.

"This is Martin Darius."

"Look carefully at this newspaper picture of Peter Lake and tell me what you think."

Page studied the two pictures. He imagined Lake with a beard and Darius without one. He tried to judge the size of the two men and compare builds.

"They could be the same person," he said.

"They are the same person. And the man who is murdering your women is the same man who murdered the women in Hunter's Point. We never released the color of the rose or the contents of the notes. Whoever is killing your women has information known only by the members of the Hunter's Point task force and the killer."

Gordon took a fingerprint card from the briefcase and handed it to Page.

"These are Lake's fingerprints. Compare them to Darius's. You must have some on file."

"How did you find Lake here?" Page asked.

Gordon took a sheet of stationery out of her briefcase and laid it on the coffee table next to the photograph.

"I've had it dusted for prints," she said. "There aren't any."

Page picked up the letter. It had been written on a word processor. The stationery looked cheap, probably the type sold in hundreds of chain stores and impossible to trace. The note read: "Women in Portland, Oregon are 'Gone, But Not Forgotten.'" The first letters of each word were capitalized like those in the notes found in the homes of the victims.

"I received this yesterday. The envelope was post-marked from Portland. The photograph of Darius and an *Oregonian* profile of him were inside. I knew it was Lake the minute I saw the picture. The envelope also con-tained a clipping about you, Mr. Page, your address and a ticket for a United Airlines flight. No one met me at the airport, so I came to see you."

"What do you suggest we do, Detective Gordon? We certainly can't bring Darius in for questioning with what you've given me."

"No!" Gordon said, alarmed. "Don't spook him. You have to stay away from Martin Darius until your case is airtight. You have no idea how clever he is."

Page was startled by Gordon's desperation.

"We know our business, Detective," he assured her.

"You don't know Peter Lake. You've never dealt with anyone like him."

"You said that before."

"You must believe me."

"Is there something else you aren't telling me?"

Gordon started to say something, then she shook her head.

"I'm exhausted, Mr. Page. I need to rest. You don't know what this is like for me. To have Lake surface after all these years. If you had seen what he did to Patricia Cross . . ."

There was a long pause and Page said nothing.

"I need a place to stay," Gordon said abruptly. "Can you suggest a motel? Someplace quiet."

"There's the Lakeview. We keep out-of-town witnesses there. I can drive you."

"No, don't. I'll take a cab. Can you call one for me?"

"Sure. My phone book is in my bedroom. I'll be right out."

"I'll leave you the fingerprint card, the photograph and the newspaper clipping. I have copies," Gordon said as she gathered up the note.

"You're certain you don't want me to drive you? It's no trouble."

Gordon shook her head. Page went into the bedroom and called for a cab. When he returned to the living room, Gordon was slumped on the couch, her eyes closed.

"They'll be here in ten minutes," he said.

Gordon's eyes snapped open. She looked startled, as if she had drifted off for a few minutes and had been scared awake.

"It's been a long day," the detective said. She looked embarrassed.

"Jet lag," Page said to make conversation. "I hope you're right about Darius."

"I am right," Gordon answered, her features rigid. "I am one hundred percent right. You believe that, Mr. Page. The lives of a lot of women depend on it."

Chapter Seven

I

Something was definitely wrong with Gordon's story. It was like a book with a great plot and a flat ending. And there were inconsistencies. The way Gordon told it, she, Grimsbo and Turner were dedicated detectives. If they were convinced Lake murdered six women and framed Waters, how could they simply let the case go? And why would Lake suddenly leave a thriving practice and disappear, if he thought he was in the clear? Had he ever followed up on his romantic interest in Gordon? She hadn't mentioned any contact after the night of Waters's arrest. Finally, there was the question Page had forgotten to ask. What about the women? Gordon had not told him what happened to the missing women.

While he waited for someone in the Hunter's Point Detective Bureau to pick up the phone, Page listed these points on a yellow legal pad. Rolling black storm clouds were coming in from the west. Page was awfully tired of the rain. Maybe these clouds would give him a break and float across the city before dropping their load. Maybe they would leave a space for the sun to shine through when they left.

"Roy Lenzer."

Page laid his pen down on the pad.

"Detective Lenzer, I'm Alan Page, the Multnomah County district attorney. That's in Portland, Oregon."

"What can I do for you?" Lenzer asked cordially.

"Do you have a detective in your department named Nancy Gordon?"

"Sure, but she's on vacation. Won't be back for a week or so."

"Can you describe her?"

Lenzer's description matched the woman who had visited Page's apartment.

"Is there something I can help you with?" he asked.

"Maybe. We have an odd situation here. Three women have disappeared. In each case, we found a note in the bedroom pinned down by a rose. Detective Gordon told me she was involved with an identical case in Hunter's Point, approximately ten years ago."

"It seems to me I heard something about the case, but I've only been on the force for five years. Moved here from Indiana. So I wouldn't be much help."

"What about Frank Grimsbo or Wayne Turner? They were the other detectives."

"There's no Grimsbo or Turner in the department now."

Page heard a rumble of thunder and looked out the window. A flag on the building across the way was snapping back and forth. It looked like it might rip off the pole.

"I don't suppose there's any chance I can get a copy of the file. The guy who was eventually arrested was Henry Waters . . ."

"W-A-T-E-R-S?"

"Right. He was shot resisting. I think there were six dead women. One of them was named Patricia Cross. Then there was Melody Lake, a young girl, and Sandra Lake, her mother. I don't remember the names of the others."

"If this happened ten years ago, the file is in storage. I'll get on it and let you know when I find it. What's your address and phone number?"

Page was telling them to Lenzer when Randy Highsmith, the chief criminal deputy, opened the door for William Tobias, the chief of police, and Ross Barrow, the detective in charge of the black rose case. Page motioned them into seats, then hung up.

"We may have a break in the case of the missing women," Page said. He started relating Gordon's version of the Hunter's Point case.

"Before the body was found at Waters's house, the chief suspect was Peter Lake, a husband of one of the victims," Page concluded. "There was enough circumstantial evidence to raise the possibility that Lake framed Waters. Shortly after the case was officially closed, Lake disappeared.

"Two days ago, Gordon received an anonymous note with the words 'Women in Portland, Oregon are "Gone, But Not Forgotten."' The first letter in each word was capitalized, just the way our boy does it. Enclosed was a photograph of Martin Darius leaving a motel room. Martin Darius may be Peter Lake. Gordon thinks he's our killer."

"I know Martin Darius," Tobias said incredulously.

"Everyone knows Darius," Page said, "but how much do we know about him?"

Page pushed the photograph of Darius and the newspaper with Lake's picture across the desk. Barrow, Tobias and Highsmith huddled over them.

"Boy," Highsmith said, shaking his head.

"I don't know, Al," Tobias said. "The news photo isn't that clear."

"Gordon left me Lake's prints for comparison. Can you run them, Ross?"

Barrow nodded and took the print card from Page.

"I'm having a hard time buying this," Tobias said. "I'd like to talk to your detective."

"Let me call her in. I'd like you to hear her tell the story," Page said, not revealing his doubts, because he wanted them to have an open mind when they heard Gordon.

Page dialed the number for the Lakeview Motel. He asked to be connected with Gordon's room, then leaned back while the desk clerk rang it.

"She's not? Well, this is very important. Do you know when she left? I see. Okay, tell her to call Alan Page as soon as she gets back."

Page left his number and hung up. "She checked in last night around one, but she's not in now. It's possible she's having breakfast."

"What do you want to do, Al?" Highsmith asked.

"I'd like a twenty-four-hour surveillance on Darius, in case Gordon is right."

"I can do that," Barrow said.

"Make sure you use good people, Ross. I don't want Darius to suspect we're watching him.

"Randy, run a background check on Darius. I want his life story as quickly as you can get it."

Highsmith nodded.

"As soon as Gordon calls, I'll get back to you."

Highsmith led Tobias and Barrow out of the office and closed the door. Page thought of dialing the Lakeview again, but it was too soon after the first call. He swiveled toward the window. It was pouring.

Why hadn't he spotted the flaws in Gordon's story last night? Was it Gordon? She seemed barely in control, on edge, as if electrical charges were coursing through her. He could not take his eyes off her when she talked. It was not a physical attraction. Something else drew him to her. Her passion, her desperation. Now that she was out of sight, he could think more clearly. When she was near him, she created a disturbance in the field, like the lightning flashing over the river.

2

Betsy scanned the restaurant for single women as she followed the hostess between a row of tables. She noticed a tall, athletic woman wearing a bright yellow blouse and a navy blue suit seated in a booth against the wall. As Betsy drew near, the woman stood up.

"You must be Nora Sloane," Betsy said as they shook hands. Sloane's complexion was pale. So were her blue eyes. She wore her chestnut-colored hair short. Betsy noticed a few gray streaks, but she guessed they were about the same age.

"Thank you for meeting me, Mrs. Tannenbaum."

"It's Betsy and you're a good saleswoman. When you called this morning and mentioned a free lunch, you hooked me."

Sloane laughed. "I'm glad you're this easy, because a free lunch is about all you're going to get out of me. I'm writing this article on spec. I got the idea when I covered your suit against the anti-abortion protestors for the *Arizona Republic*."

"You're from Phoenix?"

"New York, originally. My husband got a job in

Phoenix. We separated a year after we moved. I was never crazy about Arizona, especially with my ex living there, and I fell in love with Portland while I was covering your case. So, a month ago I quit my job and moved. I'm living on savings and looking for a job and I decided now was as good a time as any to write this article. I ran the idea by Gloria Douglas, an editor at *Pacific West* magazine, and she's definitely interested. But she wants to see a draft of the article before she commits."

"What exactly will the article cover?"

"Women litigators. And I want to use you and your cases as the centerpiece."

"I hope you're not going to make too much of me."

"Hey, don't get bashful on me," Sloane said with a laugh. "Until recently, women attorneys were relegated to the probate department or handled divorces. Stuff that was acceptable as 'woman's work.' My whole point is that you're at the vanguard of a new generation of women who are trying murder cases and getting million-dollar verdicts in civil cases. Areas that have traditionally been male-dominated."

"It sounds interesting."

"I'm glad you think so, because people want to read about you. You're really the hook for the article."

"What will I have to do?"

"Not much. Mostly, it will be talking to me about Hammermill and your other cases. On occasion, I may want to tag along when you go to court."

"That sounds okay. Actually, I think talking through my cases might help me put them in perspective. I was so close to what was happening when they were going on."

The waiter arrived. Sloane ordered a Caesar salad and a glass of white wine. Betsy ordered yellowfin tuna on pasta, but passed on the wine.

"What did you want to do today?" Betsy asked, as soon as the waiter left.

"I thought we'd go over some background material. I read the piece in *Time*, but I felt it was superficial. It didn't tell me what made you the way you are today. For instance, were you a leader in high school?"

Betsy laughed. "God, no. I was so shy. A real gawk."

Sloane smiled. "I can understand that. You were tall, right? I had the same problem."

"I towered over everyone. In elementary school, I walked around with my eyes down and my shoulders hunched, wishing I could disappear. In junior high, it got worse, because I had these Coke-bottle glasses and braces. I looked like Frankenstein."

"When did you start to feel self-confident?"

"I don't know if I ever feel that way. I mean, I know I do a good job, but I always worry I'm not doing enough. But I guess it was my senior year in high school that I started believing in myself. I was near the top of my class, the braces were gone, my folks got me contacts and boys started noticing me. By the time I graduated Berkeley I was much more outgoing."

"You met your husband in law school, didn't you?"

Betsy nodded. "We're separated, now."

"Oh. I'm sorry."

Betsy shrugged. "I really don't want to talk about my personal life. Will that be necessary?"

"Not if you don't want to. I'm not writing this for the *Enquirer*."

"Okay, because I don't want to discuss Rick."

"I understand you one hundred percent. I went through the same thing in Phoenix. I know how difficult it can be. So, let's move on to something else."

The waiter arrived with their food and Sloane asked

Betsy some more questions about her childhood while they ate.

"You didn't go into private practice right out of law school, did you?" Sloane asked after the waiter cleared their plates.

"No."

"Why not? You've done so well at it."

"That's been all luck," Betsy answered, blushing slightly. "I never thought of going out on my own, back then. My law school grades were all right, but not good enough for a big firm. I worked for the attorney general doing environmental law for four years. I liked the job, but I quit when I became pregnant with Kathy."

"How old is she?"

"Six."

"How did you get back into law?"

"I was bored sitting home when Kathy started pre-school. Rick and I talked it over and we decided I would practice out of our home, so I would be there for Kathy. Margaret McKinnon, a friend of mine from law school, let me use her conference room to meet clients. I didn't have much of a caseload. A few court-appointed misdemeanors, some simple divorces. Just enough to keep me busy.

"Then Margaret offered me a windowless office about the size of a broom closet, rent free, in exchange for twenty hours of free legal work each month. I agonized over that, but Rick said it was okay. He thought it would be good for me to get out of the house, as long as I kept my caseload low enough to pick up Kathy at day care and stay home with her if she got sick. You know, still be a mom. Anyway, it worked out fine and I started picking up some felonies and a few contested divorces that paid better."

"The Peterson case was your big break, right?"

"Yeah. One day I was sitting around without much to

do and the clerk who assigns court-appointed cases asked me if I'd represent Grace Peterson. I didn't know much about the battered woman's syndrome, but I remembered seeing Dr. Lenore Walker on a TV talk show. She's the expert in this area. The court authorized the money and Lenore came out from Denver and evaluated Grace. It was pretty horrible, what her husband did. I'd led a sheltered life, I guess. No one where I grew up did things like that."

"No one you knew about."

Betsy nodded sadly. "No one I knew about. Anyway, the case attracted a lot of publicity. We had the support of some women's groups and the press was behind us. After the acquittal, my business really picked up. Then Andrea hired me because of the verdict in Grace's case."

The waiter arrived with their coffee. Sloane looked at her watch. "You said you had a one-thirty appointment, didn't you?"

Betsy glanced at her own watch. "Is it one-ten already? I really got wrapped up in this."

"Good. I was hoping you'd be as excited about the project as I am."

"I am. Why don't you call me and we can talk again soon?"

"Great. I'll do that. And thanks for taking the time. I really appreciate it."

3

Randy Highsmith shook the rain off his umbrella and laid it on the floor under the dashboard as Alan Page drove out of the parking garage. The umbrella hadn't helped much in the gusting rain and Highsmith was cold and wet.

Highsmith was slightly overweight, studious-looking, a staunch conservative and the best prosecutor in the office, Page included. While earning a law degree from Georgetown he'd fallen in love with Patty Archer, a congressional aide. He then fell in love with Portland when he traveled there to meet Patty's family. When her congressman decided not to run for reelection, the newlyweds moved west, where Patty opened a political consulting firm and Randy was snapped up by the office of the Multnomah County district attorney.

"Tell me about Darius," Page said as they got on the freeway.

"He moved to Portland eight years ago. He had money to start with and borrowed on his assets. Darius made his name, and increased his fortune, by gambling on the revitalization of downtown Portland. His first big success was the Couch Street Boutique. He bought a block of dilapidated buildings for a song, converted them to an indoor mall, then changed the area surrounding the boutique into the trendiest section in Portland by leasing renovated buildings to upscale shops and restaurants at low rents. As business increased, so did the rents. The upper floors of a lot of the buildings were converted to condos. That's been his pattern. Buy up all the buildings in a slum area, set up a core attraction, then build around it. Recently he's branched out into suburban malls, apartment complexes, and so on.

"Two years ago, Darius married Lisa Ryder, the daughter of Oregon Supreme Court justice Victor Ryder. Ryder's old firm, Parish, Marquette and Reeves, handles his legal work. I talked to a few friends over there in confidence. Darius is brilliant and unscrupulous. Half the firm's energy is spent keeping him honest. The other half is spent defending lawsuits when they fail."

"What's 'unscrupulous' mean? Law violations, ethics, what?"

"Nothing illegal. But he has his own set of rules and a total disregard for the feelings of others. For instance, earlier this year he bought up a street of historically significant houses over in the Northwest, so he could tear them down and build town houses. There were several citizen groups up in arms. They got a temporary injunction and were trying to get the houses landmark status. A smart young lawyer at Parish, Marquette convinced the judge to drop the injunction. Darius moved bulldozers in at night and leveled the block before anyone knew what was going on."

"A guy like that must have done something illegal."

"The closest I've got is a rumor that he's friendly with Manuel Ochoa, a Mexican businessman who the D.E.A. thinks is laundering money for a South American drug cartel. Ochoa may be lending Darius money for a big project downstate that was risky enough to scare off some of the banks."

"What about his past?" Page asked as they drove into the parking lot of the Lakeview Motel.

"Doesn't have one, which makes sense if he's Lake."

"Did you check newspaper stories, profiles?"

"I did better than that. I spoke to the *Oregonian*'s top business reporter. Darius does not give interviews about his private life. For all anyone knows, he was born eight years ago."

Page pulled into a parking spot in front of the motel office. The dashboard clock read five twenty-six.

"Stay here. I'll see if Gordon's back."

"Okay. But there's one other thing you should

know." Page waited with the car door half-open. "We've got a link between our missing women and Darius."

Page closed the door. Highsmith smiled.

"I saved the best for last. Tom Reiser, the husband of Wendy Reiser, works for Parish, Marquette. He's the lawyer who convinced the judge to drop the injunction. Last Christmas, the Reisers attended a party at the Darius estate. This summer, they were invited to a bash to celebrate the opening of a mall, two weeks before the disappearances started. Reiser has had numerous business dealings with Darius.

"Larry Farrar's accounting firm has Darius Construction for a client. He and Laura Farrar were at the party for the mall opening too. He's done a lot of work for Darius.

"Finally, there's Victoria Miller. Her husband, Russell, works for Brand, Gates and Valcroft. That's the advertising firm that represents Darius Construction. Russell was just put in charge of the account. They've been on Darius's yacht and to his house. They were also at the mall opening party."

"That's unbelievable. Look, I want a list of the women at that party. We've got to alert Bill Tobias and Barrow."

"I already have. They're putting a second team on Darius."

"Good work. Gordon could be the key to wrapping this up."

Highsmith watched Page duck into the manager's office. A chubby man in a plaid shirt was standing behind the counter. Page showed the manager his i.d. and asked him a question. Highsmith saw the manager shake his head. Page said something else. The manager disappeared into a back room and reappeared in a raincoat. He grabbed a key from a hook on the wall. Page followed the manager outside and gestured to Highsmith.

Highsmith slammed the car door and raced under the protection afforded by the second-floor landing. Gordon's room was around the side of the motel on the ground floor. He arrived just as the manager knocked on the door and called out Gordon's name. There was no answer. A window faced into the parking lot. The green drapes were closed. There was a "Do Not Disturb" sign hanging from the doorknob.

"Miss Gordon," the manager called again. They waited a minute and he shrugged. "She hasn't been in all day, as far as I know."

"Okay," Page said, "let us in."

The manager opened the door with his key and stood aside. The room was dark, but someone had left the bathroom light on and it cast a pale glow over the empty motel room. Page flipped the light switch and looked around the room. The bed was undisturbed. Gordon's tan valise lay open on a baggage stand next to the dresser. Page walked into the bathroom. A toothbrush, a tube of toothpaste and makeup were set out on the bathroom counter. Page pulled back the shower curtain. A bottle of shampoo rested on a ledge. Page stepped out of the bathroom.

"She unpacked in here. There's a shampoo bottle in the bathtub. It's not a motel sample. Looks like she was planning to take a shower."

"Someone interrupted her," Highsmith said, pointing at a half-opened dresser drawer. Some of Gordon's clothes lay in it, while others remained in the valise.

"She had a briefcase with her when we talked at my place. Do you see it?"

The two men searched the room, but they did not find the briefcase.

"Look at this," Highsmith said. He was standing next to the night table. Page looked at a notepad with the motel logo that was next to the phone.

"Looks like directions. An address."

"Let's not touch it. I want a lab tech to dust the room. Treat it as a crime scene, until we know better."

"There's no sign of a struggle."

"There wasn't any at the homes of the missing women, either."

Highsmith nodded. "I'll call from the manager's office, in case there are prints on the phone."

"Do you have any idea where this is?" Page asked, as he reread the notes on the pad.

Highsmith's brow furrowed for a moment, then he frowned.

"As a matter of fact, I do. Remember I told you about the houses Darius bulldozed? This sounds like the address."

"What's there now?"

"A block-wide empty lot. As soon as the neighbors saw what Darius did, they went nuts. There have been protests, lawsuits. Darius went ahead with construction anyway and had three units built, but someone torched them. Construction's been halted ever since."

"I don't like this. How would anyone know where Gordon was? I'm the one who suggested the Lakeview."

"She could have phoned someone."

"No. I asked the manager. There weren't any outgoing calls. Besides, she doesn't know anyone in Portland. That's why she came to my place. She assumed the person who sent her the anonymous letter would meet her at the airport, but no one showed. A clipping about me and my address were in with the note. If she knew anyone else, she would have spent the night with them."

"Then someone must have followed her from the airport to your place and from your place here."

"That's possible."

"What if that person waited until she was in the room, then phoned Gordon and asked her to come to the construction site."

"Or came here and talked Gordon into going with him or took her by force."

"Gordon's a detective," Highsmith said. "I mean, you'd think she would have enough sense to be careful."

Page thought about Gordon. Her edge, the tension in her body.

"She's driven, Randy. Gordon told me she stayed a cop so she could track down Lake. She's been on this case for ten years and she dreams about it. Gordon's smart, but she might not be smart where this case is concerned."

The building site was larger than Page imagined. The houses Darius had destroyed were built along a bluff overlooking the Columbia River. The land included a steep wooded hill that angled down toward the water. A high, chain link fence surrounded the property. A "Darius Construction—Absolutely No Trespassing" sign was fastened to the fence. Page and Highsmith huddled under their umbrellas, the collars of their raincoats turned up around their cheeks, and studied the padlock on the gate. The moon was full, but storm clouds scudded across it with great frequency. The heavy rain made the night as dark as it would have been with no moon.

"What do you think?" Highsmith asked.

"Let's walk along the fence to see if there's another entrance. There's no sign she came in here."

"These are new shoes," Highsmith complained.

Page started off along the periphery without answering. The ground had been stripped bare of grass during construction. Page felt the mud oozing around his shoes. He peered through the fence as he walked, occasionally shining his flashlight inside the site. Most of the land was empty and flat where the bulldozers had done their work. At one point, he saw a shack. At another, his beam highlighted broken and burned timbers that had once been the framework of a Darius town house.

"Al, bring your light here," Highsmith shouted. He had walked ahead and was pointing at a section of fence that had been sheared through and folded back. Page ran over. He paused just before he reached Highsmith. A gust of cold wind struck his face. Page turned away for a second and clutched his collar closer to his neck.

"Look at this," Page said. He was standing under an ancient oak tree pointing the flashlight beam toward the ground. Tire tracks had gouged out the mud where they were standing. The canopy formed by the leaves covered the tracks. Page and Highsmith followed them away from the fence.

"Someone drove off the road across the field in this mud," Page said.

"Not necessarily tonight, though."

The tracks stopped at the street and disappeared. The rain would have washed away the mud from the asphalt.

"I think the driver backed up to the fence, Al. There's no sign that he turned around."

"Why back up? Why drive over to the fence at all and risk getting stuck in the mud?"

"What's in the back of a car?"

Page nodded, imagining Nancy Gordon folded in the confined space of a car trunk.

"Let's go," he said, heading back toward the hole in

the fence. In his heart, Page knew she was down there, buried in the soft earth.

Highsmith followed him through. As he ducked, he snagged his coat on a jagged piece of wire. By the time he freed himself, Page was well ahead, obscured by the darkness, only the wavering beam of the flashlight showing his location.

"Do you see any tracks?" Highsmith asked when he caught up.

"Look out!" Page cried, grabbing Highsmith by his coat. Highsmith pulled up. Page shone his light down. They were on the edge of a deep pit that had been gouged out of the earth for a foundation. Muddy walls sloped down toward the bottom, which was lost in darkness. Suddenly the moon appeared, bathing the bottom of the pit in a pale glow. The uneven surface cast shadows over rocks and mounds of dirt.

"I'm going down," Page said, as he went over the rim. He edged along the wall of the pit sideways, leaning into the slope and digging in with the sides of his shoes. Halfway down, he slipped to one knee and slid along the smooth mud, stopping his descent by grabbing a protruding root. The root had been severed by a bulldozer blade. The end came free of the mud, but Page slowed enough to dig in and stop his slide.

"You okay?" Highsmith called into the wind.

"Yeah. Randy, get down here. Someone's been digging recently."

Highsmith swore, then started edging down the slope. When he reached the bottom, Page was wandering slowly over the muddy ground, studying everything that entered the beam of his flashlight. The ground looked as if it had been turned over recently. He examined it as closely as he could in the dark.

The wind died suddenly and Page thought he heard

a sound. Something slithering in the shadows just out of
his line of sight. He tensed, trying to hear above the
wind, peering helplessly into the darkness. When he convinced himself he was the victim of his imagination, he
turned around and shone the light near the base of a steel
girder. Page straightened suddenly and took a step back,
catching his heel on a timber half-concealed in the mud.
He stumbled and the flashlight fell, its beam fanning out
over the rain-soaked earth, catching something white in
the light. A rock or a paper cup. Page knelt quickly and
recovered the flashlight. He walked over to the object
and squatted next to it. His breath caught in his chest.
Protruding from the earth was a human hand.

The sun was just coming up when they dug the last body
out of the ground. The horizon took on a scarlet tinge as
two officers lifted the corpse onto a stretcher. Around
them, other officers walked slowly over the muddy floor
of the construction site in search of more graves, but the
area had been scoured so thoroughly that no one expected to find one.

A prowl car perched on the edge of the pit. The door
on the driver's side was open. Alan Page sat in the front
seat with one foot on the ground, holding a paper cup
filled with scalding, black coffee, trying not to think about
Nancy Gordon and thinking of nothing else.

Page rested his head against the back of the seat. As
the darkness retreated, the river began taking on dimen-
sion. Page watched the flat black ribbon turn liquid and
turbulent in the red dawn. He believed Nancy Gordon
was in the pit, buried under layers of mud. He wondered
if there was something he could have done to save her.
He imagined Gordon's frustration and rage when she
died at the hands of the man she had sworn to stop.

The rain had ended shortly after the first police car arrived. Ross Barrow took charge of the crime scene, after consulting with the lab techs about the best way to handle the evidence. Floodlights shone down on the workers from the rim of the pit. Designated search areas were fenced off with yellow tape. Sawhorses had been erected as barriers against the curious. As soon as Page was certain Barrow could get along without him, he and Highsmith had grabbed a quick dinner at a local restaurant. By the time they returned, Barrow had positively identified Wendy Reiser's body and an officer had located a second grave.

Through the windshield, Page watched Randy Highsmith trudge toward the car. He had been in the pit observing while Page took a break.

"That's the last one," Highsmith said.

"What have we got?"

"Four bodies and positive i.d.s on Laura Farrar, Wendy Reiser and Victoria Miller."

"Were they killed like Patricia Cross?"

"I didn't look that closely, Al. To tell the truth, I almost lost it. Dr. Gregg is down there. She can give you the straight scoop when she comes up."

Page nodded. He was used to dealing with the dead, but that didn't mean he liked looking at a corpse any more than Highsmith.

"What about the fourth woman?" Page asked hesitantly. "Does she match my description of Nancy Gordon?"

"It's not a woman, Al."

"What!"

"It's an adult male, also naked, and his face and fingertips were burned away with acid. We'll be lucky to identify him."

Page saw Ross Barrow slogging through the mud and got out of the car.

"You're not stopping, Ross?"

"There's nothing more down there. You can look if you want."

"I was sure that Gordon . . . It doesn't make sense. She wrote the address."

"Maybe she met someone here and left with them," Barrow suggested.

"We didn't find any footprints," Highsmith reminded him. "She may not have found a way in."

"Did you find anything down there that'll help us figure out who did this?"

"Not a thing, Al. I'm guessing all four were killed elsewhere and transported here."

"Why's that?"

"Some of the bodies are missing organs. We haven't found them or any pieces of bone or excess flesh. No one could clean the area that thoroughly."

"Do you think we have enough to arrest Darius?" Page asked Highsmith.

"Not without Gordon or some solid evidence from Hunter's Point."

"What if we don't find her?" Page asked anxiously.

"In a pinch, you could swear to what she told you. We might get a warrant out of a judge with that. She's a cop. She'd be reliable. But, I don't know. With something like this, we shouldn't rush."

"And we don't really have a solid connection between Darius and the victims," Barrow added. "Finding them at a site owned by Darius Construction doesn't mean a thing. Especially when it's deserted and anyone could have gotten in."

"Do we know if Darius is Lake?" Page asked Barrow.

"Yeah. The prints match."

"Well, that's something," Highsmith said. "If we can get a match between those tire tracks and one of Darius's cars . . ."

"And if we can find Nancy Gordon," Page said, staring into the pit. He desperately wanted Gordon to be alive, but he had been in the business of violent death and lost hopes too long to grasp at straws.

Chapter Eight

I

"Detective Lenzer, this is Alan Page from Portland, Oregon. We talked the other day."

"Right. I was going to call you. That file you asked for is missing. We switched to computers seven years ago, but I did a search anyway. When I couldn't find it listed, I had a secretary go through the old files in storage. There's no file card and no file."

"Did someone check it out?"

"If they did, they didn't follow procedure. You're supposed to fill in a log sheet in case someone else needs the file, and there's no log entry."

"Could Detective Gordon have checked it out? She had a fingerprint card with her. It probably came from the file."

"The file isn't with her stuff in the office and it's against departmental policy to take files home unless you log them out. There's no record showing anyone logged it out. Besides, if there were six dead women it would be the highest victim count we've ever had here. We're probably talking about a file that would take up an entire shelf. Maybe more. Why would she be lugging around something that big? Hell, you'd need a couple of suitcases to get it home."

Page thought that over. "You're certain it's not in storage and just misplaced?"

"The file's not in storage, believe me. The person who looked for it did a real thorough job and I even went down there for a while."

Page was silent for a moment. He decided to tell Lenzer everything.

"Detective Lenzer, I'm pretty sure Nancy Gordon's in danger. She may even be dead."

"What?"

"I met her for the first time two nights ago and she told me about the Hunter's Point murders. She was convinced the man who committed them is living in Portland under a different name, committing similar crimes here.

"Gordon left my apartment a little after midnight and took a cab to a motel. Shortly after checking in, she left in a hurry. We found an address on a pad in her motel room. It's a construction site. We searched it and discovered the bodies of three missing Portland women and an unidentified man. They were tortured to death. We have no idea where Gordon is, and I'm thinking she was right about your killer being in Portland."

"Jesus. I like Nancy. She's a little intense, but she's a very good cop."

"The key to this case could be in the Hunter's Point files. She may have brought them home. I would suggest searching her house."

"I'll do anything I can to help."

Page told Lenzer to call him anytime, gave him his home number, then hung up. Lenzer had characterized Gordon as intense and Page had to agree. She was also dedicated. Ten years on the trail and still burning with that fire. Page had been like that once, but the years were getting to him. Tina's affair and the divorce had sucked him dry emotionally, but he had been losing ground even before her infidelity took over his life. Fighting for the office of district attorney had been great. Every day was exciting. Then he woke up one morning with the responsibilities of the job and the fear that he might not be able to fulfill them. He had mastered those fears through hard work, and he had mastered the job, but the thrill was gone. The days were all getting to be the same, and he was starting to think about what he would be doing ten years down the road.

The intercom buzzed and Page hit the com button.

"There's a man on line three with information about one of the women who was killed at the construction site," his secretary said. "I think you should talk to him."

"Okay. What's his name?"

"Ramon Gutierrez. He's the clerk at the Hacienda Motel in Vancouver, Washington."

Page hit the button for line three and talked to Ramon Gutierrez for five minutes. When he was done, he called Ross Barrow, then headed down the hall to Randy Highsmith's office. Fifteen minutes later, Barrow picked up Highsmith and Page on the corner and they headed for Vancouver.

2

"Can I watch TV?" Kathy asked.

"Did you have enough pizza?"

"I'm stuffed."

Betsy felt guilty about dinner, but she had put in an

exhausting day in court and didn't have the energy to cook.

"Is Daddy going to come home tonight?" Kathy asked, looking up at Betsy expectantly.

"No," Betsy answered, hoping Kathy would not ask her anymore about Rick. She had explained the separation to Kathy a number of times, but Kathy would not accept the fact that Rick was most probably never going to live with them again.

Kathy looked worried. "Why won't Daddy stay with us?"

Betsy picked up Kathy and carried her to the living room couch.

"Who's your best friend?"

"Melanie."

"Remember the fight you two had, last week?"

"Yeah."

"Well, Daddy and I had an argument too. It's a serious one. Just like the one you had with your best friend."

Kathy looked confused. Betsy held Kathy on her lap and kissed the top of her head.

"Melanie and me made up. Are you and Daddy going to make up?"

"Maybe. I don't know right now. Meanwhile, Daddy is living someplace else."

"Is Daddy mad at you because he had to pick me up at day care?"

"What made you ask that?"

"He was awful mad the other day and I heard you arguing about me."

"No, honey," Betsy said, hugging Kathy tight to her. "This doesn't have anything to do with you. It's just us. We're mad at each other."

"Why?" Kathy asked. Her jaw was quivering.

"Don't cry, honey."

"I want Daddy," she said, sobbing into Betsy's shoulder. "I don't want him to go away."

"He won't go away. He'll always be your daddy, Kathy. He loves you."

Suddenly Kathy pushed away from Betsy and wriggled off her lap.

"It's your fault for working," she yelled.

Betsy was shocked. "Who told you that?"

"Daddy. You should stay home with me like Melanie's mom."

"Daddy works," Betsy said, trying to stay calm. "He works more than I do."

"Men are supposed to work. You're supposed to take care of me."

Betsy wished Rick was here so she could smash him with her fists.

"Who stayed home with you when you had the flu?" Betsy asked.

Kathy thought for a moment. "You, Mommy," she answered, looking up at Betsy.

"And when you hurt your knee at school, who came to take you home?"

Kathy looked down at the floor.

"What do you want to be when you grow up?"

"An actress or a doctor."

"That's work, honey. Doctors and actresses work just like lawyers. If you stayed home all day, you couldn't do that work."

Kathy stopped crying. Betsy picked her up again.

"I work because it's fun. I also take care of you. That's more fun. I love you much more than I like my work. It's no contest. But I don't want to stay home all day doing nothing while you're at school. It would be boring, don't you think?"

Kathy thought about that.

"Will you make up with Daddy, like I did with Melanie?"

"I'm not sure, honey. But either way, you'll see plenty of Daddy. He still loves you very much and he'll always be your dad.

"Now, why don't you watch a little TV and I'll clean up, then I'll read you another chapter of *The Wizard of Oz*."

"I don't feel like TV, tonight."

"Do you want to help me in the kitchen?"

Kathy shrugged.

"How about a hot chocolate? I could make one while we're cleaning the dishes."

"Okay," Kathy said without much enthusiasm. Betsy followed her daughter into the kitchen. She was too small to have to carry the heavy burden of her parents' problems, but she was going to anyway. That was the way it worked and there was nothing Betsy could do about it.

After they were finished in the kitchen, Betsy read Kathy two chapters of *The Wizard of Oz*, then put her to bed. It was almost nine o'clock. Betsy looked at the TV listings and was about to turn on the set when the phone rang. She walked into the kitchen and picked up on the third ring.

"Betsy Tannenbaum?" a man asked.

"Speaking."

"This is Martin Darius. The police are at my home with a search warrant. I want you over here immediately."

A high brick wall surrounded the Darius estate. A policeman in a squad car was parked next to a black wrought-iron gate. As Betsy turned the Subaru into the driveway, the policeman got out of his car and walked over to her window.

"I'm afraid you can't go in, ma'am."

"I'm Mr. Darius's attorney," Betsy said, holding her Bar card out the window. The officer examined the card for a second, then returned it to her.

"My orders are to keep everyone out."

"I can assure you that doesn't include Mr. Darius's attorney."

"Ma'am, there's a search being conducted. You'd be in the way."

"I'm here because of the search. A warrant to search doesn't give the police the right to bar people from the place being searched. You have a walkie-talkie in your car. Why don't you call the detective in charge and ask him if I can come in."

The officer's patronizing smile was replaced by a Clint Eastwood stare, but he walked back to his car and used the walkie-talkie. He returned less than a minute later, and he did not look happy.

"Detective Barrow says you can go in."

"Thank you," Betsy answered politely. As she drove off, she could see the cop glaring at her in the rearview mirror.

After seeing the old-fashioned brick wall and the ornate scrollwork on the wrought-iron gate, Betsy assumed Darius would live in a sedate, colonial mansion, but she found herself staring at a collection of glass and steel fashioned into sharp angles and delicate curves that had nothing to do with the nineteenth century. She parked next to a squad car near the end of a curved driveway. A bridge covered by a blue awning connected the driveway with the front door. Betsy looked down through a glass roof as she walked along the bridge and saw several officers standing around the edge of an indoor pool.

A policeman was waiting for her at the front door. He guided her down a short set of stairs into a cavernous living room. Darius was standing under a giant abstract painting in vivid reds and garish greens. Beside him was a slender woman in a black dress. Her shiny black hair cascaded over her shoulders and her tan spoke of a recent vacation in the tropics. She was stunningly beautiful.

The man standing next to Darius was not. He had a beer gut and a face that would be more at home in a sports bar than a condo in the Bahamas. He was dressed in an unpressed brown suit and white shirt. His tie was askew and his raincoat was draped unceremoniously over the back of a snow-white sofa.

Before Betsy could say anything, Darius thrust a rolled-up paper at her.

"Is this a valid warrant? I'm not going to permit an invasion of my privacy until you've looked at the damn thing."

"I'm Ross Barrow, Ms. Tannenbaum," said the man in the brown suit. "This warrant's been signed by Judge Reese. The sooner you tell your client we can go through with this, the sooner we'll be out of here. I could have started already, but I waited for you to make certain Mr. Darius had representation during the search."

If Darius was a black dope dealer instead of a prominent white socialite and businessman, Betsy knew the house would have been a shambles by the time she arrived. Somebody had ordered Barrow to go very slowly with this case.

"The warrant seems okay, but I'd like to see the affidavit," Betsy said, asking for the document the police prepare to convince a judge that there is probable cause for the issuance of a warrant to search someone's house.

The affidavit would contain the factual basis for the suspicion that somewhere in the Darius mansion was evidence of a crime.

"Sorry, the affidavit's been sealed."

"Can you at least tell me why you're searching? I mean, what are the charges?"

"There aren't any charges yet."

"Let's not play games, Detective. You don't roust someone like Martin Darius without a reason."

"You're going to have to ask District Attorney Page about the case, Ms. Tannenbaum. I've been told to refer all inquiries to him."

"Where can I reach him?"

"I'm afraid I don't know that. He's probably home, but I'm not authorized to give out that number."

"What kind of bullshit is this?" Darius asked angrily.

"Calm down, Mr. Darius," Betsy said. "The warrant is legal and he can search. There's nothing we can do now. If it turns out that the affidavit is faulty, we'll be able to suppress any evidence they find."

"Evidence of what?" Darius demanded. "They refuse to tell me what they're looking for."

"Martin," the woman in black said, laying a hand on his forearm, "let them search. Please. I want them out of here, and they're not going to leave until they're through."

Darius pulled his arm away. "Search the damn house," he told Barrow angrily, "but you'd better get yourself a good lawyer, because I'm going to sue your ass all over this state."

Detective Barrow walked away, the insults bouncing ineffectively off his broad back. Just as he reached the steps leading out of the living room, a gray-haired man in a windbreaker entered the house.

"The tread on the BMW matches and there's a black

Ferrari in the garage," Betsy heard him say. Barrow motioned to two uniforms who were standing in the entryway. They followed him back to Darius.

"Mr. Darius, I'm placing you under arrest for the murders of Wendy Reiser, Laura Farrar and Victoria Miller."

The color drained from Darius's face and the woman's hand flew to her mouth, as if she was going to be sick.

"You have the right to remain silent . . ." Barrow said, reading from a laminated card he had taken from his wallet.

"What the fuck is this?" Darius exploded.

"What is he talking about?" the woman asked Betsy.

"I have to inform you of these rights, Mr. Darius."

"I think we're entitled to an explanation, Detective Barrow," Betsy said.

"No, ma'am, you're not," Barrow responded. Then he finished reading Darius his *Miranda* rights.

"Now, Mr. Darius," Barrow went on, "I'm going to have to handcuff you. This is procedure. We do it with everyone we arrest."

"You're not handcuffing anyone," Darius said, taking a step back.

"Mr. Darius, don't resist," Betsy said. "You can't do that, even if the arrest is illegal. Go with him. Just don't say a thing.

"Detective Barrow, I want to accompany Mr. Darius to the station."

"That won't be possible. I assume you don't want him questioned, so we'll book him in as soon as we get downtown. I wouldn't go down to the jail until tomorrow morning. I can't guarantee when he'll finish the booking process."

"What's my bail?" Darius demanded.

"There isn't any for murder, Mr. Darius," Barrow answered calmly. "Ms. Tannenbaum can ask for a bail hearing."

"What's he saying?" the woman asked in disbelief.

"May I talk with Mr. Darius for a moment in private?" Betsy asked.

Barrow nodded. "You can go over there," he said, pointing to a corner of the living room away from the windows. Betsy led Darius to the corner. The woman tried to follow, but Barrow told her she could not join them.

"What's this about no bail? I'm not sitting in some jail with a bunch of drug dealers and pimps."

"There's no automatic bail for murder or treason, Mr. Darius. It's in the Constitution. But there is a way to get a judge to set bail. I'll schedule a bail hearing as soon as possible and I'll see you first thing in the morning."

"I don't believe this."

"Believe it and listen to me. Anything you tell anyone will be used to convict you. I don't want you talking to a soul. Not the cops, not a cell mate. No one. There are snitches at the jail who'll trade you to beat their case and every guard will repeat every word you say to the d.a."

"Goddamn it, Tannenbaum. You get me out of this fast. I paid you to protect me. I'm not going to rot in jail."

Betsy saw Detective Barrow motion the two officers toward them.

"Remember, not a word," she said as Barrow reached them.

"Hands behind you, please," said one of the uniforms. Darius complied and the officer snapped on the cuffs. The woman watched in wide-eyed disbelief.

"I'll expect you first thing in the morning," Darius said as they led him away.

"I'll be there."

Betsy felt a hand on her arm.

"Mrs. Tannenbaum . . . ?"

"It's Betsy."

"I'm Martin's wife, Lisa. What's happening? Why are they taking Martin away?"

Lisa Darius looked bewildered, but Betsy did not see any tears. She seemed more like a hostess whose party has been a stunning flop, than a wife whose husband had just been arrested for mass murder.

"You know as much as I do, Lisa. Did the police mention anything about why they were at your home?"

"They said . . . I can't believe what they said. They asked us about the three women who were found at Martin's construction site."

"That's right," Betsy said, suddenly remembering why the names Barrow had spoken sounded so familiar.

"Martin couldn't have had anything to do with that. We know the Millers. They were out on our yacht this summer. This has to be a mistake."

"Mrs. Darius?"

Betsy and Lisa Darius looked toward the living room stairs. A black detective dressed in jeans and a black and red Portland Trail Blazers jacket was walking toward them.

"We're going to seize your BMW. May I have your key, please?" he asked politely, handing her a yellow carbon of a property receipt.

"Our car? Can they do this?" Lisa asked Betsy.

"The warrant mentioned cars."

"Oh, God. Where will this end?"

"I'm afraid my men are going to have to search your house," the detective told her apologetically. "We'll try to be neat and put everything back that we don't take. If you like, you can come along with us."

"I can't. Just be quick, please. I want you out of my house."

The detective was embarrassed. He looked down at the carpet as he walked off. Barrow had taken his raincoat with him, but there was a damp spot on the sofa where it had lain. Lisa Darius looked at the spot with distaste and sat as far from it as she could. Betsy sat next to her.

"How long is Martin going to be in jail?"

"That depends. The State has the burden of convincing the court that it's got a damn good case, if it wants to hold Martin without bail. I'll ask for an immediate hearing. If the State can't meet its burden, he'll be out quickly. If they meet it, he won't get out at all, unless we get a not guilty verdict."

"This is unbelievable."

"Lisa," Betsy asked cautiously, "did you have any idea something like this might happen?"

"What do you mean?"

"It's been my experience that the police usually don't act unless they have a pretty good case. They make mistakes, of course, but that's rarer than you'd think from the way they're portrayed on television. And your husband's no street punk. I can't imagine Alan Page rousting someone of Martin's stature in the community without some pretty strong evidence. Especially on a charge like this."

Lisa stared openmouthed at Betsy for a moment.

"Are you suggesting . . . ? I thought you were Martin's lawyer. If you don't believe him, you have no business handling his case. I don't know why he hired you, anyway. Daddy says Oscar Montoya and Matthew Reynolds are the best criminal lawyers in Oregon. He could have had either one of them."

"A lawyer who only thinks what her client wants her to think isn't doing her job," Betsy said calmly. "If there's something you know about these charges, I have to know it, so I can defend Martin properly."

"Well, there isn't," Lisa answered, looking away from Betsy. "The whole thing is outrageous."

Betsy decided not to push. "Do you have anyone who can stay with you?" she asked.

"I'll be fine by myself."

"This will get rough, Lisa. The press will be hounding you night and day, and living in a spotlight is much worse than most people imagine. Do you have an answering machine you can use to screen your calls?"

Lisa nodded.

"Good. Put it on and don't take any calls from the media. Since we don't have any idea of the case against Martin, we don't know what can hurt him. For instance, where Martin was on a certain date might be crucial. If you tell the press he wasn't with you on that date, it could destroy an alibi. So don't say anything. If a reporter does get through to you, refer her to me. And never talk to the police or someone from the d.a.'s office. There's a privilege for husband-wife communications and you have a right to refuse to talk to anyone. Do you understand?"

"Yes. I'll be okay. And I'm sorry I said that. About how Martin could have gotten someone better. I'm just . . ."

"No need to apologize or explain. This must be very difficult for you."

"You don't have to stay with me."

"I'll stay until the search is finished. I want to see what they're taking. It might tell us why they think Martin's involved. I heard one officer tell Barrow they matched the tread on the BMW to something. That means they've placed Martin's car somewhere. Maybe the crime scene."

"So what? He drives to his construction sites all the time. This whole thing is ridiculous."

"We'll see soon enough," Betsy said, but she was worried. Lisa Darius may have been shocked and surprised by her husband's arrest, but Betsy knew Martin Darius was not. No one gives a $58,000 retainer to a lawyer in anticipation of being arrested for shoplifting. That was the type of retainer a good lawyer received for representing someone on a murder charge.

Chapter Nine

"It's a pleasure to meet you, Mrs. Tannenbaum," Alan Page said when Betsy was seated across his desk from him. "Randy Highsmith was very impressed with the way you handled the Hammermill case. He had nothing but nice things to say about you. That's really high praise, because Randy hates to lose."

"I think Randy might not have brought the charges if he knew how brutal Andrea's husband was."

"That's being charitable. Let's face it. Randy thought he'd run over you. You taught him a good lesson. Losing 'Hammermill' will make Randy a better prosecutor. But you're not here to talk about old business, are you? You're here to talk about Martin Darius."

"Detective Barrow must have called you at home at the phone number he wouldn't give me."

"Ross Barrow's a good cop who knows how to follow orders."

"Do you want to tell me why you've arrested my client?"

"I think he murdered the four people we found buried at his construction site."

"That's obvious, Mr. Page . . ."

"Why don't you call me Al?"

"I'd be glad to. And you may call me Betsy. Now that we're on a first-name basis, how about telling me why you searched Martin's house and arrested him?"

Page smiled. "'Fraid I can't do that."

"Won't, you mean."

"Betsy, you know you're not entitled to discovery of our police reports until I've filed an indictment."

"You're going to have to tell the judge what you've got at the bail hearing."

"True. But that's not scheduled yet and there's no indictment, so I'm going to stick to the letter of the discovery statutes."

Betsy leaned back in her chair and smiled sweetly.

"You must not have much confidence in your case, Al."

Page laughed to cover his surprise that Betsy had seen through him so easily.

"I've got plenty of confidence in our case," he lied. "But I also have a healthy respect for your abilities. I won't make Randy's mistake of underestimating you. I must confess, though, that with your commitment to feminism I was surprised when Ross told me you were defending Darius."

"What does feminism have to do with my representation of Martin Darius?"

"Hasn't he told you what he's done?"

"Martin Darius has no idea why you're holding him and neither do I."

Page looked at her for a moment, then made a decision.

"I guess it's not fair leaving you completely in the dark, so I'll tell you that we plan to indict your client for the kidnapping, torture and murder of three women and one man."

Page took a color photo of Wendy Reiser's body out of a manila envelope and handed it to Betsy. She blanched. The picture had been taken right after the body had been dug up. The naked woman was sprawled in the mud. Betsy could see the incisions on her stomach and the cuts and burn marks on her legs. She could also see Wendy Reiser's face clearly. Even in death, she seemed to be suffering.

"That's what Martin Darius does to women, Betsy, and this may not be the first time he's done it. We have pretty solid information that ten years ago a man named Peter Lake murdered six women in Hunter's Point, New York, in much the same way these victims were murdered. We also have conclusive proof that Peter Lake and Martin Darius are the same person. You might want to ask your client about that.

"One other thing. There's another missing woman. This is a one-time offer: If she's alive and Darius tells us where she is, we might be able to deal."

The jail elevator opened onto a narrow concrete hallway painted in yellow and brown pastels. Across from the elevator were three solid doors. Betsy used the key the guard had given her when she checked in at the visitor's desk. The middle door opened into a tiny room. In front of her was a wall divided in half by a narrow ledge. Below the ledge was concrete; above, a slab of bulletproof glass. Betsy placed her legal pad on the ledge, sat down on an uncomfortable metal folding chair and picked up the receiver on the phone that was attached to the wall to her left.

On the other side of the glass, Martin Darius lifted his receiver. He was dressed in an orange jumpsuit, but he still looked as imposing as he had in her office. His hair and beard were combed and he sat erect and at ease. Darius leaned forward until he was almost touching the glass. His eyes looked a little wild, but that was the only sign of discontent.

"When is the bail hearing scheduled?" Darius asked.

"It isn't."

"I told you I wanted out of here. You should have scheduled the hearing first thing this morning."

"This isn't going to work. I'm an attorney, not a gofer. If you want someone to order around I'll refer you to a maid service."

Darius stared at Betsy for a moment, then flashed an icy smile of concession.

"Sorry. Twelve hours in this place doesn't help your disposition."

"I met with Alan Page, the district attorney, this morning. He had some interesting things to tell me. He also showed me the crime scene photographs. The three women were tortured, Martin. I've seen a lot of cruelty, but nothing like this. The killer didn't just end their lives, he slaughtered them. Tore them open . . ."

Betsy stopped, as the memory of what she'd seen took her breath away. Darius watched her. She waited for him to say something. When he didn't, she asked:

"Does any of this sound familiar?"

"I didn't kill those women."

"I didn't ask you if you killed them. I asked if anything about the crimes sounded familiar."

Darius studied Betsy. She didn't like the way he made her feel like a lab specimen.

"Why are you interrogating me?" Darius asked. "You work for me, not the d.a."

"Mr. Darius, I decide whom I work for and right now I'm not so sure I want to work for you."

"Page said something, didn't he. He played with your head."

"Who is Peter Lake?"

Betsy expected a reaction, but not the one she got. The look of icy calm deserted Darius. His lip trembled. He looked, suddenly, like a man on the verge of tears.

"So Page knows about Hunter's Point."

"You haven't been honest with me, Mr. Darius."

"Is that what this is all about?" Darius asked, pointing at the bulletproof glass. "Is that why you didn't ask for a contact visit? Are you afraid to be locked in with me? Afraid I'll . . ."

Darius stopped. He put his head in his hands.

"I don't think I'm the right person to represent you," Betsy told him.

"Why?" Darius asked, his voice filled with pain. "Because Page claims I raped and murdered those women? Did you refuse to represent Andrea Hammermill when the district attorney said she murdered her husband?"

"Andrea Hammermill was the victim of a husband who beat her constantly during her marriage."

"But she killed him, Betsy. I did *not* murder those women. I swear it. I did *not* kill anyone in Hunter's Point. I was Peter Lake, but, do you know who Peter Lake was? Did Page tell you that? Does he even know?

"Peter Lake was married to the most wonderful woman in the world. He was the father of a perfect child. A little girl who never hurt anyone. And his wife and daughter were murdered by a madman named Henry Waters for an insane reason Peter could never fathom.

"Peter was a lawyer. He made money hand over fist. He lived in a magnificent house and drove a fancy car, but all that money and everything he owned couldn't make him forget the wife and daughter who'd been taken from him. So he ran away. He assumed a new identity and started a new life, because his old life was impossible to bear."

Darius stopped talking. There were tears in his eyes. Betsy did not know what to think. Moments ago, she was convinced Darius was a monster. Now, seeing his pain, she wasn't so sure.

"I'll make you a deal, Betsy," Darius said, his voice barely above a whisper. "If you reach the point where you don't believe I'm innocent, you can walk away from my case with my blessing, and you can keep your retainer."

Betsy did not know what to say. Those pictures. She couldn't stop wondering how the women felt in those first, long moments of terror, knowing that the best that could ever happen to them in the rest of their lives was a death that would bring an end to their pain.

"It's all right," Darius said, "I know how you feel. You only saw the pictures. I saw the dead bodies of my wife and my child. And I still see them, Betsy."

Betsy felt ill. She took a deep breath. She could not stay in the narrow room any longer. She needed air. And she needed to find out a lot more about Peter Lake and what happened in Hunter's Point.

"Are you okay?" Darius asked.

"No, I'm not. I'm very confused."

"I know you are. Page laid a heavy trip on you. They said I'd be arraigned tomorrow. You get a good night's sleep and tell me what you've decided to do, then."

Betsy nodded.

"Two things, though," Darius said, looking directly at Betsy.

"What's that?"

"If you decide to keep me as a client, you've got to fight like hell for me."

"And the other thing?"

"From now on, I want every visit to be a contact visit. No more glass cage. I don't want my lawyer treating me like a zoo animal."

Chapter Ten

As soon as Rita Cohen opened the door wide enough, Kathy squeezed through and raced into the kitchen.

"You didn't buy that bubble-gum-flavored cereal again, did you, Mom?" Betsy asked.

"She's a little kid, Betsy. Who could stand that healthy stuff you feed her all the time? Let her live."

"That's what I'm trying to do. If it was up to you, she'd be on an all-cholesterol diet."

"When I was growing up, we didn't know from cholesterol. We ate what made us happy, not the same stuff you feed horses. And look at me. Seventy-four and still going strong."

Betsy hugged her mother and gave her a kiss on the forehead. Rita was only five feet four, so Betsy had to bend down to do it. Betsy's dad never topped five feet nine. No one could figure where Betsy got her height.

"How come there's no school?" Rita asked.

"It's another teacher planning day. I forgot to read the flyer they sent home, so I didn't know until yesterday evening, when Kathy mentioned it."

"You have time for a cup of coffee?" Rita asked.

Betsy looked at her watch. It was only seven-twenty. They would not let her into the jail to see Darius until eight.

"Sure," she said, dropping the backpack with Kathy's things on a chair and following her mother into the living room. The television was already on, tuned to a morning talk show.

"Don't let her watch too much TV," Betsy said, sitting down on the couch. "I packed some books and games for her."

"A little television isn't going to kill her any more than that cereal."

Betsy laughed. "One day with you undoes all the good habits I've instilled in a year. You're an absolute menace."

"Nonsense," Rita answered gruffly, pouring two cups of coffee from the pot she had prepared in expectation of Betsy's visit. "So, what are you doing this morning that's so important you had to abandon that lovely angel to such an ogre?"

"You've heard of Martin Darius?"

"Certainly."

"I'm representing him."

"What did he do?"

"The d.a. thinks Darius raped and killed the three women they found at his construction site. He also thinks Darius tortured and killed six women in Hunter's Point, New York, ten years ago."

"Oh, my God! Is he guilty?"

"I don't know. Darius swears he's innocent."

"And you believe him?"

Betsy shook her head. "It's too early to say."

"He's a rich man, Betsy. The police wouldn't arrest someone that important without proof."

"If I took the State's word for everything, Andrea Hammermill and Grace Peterson would be in prison today."

Rita looked concerned. "Should you be representing

a man who rapes and tortures women after all the work you've done for women's rights?"

"We don't know that he tortured anyone, Mom, and that feminist label is something the press stuck on me. I want to work for women's rights, but I'm not just a woman's lawyer. This case will help me be seen as more than one-dimensional. It could make my career. And, more important, Darius may be innocent. The d.a. won't tell me why he thinks Darius is guilty. That makes me very suspicious. If he had the goods on Darius he'd be confident enough to tell me what he's got."

"I just don't want to see you get hurt."

"I won't get hurt, Mom, because I'll do a good job. I learned something when I won Grace's case. I have a talent. I'm a very good trial attorney. I have a knack for talking to jurors. I'm damned good at cross-examination. If I win this case, people across the country are going to know how good I am, and that's why I want this case so badly. But I'm going to need your help."

"What do you mean?"

"The case is going to go on for at least a year. The trial could last for months. With the State asking for the death penalty, I'm going to have to fight every step of the way, and the case is extremely complicated. It's going to take all my time. We're talking about events that occurred ten years ago. I've got to find out everything there is to know about Hunter's Point, Darius's background. That means I'll be working long hours and weekends and I'm going to need help with Kathy. Someone has to pick her up from day care, if I'm tied up in court, make her dinner . . ."

"What about Rick?"

"I can't ask him. You know why."

"No, I don't know why. He's Kathy's father. He's also your husband. He should be your biggest fan."

"Well, he's not. He's never accepted the fact that I'm a real lawyer with a successful practice."

"What did he think you'd be doing when you hung out your shingle?"

"I think he thought it was going to be a cute hobby like stamp collecting, something to keep me occupied when I wasn't cooking dinner or cleaning."

"Well, he is the man of the house. Men like to feel they're in charge. And here you are, getting all the headlines and talking on the television."

"Look, Mom, I don't want to discuss Rick. Do you mind? I just get angry."

"All right, I won't discuss him and, of course, I'll help."

"I don't know how I'd make it without you, Mom."

Rita blushed and waved a hand at Betsy. "That's what mothers are for."

"Granny," Kathy yelled from the kitchen, "I can't find the chocolate syrup."

"Why would she want chocolate syrup at seven-thirty in the morning?" Betsy asked menacingly.

"None of your business," Rita answered imperiously. "I'm coming, sweetheart. It's too high up. You can't reach it."

"I've got to go," Betsy said, with a resigned shake of the head. "And please keep the TV to a minimum."

"We're only reading Shakespeare and studying algebra this morning," Rita answered as she disappeared into the kitchen.

Reggie Stewart was waiting for Betsy on a bench near the visitor's desk at the jail. Stewart had worked at several unsatisfying jobs before discovering a talent for investigation. He was a slender six-footer with shaggy brown hair

and bright blue eyes who was most comfortable in plaid
flannel shirts, cowboy boots and jeans. Stewart had an
odd way of looking at events and a sarcastic air that put
off some people. Betsy appreciated the way he used his
imagination and his knack for making people trust him.
These attributes proved invaluable in the Hammermill
and Peterson cases, where the best evidence of abuse
came from the victims' relatives and would have remained buried under layers of hate and family pride if it
was not for Reggie's persuasiveness and persistence.

"Ready, Chief?" Stewart asked, smiling as he un-
wound from the bench.

"Always," Betsy answered with a smile.

Stewart had filled out visitor's forms for both of
them. A guard sat behind a glass window in a control
room. Betsy pushed the forms and their i.d. through a slot
in the window and asked for a contact visit with Martin
Darius. As soon as the guard told them it was set, she and
Reggie emptied the metal objects from their pockets,
took off their watches and jewelry and walked through
the metal detector. The guard checked Betsy's briefcase,
then called for the elevator. When it came, Betsy inserted
the key for the seventh floor in a lock and turned it. The
elevator rode up to seven and the doors opened on the
same narrow hall Betsy had stepped into the day before.
This time, she walked to the far end and waited in front
of a thick metal door with an equally thick piece of glass
in the upper half. Through the glass, she could see the
two seventh-floor contact rooms. They were both empty.

"Darius is going to be a demanding client," Betsy
told Stewart as they waited for the guard. "He's used to
being in charge, he's very bright and he's under tremen-
dous pressure."

"Gottcha."

"Today, we listen. The arraignment isn't until nine,

so we have an hour. I want to get his version of what happened in Hunter's Point. If we're not done by nine, you can finish up later."

"What's he facing?"

Betsy pulled a copy of the indictment from her brief-case.

"This don't look good, Chief," Stewart said after reading the charges. "Who's 'John Doe'?"

"The man. The police have no idea who he is. His face and fingertips were disfigured with acid and the killer even smashed his teeth with a hammer to try and prevent an i.d. from his dental records."

Stewart grimaced. "This is one set of crime scene photos I'm not lookin' forward to seeing."

"They're the worst, Reg. Look at them before break-fast. I almost lost mine."

"How do you dope it out?"

"You mean, do I think Darius did it?" Betsy shook her head. "I'm not sure. Page is convinced, but either Darius put on a great performance for me yesterday, or he's not guilty."

"So we have a real whodunit?"

"Maybe."

Out of their sight, a heavy lock opened with a loud snap. Betsy craned her neck and saw Darius precede the guard into the narrow space in front of the two contact rooms. When her client was locked in one of them, the guard let Betsy and Stewart into the contact area, then secured the door to the hall where they had been waiting. After locking them in with Darius, the guard left the contact visiting area by the door through which he had entered.

The contact room was small. Most of the space in it was taken up by a large circular table and three plastic chairs. Darius was sitting in one of them. He did not stand up when Betsy entered.

"I see you brought a bodyguard," Darius said, studying Stewart carefully.

"Martin Darius meet Reggie Stewart, my investigator."

"You're only using one?" Darius asked, ignoring Reggie's outstretched hand. Stewart pulled his hand back slowly.

"Reggie is very good. I wouldn't have won 'Hammermill' without him. If I think you need more investigators, you'll get them. Here's a copy of the indictment."

Darius took the paper and read it.

"Page is charging you under several theories in the death of each person: personally killing a human being during the commission of the felony crime of kidnapping; torture killing; more than one victim. If he gets a conviction on any theory of Aggravated Murder, we go into a second, or penalty, phase of the trial. That's a second trial on the issue of punishment.

"In the penalty phase, the State has to convince the jurors that you committed the murder deliberately, that the victim's provocation, if any, did not mitigate the killing and that there's a probability that you'll be dangerous in the future. If the jurors answer 'yes' unanimously to these three questions, you'll be sentenced to death, unless there is some mitigating circumstance that convinces any juror that you should not get a death sentence.

"If any juror votes 'no' on any question, the jurors then decide on whether you get life without parole or life with a thirty-year minimum sentence. Any questions, so far?"

"Yes, Tannenbaum," Darius said, looking at her with an amused smile. "Why are you wasting your time on an explanation of the penalty phase? I did not kidnap, torture or kill these women. I expect you to explain that to our jury."

"What about Hunter's Point?" Betsy asked. "That's going to play a huge part in your trial."

"A man named Henry Waters was the killer. He was shot trying to escape arrest. They found the body of one of his victims disemboweled in his basement. Everyone knew Waters was guilty and the case was closed."

"Then why is Page convinced you killed the Hunter's Point women?"

"I have no idea. I was a victim, for God's sake. I told you. Waters killed Sandy and Melody. I was part of the task force that investigated the killings."

"How did that happen?" Betsy asked, surprised.

"I volunteered. I was an excellent lawyer and I did a lot of criminal defense when I started out. I felt I could provide a unique insight into the criminal mind. The mayor agreed."

"Why didn't you set up a law practice in Oregon?"

Darius stopped smiling. "Why is that important?"

"It looks like you're trying to hide. So does dyeing your hair black."

"My wife and child were murdered, Tannenbaum. I found their bodies. Those deaths were part of my old life. When I moved here, it was my chance to start over. I didn't want to see my old face in the mirror, because I would remember how Sandy and Melody looked beside me in old photographs. I didn't want to work at the same job, because there were too many associations between that job and my old life."

Darius leaned forward. He rested his elbows on the table and supported his head on his lean fingers, massaging his forehead, as if he was trying to wipe away painful memories.

"I'm sorry if that sounds crazy, but I was a little

crazy for a while. I'd been so happy. Then that maniac . . ."

Darius closed his eyes. Stewart studied him carefully. Betsy was right. Either the guy was a great actor or he was innocent.

"We'll need the old files from Hunter's Point," Betsy told Stewart. "You'll probably have to go back there to talk to the detectives who worked the case. Page's theory falls apart if Martin didn't kill the Hunter's Point women."

Stewart nodded, then he leaned toward Darius.

"Who are your enemies, Mr. Darius? Who hates you enough to frame you for these murders?"

Darius shrugged. "I've made lots of enemies. There are those fools who are tying up the project where the bodies were found."

"Mr. Darius," Stewart said patiently, "with all due respect, you're not seriously suggesting a group dedicated to preserving historic buildings is responsible for framing you, are you?"

"They torched three of my condos."

"You don't see a difference between setting fire to an inanimate object and torturing three women to death? We're looking for a monster here, Mr. Darius. Who do you know who has no conscience, no compassion, who thinks people are no more valuable than bugs and hates your guts?"

Betsy did not expect Darius to put up with Stewart's insolence, but he surprised her. Instead of getting mad, he leaned back in his chair, his brow furrowing in frustration as he tried to think of an answer to Stewart's question.

"What I say doesn't leave here, right?"

"Reggie is our agent. The attorney-client privilege applies to anything you tell him."

"Okay. One name comes to mind. There's a project in Southern Oregon I couldn't fund. The banks didn't trust my judgment. So I went to Manuel Ochoa. He's a man who doesn't do much but has lots of money. I never asked where it came from, but I've heard rumors."

"Are we talking Colombians, Mr. Darius? Cocaine, tar heroin?" Reggie asked.

"I don't know and I didn't want to. I asked for the money, he gave me the money. There were terms I agreed to that I'll have trouble meeting if I stay in jail. If Darius Construction defaults, Ochoa will make a lot of money."

"And druggies would snuff a woman or two without thinking twice," Stewart added.

"Does Ochoa know about Hunter's Point?" Betsy asked suddenly. "We're not just looking for a psychopath. We're looking for a psychopath with intimate knowledge of your secret past."

"Good point," Stewart said. "Who knew about Hunter's Point besides you?"

Darius suddenly looked ill. He rested his elbows on the table again and let his head fall heavily into his open palms.

"That's the question I've been asking myself, Tannenbaum, ever since I realized I was being framed. But it's a question I can't answer. I've never told anyone in Portland about Hunter's Point. Never. But the person who's framing me knows all about it, and I just don't know how that's possible."

"Coffee, black," Betsy told her secretary as she flew through the front door, "and get me a turkey, bacon and swiss from the Heathman Pub."

Betsy tossed her attaché case on her desk and took a

brief look at the mail and messages Ann had stacked in the center of the blotter. Betsy tossed the junk mail in the wastebasket, placed the important letters in her in-box and decided that none of the callers needed to be phoned immediately.

"The sandwich will be ready in fifteen minutes," Ann said as she put a cup of coffee on Betsy's desk.

"Great."

"How did the arraignment go?"

"A zoo. The courthouse was swarming with reporters. It was worse than 'Hammermill.' "

Ann left. Betsy sipped some coffee, then punched out the phone number of Dr. Raymond Keene, a former state medical examiner who was now in private practice. When a defense attorney needed someone to check the m.e.'s results, they went to Dr. Keene.

"What ya got for me, Betsy?"

"Hi, Ray. I've got the Darius case."

"No kidding."

"No kidding. Three women and one man. All brutally tortured. I want to know everything about how they died and what was done to them before they died."

"Who did the autopsies?"

"Susan Gregg."

"She's competent. Is there some special reason you want her findings checked?"

"It's not so much her findings. The d.a. thinks Darius did this before, ten years ago, in Hunter's Point, New York. Six women were murdered there, as far as I can tell. There was a suspect in that case who was killed resisting arrest. Page doesn't believe the suspect was the murderer. When we get the Hunter's Point autopsy reports, I want you to compare the cases to see if there is a similar m.o."

"Sounds interesting. Did Page clear it?"

"I asked him after the arraignment."

"I'll call Sue and see if I can get over to the morgue this afternoon."

"The quicker the better."

"You want me to perform another autopsy or just review her report?"

"Do everything you can think of. At this point, I have no idea what might be important."

"What lab tests has Sue done?"

"I don't know."

"Probably not as many as she should. I'll check it out. The budget pressures don't encourage a lot of lab work."

"We don't have to worry about a budget. Darius will go top dollar."

"That's what I like to hear. I'll call as soon as I have something to tell you. Give 'em hell."

"I will, Ray."

Betsy hung up the phone.

"Are you ready for lunch?" Nora Sloane asked hesitantly from the office doorway. Betsy looked up, startled.

"Your receptionist wasn't in. I waited for a few minutes."

"Oh, I'm sorry, Nora. We did have a lunch date, didn't we?"

"For noon."

"I apologize. I forgot all about it. I just picked up a new case that's taking all my time."

"Martin Darius. I know. It's the headline in the *Oregonian.*"

"I'm afraid today isn't good for lunch. I'm really swamped. Can we do it another day?"

"No problem. In fact, I was sure you'd want to cancel. I was going to call, but . . . Betsy," Sloane said excitedly, "could I tag along on this case, sit in on conferences, talk to your investigator? It's a fantastic opportunity to see how you work on a high profile case."

"I don't know . . ."

"I wouldn't say anything, of course. I'd keep your confidences. I only want to be a fly on the wall."

Sloane seemed so excited, Betsy did not want to turn her down, but a leak about defense strategy could be devastating. The front door opened and Ann appeared in the doorway carrying a brown paper bag. Sloane looked over her shoulder.

"Sorry," Ann said, backing away. Betsy motioned her to stop.

"I'll talk to Darius," Betsy said. "He'll have to give his okay. Then I'll think about it. I won't do anything that could endanger a client's case."

"I understand perfectly," Sloane said. "I'll call in a few days to see what you decide."

"Sorry about lunch."

"Oh, no. That's okay. And thank you."

There was a van with a CBS logo and another from ABC in Betsy's driveway when she pulled in.

"Who are they, Mom?" Kathy asked, as two beautifully dressed blondes with perfect features approached the car. The women held microphones and were followed by muscular men armed with portable television cameras.

"Monica Blake, CBS, Mrs. Tannenbaum," the shorter woman said as Betsy pushed open the door. Blake stepped back awkwardly and the other woman took advantage of the break.

"How do you explain a woman who is known for her strong feminist views defending a man who is alleged to have kidnapped, raped, tortured and killed three women?"

Betsy flushed. She turned abruptly and glared at the reporter from ABC, ignoring the microphone thrust in her face.

"First, I don't have to explain anything. The State does. Second, I'm an attorney. One of the things I do is defend people—male or female—who have been accused of a crime. Sometimes these people are unjustly accused, because the State makes a mistake. Martin Darius is innocent and I am proud to be representing him against these false accusations."

"What if they're not false?" asked the CBS reporter. "How can you sleep nights, knowing what he did to these women?"

"I suggest you read the Constitution, Ms. Blake. Mr. Darius is presumed innocent. Now, I have dinner to make and a little girl to take care of. I won't answer any questions at my house. I consider this an invasion of my privacy. If you want to talk to me, call my office for an appointment. Please don't come to my house again."

Betsy walked around the car and opened Kathy's door. She jumped out, looking over her shoulder at the cameras as Betsy dragged her toward the house. The two reporters continued to shout questions at her back.

"Are we gonna be on TV?" Kathy asked, as Betsy slammed the door.

Chapter Eleven

I

Alan Page was trapped in a car, careening downhill through traffic at breakneck speed on a winding turnpike, brakes screeching, tires smoking, twisting the wheel furiously to avoid an inevitable collision. When he sat up in bed, he was inches from the burning headlights of a massive semi. Sweat glued his flannel pajamas to his damp skin and he could feel the thunderous pounding of his heart. Page gulped down lungfuls of air, still uncertain where he was and half-expecting to die in a fireball of lacerated steel and shattered glass.

"Jesus," he gasped when he was oriented. The clock read four fifty-eight, an hour and a half before the alarm would go off, four and a half hours before the bail hearing. He fell back onto his pillow, anxious and sure sleep was impossible, haunted by the question that had hounded him since the arrest of Martin Darius. Had he moved too soon? Was there "clear and convincing" evidence that Martin Darius was a murderer?

Ross Barrow and Randy Highsmith had argued against searching Darius's house, even after hearing what

Gutierrez had to say. They wanted to wait until Nancy Gordon was found and they had a stronger case, but he had overridden them and instructed Barrow to make an arrest if the tire tracks at the scene matched the treads on Darius's car. Now, he wondered if Barrow and Highsmith hadn't been right all along. He had counted on finding Nancy Gordon for the bail hearing, but even with three detectives working around the clock, they were striking out.

If he could not sleep, he could rest. Page closed his eyes and saw Nancy Gordon. He had thought of the detective constantly since learning that her body was not in the pit. If she was alive, she would have gotten in touch with him as soon as she learned of Darius's arrest. If she was alive, she would have returned to the Lakeview. Was she dead, a look of unimaginable suffering on her face? Darius knew the answer to Page's questions, but the law forbade Alan to talk to him.

Page would need all of his energy in court, but the fear in his belly would not let him rest. He decided he would shower, shave, eat breakfast, then dress in his best suit and a crisp, starched shirt, fresh from the laundry. A shower and a big breakfast would make him feel human. Then he would drive to the courthouse and try to convince the Honorable Patrick Norwood, judge of the Multnomah County Circuit Court, that Martin Darius was a serial killer.

2

Martin Darius slept peacefully and felt well rested when he awoke with the other inmates of the Multnomah County Jail. Betsy Tannenbaum had arranged to have his hair cut by his barber, and the watch commander was permitting him an extra shower before court. Only a breakfast of sticky pancakes soaked in gluey, jailhouse syrup spoiled his mood. Darius used the acidic taste of the jail coffee to cut the sweetness and ate them anyway, because he knew it would be a long day in court.

Betsy had exchanged a full wardrobe for the clothes in which Darius was arrested. When Darius met her in the interview room before court, he was attired in a double-breasted, chalk-striped, dark wool suit, a cotton broadcloth shirt and a navy blue, woven silk tie with white pinpoint dots. Betsy wore a single-breasted jacket and matching skirt of black and white, windowpane plaid and a white silk blouse with a wide collar. When they walked down the courthouse corridor in the glare of the television lights, they would look like a couple you might see on "Lifestyles of the Rich and Famous," rather than a suspected mass murderer and his mouthpiece.

"How are you feeling?" Darius asked.

"Fine."

"Good. I want you at your best today. Jail is interesting, if you treat it as an educational experience, but I'm ready to graduate."

"I'm glad to see you're keeping your sense of humor."

Darius shrugged. "I have faith in you, Tannenbaum. That's why I hired you. You're the best. You won't let me down."

The praise made Betsy feel good. She basked in it and believed what Darius told her. She was the best. That was why Darius chose her over Matthew Reynolds, Oscar Montoya and the other established criminal defense lawyers.

"Who's our judge?" Darius asked.

"Pat Norwood."

"What's he like?"

"He's a crusty old codger who's nearing retirement. He looks like a troll and acts like an ogre in court. He's no legal scholar, either. But he is completely impartial. Norwood's rude and impatient with the prosecution and the defense and he won't be buffaloed by Alan Page or the press. If Page doesn't meet his burden of proof on the bail issue, Norwood will do the right thing."

"Do you think the State will meet its burden?" Darius asked.

"No, Martin, I don't think they will."

Darius smiled. "That's what I wanted to hear." Then the smile faded as he changed the subject. "Is Lisa going to be in court?"

"Of course. I talked to her yesterday."

"Looks like you're having more luck getting in touch with my wife than I am."

"Lisa's staying with her father. She didn't feel comfortable alone in the house."

"That's funny," Darius said, flashing Betsy a chilly smile. "I called His Honor last night and he told me she wasn't home."

"She may have been out."

"Right. The next time you talk to my wife, please ask her to visit me, will you?"

"Sure. Oh, before I forget, there's a woman named Nora Sloane who's writing an article about women defense attorneys. She wants to follow me through your case. If I let her, there's a chance she might learn defense strategy or attorney-client confidences. I told her I had to ask your permission before I let her get involved. Do you have any objections to her tagging along?"

Darius considered the question for a moment, then shook his head.

"I don't mind. Besides"—he grinned—"you'll have

more incentive to do a great job for me if someone is writing about you."

"I never thought of it that way."

"That's why I'm a millionaire, Tannenbaum. I always figure the angles."

3

There were several new courtrooms outfitted with state-of-the-art video equipment and computer technology that Patrick L. Norwood could have commandeered because of his senior status, but Judge Norwood preferred the courtroom where he had ruled with an iron fist for twenty years. It had high ceilings, grand marble columns and a hand-carved wooden dais. It was an old-fashioned court-room, perfect for a man with the judicial temperament of a nineteenth-century hanging judge.

The courtroom was filled to capacity for the Martin Darius bail hearing. Those who were too late to find a seat stood in line in the hall. Spectators had to pass through a metal detector before entering the courtroom and there were extra security guards inside, because of death threats.

Harvey Cobb, an elderly black man, called the court to order. He had been Norwood's bailiff from the day the judge was appointed. Norwood came out of his chambers through a door behind the bench. Short and squat, he was ugly as sin, but his toadlike face was crowned by a full head of beautiful snowy white hair.

"Be seated," Cobb said. Betsy took her place beside Martin Darius and glanced briefly at Alan Page, who was sitting next to Randy Highsmith.

"Call your first witness, Mr. Page," Norwood ordered.

"The State calls Ross Barrow, Your Honor."

Harvey Cobb had Detective Barrow raise his right hand and swear to tell the truth. Barrow sat in the witness box and Page established his credentials as a homicide investigator.

"Detective Barrow, sometime in mid-August did you become aware of a series of unusual disappearances?"

"Yes, I did. In August a detective from our missing persons bureau told me that a woman named Laura Farrar was reported missing by her husband, Larry Farrar. Larry told the detective that . . ."

"Objection, hearsay," Betsy said, standing.

"No," Norwood ruled. "This is a bail hearing, not a trial. I'm going to permit the State some leeway. If you need to examine some of these witnesses, you can subpoena them. Let's move on, Mr. Page."

Page nodded at Barrow, who continued with his account of the investigation.

"Farrar told the detective that he had come home from work on August tenth, about eight o'clock. His house looked perfectly normal, but his wife was missing. None of her clothes was missing or her makeup. In fact, nothing was missing from the house, as far as he could tell. The only unusual circumstance was a rose and a note Mr. Farrar found on his wife's pillow."

"Was there anything odd about the rose?"

"Yes, sir. A lab report on the rose indicates that it had been dyed black."

"What did the note say?"

" 'Gone, But Not Forgotten.' "

Page handed a document and a photograph to the judge's clerk.

"This is a photocopy of the Farrar note and a photograph of the rose, Your Honor. The originals are still at the lab. I talked about this with Mrs. Tannenbaum and she's willing to stipulate to the introduction of these and other copies, solely for purposes of this hearing."

"Is that so?" Norwood asked Betsy. She nodded.

"The exhibits will be received."

"Did the detective from missing persons tell you about a second disappearance in mid-September?"

"Yes, sir. Wendy Reiser, the wife of Thomas Reiser, was reported missing by her husband under identical circumstances."

"Nothing disturbed in the house or missing?"

"Correct."

"Did Mr. Reiser find a black rose and a note on his wife's pillow?"

"He did."

Page introduced a photocopy of the Reiser note and a photograph of the Reiser rose.

"What did the lab say about the second note and rose?"

"They are identical to the note and rose found at the Farrar house."

"Finally, Detective, did you learn about a third, recent disappearance?"

"Yes, sir. Russell Miller reported his wife, Victoria, missing under circumstances that were identical to the other cases. Note and rose on the pillow. Nothing disturbed or missing in the house."

"Several days ago, did you learn where the women were?"

Barrow nodded gravely. "The three women and an unidentified male were found buried in a construction site owned by Darius Construction."

"Who owns Darius Construction?"

"Martin Darius, the defendant."

"Was the gate to the site locked?"

"Yes, sir."

"Was a gaping hole located in the fence near the area where the bodies were found?"

"Yes, sir."

"Were tire tracks located near that hole?"

"They were."

"On the evening Mr. Darius was arrested, did you execute a search warrant at his residence?"

"Yes, sir."

"Did you locate any vehicles during the search?"

"We located a station wagon, a BMW and a black Ferrari."

"Move to introduce exhibits ten to twenty-three, which are photographs of the construction site, the hole in the fence, the tire tracks, the burial site and the bodies being removed from it, and the vehicles."

"No objection," Betsy said.

"Received."

"Was a cast made of the tire tracks?"

"It was. The tracks at the site match the tread on the BMW we found at Darius's house."

"Was the trunk of the BMW examined for trace evidence, such as hairs and fibers, that might have belonged to any of the victims?"

"Yes, sir. None was found."

"Did the lab report explain why?"

"The trunk had been recently vacuumed and cleaned."

"How old was the BMW?"

"A year old."

"Not a brand-new car?"

"No, sir."

"Detective Barrow, are you aware of any connections between the defendant and the murdered women?"

"I am. Yes. Mr. Reiser works for the law firm that represents Darius Construction. He and his wife met the defendant at a party Mr. Darius threw this summer to celebrate the opening of a new mall."

"How soon before the disappearance of the first woman, Laura Farrar, was this party?"

"Approximately three weeks."

"Were Mr. and Mrs. Farrar at that party?"

"They were. Mr. Farrar works for the accounting firm that Mr. Darius uses."

"And Russell and Victoria Miller?"

"They were at the party too, but they have closer ties with the defendant. Mr. Miller was just put in charge of the Darius Construction account at Brand, Gates and Valcroft, the advertising agency. They also socialized with Mr. and Mrs. Darius."

Page checked his notes, conferred with Randy Highsmith, then said, "Your witness, Mrs. Tannenbaum."

Betsy looked at a legal pad on which she had listed several points she wanted to bring out through Barrow. She selected several police reports from the discovery she received from the district attorney.

"Good morning, Detective Barrow. Teams of criminalists from the Oregon State Crime Lab went through the houses of all three women, did they not?"

"That's true."

"Isn't it also true that none of these fine scientists found a single piece of physical evidence connecting Martin Darius to the homes of Laura Farrar, Victoria Miller or Wendy Reiser?"

"The person who murdered these women is very clever. He knows how to clean up a crime scene."

"Your Honor," Betsy said calmly, "will you please direct Detective Barrow to listen to the questions I ask him and respond to those questions? I'm sure Mr. Page will try to explain the problems with his case during argument."

Judge Norwood glared at Betsy. "I don't need an editorial from you, Mrs. Tannenbaum. Just make your objections." Then Norwood swiveled toward the witness. "And you've testified enough times to know you only answer what you're asked. Save the clever answers. They don't impress me."

"So, Detective Barrow, what's your answer? Was a single shred of physical evidence linking my client to any victim found at any of the homes of the missing women?"

"No."

"How about on the bodies?"

"We found the tire tracks."

"Your Honor?" Betsy asked.

"Detective Barrow, were there tire tracks on the body of any of those women?" the judge asked sarcastically.

Barrow looked embarrassed. "Sorry, Your Honor."

"Are you catching on, Detective?" Judge Norwood asked.

"There was no physical evidence at the burial site connecting the defendant with any of the women," Detective Barrow answered.

"A dead man was also found at the burial site?"

"Yes."

"Who is he?"

"We don't know."

"So there's nothing connecting this man to Martin Darius?"

"We don't know that. Until we find out who he is, we can't investigate his possible connection with your client."

Betsy was going to object but decided to let the remark pass. If Barrow kept fencing, he'd keep pissing off the judge.

"You told the judge about the tire tracks you found near the fence. Don't you think you should tell him about the interview you had with Rudy Doschman?"

"I interviewed him. What about it?"

"Do you have your report of that interview?" Betsy asked, as she walked toward the witness stand.

"Not with me."

"Why don't you take my copy and read this paragraph?" Betsy said, handing the detective a police report she had found in the discovery material. Barrow read the report and looked up.

"Mr. Doschman is a foreman with Darius Construction who was working on the site where the bodies were found?" Betsy asked.

"Yes."

"He told you Mr. Darius visited the site on many occasions, did he not?"

"Yes."

"In his BMW?"

"Yes."

"He also explained that the hole in the fence was there for some time?"

"Yes."

"In fact, it may have been the way the arsonists who burned down some of Mr. Darius's town houses entered the site several weeks ago?"

"It could be."

"There is no evidence connecting Mr. Darius to the roses or the notes?"

Barrow looked like he was going to say something, but he choked it back and shook his head.

"And you stand by that statement, even though officers of the Portland Police Bureau made a thorough search, pursuant to a warrant, of Mr. Darius's home."

"We found nothing connecting him to the roses or the notes," Barrow answered tersely.

"No murder weapons either?"

"No."

"Nothing in the trunk of the BMW connecting him to the crimes?"

"No."

Betsy turned to Darius. "Anything else you want me to ask?"

Darius smiled. "You're doing just fine, Tannenbaum."

"No further questions."

Barrow hoisted himself out of the witness box and walked quickly to the back of the courtroom as Page called his next witness.

"Dr. Susan Gregg," Page said. An attractive woman in her early forties with salt-and-pepper hair, wearing a conservative gray suit, took the witness stand.

"Will counsel stipulate to Dr. Gregg's qualifications for purposes of this hearing?" Page asked Betsy.

"We assume Dr. Gregg is well known to the court," Betsy said, "so, for purposes of this hearing only, we stipulate that Dr. Gregg is the state medical examiner and qualified to give opinions on cause of death."

"Thank you," Page said to Betsy. "Dr. Gregg, were you called to a construction site owned by Darius Construction, earlier this week, to examine the remains of four individuals who were found buried there?"

"I was."

"And you conducted the autopsies of all four victims?"

"Yes."

"What is an autopsy, Dr. Gregg?"

"It's an examination of a body after death to determine, among other things, cause of death."

"Will you explain what your autopsy involved?"

"Certainly. I examined the bodies carefully for serious injuries, natural diseases and other natural causes of death."

"Did any of the victims die a natural death?"

"No."

"What injuries did you observe?"

"All four individuals had numerous burns and cutting injuries on various parts of their bodies. Three of the male's fingers had been severed. There was evidence of sharp cuts on the women's breasts. The nipples on the women had been mutilated, as had the genitalia of the man and the women. Do you want me to go into detail?"

"That won't be necessary for this hearing. How did the three women die?"

"Their abdomens had been deeply cut, resulting in serious injuries to their bowel and abdominal viscera."

"When a person is disemboweled, do they die quickly?"

"No. A person can stay alive for some time in this condition."

"Can you give the court a rough estimate?"

Gregg shrugged. "It's hard to say. Two to four hours. Eventually they die from shock and loss of blood."

"And that was the cause of death of these women?"

"Yes."

"And the male?"

"He suffered a fatal gunshot wound to the back of his head."

"Did you order laboratory tests?"

"Yes. I had the blood tested for alcohol. The results were negative for all of the victims. I ordered a urine screen for drugs of abuse. This involves testing the urine for the presence of five drugs: cocaine, morphine, marijuana, amphetamine and PCP. Our results were all negative."

Page studied his notes and conferred with Highsmith before turning the witness over to Betsy. She reread a portion of the autopsy report and frowned.

"Dr. Gregg, I'm confused by some remarks you made on page four of your report. Were the women raped?"

"That's hard to say. I found bruises and tears around the genitalia and rectum. Tearing that would indicate invasion by a foreign object."

"Did you test for semen?"

"I did not find any traces of seminal fluid."

"So you can't say conclusively that the women were raped?"

"I can only say there was penetration and violent injury. There was no evidence of male ejaculation."

"Did you draw a conclusion concerning whether the women were murdered at the construction site?"

"I believe they were killed elsewhere."

"Why?"

"There would have been a large amount of blood at the murder scene because of their massive cutting injuries. There were also organs removed from two of the women."

"Would the rain obscure traces of their blood?"

"No. They were buried. The rain would have washed away the blood on the surface, but we should have found larger quantities under the bodies in the graves."

"So you believe the women were killed someplace else and transported to the site?"

"Yes."

"If they were transported in the trunk of a BMW, could you erase all traces of blood from the trunk?"

"Objection," Page said. "Dr. Gregg is not qualified to answer that question. She is a medical doctor, not a forensic chemist."

"I'll let her answer, if she can," the judge ruled.

"I'm afraid that's outside my area of expertise," the doctor answered.

"The male was not disemboweled?"

"No."

"Nothing further."

Alan Page stood. He looked a little unsure of himself. "Your Honor, I'm going to call myself as a witness. Mr. Highsmith will examine."

"Objection, Your Honor. It's unethical for an attorney to testify as a witness in a case he's trying."

"That might be true in a trial before a jury, Your Honor," Page replied, "but the court is not going to have any trouble deciding my credibility as a witness, if that comes into question, simply because I'm also arguing the State's position."

Norwood looked troubled. "This is unusual. Why do you have to testify?"

"What's he up to?" Darius whispered in Betsy's ear.

Betsy shook her head. She was studying Page. He looked ill at ease and grim. Something was troubling the district attorney.

"Your Honor, I'm in possession of evidence you must hear if you are going to make a reasoned decision on the issue of bail. Unless I testify, you'll be without the most important evidence we have that Martin Darius is the man who killed Laura Farrar, Wendy Reiser and Victoria Miller."

"I'm confused, Mr. Page," Norwood said testily.

"How can you have this evidence? Were you an eyewitness?" Norwood shook his head. "I don't get it."

Page cleared his throat. "Your Honor, there is a witness. Her name is Nancy Gordon." Darius took a deep breath and leaned forward intently. "Ten years ago, an identical series of murders occurred in Hunter's Point, New York. The day before we found the bodies, Detective Gordon told me about those murders and why she believed Martin Darius committed them."

"Then call Detective Gordon," Norwood said.

"I can't. She's missing and she may be dead. She checked into a motel room after leaving me. I called her several times starting around eight, eight-thirty, the next morning. I think something happened to her shortly after she checked in. It looks like she was unpacking when something interrupted her. All of her possessions were in the room, but she hasn't come back for them. I have a team of detectives looking for her, but we've had no luck so far."

"Your Honor," Betsy said, "if Mr. Page is going to testify about this woman's statements to prove my client murdered some women ten years ago, it will be pure hearsay. I know the court is giving Mr. Page leeway, but Mr. Darius has state and federal constitutional rights to confront the witnesses against him."

Norwood nodded. "That's true, Mrs. Tannenbaum. I'll tell you, Mr. Page, this bothers me. Isn't there another witness from Hunter's Point you can call who can testify about these other crimes?"

"Not on such short notice. I know the names of the other detectives who worked on the case, but they don't work for the Hunter's Point police anymore and I haven't traced them."

Norwood leaned back and almost disappeared from view. Betsy was dying to know what the missing detec-

tive had told Page, but she had to keep the testimony out
if it was the ammunition Page needed to keep Martin
Darius in jail.

"It's eleven-fifteen, folks," Norwood said. "We'll adjourn until one-thirty. I'll hear legal argument then."

Norwood stood up and walked out of the courtroom.
Harvey Cobb rapped the gavel and everyone stood.

"Now I know why Page thinks I killed those
women," Darius whispered to Betsy. "When can we
talk?"

"I'll come up to the jail right now."

Betsy turned to one of the guards. "Can you put Mr.
Darius in the interview room? I want to talk to him."

"Sure, Mrs. Tannenbaum. We're gonna wait for the
court to clear before taking him up. You can ride with us
in the jail elevator if you want."

"Thanks, I will."

The guard handcuffed Darius. Betsy glanced toward
the back of the courtroom. Lisa Darius was standing near
the door, talking to Nora Sloane. Lisa glanced toward
Betsy. Betsy smiled. Lisa did not smile back, but she did
nod toward her. Betsy raised a hand to let Lisa know she
would be right with her. Lisa said something to Sloane.
Sloane smiled and patted Lisa's shoulder, then left the
courtroom.

"I'm going to talk to Lisa for a moment," Betsy told
Darius. Lisa was waiting just inside the door, looking nervously through the glass at the waiting reporters.

"That woman said she's working with you on an article for *Pacific West*," Lisa said.

"That's right. She's going to tag along while I try
Martin's case to see how I work."

"She said she'd like to talk to me. What should I
do?"

"Nora seems responsible, but you make up your own mind. How are you holding up?"

"This is terrible. The reporters won't leave me alone. When I moved to Daddy's house I had to sneak out of the estate through the woods so they wouldn't know where I was going."

"I'm sorry, Lisa. This isn't going to get any easier for you."

Lisa hesitated, then she asked, "Will the judge let Martin out on bail?"

"There's a good chance he'll have to. The State's evidence has been pretty weak, so far."

Lisa looked worried.

"Is something troubling you?"

"No," Lisa answered too quickly.

"If you know anything about this case, please tell me. I don't want any surprises."

"It's the reporters, they've really gotten to me," Lisa said, but Betsy knew she was lying.

"We're ready," the guard told Betsy.

"I've got to talk to Martin. He wants you to visit him."

Lisa nodded, but her thoughts seemed far away.

"Who is Nancy Gordon?" Betsy asked Darius. They were sitting next to each other in the narrow confines of the courthouse jail visiting room.

"One of the detectives on the task force. I met her the night Sandy and Melody died. She interviewed me at the house. Gordon was engaged to another cop, but he was killed a few weeks before the wedding. She was still grieving when I joined the task force and she tried to help me deal with my grief.

"Nancy and I were thrown together on several occasions. I didn't realize it, but she took my friendliness as something else and, well . . ." Darius looked into Betsy's eyes. Their knees were almost touching. His head bent toward her. "I was vulnerable. We both were. You can't understand what it feels like to lose someone you love like that, until it happens to you.

"I became convinced Waters was the rose killer and I did a stupid thing. Without telling anyone, I started following him. I even staked out his house, hoping I'd catch him in the act." Darius smiled sheepishly. "I made a mess of things and almost blew the investigation. I was so obvious, a neighbor called the police to complain about this strange man who was camped outside their house. The police came. I felt like an idiot. Nancy bailed me out. We met at a restaurant near the police station and she let me have it.

"By the time we'd finished eating, it was late. I offered to drive her home because her car was in for repairs. We'd both had a few beers. I don't even remember who started it. The bottom line is, we ended up in bed."

Darius looked down at his hands, as if he was ashamed. Then he shook his head.

"It was a stupid thing to do. I should have known she would take it too seriously. I mean, it was good for us to have someone to spend the night with. We were both so lonely. But she thought I loved her, and I didn't. It was too soon after Sandy. When I didn't want to continue the relationship, she grew bitter. Fortunately Waters was caught soon after that and my involvement with the task force ended, so there was no reason for us to see each other. Only, Nancy couldn't let go. She called me at home and at the office. She wanted to meet and talk about us. I told her there was no 'us,' but it was hard for her to accept."

"Did she accept it?"

Darius nodded. "She stopped calling, but I knew she was bitter. What I can't understand is how she could possibly think I killed Sandy and Melody."

"If the judge lets Page testify," Betsy said, "we'll soon find out."

Chapter Twelve

"Let me tell you how I see it, Mrs. Tannenbaum," Judge Norwood said. "I know what the Constitution says about confronting the witnesses and I'm not saying you don't have a point, but this is a bail hearing and the issues are different at trial. What Mr. Page is trying to do is convince me he's got so much evidence a guilty verdict at the trial is almost a sure thing. He thinks some of this trial evidence is going to come from this missing detective or from someone else in New York. I'm going to let him tell me what the evidence is, but I'm also going to take into account that he doesn't have his witness and may not be able to produce her, or these other detectives, at trial. So, I'll decide what weight to give to this testimony, but I'm going to let it in. If you don't like my ruling, I don't blame you. I might be wrong. That's why we have appeals courts. But, right now, Mr. Page can testify."

Betsy had already made her objections for the record, so she said nothing more when Alan Page was sworn in.

"Mr. Page," Randy Highsmith asked, "the evening before the bodies of Victoria Miller, Wendy Reiser, Laura Farrar and an unknown male were unearthed at a construction site owned by the defendant, did a woman visit you at your residence?"

"Yes."

"Who was this woman?"

"Nancy Gordon, a detective with the Hunter's Point Police Department in New York."

"At the time of Detective Gordon's visit were the details surrounding the disappearances of the three Portland women widely known?"

"To the contrary, Mr. Highsmith. The police and the district attorney's office weren't certain of the status of the missing women, so we were treating them as missing persons cases. No one in the press knew of the links between the cases and the husbands were cooperating with us by not divulging details of the disappearances."

"What were the links you spoke of?"

"The black roses and the notes that said 'Gone, But Not Forgotten.' "

"What did Detective Gordon say that led you to believe she had information that could be useful in solving the mystery surrounding these disappearances?"

"She knew about the notes and the roses."

"Where did she say she had acquired this knowledge?"

"Ten years ago in Hunter's Point, when an almost identical series of disappearances occurred."

"What was her connection with the Hunter's Point case?"

"She was a member of a task force assigned to that case."

"How did Detective Gordon learn about our disappearances and the similarities between the cases?"

"She told me she received an anonymous note that led her to believe that the person who was responsible for the Hunter's Point murders was living in Portland."

"Who was this person?"

"She knew him as Peter Lake."

"Did she give some background information on Peter Lake?"

"She did. He was a successful lawyer in Hunter's Point. He was married to Sandra Lake and they had a six-year-old daughter, Melody. The wife and child were murdered and a 'Gone, But Not Forgotten' note and black rose were found on the floor near the mother's body. Lake had a lot of political clout and the mayor of Hunter's Point ordered the police chief to put him on the task force. Lake soon became the primary suspect, though he was not aware of that fact."

"Have the prints of Peter Lake been compared to the fingerprints of Martin Darius?"

"Yes."

"With what results?"

"Martin Darius and Peter Lake are the same person."

Highsmith handed the clerk two fingerprint cards and a report from a fingerprint expert and introduced them into evidence.

"Mr. Page, did Detective Gordon tell you why she believed the defendant murdered the Hunter's Point women?"

"She did."

"Tell the court what she told you."

"Peter Lake had a connection to each of the women who disappeared in Hunter's Point. Gloria Escalante sat on one of Lake's juries. Samantha Reardon belonged to the same country club as the Lakes. Anne Hazelton's husband was an attorney and the Lakes and Hazeltons had been to some of the same Bar Association functions. Patricia Cross and Sandra Lake, Peter's wife, were both in the Junior League.

"Detective Gordon met Lake the evening Sandra and Melody Lake were murdered. This was the first time a body was discovered. In all the other cases, when the women disappeared, the note and rose were found on the woman's pillow in her bedroom. None of these notes had fingerprints on them. The note found at Lake's house had Sandra Lake's prints on it. The detectives believed that Sandra Lake discovered the note and was killed by her husband so she would not connect him to the disappearances when the notes were made public. They also believed Melody saw her mother killed and was murdered because she was a witness."

"Was there a problem with the time that Peter Lake reported the murders to the police?"

"Yes. Peter Lake told the police that he discovered the bodies right after he entered the house, that he sat down on the steps for a while, in shock, then called 911. The 911 call came in at eight-fifteen, but a neighbor, who lived near the Lakes, saw Peter Lake arrive home shortly after seven-twenty. The task force members believed it took Lake fifty-five minutes to report the murders because the victims were alive when Lake got home."

"Was there anything else that implicated Lake?"

"A man named Henry Waters worked for a florist. His truck was seen near the Escalante house on the day she disappeared. Waters had a sex offender record as a Peeping Tom. The body of Patricia Cross was found in the basement of Waters's house. She was disemboweled, just like the three Portland women.

"Waters was never really a suspect, but Lake didn't know that. Waters was borderline retarded and had no history of violence. There wasn't any connection between him and any other victim. Without telling anyone, Lake staked out Waters's house and followed him for days before the body of Patricia Cross was discovered."

"What led the police to Waters's house?"

"An anonymous male caller, who was never identified. The task force members believed Lake brought Cross to Waters's house, murdered her in the basement, then made the phone call to the police."

"Why wasn't Lake prosecuted in Hunter's Point?"

"Waters was killed during his arrest. The police chief and the mayor made a public statement labeling Waters as the rose killer. There were no more murders and the cases were closed."

"Why did Detective Gordon come to Portland?"

"When she learned about the Portland notes and roses, she knew the same person had to be responsible for the Hunter's Point and Portland crimes, because the color of the rose and the contents of the notes were never made public in Hunter's Point."

"Where did Detective Gordon go after she left your residence?"

"The Lakeview Motel. The manager said she checked in about twenty minutes after leaving my place."

"Have you seen or talked to Detective Gordon since she left your residence?"

"No. She's disappeared."

"Have you searched her room at the motel?"

Page nodded. "It looked like she was in the midst of unpacking when something happened. When she was at my place, she had an attaché case with a lot of material relating to the case. It was missing. We also found the address of the construction site where the bodies were found on a pad next to the phone."

"What conclusion do you draw from that?"

"Someone called her with the address."

"What do you believe happened then?"

"Well, she had no car. We've checked all of the taxi

companies. None of them picked her up from the Lakeview. I believe the person who called her picked her up."

"No further questions, Your Honor."

Betsy smiled at Page, but he did not smile back. He looked grim and sat stiffly, back straight, with his hands folded in his lap.

"Mr. Page, there was a lengthy investigation in Hunter's Point, wasn't there?"

"That's what Detective Gordon said."

"I assume you've read the police reports from that investigation."

"No, I haven't," Page answered, shifting uncomfortably on his seat.

"Why is that?"

"I don't have them."

"Have you ordered them from Hunter's Point?"

"No."

Betsy's brow furrowed. "If you're planning on having Detective Gordon testify, you'll have to produce her reports."

"I know that."

"Is there a reason you haven't ordered them?"

Page colored. "They've been misplaced."

"Excuse me?"

"The Hunter's Point police are looking for them. The reports were supposed to be in a storage area, but they aren't. We think Detective Gordon may know where they are, because she gave me some items—including Peter Lake's fingerprint card—we assume came from the file."

Betsy decided to switch to another topic.

"On direct examination, you repeatedly said, 'The task force members believed . . .' Have you talked to these task force members?"

"No, other than Detective Gordon."

"Do you even know where they are?"

"I just learned that Frank Grimsbo is the head of security at Marlin Steel."

"Where is his office located?"

"Albany, New York."

Betsy made a note.

"You haven't talked to Grimsbo?"

"No."

"What are the names of the other detectives?"

"Besides Gordon and Grimsbo, there was a criminalist named Glen Michaels and another detective named Wayne Turner."

Betsy wrote down the names. When she looked up Page was stone-faced.

"Mr. Page, isn't it true that you have no support for the story your mysterious visitor told you?"

"Other than what the detective said, no."

"What detective?"

"Nancy Gordon."

"This was the first time you saw this woman, correct?"

Page nodded.

"Have you ever seen a photograph of Nancy Gordon?"

"No."

"So you can't say that the person who introduced herself as Detective Nancy Gordon is really Nancy Gordon, can you?"

"A Nancy Gordon works for the Hunter's Point Police Department."

"I don't doubt that. But we don't know that she is the person who visited you, do we?"

"No."

"There's also no proof that this woman is dead or even a victim of foul play, is there?"

"She's missing."

"Was there blood found in her room?"

"No."

"Or signs of a struggle?"

"No," Page answered grudgingly.

"Were there any witnesses to the murders of Melody and Sandra Lake?"

"Your client may have witnessed the killings," Page answered defiantly.

"You have nothing but theories propounded by your mystery woman to support that position."

"That's true."

"Isn't it also true that the chief of police and the mayor of Hunter's Point officially declared Henry Waters to be the murderer of all the women?"

"Yes."

"That would include Sandra and Melody Lake?"

"Yes."

"Which would make Mr. Lake—Mr. Darius—a victim, wouldn't it?"

Page did not answer and Betsy did not force him to.

"Mr. Page, there were six victims in Hunter's Point, including a six-year-old girl. Can you think of any reason why a responsible public official would close a case like that and publicly declare an individual to be the killer, if there was any possibility that the murderer was still at large?"

"Maybe the officials wanted to allay the fears of the community."

"You mean the public announcement might be part of a ruse to make the killer lower his guard while the investigation continued?"

"Exactly."

"But the investigation didn't continue, did it?"

"Not according to Detective Gordon."

"And the murders stopped after Mr. Waters was killed, didn't they?"

"Yes."

Betsy paused and looked directly at Judge Norwood. "No further questions, Your Honor."

"Mr. Highsmith?" Judge Norwood asked.

"I have nothing further of Mr. Page."

"You can step down, Mr. Page."

Page stood slowly. Betsy thought he looked tired and defeated. She took satisfaction in this. Betsy did not enjoy humiliating Page—he seemed a decent sort—but Page deserved any pain she inflicted. It was clear he had arrested Martin Darius on the flimsiest evidence, made him spend several days in jail and slandered him. A public defeat was a small price to pay for that kind of callous disregard of his public duty.

"Any other witnesses?" the judge asked.

"Yes, Your Honor. Two, both brief," Highsmith answered.

"Proceed."

"The State calls Ira White."

A chubby man in an ill-fitting brown suit hurried forward from the back of the courtroom. He smiled nervously as he was sworn. Betsy guessed he was in his early thirties.

"Mr. White, what do you do for a living?" Randy Highsmith asked.

"I'm a salesman for Finletter Tools."

"Where is your home office?"

"Phoenix, Arizona, but my territory is Oregon, Montana, Washington, Idaho and parts of Northern California, near the Oregon border."

"Where were you at two p.m. on October eleventh of this year?"

The date rang a bell. Betsy checked the police reports. Victoria Miller was reported missing that evening.

"In my room at the Hacienda Motel," White said.

"Where is that motel located?"

"It's in Vancouver, Washington."

"Why were you in your room?"

"I just checked in. I had a meeting scheduled for three and I wanted to unpack, take a shower and change out of my traveling clothes."

"Do you remember your room number?"

"Well, you showed me a copy of the ledger, if that's what you mean."

Highsmith nodded.

"It was 102."

"Where is that located in relation to the manager's office?"

"Right next to it on the ground floor."

"Mr. White, at approximately two p.m. did you hear anything in the room next to yours?"

"Yeah. There was a woman yelling and crying."

"Tell the judge about that."

"Okay," White said, shifting so he could look up at Judge Norwood. "I didn't hear anything until I got out of the shower. That's because the water was running. As soon as I turned it off, I heard a shriek, like someone was in pain. It startled me. The walls in that motel aren't thick. The woman was begging not to be hurt and she was crying, sobbing. It was hard to hear the words, but I'd catch a few. I could hear her crying, though."

"How long did this go on?"

"Not long."

"Did you ever see the man or the woman in the next room?"

"I saw the woman. I was thinking of calling the manager, but everything quieted down. Like I said, it didn't last long. Anyway, I dressed for my appointment and I left around two-thirty. She was coming out at the same time."

"The woman in the next room?"

White nodded.

"Do you remember what she looked like?"

"Oh, yeah. Very attractive. Blonde. Good figure."

Highsmith crossed over to the witness and showed him a photograph.

"Does this woman look familiar?"

White looked at the photograph. "That's her."

"How certain of that are you?"

"Absolutely positive."

"Your Honor," Highsmith said, "I offer State's exhibit thirty-five, a photograph of Victoria Miller."

"No objection," Betsy said.

"No further questions," Highsmith said.

"I don't have any questions for Mr. White," Betsy told the judge.

"You're excused, Mr. White," Judge Norwood told the witness.

"State calls Ramon Gutierrez."

A neatly-dressed, dark-skinned young man with a pencil-thin mustache took the stand.

"Where do you work, sir?" Randy Highsmith asked.

"The Hacienda Motel."

"That's in Vancouver?"

"Yes."

"What's your job there?"

"I'm the day clerk."

"What are you doing in the evenings?"

"I'm in college at Portland State."

"What's your field of study?"

"Premed."

"So you're working your way through?" Highsmith asked with a smile.

"Yes."

"That sounds tough."

"It isn't easy."

"Mr. Gutierrez, were you working at the Hacienda on October eleventh of this year?"

"Yes."

"Describe the layout of the motel."

"It's two stories. There's a landing that goes around the building on the second floor. The office is at the north end on the ground floor, then we have the rooms."

"How are the rooms numbered on the ground floor?"

"The room next to the office is 102. The one next to that is 103 and so on."

"Have you brought the check-in sheet for October eleventh?"

"Yes," Gutierrez said, handing the deputy district attorney a large, dull-yellow ledger page.

"Who was checked into Room 102 that afternoon?"

"Ira White from Phoenix, Arizona."

Highsmith turned his back to the witness and looked at Martin Darius.

"Who was checked into Room 103?"

"An Elizabeth McGovern from Seattle."

"Did you check in Ms. McGovern?"

"Yes."

"At what time?"

"A little after noon."

"I am handing the witness State's exhibit thirty-five. Do you recognize that woman?"

"That's Ms. McGovern."

"You're certain?"

"Yeah. She was a looker," Gutierrez said sadly.

"Then, I saw her picture in the *Oregonian*. I knew her right away."

"To what picture are you referring?"

"The picture of the murdered women. Only it said her name was Victoria Miller."

"Did you call the district attorney's office as soon as you read the paper?"

"Right away. I talked with Mr. Page."

"Why did you call?"

"It said she disappeared that night, the eleventh, so I thought the police might want to know about the guy I saw."

"What guy?"

"The one who was in the room with her."

"You saw a man in the room with Mrs. Miller?"

"Well, not in the room. But, I saw him go in and come out. He'd been there before."

"With Mrs. Miller?"

"Yes. Like once or twice a week. She would register and he would come later." Gutierrez shook his head. "What I couldn't figure out is, if he wanted to sneak around, why did he drive that car?"

"What car?"

"This fantastic black Ferrari."

Highsmith searched for a photograph among the exhibits on the clerk's desk, then handed it to the witness.

"I'm handing you State's exhibit nineteen, which is a photograph of Martin Darius's black Ferrari and I ask you if it looks like the car driven by the man who went into the room with Mrs. Miller?"

"I know it's the car."

"How do you know?"

Gutierrez pointed at the defense table. "That's Martin Darius, right?"

"Yes, Mr. Gutierrez."

"He's the guy."

"Why didn't you tell me about Victoria Miller?" Betsy asked Martin Darius as soon as they were alone in the visiting room.

"Calm down," Darius said patiently.

"Don't you tell me to calm down," Betsy responded, infuriated by her client's icy composure. "Damn it, Martin, I'm your lawyer. Don't you think I would find it interesting that you were screwing one of the victims, and beat her up, the day she disappeared?"

"I didn't beat up Vicky. I told her I didn't want to see her anymore and she became hysterical. She attacked me and I had to control her. Besides, what does my fucking Vicky have to do with getting bail?"

Betsy shook her head. "This could sink you, Martin. I know Norwood. He's straight-laced. Real old-fashioned. The guy's been married to the same woman for forty years and goes to church on Sunday. If you'd told me, I could have softened the impact."

Darius shrugged. "I'm sorry," he said, without meaning it.

"Were you having sex with Laura Farrar or Wendy Reiser?"

"I hardly knew them."

"What about this party for the mall?"

"There were hundreds of people there. I don't even remember talking to Farrar or Reiser."

Betsy leaned back in her seat. She felt very uncomfortable alone with Darius in the narrow confines of the visiting room.

"Where did you go after you left the Hacienda Motel?"

Darius smiled sheepishly. "To a meeting at Brand, Gates and Valcroft with Russ Miller and the other people working on the advertising for Darius Construction. I'd just seen to it that Russ was put in charge of the account. I guess that won't work anymore."

"You are one cold son-of-a-bitch, Martin. You screw Miller's wife, then throw him a bone. Now you're joking about her when she's been murdered. Dr. Gregg said she could have been alive for hours, sliced open, in the most godawful pain. Do you know how much she must have suffered before she died?"

"No, Tannenbaum, I don't know how much she suffered," Darius said, the smile leaving his face, "because I didn't kill her. So how about spreading a little of your sympathy in my direction? I'm the one who's being framed. I'm the one who wakes up every morning to this jail stench and has to eat the slop that passes for food."

Betsy glared at Darius and stood up. "Guard!" she shouted, pounding on the door. "I've had enough of you for today, Martin."

"Suit yourself."

The guard bent down to put the key in the lock.

"The next time we talk, I want the truth about everything. And that includes Hunter's Point."

The door opened. As Darius watched her walk away, the thinnest smile creased his lips.

Chapter Thirteen

I

International Exports was on the twenty-second floor of the First Interstate Bank Tower in a small suite of offices tucked away in a corner next to an insurance company. A middle-aged Hispanic woman looked up from her word processor when Reggie Stewart opened the door. She looked surprised, as if visitors were an uncommon sight.

Moments later, Stewart was seated across the desk from Manuel Ochoa, a well-dressed, heavy-set Mexican with a swarthy complexion and a bushy, salt-and-pepper mustache.

"This business with Martin is so terrible. Your district attorney must be insane to arrest someone so prominent. Certainly there is no evidence against him?" Ochoa said as he offered Stewart a slender cigarillo.

Stewart raised his hand, declining the smoke.

"Frankly, we don't know what Alan Page has. He's playing his cards close to the vest. That's why I'm talking to people who know Mr. Darius. We're trying to figure out what in the world Page is thinking."

Ochoa shook his head sympathetically. "I'll do anything I can to help, Mr. Stewart."

"Why don't you explain your relationship to Darius."

"We are business partners. He wanted to build a shopping mall near Medford and the banks would not finance it, so he came to me."

"How's the venture going?"

"Not well, I'm afraid. Martin has been having trouble lately. There is the unfortunate business with the site where the bodies were discovered. He has a lot of money tied up in the town house project. His debts are mounting. Our venture has also been stalled."

"How serious is Darius's financial situation?"

Ochoa blew a stream of smoke at the ceiling. "Serious. I am concerned for my investment, but, of course, I am protected."

"If Mr. Darius stays in jail or is convicted, what will happen to his business?"

"I can't say. Martin is the genius behind his firm, but he does have competent men working for him."

"How friendly are you with Mr. Darius?"

Ochoa took a long drag on his cigarillo.

"Until recently, you could say we were friends, but not close friends. Business acquaintances would be more accurate. I have had Martin to my home, we socialized occasionally. However, business pressures have strained our relationship."

Stewart laid photographs of the three women and a sheet of paper with the dates of their disappearances on the blotter.

"Were you with Mr. Darius on any of these dates?"

"I don't believe so."

"What about the photographs? Have you ever seen Mr. Darius with any of these women?"

Ochoa studied the photos, then shook his head. "No,

but I have seen Martin with other women." Stewart took out a pad. "I have a large house and I live alone. I enjoy getting together with friends. Some of these friends are attractive, single women."

"Do you want to spell this out for me, Mr. Ochoa?"

Ochoa laughed. "Martin likes young women, but he is always discreet. I have guest bedrooms for my friends."

"Did Mr. Darius use drugs?"

Ochoa eyed Stewart curiously. "What does that have to do with your case, Mr. Stewart?"

"I need to know everything I can about my client. You never know what's important."

"I have no knowledge of drugs and," Ochoa said, looking at his Rolex, "I'm afraid I have another appointment."

"Thanks for taking the time to see me."

"It was my pleasure. If I can be of further help to Martin, let me know. And wish him the best for me."

2

Nora Sloane was waiting for Betsy on a bench outside the courthouse elevator.

"Did you talk to Mr. Darius?"

"Martin says you can tag along."

"Great!"

"Let's meet after court and I'll set up some ground rules."

"Okay. Do you know how Judge Norwood is going to rule?"

"No. His secretary just said to be here at two."

Betsy turned the corner. Judge Norwood's court was

at the far end of the hall. Most of the people in the corridor were congregating outside the courtroom door. Television crews were grouped around the entrance and a guard was checking people through the metal detector. Betsy flashed her Bar card at the guard. He stood aside. Betsy and Sloane cut behind him and went into the courtroom without having to go through the metal detector.

Martin Darius and Alan Page were in court. Betsy slid into the chair next to Darius and took her files and a pad out of her attaché case.

"Have you seen Lisa?" he asked.

Betsy scanned the packed courtroom. "I told my secretary to call her, but she's not here yet."

"What's he going to do, Tannenbaum?"

Darius was trying to sound casual, but there was an edge to his voice.

"We'll soon find out," Betsy said as Harvey Cobb rapped the gavel.

Judge Norwood strode out of his chambers. He was clutching several sheets of yellow, lined paper. Norwood was a shoot-from-the-hip guy. If he'd taken the time to write out the reasons for his decision, he was expecting it to be appealed.

"This is a very troubling case," the judge said without preliminaries. "Someone brutally tortured and murdered four innocent people. That person should not be roaming our streets. On the other hand, we have a presumption in this country that a person is innocent until proven guilty. We also have a guarantee of bail in our Constitution, which can be denied a defendant in a murder case only on a showing by the State that there is clear and convincing evidence of guilt.

"Mr. Page, you proved these people were murdered.

You proved they were buried at a site owned and visited by Mr. Darius. You proved Mr. Darius knew the three women victims. You also proved he was having an affair with one of them and may have beaten her the day she disappeared. What you have not shown, by clear and convincing evidence, is a connection between the defendant and the murders.

"No one saw Mr. Darius kill these people. There is no scientific evidence connecting him to any of the bodies or the homes from which they disappeared. You have matched the tires on the BMW to the tracks left at the murder site, but Mr. Darius visited that site frequently. Granted, it is suspicious that the tracks led up to the hole in the fence, but that's not enough, especially when there is no evidence connecting the BMW with any victim.

"Now I know you'll tell me that Mr. Darius destroyed the evidence by cleaning the trunk of his car, and that looks suspicious. But the standard I must use to deny bail is clear and convincing evidence, and the absence of evidence, no matter how suspicious the circumstances, is not a substitute for evidence.

"Really, Mr. Page, the crux of your case is the information given to you by this Gordon woman. But she wasn't here to be cross-examined by Mrs. Tannenbaum. Why isn't she here? We don't know. Is it because of foul play or because she made up the story she told you and is smart enough to avoid committing perjury?

"Even if I accept what you say, Mr. Darius is guilty of the Hunter's Point murders only if we accept Detective Gordon's theory. This Henry Waters fellow was named by the Hunter's Point police as the killer. If Waters is the killer, then Mr. Darius was a victim of the man."

Judge Norwood paused to take a sip of water. Betsy

choked back a victory grin. She glanced to her left. Alan Page was sitting stiffly, eyes straight ahead.

"Bail will be set in the sum of one million dollars. Mr. Darius may be released if he posts ten percent."

"Your Honor," Page exclaimed, leaping to his feet.

"This won't help you, Mr. Page. I've made up my mind. Personally, I'm surprised to see you force this hearing with such a skimpy case."

Judge Norwood turned his back on the prosecutor and walked off the bench.

"I knew I did the right thing hiring you, Tannenbaum," Darius exclaimed. "How long will it take to get me out of here?"

"As long as it takes you to post the bail and the jail to process you."

"Then call Terry Stark, my accountant at Darius Construction. He's waiting to hear from you. Tell him the amount he has to post and tell him to get it down here immediately."

Nora Sloane watched Betsy field questions from the press, then walked with her toward the elevators.

"You must feel great," Sloane said.

Betsy was tempted to feed Sloane the same upbeat line she had given to the reporters, but she liked Nora and felt she could confide in her.

"Not really."

"Why is that?"

"I admit, winning gives me a rush, but Norwood is right. Page's case was very skimpy. Anyone would have won this hearing. If this is the best Page can do, he won't get his case to a jury.

"Also, I don't know who Martin Darius is. If he's a husband and father who found his wife and child brutally murdered, then I did something good today. But what if he really murdered the women in the pit?"

"You think he's guilty?"

"I didn't say that. Martin insists he's innocent and I haven't seen anything to convince me otherwise. What I mean is, I still don't know for certain what happened here or in Hunter's Point."

"If you knew for certain that Darius was the rose killer, would you still represent him?"

"We have a system in America. It's not perfect, but it's worked for two hundred years and it depends on giving a fair trial to every person who goes through the courts, no matter what they've done. Once you start discriminating, for any reason, the system breaks down. The real test of the system is when it deals with a Bundy or a Manson, someone everyone fears and despises. If you can try that person fairly, then you send a message that we are a nation of law."

"Can you imagine a case you wouldn't take?" Sloane asked. "A client you might find so repulsive that your conscience would not let you represent him?"

"That's the question you confront when you choose to practice criminal law. If you can't represent that client, you don't belong in the business."

Betsy checked her watch. "Look, Nora, that's going to have to be it for today. I've got to make certain Martin's bail is posted, and my mother's watching Kathy, so I've got to leave the office a little early."

"Kathy is your daughter?"

Betsy smiled.

"I'd like to meet her."

"I'll introduce you to Kathy soon. My mom, too. You'll like them. Maybe I'll have you over for dinner."

"Great," Sloane said.

3

"Lisa Darius is waiting for you in your office," Ann said as soon as Betsy walked in. "I hope you don't mind. She's very upset about something and she was afraid to sit in the waiting room."

"That's okay. Does she know Martin's going to be released on bail?"

"Yes. I asked her how the judge ruled when she came in and she said you won."

"I didn't see her in court."

"I called her about the court appearance as soon as you told me to."

"I'm sure you did. Look, call Terry Stark at Darius Construction," Betsy said, writing down the name and phone number. "I told him how to post the bail a few days ago. He'll need a cashier's check for one hundred thousand. If there are any problems, buzz me."

Betsy did not recognize Lisa at first. She wore tight jeans, a blue turtleneck and a multicolored ski sweater. Her long hair was pulled back in a French braid, her emerald eyes were red from crying.

"Lisa, are you all right?"

"I never thought they'd let him out. I'm so scared."

"Of Martin? Why?"

Lisa put her hands to her face. "He's so cruel. No one knows how cruel. In public, he's charming. And sometimes he's just as charming with me when we're alone. He surprises me with flowers, jewelry. When he wants to, he treats me like a queen and I forget what he's really like inside. Oh God, Betsy, I think he killed those women."

Betsy was stunned. Lisa started to cry.

"Do you want some water?" Betsy asked.

Lisa shook her head. "Just give me a moment."

They sat quietly while Lisa caught her breath. Outside, a winter sun was shining and the air was so crisp and brittle, it seemed you could crack it into a million pieces. When Lisa spoke, her words came in a rush.

"I understand what Andrea Hammermill went through. Taking it, because you don't want anyone to know how bad it is and because there are good times and . . . and you love him."

Lisa sobbed. Her shoulders shook. Betsy wanted to comfort Lisa, but not as much as she wanted to learn what Darius had done to her to put her in this state, so she sat stiffly, waiting for Lisa to regain her composure.

"I do love him and I hate him and I'm scared of him," Lisa said hopelessly. "But this . . . If he . . ."

"Wife-beating is very common, Lisa. Serial murder isn't. Why do you think Martin may have killed these women?"

"It's more than beatings. There's a perverted side to . . . to what he does. His sexual needs . . . One time . . . This is very hard for me."

"Take your time."

"He wanted sex. We'd been to a party. I was tired. I told him. He insisted. We had an argument. No. That's not true. He never argues. He . . . he . . ."

Lisa closed her eyes. Her hands were clenched in her lap. Her body was rigid. When she spoke, she kept her eyes shut.

"He told me very calmly that I would have sex with him. I was getting angrier and angrier. The way he was speaking, it's the way you talk to a very small child or someone who's retarded. It enraged me. And the more I screamed, the calmer he became.

"Finally he said, 'Take off your clothes,' the way you'd command a dog to roll over. I told him to go to hell. The next thing I knew, I was on the floor. He hit me in the stomach. I lost my air. I was helpless.

"When I started to breathe, I looked up. Martin was smiling. He ordered me to take my clothes off again in that same voice. I shook my head. I couldn't talk yet, but I was damned if I was going to give in. He knelt down, grabbed my nipple through my blouse and squeezed. I almost blacked out from the pain. I was crying now and thrashing around on the floor. He did it to my other nipple, and I couldn't stand it. The horrible thing was how methodical he was. There was no passion in it. And he had the tiniest smile on his face, as if he was enjoying himself immensely but didn't want anyone to know.

"I was on the verge of passing out when he stopped. I sprawled on the floor, exhausted. I knew I couldn't fight him anymore. The next time he ordered me to, I took off my clothes."

"Did he rape you?" Betsy asked. She felt queasy.

Lisa shook her head. "That was the worst thing. He looked at me for a moment. There was a smile of satisfaction on his face I will never forget. Then he told me that I must always submit to him when he wanted sex and that I would be punished anytime I disobeyed him. He told me to get on all fours. I thought he was going to take me from behind. Instead, he made me crawl across the floor like a dog.

"We have a clothes closet in our bedroom. He opened the door and made me go in, naked. He said I would have to stay there without making a sound until he let me out. He told me I would be severely punished if I made any sound."

Lisa started sobbing again.

"He kept me in the closet all weekend without food. He put in some toilet paper and a bucket to . . . to use if I . . . I was so hungry and so scared.

"He told me that he would open the door when he was ready and I would immediately have sex with him or I would go back. When he opened the door I just crawled out and . . . and did anything he wanted. When he was through with me, he led me into the bathroom and bathed me, as if I was a baby. There were clothes laid out on the bed. Evening clothes. And a bracelet. It must have cost a fortune. Diamonds, rubies, gold. It was my reward for obedience. When I was dressed, he took me to a restaurant for a lavish dinner. All evening, he treated me like a queen.

"I was certain he would want me again when we got home. It's all I thought about at dinner. I had to force myself to eat, because I was nauseous thinking of what was coming but I was afraid he would do something to me if I didn't eat. Then when we got home he just went to sleep and he didn't touch me for a week."

"Did he ever do anything like that to you again?"

"No," Lisa said, hanging her head. "He didn't have to. I learned my lesson. If he said he wanted sex, I did what he wanted. And I received my rewards. And no one knew, until now, what I've been going through."

"Did you ever think of leaving him?" Betsy asked.

"He . . . he told me if I told anyone the things he did, or tried to run away, he would kill me. If you heard the way he said it, so calm, so detached . . . I knew he'd do it. I knew."

Lisa took deep breaths until she was back in control.

"There's something else," Lisa said. Betsy noticed a shopping bag lying next to Lisa's chair. Lisa leaned over and took a scrapbook out of it and placed it in her lap.

"I was certain Martin was having an affair. He never said anything and I never saw him with anyone, but I knew. One day I decided to search his things while he was at work to see if I could find proof. Instead, I found this."

Lisa tapped the cover of the scrapbook, then handed it across to Betsy. Betsy placed the book in the center of her blotter. The cover was a faded brown with a gold trim. Betsy opened the scrapbook. On the first page, under a plastic sheet, were clippings about the Hunter's Point case from the Hunter's Point paper, the New York *Times, Newsday* and other papers. Betsy flipped through some of the other pages without reading the articles. They were all about the Hunter's Point case.

"Did you ever ask Martin about this?" Betsy asked.

"No. I was too scared. I put it back. But I did do something. I hired a private detective to follow Martin and to find out about Hunter's Point."

"What's the detective's name?"

"Sam Oberhurst."

"Do you have an address and phone number where I can reach him?"

"I've got a phone number."

"No address?"

"I got his name from a friend who used him in her divorce. She gave me the number. It's an answering machine. We met at a restaurant."

"Where did you send your checks?"

"I always paid him in cash."

"Give me your friend's name and I'll have my investigator contact her if it's necessary."

"Her name is Peggy Fulton. Her divorce attorney was Gary Telford. He's the one who gave her the name. I'd rather you didn't go to her, unless you have to."

"The lawyer's better," Betsy said as she pulled a sheet of paper out of her drawer and filled in several blanks. "This is a release of information form giving me or my investigator the right to see Oberhurst's files."

While Lisa read the form, Betsy told Ann to have Reggie Stewart come to her office immediately. Lisa signed the release and handed it back to Betsy.

"What did Oberhurst tell you?"

"He was certain Martin was cheating, but he didn't have a name yet."

"And Hunter's Point?"

"He told me he hadn't started working on that aspect of the investigation."

Lisa's story had affected Betsy deeply. The thought of Darius treating his wife like an animal disgusted her and Lisa's description made Betsy physically ill. But it did not mean Darius was a murderer, and she was still his attorney.

"Why did you come to me, Lisa?"

"I don't know. I'm so confused by everything. You seemed so understanding at the house and I knew how hard you fought for Andrea Hammermill and the Peterson woman. I hoped you could tell me what to do."

"Do you plan to tell the district attorney what you've told me or to give him this book?"

Lisa looked startled. "No. Why would I do that?"

"To hurt Martin."

"No. I don't want to . . . I still love him. Or, I . . . Mrs. Tannenbaum, if Martin did those things . . . If he tortured and killed those women, I have to know."

Betsy leaned forward and looked directly into Lisa's moist green eyes.

"I'm Martin's lawyer, Lisa. My professional loyalty lies with him, even if he is guilty."

Lisa looked shocked. "You'd continue to defend him, even if he did that?"

Betsy nodded. "But he may not have, Lisa, and what you've told me could be very important. If Oberhurst was following Martin on a date when one of those women disappeared, he could provide Martin with an alibi. Page is going to argue that the same man killed all three women, and he probably did. All I have to do is show Martin didn't kill one of the victims and the d.a.'s case disappears."

"I hadn't thought of that."

"When is the last time you talked to Oberhurst?"

"A few weeks ago. I left a few messages on his machine, but he didn't return my calls."

"I'll have my investigator contact Oberhurst. Can I hold on to the scrapbook?"

Lisa nodded. Betsy walked around the desk and laid a hand on Lisa's shoulder.

"Thank you for confiding in me. I know how hard it must have been."

"I had to tell someone," Lisa whispered. "I've kept it in so long."

"I have a friend who might help you. Alice Knowland. She's very nice and very compassionate. I've sent other women with similar problems to her and she's helped some of them."

"What is she, a doctor?"

"A psychiatrist. But don't let that scare you off. Psychiatrist is just a fancy title for a good listener with experience in helping troubled people. She might be good for you. You could go to her a few times, then stop if she isn't helping. Think it over and give me a call."

"I will," Lisa said, standing. "And thank you for listening."

"You're not alone, Lisa. Remember that."

Betsy put her arms around Lisa and hugged her.

"Martin will be home late tonight. Will you stay with him?" Betsy asked.

"I can't. I'm living with my father until I decide what to do."

"Okay."

"Don't tell Martin I came, please."

"I won't if I can help it. He is my client, but I don't want to hurt you."

Lisa wiped her eyes and left. Betsy was drained. She pictured Lisa, hungry and terrified, cowering in the closet in the dark with the smell of her own urine and feces. Betsy's stomach rolled. She walked out of the office and down the hall to the rest room and ran some cold water in the sink. She splashed her face with the running water, then cupped her hands and drank.

She remembered the questions Nora and the reporters had asked. How could she sleep if she saved Martin Darius, knowing what she knew about him? What would a man who treated his wife like a dog do to a woman he did not know, if she fell under his power? Would he do what the rose killer had done to his victims? Was Martin the killer?

Betsy remembered the scrapbook and dried her face, then returned to her office. She was halfway through the scrapbook when Reggie Stewart walked in.

"Congratulations on the bail hearing."

"Pull a chair next to me. I've got something that might break Martin's case."

"Excellent."

"Lisa Darius was just here. She suspected Martin might be cheating on her, so she hired an investigator to tail him. Have you heard of a p.i. named Sam Oberhurst?"

Stewart thought for a moment, then shook his head.

"The name sounds vaguely familiar, but I'm sure we've never met."

"Here's his phone number and a release from Lisa. Oberhurst has an answering machine. If you can't get through to him, try a divorce attorney named Gary Telford. Lisa got the name from one of his clients. Tell Gary you're working for me. We know each other. Find out if Oberhurst was tailing Darius on a date when any of the women disappeared. He could be Martin's alibi."

"I'll get right on it."

Betsy pointed to the scrapbook. "Lisa found this in Martin's things when she was looking for evidence of the affair. It's filled with clippings from the Hunter's Point case."

Stewart looked over Betsy's shoulder as Betsy turned the pages. Most of the stories concerned the disappearances. There were several stories about the murders of Sandra and Melody Lake. A section was devoted to the discovery of the disemboweled body of Patricia Cross in Henry Waters's basement and Waters's death. Betsy turned to the final section of the scrapbook and stopped cold.

"My God, there were survivors."

"What? I thought all the women were murdered."

"No. Look here. It says Gloria Escalante, Samantha Reardon and Anne Hazelton were found alive in an old farmhouse."

"Where?"

"It doesn't give any other information. Wait a minute. No, there's nothing else. According to the article, the women declined to be interviewed."

"I don't get it. Didn't Darius tell you about this?"

"Not a word."

"Page?"

"He always referred to them as if they were dead."

"Maybe Page doesn't know," Stewart said.

"How is that possible?"

"What if Gordon didn't tell him?"

"Why wouldn't she? And why wouldn't Martin tell me? Something's not right, Reg. None of this makes sense. Gordon and Martin don't mention the survivors. The Hunter's Point files have disappeared. I don't like it."

"I know you love a mystery, Betsy, but I see this as our big break. The survivors will know who kidnapped and tortured them. If it wasn't Darius, we're home free."

"Maybe Martin didn't mention the survivors because he knew they'd identify him."

"There's only one way to find out," Stewart said. "Have Ann book me on an early flight to Hunter's Point."

"I want you to go to Albany, New York, first. Frank Grimsbo, one of the other detectives on the task force, is head of security at Marlin Steel. His office is in Albany."

"You got it."

Betsy buzzed Ann and told her what to do. When she got off the intercom, Stewart asked:

"What about the p.i.?"

"I'll run down Oberhurst. I want you on that flight, first thing. There's something weird about this case, Reg, and I'm betting that the answers we need are in Hunter's Point."

4

Alan Page left the courtroom in a daze. He barely heard the reporters' questions and answered them mechanically. Randy Highsmith told him not to take the loss personally, and assured him that it wasn't his fault that they couldn't find Nancy Gordon, but Highsmith and Barrow had warned him that he was making a mistake by rushing to arrest Darius. Even after they learned about the incident at the Hacienda Motel, the detective and the deputy district attorney wanted to move slowly. Page had overruled them. Now he was paying the price.

Page left work as soon as he could. There was an elevator in the rear of the district attorney's office that went to the basement. He took it and dodged across the street to the parking garage, hoping no one would see him and ask him about his public humiliation.

Page poured his first scotch as soon as he took off his raincoat. He drank it quickly, refilled his glass and carried it into the bedroom. Why was he screwing up like this? He hadn't been thinking straight since Tina left him. This was the first time his ragged thought processes had gotten him in trouble, but it had been only a matter of time. He wasn't sleeping, he wasn't eating right, he couldn't concentrate. Now, he was haunted by the ghost of a woman he had known for all of two hours.

Page settled down in front of his television in an alcoholic haze. The old movie he was watching was one he had seen many times before. He let the black and white images float across the screen without seeing them. Did he order the arrest of Martin Darius to protect Nancy Gordon? Did he think he could keep them apart and rescue her? What sense did that make? What sense did anything in his life make?

5

Martin Darius parked his Ferrari in front of his house. It was cold. The mist pressed against him when he stepped out of the car. After a week in jail, the chill, damp air felt good. Darius crossed over the bridge. The lights were out. He could barely see the placid pool water through the glass roof. The rest of the house was also dark. He opened the front door and punched in the code that turned off the alarm.

Lisa was probably hiding from him at her father's house. He didn't care. After a week crowded in with unwashed, frightened men in the stale air of the county correctional facility, a night alone would be a pleasure. He would relish the quiet and bask in the luxury of soaping off the sour jail smell that had seeped into his pores.

There was a bar in the living room, and Darius fixed himself a drink. He flipped on the outside lights and watched the rain fall on the lawn through the picture window. He hated jail. He hated taking orders from fools and living with idiots. When he was practicing criminal law in Hunter's Point, he'd had only contempt for his clients. They were losers who were not equipped to succeed in the world, so they dealt with their problems through stealing or violence. A superior man controlled his environment and bent the will of others to him.

To Darius's way of thinking, there was only one reason to tolerate inferior minds. Someone had to do menial labor. Martin wondered what the world would be like if it was ruled by the strong, with the menial work done by a slave class selected from docile, mentally inferior men and women. The men could do the heavy work. The inferior women could be bred for beauty.

It was cold in the house. Darius shivered. He thought about the women. Docile women, bred for beauty and subservience. They would make excellent pets. He imagined his female slaves instantly submitting to his commands. Of course, there would be disobedient slaves who would not do as they were told. Such women would have to be chastised.

Darius grew hard thinking about the women. It would have been easy to give in to the fantasy, to open his fly and relieve the delicious feeling of tension. But giving in would be a sign of weakness, so he opened his eyes and breathed deeply. The inferior man lived only in his fantasies, because he lacked willpower and imagination. The superior man made his fantasies a reality.

Darius took another sip, then placed the cool glass to his forehead. He had given his dilemma a lot of thought while he was locked up in jail. He was certain he knew what was coming next. He was free. The newspapers had printed Judge Norwood's opinion that the evidence was not strong enough to convict him. That meant someone else would have to die.

Darius looked at his watch. It was almost ten. Lisa would be up. Getting through to her was the problem. At the jail only collect calls were permitted. Justice Ryder had refused every one he made. Darius dialed the judge's number.

"Ryder residence," a deep voice answered after three rings.

"Please put my wife on the phone, Judge."

"She doesn't want to talk to you, Martin."

"I want to hear that from her lips."

"I'm afraid that's not possible."

"I'm out now and I don't have to put up with your interference. Lisa is my wife. If she says she doesn't want to talk to me, I'll accept that, but I want to hear it from her."

"Let me talk to him, Dad," Lisa said in the background. The judge must have covered the receiver, because Darius could hear only a muffled argument. Then Lisa was on the phone.

"I don't want you to call me, Martin."

She sounded shaky. Darius imagined her trembling.

"Judge Norwood let me out because he didn't believe I was guilty, Lisa."

"He . . . he doesn't know everything I know."

"Lisa . . ."

"I don't want to see you."

"Are you afraid?"

"Yes."

"Good. Stay afraid. There's something going on here you know nothing about." Darius heard an intake of breath and the judge asked Lisa if he was threatening her. "I don't want you to come home. It's too dangerous for you. But I don't want you staying at your father's house, either. There isn't anywhere in Portland you'll be safe."

"What are you talking about?"

"I want you to go away somewhere until I tell you to come back. If you're afraid of me, don't tell me where you go. I'll get in touch with you through your father."

"I don't understand. Why should I be afraid?"

Darius closed his eyes. "I can't tell you and you don't want to know. Believe me when I say you are in great danger."

"What kind of danger?"

Lisa sounded panicky. Justice Ryder snatched the phone from her hand. "That's it, Darius. Get off this phone or I'll call Judge Norwood personally and have you thrown back in jail."

"I'm trying to save Lisa's life and you're endangering it. It's imperative that . . ."

Ryder slammed the phone down. Darius listened to the dial tone. Ryder had always been a pompous ass. Now his bullheadedness could cost Lisa her life. If Darius explained why, the judge would never believe him. Hell, he'd use what Darius said to put him on Death Row. Darius wished he could talk over his problem with Betsy Tannenbaum. She was very bright and she might come up with a solution, but he couldn't go to her either. She'd honor the attorney-client privilege, but she would drop him as a client and he needed her.

Darius had not seen the moon all the time he was in

jail. He looked for it now, but it was obscured by clouds. He wondered what phase the moon was in. He hoped it was not full. That brought out the crazies. He should know. Martin shivered, but not from the cold. Right now, he was the only one who was not in danger, but that could change at any moment. Darius did not want to admit it, but he was afraid.

Part Four

———————

THE DEVIL'S
BARGAIN

Chapter Fourteen

I

Gary Telford had the smile and bright eyes of a young man, but his flabby body and receding hairline made him look middle-aged. He shared a suite of offices with six other lawyers in one of the thirty-story glass boxes that had sprung up in downtown Portland during the past twenty years. Telford's office had a view of the Willamette River. On clear days he could see several mountains in the Cascade range, including majestic Mount Hood and Mount St. Helens, an active volcano that had erupted in the early eighties. Today, low-lying clouds owned the sky and it was hard to see the east side of the river in the fog.

"Thanks for seeing me," Betsy said as they shook hands.

"It's been too long," Gary said warmly. "Besides, I'm dying to know how I'm connected with this Darius business."

"When you represented Peggy Fulton in her divorce, did you use a p.i. named Sam Oberhurst?"

Telford stopped smiling. "Why do you want to know?"

"Lisa Darius suspected her husband was having an affair. She asked your client for advice and Peggy gave her Oberhurst's name. He was tailing Darius. I was hoping Oberhurst was conducting surveillance when one of the women disappeared and can give Darius an alibi."

"If Lisa Darius employed Oberhurst, why do you need to talk to me?"

"She doesn't have his address. Just a phone number. I've called it several times, but all I get is an answering machine. He hasn't returned my calls. I was hoping you'd have his office address."

Telford considered this information for a moment. He looked uncomfortable. "I don't think Oberhurst has an office."

"What's he do, work out of his home?"

"I guess. We always met here."

"What about bills? Where did you send his checks?"

"Cash. He wanted cash. Up front."

"Sounds a little unusual."

"Yeah. Well, he's a little unusual." Telford paused. "Look, I'll try to help you find Oberhurst, but there's something you need to know. Some of the stuff he does isn't on the up-and-up. You follow me?"

"I'm not sure I do."

Telford leaned forward conspiratorially. "Say you want to find out what someone says when they think the conversation is private, you hire Oberhurst. See what I mean?"

"Electronics?"

Telford nodded. "Phones, rooms. He hinted he's not above a little b. and e. And the guy's got a record for it. I think he did penitentiary time down south somewhere for burglary."

"Sounds pretty unsavory."

"Yeah. I didn't like him. I only used him that one time and I'm sorry I did."

"Why?"

Telford tapped his fingers on his desk. Betsy let him decide what he wanted to say.

"Can we keep this confidential?"

Betsy nodded.

"What Peg wanted . . . Well, she was a little hysterical. Didn't take the divorce well. Anyway, I was sort of like a middleman with this. She said she wanted someone to do something, a private investigator who wouldn't ask too many questions. I hooked them up and paid him his money. I never really used him to work on the case.

"Anyway, someone beat up Mark Fulton about a week or so after I introduced Oberhurst to Peg. It was pretty bad from what I hear. The police thought it was a robbery."

"Why do you think different?"

"Oberhurst tried to shake me down. He came to my office a week after the beating. Showed me a newspaper article about it. He said he could keep me out of it for two thousand bucks.

"I told him to take a hike. I didn't know a goddamn thing about it. For all I knew, he could have been making the whole thing up. I mean, he reads the article, figures he can touch me for two grand and I won't squawk because the amount's not worth the risk."

"Weren't you afraid?"

"Damn straight. He's a big guy. He even looks like a gangster. He has a broken nose, talks tough. The whole bit. Only, I figured he was testing me. If I'd given in, he would have kept coming back. Besides, I didn't do anything wrong. Like I said, I only hooked them up."

"How do I get to Oberhurst?" Betsy asked.

"I got his name from Steve Wong at a party. Try him. Say I told you to call."

Telford thumbed through a lawyer's directory and wrote Wong's number on the back of a business card.

"Thanks."

"Glad I could help. And be careful with Oberhurst, he's bad news."

2

Betsy ate lunch at Zen, then shopped at Saks Fifth Avenue for a suit. It was one-fifteen when she returned to her office. There were several phone messages in her slot and two dozen red roses on her desk. Her first thought was that they were from Rick, and the idea made her heart pound. Rick sent her flowers when they were dating and on Valentine's Day. It was something he would do if he wanted to come home.

"Who are these from?" she asked Ann.

"I don't know. They were just delivered. There's a card."

Betsy put down her phone messages. A small envelope was taped to the vase. Her fingers trembled as she pried open the flap of the envelope and pulled out a small white card that said:

> For man's best friend, his lawyer.
> You did a bang-up job,
> **A VERY GRATEFUL CLIENT**
> Martin

Betsy put down the card. Her excitement turned sour.

"They're from Darius," she told Ann, hoping her disappointment didn't show.

"How thoughtful."

Betsy said nothing. She had wished so hard that the flowers were from Rick. Betsy debated with herself for a moment, then dialed his number.

"Mr. Tannenbaum's office," Rick's secretary said.

"Julie, this is Betsy. Is Rick in?"

"I'm sorry, Mrs. Tannenbaum, he's out of the office all day. Should I tell him you called?"

"No, thanks. That's okay."

The line went dead. Betsy held the receiver for a moment, then hung up. What would she have said if Rick had taken the call? Would she have risked humiliation and told him she wanted to get together? What would Rick have said? Betsy closed her eyes and took a few deep breaths to calm her heart. To distract herself, she looked through her phone messages. Most could be put off, but one was from Dr. Keene. When Betsy was back in control, she dialed his number.

"Sue did a good job, Betsy," the pathologist said, when they finally got down to business, "but I've got something for you."

"Let me get a pad. Okay, shoot."

"A medical examiner always collects urine samples from the body to screen for drugs. Most labs only do a d.a.u., which screens for five drugs of abuse to see if the victim used morphine, cocaine, amphetamines and so on. That's what Sue did. I had my lab do a urine screen for other substances. We came up with strong positive barbiturate readings for the women. I retested the blood. Every one of these ladies showed pentobarbital levels that were off scale."

"What does that mean?"

"Pentobarbital is not a common drug of abuse, which is why the lab didn't find it. It's an anesthetic."

"I don't follow."

"It's used in hospitals to anesthetize patients. This is not a drug these women would take themselves. Someone gave it to them. Now, this is where it gets strange, Betsy. These women all had three to four milligrams percent of pentobarbital in their blood. That's a very high level. In fact, it's a fatal level."

"What are you telling me?"

"I'm telling you that the three women died from an overdose of pentobarbital, not from their wounds."

"But they were tortured."

"They were mutilated, all right. I saw burn marks that were probably from cigarettes and electrical wires, there were cuts made with razor blades, the breasts were mutilated and there's evidence that objects had been inserted into their anus. But there's a chance the women were unconscious when these injuries were inflicted. Microscopic sections from around the wounds showed an early repair process. This tells me death occurred about twelve to twenty-four hours after the wounds were inflicted."

Betsy was quiet for a moment. When she spoke she sounded confused. "That doesn't make sense, Ray. What possible benefit is there in torturing someone who's unconscious?"

"Beats me. That's your problem. I'm just a sawbones."

"What about the man?"

"Here we have a different story. First, there's no pentobarbital. None. Second, there is evidence of repair around several wounds, indicating that he was tortured over a period of time. Death was sometime later from a gunshot wound, just like Sue said."

"How could Dr. Gregg have been fooled about the cause of death of the women?"

"Easy. You see a person cut from crotch to chest, the heart torn out, the intestines hanging out, you assume that's what killed 'em. I would have thought the same, if I hadn't found pentobarbital."

"You've given me a king-size headache, Ray."

"Take two aspirin and call me in the morning."

"Very funny."

"I'm glad I could bring some joy into your life."

They hung up, but Betsy kept staring at her notes. She doodled on the pad. The drawings made as much sense as what Dr. Keene had just told her.

3

Reggie Stewart's cross-country flight arrived late at JFK, so he had to sprint through the terminal to catch the connecting, upstate flight. He felt ragged by the time the plane landed at Albany County Airport. After checking into a motel near the airport, Stewart ate a hot meal, took a shower, and exchanged his cowboy boots, jeans and a flannel shirt for a navy blue suit, a white shirt and a tie with narrow red and yellow stripes. He was feeling human again by the time he parked his rental car in the lot of Marlin Steel's corporate headquarters, fifteen minutes before his scheduled appointment with Frank Grimsbo.

"Thanks for seeing me on such short notice," Stewart said, as soon as the secretary left him alone with the chief of security.

"Curiosity got the better of me," Grimsbo answered with an easy smile. "I couldn't figure out what a private investigator from Portland, Oregon, would want with me." Grimsbo gestured toward his wet bar. "Can I get you a drink?"

"Bourbon, neat," Stewart said, as he looked out the window at a breathtaking view of the Hudson River.

Grimsbo's office was furnished with an eight-foot rosewood desk and rosewood credenza. Old English hunting scenes hung from the walls. The couch and chairs were black leather. It was a far cry from the stuffy, converted storage area he had shared with the task force members in Hunter's Point. Like his surroundings, Grimsbo had also changed. He drove a Mercedes instead of a beat-up Chevy and he'd long since lost his taste for polyester. His conservative, gray pinstripe suits were custom-tailored to conceal what was left of a beer belly that had been dramatically reduced by dieting and exercise. He had also lost most of his hair, but he had gained in every other way. If old acquaintances thought he missed his days as a homicide detective, they were mistaken.

"So, what brings you from Portland, Oregon, to Albany?" Grimsbo asked as he handed Stewart his drink.

"I work for a lawyer named Betsy Tannenbaum. She's representing a prominent businessman who's been charged with murder."

"So you told my secretary when you called. What's that have to do with me?"

"You used to work for the Hunter's Point Police Department, didn't you?"

"I haven't had anything to do with Hunter's Point P.D. for nine years."

"I'm interested in discussing a case you worked on ten years ago. The rose killer."

Grimsbo had been raising his glass to his lips, but he stopped abruptly.

"Why are you interested in the rose killer? He's ancient history."

"Bear with me and I'll explain in a minute."

Grimsbo shook his head. "That's a hard case to forget."

"Tell me about it."

Grimsbo tilted his head back and closed his eyes, as if he was trying to picture the events. He sipped his scotch.

"We started getting reports of missing women. No signs of a struggle, nothing missing at the crime scenes, but there was always a rose and a note that said 'Gone, But Not Forgotten' left on the women's pillows. Then a mother and her six-year-old daughter were murdered. The husband found the bodies. There was a rose and a note next to the woman.

"A neighbor had seen a florist truck at the house of one of the victims, or maybe it was near the house. It's been some time now, so I may not have my facts exactly right. Anyway, we figured out who the deliveryman was. It was a guy named Henry Waters. He had a sex offender record. Then an anonymous caller said he was talking to Waters at a bar and Waters told him he had a woman in his basement. Sure enough, we found one of the missing women."

Grimsbo shook his head. "Man, that was a sight. You wouldn't believe what that bastard did to her. I wanted to kill him right there, and I would have, but fate took over and the son-of-a-bitch tried to escape. Another cop shot him and that was that."

"Was Peter Lake the husband who found the two bodies? The mother and daughter?"

"Right. Lake."

"Are you satisfied that the deliveryman was the killer?"

"Definitely. Hell, they found some of the roses and a note. And, of course, there was the body. Yeah, we got the right man."

"There was a task force assigned to investigate the case, wasn't there?"

Grimsbo nodded.

"Was Nancy Gordon a member of the task force?"

"Sure."

"Mr. Grimsbo . . ."

"Frank."

"Frank, my client is Peter Lake. He moved to Portland about eight years ago and changed his name to Martin Darius. He's a very successful developer. Very respected. About three months ago, women started disappearing in Portland. Roses and notes identical to those left in the Hunter's Point case were found on the pillows of the missing women. About two weeks ago the bodies of the missing women and a man were found buried at a construction site owned by Martin Darius. Nancy Gordon told our district attorney that Darius—Lake—killed them."

Grimsbo shook his head. "Nancy always had a bee in her bonnet about Lake."

"But you don't agree with her?"

"No. Like I said, Waters was the killer. I have no doubt about that. Now, we did think Lake might be the killer for a while. There was circumstantial evidence pointing that way, and I even had bad feelings about the guy. But it was only circumstantial evidence and the case against Waters was solid."

"What about Lake leaving Hunter's Point?"

"Can't blame him. If my wife and kid were brutally murdered, I wouldn't want to be reminded of them every day. Leaving town, starting over—sounds like the smart thing to do."

"Did the other investigators agree that Lake was innocent?"

"Everyone but Nancy."

"Was there any evidence that cleared Lake?"

"Like what?"

"Did he have an alibi for the time of any of the disappearances."

"I can't recall anything like that. Of course, it's been some time. Why don't you check the file? I'm sure Hunter's Point still has it."

"The files are missing."

"How did that happen?"

"We don't know." Stewart paused. "What kind of a person is Gordon?"

Grimsbo sipped his scotch and swiveled toward the window. It was comfortable in Grimsbo's office, but there was a thin coating of snow on the ground outside the picture window and the leafless trees were swaying under the attack of a chill wind.

"Nancy is a driven woman. That case got to all of us, but it affected her the most. It came right after she lost her fiancé. Another cop. Killed in the line of duty shortly before her wedding. Really tragic. I think that unbalanced her for a while. Then the women started disappearing and she submerged herself in the case.

"Now I'm not saying she isn't a fine detective. She is. But she lost her objectivity in that one case."

Stewart nodded and made some notes.

"How many women disappeared in Hunter's Point?"

"Four."

"And one was found in Waters's basement?"

"Right."

"What happened to the other women?"

"They were found in some old farmhouse out in the

country, if I remember correctly. I wasn't involved with that. Got stuck back at the station writing reports."

"How were they found?"

"Pardon?"

"Wasn't Waters shot almost as soon as the body was found in the basement?"

Grimsbo nodded.

"So, who told you where the other women were?"

Grimsbo paused, thinking. Then he shook his head. "You know, I honestly can't remember. It could have been his mother. Waters was living with his mother. Or he might have written something down. I just don't recall."

"Did any of the survivors positively i.d. Waters as the killer?"

"They may have. Like I said, I didn't question any of them. They were pretty messed up, if I remember. Barely alive. Tortured. They went right to the hospital."

"Can you think of any reason why Nancy Gordon wouldn't tell our d.a. there were survivors?"

"She didn't?"

"I don't think so."

"Hell, I don't know. Why don't you ask her?"

"We can't. She's disappeared."

"What?" Grimsbo looked alarmed.

"Gordon showed up at the home of Alan Page, our d.a., late one night and told him about the Hunter's Point case. Then she checked into a motel. When Page called her the next morning, she was gone. Her clothing was still in the room, but she wasn't there."

"Have they looked for her?" Grimsbo asked anxiously.

"Oh, yeah. She's Page's whole case. He lost the bail hearing when he couldn't produce her."

"I don't know what to say. Did she return to Hunter's Point?"

"No. They thought she was on vacation. She never told anyone she was coming to Portland, and they haven't heard from her."

"Jesus, I hope nothing serious happened. Maybe she took off somewhere. Didn't you say Hunter's Point P.D. thought she was on vacation?"

"If she was going on vacation she wouldn't leave her clothes and makeup."

"Yeah." Grimsbo looked solemn. He shook his head. Stewart watched Grimsbo. The security chief was very upset.

"Is there anything else I can do for you, Mr. Stewart? I'm afraid I have some work to do," Grimsbo asked.

"No, you've been a big help." Stewart laid his and Betsy's business cards on Grimsbo's desk. "If you remember anything about the case that might help our client, please call me."

"I will."

"Oh, there is one other thing. I want to talk with all the members of the Hunter's Point task force. Do you know where I can find Glen Michaels and Wayne Turner?"

"I haven't heard from Michaels in years, but Wayne will be easy to find in about two weeks."

"Oh?"

"All you gotta do is turn on your TV. He's Senator Colby's administrative assistant. He should be sitting right next to him during the confirmation hearings."

Stewart scribbled this information into his notebook, thanked Grimsbo and left. As soon as the door closed behind Stewart, Grimsbo went back to his desk and dialed a Washington, D.C., phone number. Wayne Turner answered on the first ring.

Chapter Fifteen

I

Reggie Stewart eased himself into a seat across the desk from Dr. Pedro Escalante. The cardiologist had put on weight over the past ten years. His curly black hair was mostly gray. He was still cheerful with patients, but his good humor was not second nature to him anymore.

They were meeting in the cardiologist's office in the Wayside Clinic. A diploma from Brown University and another from Tufts Medical School hung on one wall. Beneath the diplomas was a child's crayon drawing of a stick-figure girl standing next to a yellow flower that was almost as tall as she was. A rainbow stretched from one side of the picture to the other.

"That your daughter?" Stewart asked. A photograph of Gloria Escalante holding a little girl on her lap stood on one corner of the doctor's desk. Stewart figured the child for the artist and asked about her as a way of easing into a conversation that was certain to evoke painful memories.

"Our adopted daughter," Escalante replied sadly. "Gloria lost the ability to conceive after her ordeal."

Stewart nodded because he could not think of a single thing to say.

"I'm afraid you've wasted your trip, if it was made solely to talk to my wife. We have tried our best to put the past behind us."

"I appreciate why Mrs. Escalante wouldn't want to talk to me, but this is literally a matter of life and death. We have the death penalty in Oregon and there's no doubt that my client will receive it, if he's convicted."

Dr. Escalante's features hardened. "Mr. Stewart, if your client treated those women the way my wife was treated, the death penalty would be insufficient punishment."

"You knew my client as Peter Lake, Dr. Escalante. His wife and daughter were killed by Henry Waters. He suffered the same anguish you suffered. We're talking about a frame-up of the worst kind, and your wife may have information that can prove an innocent man is being prosecuted."

Escalante looked down at his desk. "Our position is firm, Mr. Stewart. My wife will not discuss what happened to her with anyone. It has taken ten years to put the past behind her and we are going to keep it behind her. However, I may be of some help to you. There are answers to questions I may be able to give you."

"Any help will be appreciated."

"I don't want you to think her hard, Mr. Stewart. We did consider your request for an interview most seriously, but it would be too much for Gloria. She is very strong. Very strong. Otherwise she would not have survived. But as strong as she is, it is only within the past few years that she has been anything like the woman she used to be. Since your call, the nightmares have returned."

"Believe me, I would never subject your wife to . . ."

"No, no. I understand why you're here. I don't blame you. I just want you to understand why I can't permit her to relive what happened."

"Dr. Escalante, the main reason I wanted to talk to your wife was to find out if she saw the face of the man who kidnapped her."

"If that's why you came, I'm afraid I must disappoint you. She was taken from behind. Chloroform was used. During her captivity, she was forced to wear a leather hood with no eyelets whenever . . . whenever her captor . . . when he came."

"She never saw his face?"

"Never."

"What about the other women? Did any of them see him?"

"I don't know."

"Do you know where I can find Ann Hazelton or Samantha Reardon?"

"Ann Hazelton committed suicide six months after she was freed. Reardon was in a mental hospital for some time. She had a complete breakdown. Simon Reardon, Samantha's husband, divorced her," Escalante said with obvious distaste. "He moved away years ago. He's a neurosurgeon. You can probably locate him through the American Medical Association. He might know where Mrs. Reardon is living."

"That's very helpful," Stewart said as he wrote the information in his notebook.

"You could ask the other investigator. He may have located her."

"Pardon?"

"There was another investigator. I wouldn't let him speak to Gloria either. He came during the summer."

"The disappearances didn't start until August."

"No, this would have been May, early June. Somewhere in there."

"What did he look like?"

"He was a big man. I thought he might have played football or boxed, because he had a broken nose."

"That doesn't sound like anyone from the d.a.'s office. But they wouldn't have been involved that early. Do you remember his name or where he was from?"

"He was from Portland and I have his card." The doctor opened the top drawer of his desk and pulled out a white business card. "Samuel Oberhurst," he said, handing the card to Stewart. The card had Oberhurst's name and a phone number, but no address. The number was the one Betsy had given him.

"Dr. Escalante, what happened to your wife and the other women after they were kidnapped?"

Escalante took a deep breath. Stewart could see his pain even after all these years.

"My wife told me that there were three women with her. They were kept in an old farmhouse. She isn't clear where the house was situated, because she was unconscious when he brought her there and she was in shock when she left. Almost dead from starvation. It was a miracle."

Escalante paused. He ran his tongue across his lips and breathed deeply, again.

"The women were kept naked in stalls. They were chained at the ankles. Whenever he would come, he was masked and he would make them put on the hoods. Then he . . . he would torture them." Escalante closed his eyes and shook his head, as if trying to clear it of images too painful to behold. "I have never asked her to tell me what he did, but I have seen my wife's medical records."

Escalante paused again.

"I don't need that information, Doctor. It's not necessary."

"Thank you."

"The important thing is the identification. If your wife can remember anything about her captor that would help us to prove he was not Peter Lake."

"I understand. I'll ask her, but I'm certain she won't be able to help you."

Dr. Escalante shook hands with Stewart and showed him out. Then he returned to his office and picked up the photograph of his wife and child.

2

Betsy had a trial scheduled to start Friday in a divorce case and she was putting the file in her attaché case to bring home when Ann told her Reggie Stewart was on the line.

"How was your trip?" Betsy asked.

"Just fine, but I'm not accomplishing much. There's something weird about this business and it's getting weirder by the minute."

"Go on."

"I can't put my finger on what's wrong, but I know I'm getting the runaround about the case when no one should have any reason to lie to me."

"What are they lying about?"

"That's just it. I have no idea. But I know something's up."

"Tell me what you've learned so far," Betsy said, and Stewart recounted his conversations with Frank Grimsbo and Dr. Escalante.

"After I left Escalante, I spent some time at the public library going over newspaper accounts of the case. I figured there would be interviews with the victims, the cops. Nothing. John O'Malley, the chief of police, was the mayor's spokesman. He said Waters did it. Case closed. The surviving women were hospitalized immediately. Reardon was institutionalized. Escalante wouldn't talk to reporters. Ditto Hazelton. A few weeks of this and interest fades. On to other stories. But you read the news reports and you read O'Malley's statements, and you still don't know what happened to those women.

"Then I talked to Roy Lenzer, a detective with Hunter's Point P.D. He's the guy who's trying to run down the case files for Page. He knows Gordon is missing. He searched her house for the files. No luck. Someone carted off all of the files in the case. I mean, we're talking a full shelf of case reports, photographs. But why? Why take a shelf-load of paper in a ten-year-old case? What was in those files?"

"Reg, did Oberhurst visit the police?"

"I asked Lenzer about that. Gave Grimsbo a call, too. As far as I can tell, Oberhurst never talked to anyone after he talked to Dr. Escalante. Which doesn't make sense. If he was investigating the case for Lisa Darius, the police would be his first stop."

"Not necessarily," Betsy said. Then she told her investigator about her meetings with Gary Telford.

"I have a very bad feeling about this, Reg. Let me run something by you. Say you're an unscrupulous investigator. An ex-con who works on the edge. Someone who's not averse to a little blackmail. The wife of a prominent businessman hires you because she thinks her husband is having an affair. She also gives you a scrapbook containing clippings about an old murder case.

"Let's suppose that this crooked p.i. flies to Hunter's Point and talks to Dr. Escalante. He's no help, but he does tell the investigator enough information so he can track down Samantha Reardon, the only other surviving victim. What if Oberhurst found Reardon and she positively identified Peter Lake as the man who kidnapped and tortured her?"

"And Oberhurst returned to Portland and what?" Stewart said. "Blackmailed a serial killer? You'd have to be nuts."

"Who's the John Doe, Reg?"

The line was quiet for a moment, then Stewart said, "Oh, shit."

"Exactly. We know Oberhurst lied to Lisa. He told her he hadn't started investigating the Hunter's Point case, but he was in Hunter's Point. And he's disappeared. I talked to every lawyer I could find who's employed him. No contact. He doesn't return calls. The John Doe is Oberhurst's size and build. What do you want to bet the corpse has a broken nose?"

"No bets. What are you going to do?"

"There's nothing we can do. Darius is our client. We're his agents. This is all confidential."

"Even if he killed the guy?"

"Even if he killed the guy."

Betsy heard a sharp intake of air, then Stewart said:

"You're the boss. What do you want me to do next?"

"Have you tried to set up a meeting with Wayne Turner?"

"No go. His secretary says he's too busy, because of the confirmation hearings."

"Damn. Gordon, Turner, Grimsbo. They all know something. What about the police chief? What was his name?"

"O'Malley. Lenzer says he retired to Florida about nine years ago."

"Okay," Betsy said with a trace of desperation.

"Keep trying to find Samantha Reardon. She's our best bet."

"I'll do it for you, Betsy. If it was someone else . . . I gotta tell you, I usually don't give a fuck, but I'm starting to. I don't like this case."

"That makes two of us. I just don't know what to do about it. We're not even certain I'm right. I have to find that out, first."

"If you are, what then?"

"I have no idea."

3

Betsy put Kathy to sleep at nine and changed into a flannel nightgown. After brewing a pot of coffee, Betsy spread out the papers in Friday's divorce case on the dining room table. The coffee was waking her up, but her mind wandered to the Darius case. Was Darius guilty? Betsy could not stop thinking about the question she had put to Alan Page during her cross-examination: With six victims, including a six-year-old girl, why would the mayor and chief of police of Hunter's Point close the case if there was any possibility that Peter Lake, or anyone else, was really the murderer? It made no sense.

Betsy pushed aside the documents in the divorce and pulled a yellow pad in front of her. She listed what she knew about the Darius case. The list stretched for three pages. Betsy came to the information she had learned from Stewart that afternoon. A thought occurred to her. She frowned.

Betsy knew Samuel Oberhurst was not above blackmail. He'd tried it on Gary Telford. If Martin Darius was the rose killer, Darius would have no compunction about killing Oberhurst if the investigator tried to blackmail him. But Betsy's assumption that John Doe was Samuel Oberhurst made sense only if Samantha Reardon identified Martin Darius as the rose killer. And that's where the difficulty lay. The police would have questioned Reardon when they rescued her. If the task force suspected that Peter Lake, not Henry Waters, was the kidnapper, they would have shown Reardon a photograph of Lake. If she identified Lake as her kidnapper, why would the mayor and the police chief announce that Waters was the killer? Why would the case be closed?

Dr. Escalante said that Reardon was institutionalized. Maybe she couldn't be interviewed immediately. But she would have been interviewed at some point. Grimsbo told Reggie that Nancy Gordon was obsessed with the case and never believed Waters was the killer. So, Betsy thought, let's assume that Reardon did identify Lake as the killer at some point. Why wouldn't Gordon, or someone, have reopened the case?

Maybe Reardon wasn't asked until Oberhurst talked to her. But wouldn't she have read about Henry Waters and known the police had accused the wrong man? She could have been so traumatized that she wanted to forget everything that happened to her, even if it meant letting Lake go free. But if that was true, why tell Oberhurst that Lake was her kidnapper?

Betsy sighed. She was missing something. She stood up and carried her coffee cup into the living room. The Sunday New York *Times* was sitting in a wicker basket next to her favorite chair. She sat down and decided to look through it. Sometimes the best way to figure out a problem was to forget about it for a while. She had read the Book Review, the Magazine and the Arts section, but she still hadn't read the Week in Review.

Betsy skimmed an article about the fighting in the

Ukraine and another about the resumption of hostilities between North and South Korea. Death was everywhere.

Betsy turned the page and started reading a profile of Raymond Colby. Betsy knew Colby would be confirmed and it upset her. There was no more diversity of opinion on the Court. Wealthy white males with identical backgrounds and identical thoughts dominated it. Men with no concept of what it was like to be poor or helpless, who had been nominated by Republican Presidents for no reason other than their willingness to put the interests of the wealthy and big government ahead of individual rights. Colby was no different. Harvard Law, c.e.o. of Marlin Steel, governor of New York, then a member of the United States Senate for the last nine years. Betsy read a summary of Colby's accomplishments as a governor and senator and a prediction of the way he would vote on several cases that were before the Supreme Court, then skimmed another article about the economy. When she was finished with the paper, she went back to the dining room.

The divorce case was a mess. Betsy's client and her husband didn't have children and they had agreed to split almost all of their property, but they were willing to go to the mat over a cheap landscape they had bought from a sidewalk artist in Paris on their honeymoon. Going to court over the silly painting was costing them both ten times its value, but they were adamant. Obviously it was not the painting that was fueling their rage. It was a case like this that made Betsy want to enter a nunnery. But, she sighed to herself, it was also cases like this that paid her overhead. She started reading the divorce petition, then remembered something she had read in the article about Raymond Colby.

Betsy put the petition down. The idea had come so fast that it made her a little dizzy. She walked back to the living room and reread Colby's biography. There it was. He had been a United States senator for nine years. Hunter's Point Chief of Police John O'Malley retired to Florida nine years ago. Frank Grimsbo had been with Marlin Steel, Colby's old company, for nine years. And Wayne Turner was the senator's administrative assistant.

The heat was on in the house, but Betsy felt like she was hugging a block of ice. She went back to the dining room and reread her list of important facts in the Darius case. It was all there. You just had to look at the facts in a certain way and it made perfect sense. Martin Darius was the rose killer. The Hunter's Point police knew that when they announced that Henry Waters was the murderer and closed the case. Now Betsy knew how Peter Lake could walk away from Hunter's Point with the blood of all those innocent people on his hands. What she could not imagine was why the governor of New York State would conspire with the police force and mayor of Hunter's Point to set free a mass murderer.

Chapter Sixteen

___

I

The sun was shining, but the temperature was a little below freezing. Betsy hung up her overcoat. Her cheeks hurt from the cold. She rubbed her hands together and asked Ann to bring her a cup of coffee. By the time Ann set a steaming mug on her coaster, Betsy was dialing Washington, D.C.

"Senator Colby's office."

"I'd like to speak to Wayne Turner, please."

"I'll connect you to his secretary."

Betsy picked up the mug. Her hand was trembling. She wanted to sound confident, but she was scared to death.

"Can I help you?" a pleasant female voice asked.

"My name is Betsy Tannenbaum. I'm an attorney in Portland, Oregon. I'd like to speak to Mr. Turner."

"Mr. Turner is very busy with the confirmation hearings. If you leave me your number, he'll call you when he gets the chance."

Betsy knew Turner would never return her call. There was only one way to force him to get on the phone.

Betsy was convinced she knew what had happened in Hunter's Point and she would have to gamble she was right.

"This can't wait. Let Mr. Turner know that Peter Lake's attorney is on the phone." Then Betsy told the secretary to tell Turner something else. The secretary made her repeat the message. "If Mr. Turner won't talk to me, tell him I'm sure the press will."

Turner's secretary put Betsy on hold. Betsy closed her eyes and tried a meditation technique she had learned in a YWCA yoga class. It didn't work, and she jumped when Turner came on the line.

"Who is this?" he barked.

"I told your secretary, Mr. Turner. My name is Betsy Tannenbaum and I'm Martin Darius's attorney. You knew him as Peter Lake when he lived in Hunter's Point. I want to talk to Senator Colby immediately."

"The senator is extremely busy with the confirmation hearings, Ms. Tannenbaum. Can't this wait until they're over?"

"I'm not going to wait until the senator is safely on the Court, Mr. Turner. If he won't speak to me, I'll be forced to go to the press."

"Damn it, if you spread any irresponsible . . ."

"Calm down, Mr. Turner. If you thought about this at all, you'd know it would hurt my client to go to the papers. I'll only do it as a last resort. But I won't be put off."

"If you know about Lake, if you know about the senator, why are you doing this?" Turner pleaded.

Betsy paused. Turner had asked a good question. Why was she keeping what she knew to herself? Why hadn't she confided in Reggie Stewart? Why was she willing to fly across the country for the answer to her questions?

"This is for me, Mr. Turner. I have to know what kind of man I'm representing. I have to know the truth. I must meet with Senator Colby. I can fly to Washington tomorrow."

Turner was silent for a few seconds. Betsy looked out the window. In the office across the street, two men in shirtsleeves were discussing a blueprint. On the floor above them, a group of secretaries were working away on word processors. Toward the top of the office building, Betsy could see the sky reflected in the glass wall. Green-tinted clouds scudded across a green-tinted sky.

"I'll talk to Senator Colby and call you back," Turner said.

"I'm not a threat, Mr. Turner. I'm not out to wreck the senator's appointment. Tell him that."

Turner hung up and Betsy exhaled. She was not used to threatening United States senators or dealing with cases that could destroy the reputations of prominent public figures. Then she thought about the Hammermill and Peterson cases. Twice she had shouldered the burden of saving a human life. There was no greater responsibility than that. Colby was just a man, even if he was a United States senator, and he might be the reason Martin Darius was free to murder three innocent women in Portland.

"Nora Sloane is on one," Ann said over the intercom.

Betsy's divorce client was supposed to meet her at the courthouse at eight forty-five and it was eight-ten. Betsy wanted to concentrate on the issues in the divorce, but she decided she could spare Sloane a minute.

"Sorry to bother you," Sloane said apologetically. "Remember I talked to you about interviewing your mother and Kathy? Do you suppose I could do that this weekend?"

"I might be out of town. My mom will probably

watch Kathy, so you could talk to them together. Mom will get a kick out of being interviewed. I'll talk to her and get back to you. What's your number?"

"Why don't I call you? I'm going to be in and out."

"Okay. I've got court in half an hour. I should be done by noon. Call me this afternoon."

Betsy checked her watch. She had twenty minutes to prepare for court and no more time to spend thinking about Martin Darius.

2

Reggie Stewart found Ben Singer, the attorney who handled Samantha Reardon's divorce, by going through the court records. Singer had not heard from Reardon in years, but he did have an address near the campus.

Most of the houses around the University were older, single-family dwellings surrounded by well-kept lawns and shaded by oak and elm trees, but there was a pocket of apartments and boardinghouses that catered to students located several blocks behind the campus near the freeway. Stewart turned into a parking lot that ran the length of a dull-gray garden apartment complex. It had snowed the night before. Stewart stepped over a drift onto the shoveled sidewalk in front of the manager's office. A woman in her early forties dressed in heavy slacks and a green wool sweater answered the door. She was holding a cigarette. Her face was flushed. There were curlers in her strawberry-red hair.

"My name is Reggie Stewart. I'm looking for the apartment manager."

"We're full," the woman answered brusquely.

Stewart handed the woman his card. She stuck her cigarette in her mouth and examined it.

"Are you the manager?" Stewart asked. The woman nodded.

"I'm trying to find Samantha Reardon. This was the last address I had for her."

"What do you want with her?" the woman asked suspiciously.

"She may have information that could clear a client who used to live in Hunter's Point."

"Then you're out of luck. She's not here."

"Do you know when she'll be back?"

"Beats me. She's been gone since the summer." The manager looked at the card again. "The other investigator was from Portland too. I remember, because you two are the only people I ever met from Oregon."

"Was this guy big with a broken nose?"

"Right. You know him?"

"Not personally. When did he show up?"

"It was hot. That's all I remember. Reardon left the next day. Paid a month's rent in advance. She said she didn't know how long she'd be gone. Then, about a week later, she came back and moved out."

"Did she store anything with you?"

"Nah. The apartment's furnished and she hardly had anything of her own." The manager shook her head. "I was up there once to fix a leak in the sink. Not a picture on the wall, not one knickknack on a table. The place looked just like it did when she moved in. Spooky."

"You ever talk to her?"

"Oh, sure. I'd see her from time to time. But it was mostly 'good morning' or 'how's it going' on my part and not much from her. She kept to herself."

"Did she have a job?"

"Yeah. She worked somewhere. I think she was a

secretary or receptionist. Something like that. Might have been for a doctor. Yeah, a doctor, and she was a bookkeeper. That was it. She looked like a bookkeeper, too. Real mousy. She didn't take care of herself. She had a nice figure if you looked hard. Tall, athletic. But she always dressed like an old maid. It looked to me like she was trying to scare men off, if you know what I mean."

"You wouldn't happen to have a picture of her?"

"Where would I get a picture? Like I said, I don't even think she had any pictures in her place. Weird. Everyone has pictures, knickknacks, things to remind you of the good times."

"Some people don't want to think about the past," Stewart said.

The manager took a drag on her cigarette and nodded in agreement. "She like that? Bad memories?"

"The worst," Stewart said. "The very worst."

3

"Let me help you with the dishes," Rita said. They had left them after dinner, so they could watch one of Kathy's favorite television shows with her, before Betsy put her to bed.

"Before I forget," Betsy said as she piled up the bread plates, "a woman named Nora Sloane may call you. I gave her your number. She's the one who's writing the article for *Pacific West*."

"Oh?"

"She wants to interview you and Kathy for background."

"Interview me?" Rita preened.

"Yeah, Mom. It's your chance at immortality."

"*You're* my immortality, honey, but I'm available if she calls," Rita said. "Who better to give her the inside story than your mother?"

"That's what I'm afraid of."

Betsy rinsed the plates and cups and Rita put them in the dishwasher.

"Do you have some time before you go home? I want to ask you about something."

"Sure."

"You want coffee or tea?"

"Coffee will be fine."

Betsy poured two cups and they carried them into the living room.

"It's the Darius case," Betsy said. "I don't know what to do. I keep on thinking about those women, what they went through. What if he killed them, Mom?"

"Aren't you always telling me that your client's guilt or innocence doesn't matter? You're his lawyer."

"I know. And that is what I always say. And I believe it. Plus I'm going to need the money I'm making on the case, if Rick and I . . . if we divorce. And the prestige. Even if I lose, I'll still be known as Martin Darius's attorney. This case is putting me in the major leagues. If I dropped out, I'd get a reputation as someone who couldn't handle the pressure of a big case."

"But you're worried about getting him off?"

"That's it, Mom. I know I can get him off. Page doesn't have the goods. Judge Norwood told him as much at the bail hearing. But I know things Page doesn't and I . . ."

Betsy shook her head. She was visibly shaken.

"Someone is going to represent Martin Darius," Rita said calmly. "If you don't do it, another lawyer will. I listen to what you say about giving everyone, even killers and drug pushers, a fair trial. It's hard for me to accept. A man who would do that to a woman. To anyone. You want to spit on them. But you aren't defending that person. Isn't that what you tell me? You're preserving a good system."

"That's the theory, but what if you feel sick inside? What if you can't sleep because you know you're going to free someone who . . . Mom, he did this same thing in Hunter's Point. I'm certain of it. And, if I get him off, who's next? I keep thinking about what those women went through. Alone, helpless, stripped of their dignity."

Rita reached across the space between them and took her daughter's hand.

"I'm so proud of what you've done with your life. When I was a girl I never thought about being a lawyer. That's an important job. You're important. You do important things. Things other people don't have the courage to do. But there's a price. Do you think the President sleeps well? And judges? Generals? So, you're finding out about the bad side of responsibility. With those battered women, it was easy. You were on God's side. Now, God is against you. But you have to do your job even if you suffer. You have to stick with it and not take the easy way out."

Suddenly Betsy was crying. Rita moved over and threw her arms around her daughter.

"I'm a mess, Mom. I loved Rick so much. I gave him everything and he walked out on me. If he was here to help me . . . I can't do it alone."

"Yes, you can. You're strong. No one could do what you've done without being strong."

"Why don't I see it that way? I feel empty, used up."

"It's hard to see yourself the way others see you. You know you're not perfect, so you emphasize your weaknesses. But you've got plenty of strengths, believe me."

Rita paused. She looked distant for a moment, then she looked at Betsy.

"I'm going to tell you something no other living soul knows. The night your father passed away, I almost took my own life."

"Mom!"

"I sat in our bedroom, after you were asleep, and I took out pills from our bathroom cabinet. I must have looked at those pills for an hour, but I couldn't do it. You wouldn't let me. The thought of you. How I would miss seeing you grow up. How I would never know what you did with your life. Not taking those pills was the smartest thing I ever did, because I got to see you the way you are now. And I am so proud of you."

"What if I'm not proud of myself? What if I'm only in this for the money or the reputation? What if I'm helping a man who is truly evil to escape punishment, so he can be free to cause unbearable pain and suffering to other innocent people?"

"I don't know what to say to you," Rita answered. "I don't know all the facts, so I can't put myself in your place. But I trust you and I know you'll do the right thing."

Betsy wiped at her eyes. "I'm sorry I laid this on you, but you're the only one I can let my hair down with now that Rick's walked out."

"I'm glad to know I'm good for something." Rita smiled back. Betsy hugged her. It had been good to cry, it had been good to talk out what she had been holding inside, but Betsy didn't feel she was any closer to an answer.

Chapter Seventeen

On Sunday afternoon Raymond Colby stood in front of the fireplace in his den waiting for the lawyer from Portland to arrive. A servant had built a fire. Colby held his hands out to catch the heat and dispel a chill that had very little to do with the icy rain that was keeping his neighbors off the streets of Georgetown.

The front door opened and closed. That would be Wayne Turner with Betsy Tannenbaum. Colby straightened his suit coat. What did Tannenbaum want? That was really the question. Was she someone with whom he could reason? Did she have a price? Turner didn't think Lake's attorney knew everything, but she knew enough to ruin his chance of being confirmed. Perhaps she would come over to their side once she knew the facts. After all, going public would not only destroy Raymond Colby, it would destroy her client.

The door to the den opened and Wayne Turner stood aside. Colby sized up his visitor. Betsy Tannenbaum was attractive, but Colby could see she was not a woman who traded on her looks. She was dressed in a severe black suit with a cream-colored blouse. All business, a little nervous, he guessed, feeling somewhat out of her league, yet willing to confront a powerful man on his own turf.

Colby smiled and held out his hand. Her handshake was firm. She was not afraid to look Colby in the eye or to look him over much the way he had scrutinized her.

"How was your flight?" Colby asked.

"Fine." Betsy looked around the cozy room. There were three high-backed armchairs drawn up in front of the fireplace. Colby motioned toward them.

"Can I get you something to take off the chill?"

"A cup of coffee, please."

"Nothing stronger?"

"No, thank you."

Betsy took the chair closest to the window. Colby sat in the center chair. Wayne Turner poured coffee from a silver urn a servant had set up on an antique, walnut side table. Betsy stared into the fire. She had barely noticed the weather on the ride from the airport. Now that she was inside, she shivered in a delayed reaction to the tension of the preceding hours. Wayne Turner handed Betsy a delicate china cup and saucer covered with finely-drawn roses. The flowers were a pale pink and the stems a tracery of gold.

"How can I help you, Mrs. Tannenbaum?"

"I know what you did ten years ago in Hunter's Point, Senator. I want to know why."

"And what did I do?"

"You corrupted the Hunter's Point task force, you destroyed police files, and you engineered a cover-up to protect a monstrous serial killer who revels in torturing women."

Colby nodded sadly. "Part of what you say is true, but not all of it. No one on the task force was corrupt."

"I know about the payoffs," Betsy answered curtly.

"What do you think you know?"

Betsy flushed. She had been spurred on by the coincidences, the improbabilities, to the only possible solution, but she did not want to sound like she was bragging. On the other hand, letting Colby know how she figured it out would make him see that she could not be fooled.

"I know that a senator's term is six years," Betsy answered, "and that you are in the middle of your second term. That means you've been a United States senator for nine years. Nine years ago, Frank Grimsbo left a low-paying job on an obscure, small city police force to assume a high-paying job at Marlin Steel, your old company. Nine years ago, John O'Malley, the police chief of that police force, retired to Florida. Wayne Turner, another member of the rose killer task force, is your administrative assistant. I asked myself how three members of the same small city police force could suddenly do so well, and why they would all do so well the year you decided to run for the United States Senate. The answer was obvious. They had been paid off to keep a secret and for destroying the files of the rose killer investigation."

Colby nodded. "Excellent deductions, but only partly correct. There were rewards, but no bribes. Frank Grimsbo earned his position as head of security after I helped him get a job on the security force. Chief O'Malley had a heart attack and was forced to retire. I'm a very wealthy man. Wayne told me John was having financial problems and I helped him out. And Wayne was working his way through law school when the kidnappings and murders occurred. He graduated two years later and I helped him get a job in Washington, but it was not on my staff. Wayne didn't come on board until a year before my first term ended. By then he had established an excellent reputation on the Hill. When Larry Merrill, my a.a., went back into law practice in Manhattan, I asked Wayne if he would take his place. So, you see, the explanations for these events are less sinister than you supposed."

"But I'm right about the records."

"Chief O'Malley took care of that."

"And the pardon?"

Colby looked very old all of a sudden.

"Everyone has something in their life they wish they could undo. I think about Hunter's Point all the time, but I can't see how it could have ended differently."

"How could you have done it, Senator? The man's not human. You had to know he would do this again, somewhere, sometime."

Colby turned his face toward her, but he was not seeing Betsy. He looked completely lost, like a man who has just been told that he has an incurable illness.

"We knew, God forgive us. We knew, but we had no choice."

Part Five

HUNTER'S POINT

Chapter Eighteen

I

Nancy Gordon heard a tinkle of glass when Peter Lake broke the lower left pane in the back door so he could reach between the jagged shards and open it from the inside. Nancy heard the rusty hinges squeak. She shifted under the covers and trained her eyes on the doorway, straining to see in the dark.

Two hours earlier, Nancy had been alone in the task force office when Lake appeared to tell her he had heard about the shooting of Henry Waters on the late news. As planned, Nancy told Lake she had suspected him of being the rose killer because of the gap between the time he had been seen driving home and the call to 911 and his stakeout of Waters's home. Lake had been alarmed, but Nancy assured him that she was satisfied that Waters was the murderer and had kept her suspicions to herself. Then she had yawned and told Lake she was heading home. Since then Nancy had been in bed, waiting.

Black slacks, a black ski mask and a black turtleneck helped Lake blend into the darkness. There was an ugly snub-nosed revolver in his hand. Nancy did not hear him cross the living room. One second, her bedroom doorway was empty, then Lake filled it. When he snapped on the light, Nancy sat up in bed, feigning surprise. Lake removed the ski mask.

"You knew, didn't you, Nancy?" She gaped at him, as if the visit was unexpected. "I really do like you, but I can't take the chance you'll reopen the case."

Nancy looked at the revolver. "You can't believe you'll get away with murdering a cop."

"I don't have much choice. You're far too intelligent. Eventually you would have realized Waters was innocent. Then you would have kept after me. You might even have dug up enough evidence to convince a jury."

Lake walked around the side of the bed. "Place your hands on top of the sheet and take it off slowly," he said, gesturing with the gun. Nancy was sleeping under a single light sheet because of the heat. She pulled away the sheet slowly, careful to gather it up near her right hip so Lake would not see the outline of the gun that was hidden there. Nancy was wearing bikini panties and a T-shirt. The T-shirt had bunched up beneath her breasts, revealing her rigid stomach muscles. Nancy heard a quiet intake of breath.

"Very nice," Lake said. "Remove the shirt."

Nancy forced herself to look at him wide-eyed.

"I'm not going to rape you," Lake assured her. "It's not that I don't want to. I've fantasized about playing with you quite a lot, Nancy. You're so different from the others. They're all so soft, cows really, and so easy to train. But you're hard. I'm certain you would resist. It would be very enjoyable. But I want the authorities to believe that Henry Waters is the rose killer, so you'll die during a burglary."

Nancy looked at Lake with disgust. "How could you kill your wife and daughter?"

"You can't think I planned that. I loved them, Nancy. But Sandy found a note and a rose I was planning to use the next day. I'm not proud of myself. I panicked. I couldn't think of a single explanation I could make to Sandy once the notes became public knowledge. She would have gone to the police and it would have been over for me."

"What's your excuse for killing Melody? She was a baby."

Lake shook his head. He looked genuinely distraught.

"Do you think that was easy?" Lake's jaw trembled. There was a tear in the corner of one eye. "Sandy screamed. I got to her before she could do it again, but Melody heard her. She was standing on the stairs, looking through the bars on the banister. I held her and hugged her while I tried to think of some way to spare her, but there wasn't a way, so I made it painless. It was the hardest thing I've ever done."

"Let me help you, Peter. They'll never find you guilty. I'll talk to the district attorney. We'll work out an insanity plea."

Lake smiled sadly. He shook his head with regret. "It would never fly, Nancy. No one would ever let me off that easy. Think about what I did to Pat. Think about the others. Besides, I'm not crazy. If you knew why I did it, you'd understand."

"Tell me. I want to understand."

"Sorry. No time. Besides, it won't make any difference to you. You're going to die."

"Please, Peter. I have to know. There has to be a reason for a plan this brilliant."

Lake smiled condescendingly. "Don't do this. It's not becoming. What's the purpose in stalling?"

"You can rape me first. Tie me up. You want to, don't

you? I'd be helpless," she begged, sliding her right hand under the sheet.

"Don't debase yourself, Nancy. I thought you had more class than the others."

Lake saw Nancy's hand move. His face clouded. "What's that?"

Nancy went for the gun. Lake brought the revolver down hard on her cheek. Bone cracked. She went blind for a second. Her closet door slammed open. Lake froze as Wayne Turner came out of the closet. Turner fired and hit Lake in the shoulder. Lake's gun dropped to the floor just as Frank Grimsbo hurtled through the bedroom door, tackling Lake into the wall.

"Stay down," Turner yelled at Nancy. He scrambled across the bed, knocking the wind out of her. Lake was pinned to the wall and Grimsbo was smashing him in the face.

"Stop, Frank!" Turner yelled. He kept his gun trained on Lake with one hand and tried to restrain Grimsbo's arm with the other. Grimsbo delivered one more clubbing blow that bounced Lake's head off the wall. Lake's head lolled sideways. A damp patch spread across the black fabric that covered his right shoulder as blood seeped from his wound.

"Get his gun," Turner said. "It's next to the bed. And check on Nancy."

Grimsbo stood up. He was shaking.

"I'm okay," Nancy said. Her cheek was numb and she could barely see out of her left eye.

Grimsbo picked up Lake's gun. He stood over Lake and his breathing increased.

"Cuff him," Turner ordered. Grimsbo stood there, the gun rising like something with a life of its own.

"Don't fuck around, Frank," Turner said. "Just put the cuffs on."

"Why?" Grimsbo asked. "He could have been shot twice when he attacked Nancy. You hit him in the shoulder when you came out of the closet and I fired the fatal shot when this piece of shit spun toward me, and, as fate would have it, caught him between the eyes."

"It didn't happen that way, because I know it didn't," Turner said evenly.

"And what? You'd turn me in and testify at my murder trial? You'd send me to Attica for the rest of my life because I exterminated this scumbag?"

"No one would know, Wayne," Nancy said quietly. "I'd back Frank."

Turner looked at Nancy. She was watching Lake with a look of pure hatred.

"I don't believe this. You're cops. What you want to do is murder."

"Not in this case, Wayne," Nancy said. "You have to take the life of a human being to commit murder. Lake isn't human. I don't know what he is, but he's not human. A human being doesn't murder his own child. He doesn't strip a woman naked, then slice her open from groin to chest, pull out her intestines and let her die a slow death. I can't even imagine what he's done to the missing women." Nancy shuddered. "I don't want to guess."

Lake was listening to the argument. He did not move his head, but his eyes focused on each speaker as his fate was debated. He saw Turner waiver. Nancy got off the bed and stood next to Grimsbo.

"He'll get out someday, Wayne," she said. "He'll convince the Parole Board to release him or he'll convince a jury he was insane and the hospital will let him out when he is miraculously cured. Do you want to wake up some morning and read about a woman who was kidnapped in Salt Lake City or Minneapolis and the note that was left on her pillow telling her husband she was 'Gone, But Not Forgotten'?"

Turner's arm fell to his side. His lips were dry. His gut was in a knot.

"It'll be me, Wayne," Grimsbo said, pulling out his service revolver and handing Nancy Lake's weapon. "You can leave the room if you want. You can even remember it like it happened the way I said, because that's the way it will really have happened, if we all agree."

"Jesus," Turner said to himself. One hand was knotted into a fist, and the one holding the gun was squeezed so tight the metal cut into his palm.

"You can't kill me," Lake gasped, the pain from his wound making it hard for him to speak.

"Shut the fuck up," Grimsbo said, "or I'll do you now."

"They're not dead," Lake managed, squeezing his eyes shut as a wave of nausea swept over him. "The other women are still alive. Kill me and they'll die. Kill me and you kill them all."

2

Governor Raymond Colby ducked under the rotating helicopter blades and ran toward the waiting police car. Larry Merrill, the governor's administrative assistant, leaped out after the governor and followed him across the runway. A stocky, red-haired man and a slender black man were standing next to the police car. The redhead opened the back door for Colby.

"John O'Malley, Governor. I'm the Hunter's Point police chief. This is Detective Wayne Turner. He's going to brief you. We have a very bad situation here."

Governor Colby sat in the rear seat of the police car and Turner slid in beside him. When Merrill was in the front, O'Malley started toward Nancy Gordon's house.

"I don't know how much you've been told, Governor."

"Start from the beginning, Detective Turner. I want to make certain I don't miss anything."

"Women have been disappearing in Hunter's Point. All married to professionals, childless. No sign of a struggle. With the first woman, we assumed we were dealing with a missing persons case. The only oddity was a note on the woman's pillow that said 'Gone, But Not Forgotten,' pinned down by a rose that had been dyed black. We figured the wife left it. Then the second woman disappeared and we found an identical rose and note.

"After the fourth disappearance, all with notes and black roses, Sandra and Melody Lake were murdered. Sandra was the wife of Peter Lake, whom I believe you know. Melody was his daughter."

"That was tragic," Colby said. "Pete's been a supporter of mine for some time. I appointed him to a board last fall."

"He killed them, Governor. He murdered his wife and daughter in cold blood. Then he framed a man named Henry Waters by bringing one of the kidnapped women to Waters's house, disemboweling her in Waters's basement, planting some roses and one of the notes in Waters's house and calling the police anonymously."

It was four a.m. and pitch-black in the car, but Turner saw Colby blanch as the car passed under a streetlight.

"Peter Lake killed Sandy and Melody?"

"Yes, sir."

"I find that hard to believe."

"What I'm going to tell you now is known only to

Chief O'Malley, Detectives Frank Grimsbo and Nancy Gordon and me. The chief created a task force to deal with the disappearances. It consists of Gordon, Grimsbo and me, plus a forensic expert. We suspected Lake might be our killer, even after we found Patricia Cross's body at Waters's house, so we set him up. Gordon told Lake she suspected him but had kept the incriminating evidence to herself. Lake panicked, as we'd hoped he would. He broke into Gordon's house to kill her. She tricked him into admitting the killings. We wired her house and we have his confession on tape. Grimsbo and I were hiding and heard it all. We arrested Lake."

"Then what's the problem?" Merrill asked.

"Three of the women are still alive. Barely. Lake's been keeping them on a starvation diet—he only feeds them once a week. He won't tell us when he fed them last or where they are unless the governor gives him a full pardon."

"What?" Merrill asked incredulously. "The governor's not going to pardon a mass murderer."

"Can't you find them?" Colby asked. "They must be in property Lake owns. Have you searched them all?"

"Lake's made a good deal of money over the years. He has vast real estate holdings. Most of them aren't in his name. We don't have the manpower or time to find and search them all before the women starve."

"Then I'll promise to pardon Peter. After he tells us where he's holding the women, you can arrest him. A contract entered into under duress won't stand up."

Merrill looked uncomfortable. "I'm afraid it might, Ray. When I was with the U.S. attorney, we gave immunity to a contract killer for the mob in exchange for testimony against a higher-up. He said he was present when the hit was ordered, but he was in Las Vegas on the day the body was found. We checked out his story. He was registered at Caesars Palace. Several honest witnesses saw him eating at the casino. We gave him his deal, he testified, the higher-up was convicted, he walked. Then we found out he did the hit, but he did it at fifteen minutes before midnight, then flew to Vegas.

"We were furious. We rearrested him and indicted him for murder, but the judge threw out the indictment. He ruled that everything the defendant told us was true. We just didn't ask the right questions. I researched the hell out of the law on plea agreements trying to get the appellate court to rule for us. No luck. Contract principles apply, but so does due process. If both sides enter into the agreement in good faith and the defendant performs, the courts are going to enforce the agreement. If you go into this with your eyes open, Ray, I think the pardon will stick."

"Then I have no choice."

"Yes, you do," Merrill insisted. "You tell him no deal. You can't pardon a serial killer and expect to be reelected. It's political suicide."

"Damn it, Larry," Colby snapped, "how do you think people would react if they found out I let three women die to win an election?"

Raymond Colby opened the door to Nancy Gordon's bedroom. Frank Grimsbo was seated next to the door, holding his weapon, his eyes on the prisoner. The shades were drawn and the bed was still unmade. Peter Lake was handcuffed to a chair. His back was to the window. No one had treated the cuts on Lake's face and the blood had dried, making him look like a badly defeated fighter. Lake should have been scared. Instead, he looked like he was in charge of the situation.

"Thanks for coming, Ray."

"What's going on, Pete? This is crazy. You murdered Sandy and Melody?"

"I had to, Ray. I explained that to the police. You know I wouldn't have killed them if I had a choice."

"That sweet little girl. How can you live with yourself?"

Lake shrugged his shoulders. "That's really beside the point, Ray. I'm not going to prison, and you're going to see to that."

"It's out of my hands, Pete. You killed three people. You're morally responsible for Waters's death. I can't do anything for you."

Lake smiled. "Then why are you here?"

"To ask you to tell the police where you're keeping the other women."

"No can do, Ray. My life depends on keeping the cops in the dark."

"You'd let three innocent women die?"

Lake shrugged. "Three dead, six dead. They can't punish me anymore after the first life sentence. I don't envy you, Ray. Believe me when I say that I wish I didn't have to put an old friend, whom I admire deeply, in this position. But I won't tell you where the women are if I don't get my pardon. And, believe me, every minute counts. Those women are mighty hungry and mighty thirsty by now. I can't guarantee how much longer they'll last without food and water."

Colby sat on the bed across from Lake. He bent forward, his forearms resting on his knees and his hands clasped in front of him.

"I do consider myself your friend, Pete. I still can't believe what I'm hearing. As a friend, I beg you to save those women. I promise I'll intercede on your behalf with the authorities. Maybe a plea to manslaughter can be worked out."

Lake shook his head. "No prison. Not one day. I know what happens in jail to a man who's raped a woman. I wouldn't last a week."

"You're expecting a miracle, Pete. How can I let you go free?"

"Look, Ray, I'll make this simple for you. I walk or the women die. There's no other alternative, and you're using up valuable time jawing with me."

Colby hunched his shoulders. He stared at the floor. Lake's smile widened.

"What are your terms?" Colby asked.

"I want a pardon for every crime I committed in New York State and immunity from prosecution for every conceivable crime the authorities can think up in the future. I want the pardon in writing and I want a videotape of you signing it. I want the original of the tape and the pardon given to a lawyer I'll choose.

"I want immunity from prosecution in federal court . . ."

"I can't guarantee that. I have no authority to . . ."

"Call the U.S. attorney or the attorney general. Call the President. This is non-negotiable. I'm not going to get hit with a federal charge for violation of civil rights."

"I'll see what I can do."

"That's all I ask. But if you don't do what I want, the women die.

"There's one other thing. I want a guarantee that the State of New York will pay any civil judgments if I get sued by the survivors or Cross's husband. I'm not going to lose any money over this. Attorney fees, too."

Lake's last remark helped the governor see Lake for what he was. The handsome, urbane young man with whom he had dined and played golf was the disguise worn by a monster. Colby felt rage replacing the numbness he'd experienced since learning Lake's true nature.

Colby stood. "I have to know how much time those women have, so I can tell the attorney general how quickly we must act."

"I'm not going to tell you, Ray. You're not getting any information from me until I have what I want. But," Lake said with a smile, "I will tell you to hurry."

3

The police cars and ambulances bounced along the unpaved back road, their sirens blaring in hopes that the captive women would hear them and take heart. There were three ambulances, each with a team of doctors and nurses. Governor Colby and Larry Merrill were riding with Chief O'Malley and Wayne Turner. Frank Grimsbo was driving another police car with Nancy Gordon riding shotgun. In the back of that car was Herb Carstairs, an attorney Lake had retained. A videotape of Governor Colby signing a pardon and a copy of the pardon with an addendum signed by the United States attorney rested in Carstairs's safe. Next to Carstairs, in leg irons and handcuffs, sat Peter Lake, who seemed indifferent to the high-speed ride.

The cavalcade rounded a curve in the country road and Nancy saw the farmhouse. It looked deserted. The front yard was overgrown and the paint was peeling. To the right of the house, across a dusty strip of yard, was a dilapidated barn.

Nancy was out and running as soon as the car stopped. She raced up the steps of the house and kicked in the front door. Medics and doctors raced after her. Lake had said the women were in the basement. Nancy found the basement door and threw it open. A stench of urine, excrement and unwashed bodies hit her and she gagged. Then she took a deep breath and yelled, "Police. You're safe," as she started down the stairs, two at a time, stopping her headlong rush the moment she saw what was in the basement.

Nancy felt like someone had punched a hole through her chest and torn out her heart. Later it occurred to her that her reaction must have been similar to the reactions of the servicemen who liberated the Nazi concentration camps. The basement windows were painted black and the only light came from bare bulbs that hung from the ceiling. A section of the basement was divided by plywood walls into six small stalls. Three of the stalls were empty. All of the stalls were covered with straw and outfitted with dirty mattresses. A videotape camera sat on a tripod outside each of the three occupied stalls. In addition to the mattress, each stall contained a cheap clock, a plastic water bottle with a plastic straw, and a dog food dish. The water bottles looked empty. Nancy could see the remains of some kind of gruel in the dishes.

Toward the rear of the basement was an open area. In it was a mattress covered with a sheet and a large table. Nancy could not make out all of the instruments on the table, but one of them was definitely a cattle prod.

Nancy stepped aside as the doctors rushed past her. She stared at the three survivors. The women were naked. Their feet were chained to the wall at the ankles. The chain extended just far enough to reach the water bottle and dog food dish. The women in the first two stalls lay on their side on their mattress. Their eyes seemed to be floating in the sockets. Nancy could see their ribs. There were burn marks and bruises everywhere. The woman in the third stall was Samantha Reardon. She huddled against the wall, her face expressionless, staring blankly at her rescuers.

Nancy walked slowly to the bottom of the stairs. She recognized Ann Hazelton only from her red hair. Her legs were drawn up to her chest in a fetal position and she was whimpering pitifully. Ann's husband had furnished a photograph of her standing on the eighteenth hole of their country club golf course, a smile on her face and a yellow ribbon holding back her long red hair.

Gloria Escalante was in the second stall. There was no expression on her face, but Nancy saw tears in her eyes as a doctor bent next to her to check her vital signs and a policeman went to work on her shackles.

Nancy began to shake. Wayne Turner walked up behind her and put his hands on her arms.

"Come on," he said gently, "we're just in the way."

Nancy let herself be led up the stairs into the light. Governor Colby had glanced into the basement for a moment, then backed out of the farmhouse into the fresh air. His skin was gray and he was sitting on one of the steps that led up to the porch, looking like he did not have the strength to stand.

Nancy looked across the yard. She spotted the car holding Lake. Frank Grimsbo was standing guard outside it. Lake's attorney had wandered off to smoke. Nancy walked past the governor. He asked her if the women were all right, but she did not answer. Wayne Turner walked beside her. "Let it be, Nancy," he said. Nancy ignored him.

Frank Grimsbo looked up expectantly. "They're all alive," Turner said. Nancy bent down and looked at Lake. The back window was open a crack, so the prisoner could breathe in the stifling heat. Lake turned toward Nancy. He was rested and at peace, knowing he would soon be free.

Lake smirked, goading her with his eyes but saying nothing. If he expected Nancy to rage at him, he was mistaken. Her face was blank, but her eyes bored into Lake. "It's not over," she said. Then she stood up and walked toward a stand of trees on the side of the house away from the barn. With her back to the farmhouse, all she could see was beauty. There was cool shade under the greenery. The smell of grass and wildflowers. A bird sang. The horror Nancy felt when she saw the captive women was gone. Her anger was gone. She knew the future and was not afraid of it. No woman would ever have to fear Peter Lake again, because Peter Lake was a dead man.

4

Nancy Gordon wore a black jogging outfit, her white Nikes were coated with black shoe polish, and her short hair was held back by a navy blue head band, making her impossible to see in the dim light of the quarter moon that hung over The Meadows. Her car was parked on a quiet side street. Nancy locked it and loped through a back yard. She was strung tight and conscious of every sound. A dog barked, but the houses on either side stayed dark.

Until Peter Lake came into her life, Nancy Gordon had never hated another human being. She wasn't even certain she hated Lake. What she felt went beyond hate. From the moment she saw those women in the farmhouse basement, Nancy knew Lake had to be removed, the same way vermin were removed.

Nancy was a cop, sworn to uphold the law. She respected the law. But this situation was so far outside normal human experience that she did not feel everyday laws applied. No one could do what Peter Lake had done to

those women and walk away. She could not be expected
to wait day after day for the newspaper that brought news
of the next disappearance. She knew the minute Lake's
body was found she would be a prime suspect. God
knows, she did not want to spend the rest of her life in
prison, but there was no alternative. If she was caught, so
be it. If she killed Lake and walked away, it was God's
will. She could live with the consequences of her act. She
could not live with the consequences of letting Peter
Lake go free.

Nancy circled behind Lake's two-story colonial by
skirting the man-made lake. The houses on either side of
Lake's were dark, but there were lights on in his living
room. Nancy glanced at her digital watch. It was three-
thirty a.m. Lake should be asleep. Nancy knew the security system in the house was equipped with automatic
timers for the lights and decided to gamble that that was
why the living room was lit.

Nancy crouched down and ran across the back yard.
When she reached the house, she pressed herself against
the side wall. She was holding a .38 Ed had seized from a
drug dealer two years ago. Ed never reported the seizure
and the gun could not be traced to her.

Nancy crept around to the front door. She had studied the crime scene photographs earlier that evening.
Mentally, she walked herself through Lake's house, remembering as much as she could about the layout from
her only visit. She had learned Lake's alarm code during
the murder investigation. The alarm panel was to the
right of the door. She would have to disarm it quickly.

The street in front of Lake's house was deserted.
Nancy had taken Sandra Lake's keys from an evidence
locker at the police station. She turned the front door key
in the lock, then took out a penlight. Nancy grasped the
doorknob with her free hand, took a deep breath, and

pushed it open. The alarm emitted a screeching sound. She trained the penlight on the keyboard and punched in the code. The sound stopped. Nancy swung around and held her gun out. Nothing. She exhaled, switched off the penlight and straightened.

A quick tour of the ground floor confirmed Nancy's guess about the lights in the living room. After making certain no one was downstairs, Nancy edged up the stairs, her gun leading the way. The second floor was dark. The first room on the left was Lake's bedroom. When she came level with the landing, she saw his door was closed.

Nancy approached the door slowly, walking carefully even though the carpet muffled her footfalls. She paused next to the door and walked through the shooting in her head. Ease open the door, switch on the light, then shoot into Lake until the gun was empty. She breathed in and exhaled as she opened the door, an inch at a time.

Her eyes adjusted to the dark. She could see the outline of the king-size bed that dominated the room. Nancy cleared her mind of hate and all other feelings. She removed herself from the action. She was not killing a person. She was shooting into an object. Just like target practice. Nancy slipped into the room, hit the switch and aimed.

Part Six

AVENGING ANGEL

Chapter Nineteen

"The bed was empty," Wayne Turner told Betsy. "Lake was gone. He started planning his disappearance the day after he murdered his wife and daughter. All but one of his bank accounts had been emptied the day after the murder and several of his real estate holdings had been sold. His lawyer was handling the sale of his house. Carstairs said he didn't know where Lake was. No one could compel him to tell, anyway, because of the attorney-client privilege. We assumed that Carstairs had instructions to send the money he collected to accounts in Switzerland or the Caymans."

"Chief O'Malley called me immediately," Senator Colby said. "I was sick. Signing Lake's pardon was the most difficult thing I've ever done, but I couldn't think of anything else to do. I couldn't let those women die. When O'Malley told me Lake had disappeared all I could think of was the innocent victims he might claim because of me."

"Why didn't you go public?" Betsy asked. "You could have let everyone know who Lake was and what he'd done."

"Only a few people knew Lake was the rose killer and we were sworn to silence by the terms of the pardon."

"Once the women were free, why didn't you say to hell with him and go public anyway?"

Colby looked into the fire. His voice sounded hollow when he answered.

"We discussed the possibility, but we were afraid. Lake said he would take revenge by killing someone if we breached our agreement with him."

"Going public would have destroyed the senator's career," Wayne Turner added, "and none of us wanted that. Only a handful of people knew about the pardon or Lake's guilt. O'Malley, Gordon, Grimsbo, me, the U.S. attorney, the attorney general, Carstairs, Merrill and the senator. We never even told the mayor. We knew how courageous Ray had been to sign the pardon. We didn't want him to suffer for it. So we took a vow to protect Ray and we've kept it."

"And you just forgot about Lake?"

"We never forgot, Mrs. Tannenbaum," Colby told her. "I used contacts in the Albany Police and the FBI to hunt for Lake. Nancy Gordon dedicated her life to tracking him down. He was too clever for us."

"Now that you know about the pardon, what are you planning to do?" Turner asked.

"I don't know."

"If the pardon, and these new murders, become public knowledge, Senator Colby cannot be confirmed. He'd lose the support of the law-and-order conservatives on the Judiciary Committee and the liberals will crucify him. This would be the answer to their prayers."

"I realize that."

"Going public can't help your client, either."

"Wayne," Colby said, "Mrs. Tannenbaum is going to have to make up her own mind about what to do with what she knows. We can't pressure her. God knows, she's under enough pressure as it is.

"But," Colby said, turning to Betsy, "I do have a question for you. I have the impression that you deduced the existence of the pardon."

"That's right. I asked myself how Lake could have walked away from Hunter's Point. A pardon was the only answer and only the governor of New York could issue a pardon. You could keep the existence of a pardon from the public, but the members of the task force would have to know about it and they're the ones who were rewarded. It was the only answer that made sense."

"Lake doesn't know you're here, does he?"

Betsy hesitated, then said, "No."

"And you haven't asked him to confirm your guess, have you?"

Betsy shook her head.

"Why?"

"Do you remember the conflicting emotions you felt when Lake asked you to pardon him? Imagine how I feel, Senator. I'm a very good attorney. I have the skills to free my client. He maintains his innocence, but my investigation turned up evidence that made me question his word. Until today, I didn't know for certain if Martin was lying. I didn't want to confront him until I knew the truth."

"Now that you know, what will you do?"

"I haven't worked that out yet. If it was any other case, I wouldn't care. I'd do my job and defend my client. But this isn't any case. This is . . ."

Betsy paused. What could she say that everyone in the room did not know firsthand.

"I don't envy you, Mrs. Tannenbaum," the senator said. "I really believe I had no choice. That is the only reason I've been able to live with what I did, even though I regret what I did every time I think of the pardon. You can walk away from Lake."

"Then I'd be walking away from my responsibilities, wouldn't I?"

"Responsibilities," Colby repeated. "Why do we take them on? Why do we burden ourselves with problems that tear us apart? Whenever I think of Lake I wish I hadn't gone into public life. Then I think of some of the good I've been able to do."

The senator paused. After a moment he stood up and held out his hand. "It's been a pleasure meeting you, Mrs. Tannenbaum. I mean that."

"Thank you for your candor, Senator."

"Wayne can drive you back to your hotel."

Wayne Turner followed Betsy out of the room. Colby sank back down into the armchair. He felt old and used up. He wanted to stay in front of the fire forever and forget the responsibilities about which he had just spoken. He thought about Betsy Tannenbaum's responsibility to her client and her responsibilities as a member of the human race. How would she live with herself if Lake was acquitted? He would haunt her for the rest of her life, the way Lake haunted him.

Colby wondered if the pardon would become public. If it did, he would be finished in public life. The President would withdraw his nomination and he would never be reelected. Strangely, he was not concerned. He had no control over Betsy Tannenbaum. His fate rested with the decisions she made.

Chapter Twenty

I

"Dr. Simon Reardon?"

"Yes."

"My name is Reginald Stewart. I'm a private investigator. I work for Betsy Tannenbaum, an attorney in Portland, Oregon."

"I don't know anyone in Portland."

Dr. Reardon sounded annoyed. Stewart thought he detected a slight British accent.

"This is about Hunter's Point and your ex-wife, Dr. Reardon. That's where I'm calling from. I hope you'll give me a few minutes to explain."

"I have no interest in discussing Samantha."

"Please hear me out. Do you remember Peter Lake?"

"Mr. Stewart, there is nothing about those days I can ever forget."

"Three women were kidnapped in Portland recently. A black rose and a note that said 'Gone, But Not Forgotten' were left at each scene. The women's bodies were dug up recently on property belonging to Peter Lake. He's been charged with the homicides."

"I thought the Hunter's Point police caught the murderer. Wasn't he some retarded deliveryman? A sex offender?"

"The Multnomah County d.a. thinks the Hunter's Point police made a mistake. I'm trying to find the Hunter's Point survivors. Ann Hazelton is dead. Gloria Escalante won't talk to me. Mrs. Reardon is my last hope."

"It's not Mrs. Reardon and hasn't been for some time," the doctor said with distaste, "and I have no idea how you can find Samantha. I moved to Minneapolis to get away from her. We haven't spoken in years. The last I heard, she was still living in Hunter's Point."

"You're divorced?"

Reardon laughed harshly. "Mr. Stewart, this was more than a simple divorce. Samantha tried to kill me."

"What?"

"She's a sick woman. I wouldn't waste my time on her. You can't trust anything she says."

"Was this entirely a result of the kidnapping?"

"Undoubtedly her torture and captivity exacerbated the condition, but my wife was always unbalanced. Unfortunately I was too much in love with her to notice until we were married. I kept rationalizing and excusing . . ." Reardon took a deep breath. "I'm sorry. She does that to me. Even after all these years."

"Dr. Reardon, I don't want to make you uncomfortable, but Mr. Lake is facing a death sentence and I need to know as much about Hunter's Point as I can."

"Can't the police tell you what you want to know?"

"No, sir. The files are missing."

"That's strange."

"Yes, it is. Believe me, if I had those files I wouldn't be bothering you. I'm sure it's painful having me dig up this period in your life, but this is literally a matter of life and death. Our d.a. has a bee in his bonnet about Mr. Lake. Peter was a victim, just like you, and he needs your help."

Reardon sighed. "Go ahead. Ask your questions."

"Thank you, sir. Can you tell me about Mrs. Reardon, or whatever she calls herself now?"

"I have no idea what her name is. She still called herself Reardon when I left Hunter's Point."

"When was that?"

"About eight years ago. As soon as the divorce was final."

"What happened between you and your wife?"

"She was a surgical nurse at University Hospital. Very beautiful, very wanton. Sex was what she was best at," Reardon said bitterly. "I was so caught up in her body that I was oblivious to what was going on around me. The most obvious problem was the stealing. She was arrested for shoplifting twice. Our lawyer kept the cases out of court and I paid off the stores. She was totally without remorse. Treated the incidents like jokes, once she was in the clear.

"Then there was the spending. I was making good money, but we were in debt up to our ears. She drained my savings accounts, charged our credit cards to the limit. It took me four years after the divorce to get back on my feet. And you couldn't reason with her. I showed her the bills and drew up a budget. She'd get me in bed and I'd forget what I'd told her, or she'd throw a tantrum or lock me out of the bedroom. It was the worst three years of my life.

"Then she was kidnapped and tortured and she got

worse. Whatever slender string kept her tethered to reality snapped during the time she was a prisoner. I can't even describe what she was like after that. They kept her hospitalized for almost a year. She rarely spoke. She wouldn't let men near her.

"I should have known better, but I took her home after she was released. I felt guilty because of what had happened. I know I couldn't have protected her—I was at the hospital when she was kidnapped—but, still, you can see how   "

"That's very common, that feeling."

"Oh, I know. But knowing something intellectually and dealing with it emotionally are two different things. I wish I had been wiser."

"What happened after she came home?"

"She wouldn't share a bedroom with me. When I was home, she would stay in her room. I have no idea what she did when I was at work. When she did speak, she was clearly irrational. She insisted that the man who kidnapped her was still at large. I showed her the newspaper articles about Waters's arrest and the shooting, but she said he wasn't the man. She wanted a gun for protection. Of course I refused. She started accusing me of being in a conspiracy with the police. Then she tried to kill me. She stabbed me with a kitchen knife when I came home from the hospital. Fortunately a colleague was with me. She stabbed him too, but he hit Samantha and stunned her. We wrestled her to the floor. She was writhing and screeching about . . . She said I was trying to kill her . . . It was very hard for me. I had to commit her. Then I decided to get out."

"I don't blame you. It looks like you went above and beyond the call."

"Yes, I did. But I still feel bad about deserting her, even though I know I had no choice."

"You said you committed her. Which hospital was that?"

"St. Jude's. It's a private psychiatric hospital near Hunter's Point. I moved and cut off contact with her completely. I know she was there for several years, but I believe she was released."

"Did Samantha try to contact you after she was released?"

"No. I dreaded the possibility, but it never happened."

"Would you happen to have a photo of Samantha? There weren't any in the newspaper accounts."

"When I moved to Minnesota, I threw them away, along with everything else that might remind me of Samantha."

"Thank you for your time, Doctor. I'll try St. Jude's. Maybe they have a line on your ex-wife."

"One other thing, Mr. Stewart. If you find Samantha, please don't tell her you talked with me or tell her where I am."

2

Randy Highsmith drove straight to the district attorney's office from the airport. He was feeling the effects of jet lag and wouldn't have minded going home, but he knew how badly Page wanted to hear what he had found out in Hunter's Point.

"It's not good, Al," Highsmith said as soon as they were sitting down. "I was a day behind Darius's investigator everywhere I went, so he knows what we know."

"Which is?"

"Nancy Gordon wasn't straight with you. Frank

Grimsbo and Wayne Turner told me only Gordon considered Lake a serious suspect. She was fixated on him and never accepted Waters as the rose killer, but everyone else did.

"There's something else she didn't tell us. Three of the Hunter's Point women didn't die. Hazelton, Escalante and Reardon were found alive in an old farmhouse. And, before you ask, Hazelton is dead, I haven't located Reardon and Escalante never saw the face of the man who abducted her."

"Why did she let me think all the Hunter's Point women were murdered?"

"I have no idea. All I know is that our case against Martin Darius is turning to shit."

"It doesn't make sense," Page said, more to himself than to Highsmith. "Waters is dead. If he was the rose killer, who murdered the women we found at the construction site? It had to be someone who knew details about the Hunter's Point case that only the police knew. That description only fits one person, Martin Darius."

"There is one other person it fits, Al," Highsmith said.

"Who?"

"Nancy Gordon."

"Are you crazy? She's a cop."

"What if she's crazy? What if she did it to frame Darius? Think about it. Would you have considered Darius a suspect if she didn't tell you he was Lake?"

"You're forgetting the anonymous letter that told her that the killer was in Portland."

"How do we know she didn't write it herself?"

"I don't believe it."

"Well, believe it or not, our case is disappearing. Oh, and there's a new wrinkle. A Portland private investigator named Sam Oberhurst was looking into the Hunter's Point murders about a month before the first Portland disappearance."

"Whom did he represent?"

"He didn't say and he didn't tell anyone why he was asking about the case, but I'm going to ask him. I have his phone number and I'll get the address through the phone company."

"Have they had any luck with the files?"

"None at all."

Page closed his eyes and rested his head against the back of his chair.

"I'm going to look like a fool, Randy. We'll have to dismiss. I should have listened to you and Ross. We never had a case. It was all in my head."

"Don't fold yet, Al. This p.i. could know something."

Page shook his head. He had aged since his divorce. His energy had deserted him. For a while this case had recharged him, but Darius was slipping away and he would soon be a laughingstock in the legal community.

"We're going to lose this one, Randy. I can feel it. Gordon was all we had and now it looks like we never had her."

3

"Hi, Mom," Betsy said, putting down her suitcase and hugging Rita Cohen.

"How was your flight? Have you had anything to eat?"

"The flight was fine and I ate on the plane."

"That's not food. You want me to fix you something?"

"Thanks, but I'm not hungry," Betsy said as she hung up her coat. "How was Kathy?"

"So-so. Rick took her to the movies on Saturday."

"How is he?" Betsy asked, hoping she sounded disinterested.

"The louse wouldn't look me in the eye the whole time he was here. He couldn't wait to escape."

"You weren't rude to him?"

"I didn't give him the time of day," Rita answered pointing her nose in the air. Then she shook her head.

"Poor kid. Kathy was all excited when she left with him, but she was down in the dumps as soon as he dropped her off. She moped around, picked at her food at dinner."

"Did anything else happen while I was gone?" Betsy asked, hoping there had been some good news.

"Nora Sloane came by, Sunday evening," Rita said, smiling mischievously. "I told all."

"What did she ask about?"

"Your childhood, your cases. She was very good with Kathy."

"She seems like a nice woman. I hope her article sells. She's certainly working hard enough on it."

"Oh, before I forget, when you go to school, talk to Mrs. Kramer. Kathy was in a fight with another little girl and she's been disruptive in class."

"I'll see her this afternoon," Betsy said. She sounded defeated. Kathy was usually an angel at school. You didn't have to be Sigmund Freud to see what was happening.

"Cheer up," Rita told her. "She's a good kid. She's just going through a rough time. Look, you've got an hour before school lets out. Have some coffee cake. I'll make you a cup of decaf and you can tell me about your trip."

Betsy glanced at her watch and decided to give in

Eating cake was a surefire way of dealing with depression.

"Okay. I am hungry, I guess. You fix everything. I want to change."

"Now you're talking," Rita said with a smile. "And, for your information, Kathy won the fight. She told me."

Chapter Twenty-one

When Betsy Tannenbaum was a very little girl, she would not go to sleep until her mother showed her that there were no monsters in her closet or under her bed. The stage passed quickly. Betsy stopped believing in monsters. Then she met Martin Darius. What made Darius so terrifying was his dissimilarity to the slavering, fanged deformities that lurked in the shadows in her room. Give one hundred people the autopsy photographs and not one of them would believe that the elegantly-dressed gentleman standing in the doorway to Betsy's office was capable of cutting off Wendy Reiser's nipples or using a cattle prod to torture Victoria Miller. Even knowing what she knew, Betsy had to force herself to make the connection. But Betsy did know, and the shining winter sun could not keep her from feeling as frightened as the very little girl who used to listen for monsters in the dark.

"Sit down Mr. Darius," Betsy said.

"We're back to Mr. Darius, are we? This must be serious."

Betsy did not smile. Darius looked at her quizzically, but took a seat without making any more remarks.

"I'm resigning as your attorney."

"I thought we agreed that you'd only do that if you

believed I was guilty of murdering Farrar, Reiser and Miller."

"I firmly believe you killed them. I know everything about Hunter's Point."

"What's everything?"

"I spent the weekend in Washington, D.C., talking to Senator Colby."

Darius nodded appreciatively. "I'm impressed. You unraveled the whole Hunter's Point affair in no time at all."

"I don't give a damn for your flattery, Darius. You lied to me from day one. There are some lawyers who don't care whom they represent as long as the fee is large enough. I'm not one of them. Have your new attorney call me so I can get rid of your file. I don't want anything in my office that reminds me of you."

"My, aren't we self-righteous. You're sure you know everything, aren't you?"

"I know enough to distrust anything you tell me."

"I'm a little disappointed, Tannenbaum. You worked your way through this puzzle part of the way, then shut down that brilliant mind of yours just as you came to the part that needs solving."

"What are you talking about?"

"I'm talking about having faith in your client. I'm talking about not walking away from someone who desperately needs your help. I am *not* guilty of killing Reiser, Farrar and Miller. If you don't prove I'm innocent, the real killer is going to walk away, just the way I did in Hunter's Point."

"You admit you're guilty of those atrocities in Hunter's Point?"

Darius shrugged. "How can I deny it, now that you've talked to Colby?"

"How could you do it? Animals don't treat other animals like that."

Darius looked amused. "Do I fascinate you, Tannenbaum?"

"No, Mr. Darius, you disgust me."

"Then why ask me about Hunter's Point?"

"I want to know why you thought you had the right to walk into someone else's life and turn the rest of their days on Earth into Hell. I want to understand how you could destroy the lives of those poor women so casually."

Darius stopped smiling. "There was nothing casual about what I did."

"What I can't understand is how a mind like yours or Speck's or Bundy's works. What could possibly make you feel so badly about yourself that you can only keep going by dehumanizing women?"

"Don't compare me to Bundy or Speck. They were pathetic failures. Thoroughly inadequate personalities. I'm neither insane nor inadequate. I was a successful attorney in Hunter's Point and a successful businessman here."

"Then why did you do it?"

Darius hesitated. He seemed to be in a debate with himself. "Am I still covered by the attorney-client privilege?" Betsy nodded. "Anything I tell you is between us?" Betsy nodded again. "Because I'd like to tell you. You have a superior mind and a female viewpoint. Your reactions would be informative."

Betsy knew she should throw Darius out of her office and her life, but her fascination with him paralyzed her intellect. When she remained silent, Darius settled back in his chair.

"I was conducting an experiment, Tannenbaum. I wanted to know what it felt like to be God. I don't remember the exact moment the idea for the experiment germinated. I do remember a trip Sandy and I took to Barbados. Lying on the beach, I thought about how perfect my life was. There was my job, which provided me with more money than I ever dreamed of, and there was Sandy, still sexy as all get-out, even after bearing my lovely Melody. My Sandy, so willing to please, so mindless. I'd married her for her body and never checked under the hood until it was too late."

Darius shook his head wistfully.

"Perfect is boring, Tannenbaum. Sex with the same woman, day after day, no matter how beautiful and skilled she is, is boring. I've always had an intense fantasy life and I wondered what it would be like if my fantasy world was real. Would my life be different? Would I discover what I was searching for? I decided to find out what would happen if I brought my fantasy world to life.

"It took me months to find the farmhouse. I couldn't trust workmen, so I built the stalls myself. Then I selected the women. I chose only worthless women. Women who lived off their husbands like parasites. Beautiful, spoiled women who used their looks to entice a man into marriage, then drained him of his wealth and self-respect. These women were born again in my little dungeon. Their stall became their world and I became their sun, moon, wind and rain."

Betsy remembered Colby's description of the women he had seen. Their hollow eyes, the protruding ribs. She remembered the vacant stares on the faces of the dead women in the photographs.

"I admit I was cruel to them, but I had to dehumanize them so they could be molded in the image I chose. When I appeared, I wore a mask and I made them wear leather masks with no eyeholes. Once a week I doled out rations scientifically calculated to keep them on the brink of starvation. I limited the hours they could sleep.

"Did Colby mention the clocks and the videotape machines? Did you wonder what they were for? It was my crowning touch. I had a wife and child and a job, so I could only be with my subjects for short periods each week, but I wanted total control, omniscience, even when I was gone. So I rigged the videotapes to run when I wasn't there and I gave the women commands to perform. They had to watch the clock. Every hour, at set times, they would bow to the camera and perform dog tricks, rolling over, squatting, masturbating. Whatever I commanded. I reviewed the tapes and I punished deviations firmly."

Darius had an enraptured look on his face. His eyes were fixed on a scene no sane person could imagine. Betsy felt she would shatter if she moved.

"I changed them from demanding cows to obedient puppies. They were mine completely. I bathed them. They ate like dogs from a doggy bowl. They were forbidden to speak unless I told them to, and the only time I let them was to beg me for punishment and thank me for pain. In the end they would do anything to escape the pain. They pleaded to drink my urine and kissed my foot when I let them."

Darius's face was so tight Betsy thought his skin might rip. A wave of nausea made her stomach roll.

"Some of the women resisted, but they soon learned that there can be no negotiations with a god. Others obeyed immediately. Cross, for instance. She was no challenge at all. A perfect cow. As docile and unimaginative as a lump of clay. That's why I chose her for my sacrifice."

Before Darius started speaking, Betsy assumed there was nothing he could say that she would not be able to handle, but she did not want to hear any more.

"Did your experiment bring you peace?" Betsy

asked to stop Darius from talking about the women. Her breathing was ragged and she felt light-headed. Darius snapped out of his trance.

"The experiment brought me the most exquisite pleasure, Tannenbaum. The moments I shared with those women were the finest moments in my life. But Sandy found the note and it had to end. There was too much danger of being caught. Then I was caught, and then I was free, and that freedom was exhilarating."

"When was the next time you repeated the experiment, Martin?" Betsy asked coldly.

"Never. I wanted to, but I learn from experience. I had one lucky break and I was not going to risk life in prison or the death penalty."

Betsy stared at Darius with contempt.

"I want you out of my office. I don't ever want to see you again."

"You can't quit, Tannenbaum. I need you."

"Hire Oscar Montoya or Matthew Reynolds."

"Oscar Montoya and Matthew Reynolds are good lawyers, but they aren't women. I'm banking that no jury will believe that an ardent feminist would represent a man who treated a woman the way the murderer treated Reiser, Farrar and Miller. In a close case, you're my edge."

"Then you just lost your edge, Darius. You're the most vile person I've ever known. I don't ever want to see you again, let alone defend you."

"You're reneging on our deal. I told you, I did not murder Farrar, Reiser or Vicky Miller. Someone is framing me. If I'm convicted, this case will be closed and you'll be responsible for the killer's next victim and the one after that."

"Do you think I'll believe anything you say after what you just told me, after all your lies?"

"Listen, Tannenbaum," Darius said, leaning across the desk and pinning Betsy with an intense stare, "I did not kill those women. I'm being set up by someone and I'm pretty certain I know who she is."

"She?"

"Only Nancy Gordon knows enough about this case to frame me. Vicky, Reiser, those women would never have suspected her. She's female. She'd flash her badge. They'd let her in easy. That's why there were no signs of a struggle at the crime scenes. They probably went with her willingly and didn't know what was happening until it was too late."

"No woman would do what was done to those women."

"Don't be naive. She's been obsessed with me since Hunter's Point. She's probably insane."

Betsy remembered what she had learned about Nancy Gordon. The woman had tried to murder Darius in Hunter's Point. She had dedicated her life to finding him. But, to frame him like this? From what she knew, it was more likely that Gordon would have walked up to Darius and shot him.

"I don't buy it."

"You know Vicky left the Hacienda Motel at two-thirty. I was with Russell Miller and several other people at the advertising agency until almost five."

"Who can alibi you after you left the ad agency?"

"Unfortunately, no one."

"I'm not going to do it. You stand for everything in life I find repulsive. Even if you didn't kill the women in Portland, you did commit those inhuman crimes in Hunter's Point."

"And you are going to be responsible for murdering the next victim in Portland. Think about it, Tannenbaum. There's no case against me now. That means another woman will have to die to supply the evidence the State can use to convict me."

That evening Kathy snuggled close to Betsy, her attention riveted on a cartoon special. Betsy kissed the top of her daughter's head and wondered how this peaceful scene could coexist with a reality where women, curled up in the dark, waited for a torturer to bring them unbearable pain? How could she meet with a man like Martin Darius at work and watch Disney with her daughter at home without losing her sanity? How could Peter Lake spend the morning as the horror god of a warped fantasy and the evening playing with his own little girl?

Betsy wished there was only one reality: the one where she and Rick sat watching Disney with Kathy squirreled between them. The one she thought was reality before Rick walked out on her and she met Martin Darius.

Betsy had always been able to separate herself from her work. Before Darius, her criminal clients were more pathetic than frightening. She represented shoplifters, drunk drivers, petty thieves and scared juveniles. She was still friendly with the two women she had saved from homicide charges. Even when she brought her work home with her, she saw it as something that was only temporarily in her house. Darius was in Betsy's soul. He had changed her. She no longer believed she was safe. And much worse, she knew Kathy was not safe either.

Chapter Twenty-two

I

St. Jude's looked more like an exclusive private school than a mental hospital. A high, ivy-covered wall stretched back into deep woods. The administration building, once the home of millionaire Alvin Piercy, was red brick, with recessed windows and gothic arches. Piercy, a devout Catholic, died a bachelor in 1916 and left his fortune to the church. In 1923 the mansion was converted into a retreat for priests in need of counseling. In 1953 a small, modern psychiatric hospital was constructed behind the house, which became the home of St. Jude's administration. From the gate, Reggie Stewart could see the administration building through the graceful limbs of the snow-covered trees that were scattered across the grounds. In the fall, the lawn would be a carpet of green and the tree limbs would be graced with leaves of gold and red.

Dr. Margaret Flint's office was at the end of a long corridor on the second floor. The window faced away from the hospital and toward the woods. Dr. Flint was an angular, horse-faced woman with shoulder-length gray hair.

"Thank you for seeing me," Stewart said.

Dr. Flint responded with an engaging smile that softened her homely features. She took Stewart's hand in a firm grip, then motioned him into one of two armchairs that were set up around a coffee table.

"I've often wondered what became of Samantha Reardon. She was such an unusual case. Unfortunately there was no follow-up, once she was released."

"Why is that?"

"Her husband refused to pay after the divorce and it wasn't covered by insurance. In any event, I doubt Samantha would have permitted me to pry into her affairs after she gained her freedom. She hated everything associated with the hospital."

"What can you tell me about Mrs. Reardon?"

"Normally I wouldn't tell you a thing, because of patient-doctor confidentiality rules, but your phone call raised the possibility that she may be a danger to others, and that takes precedence over those rules in certain circumstances."

"She may be involved in a series of murders in Portland."

"So you said. Is there a connection between the murders and her captivity in Hunter's Point?" Dr. Flint asked.

"Yes. How did you know?"

"I'll tell you in a moment. Please bear with me. I need to know the background of your request for information."

"A man named Peter Lake was the husband of one of the Hunter's Point victims and the father of another. He moved to Portland eight years ago so he could start a new life. Someone is duplicating the Hunter's Point m.o. in

Portland. Are you familiar with the way the Hunter's Point women were treated?"

"Of course. I was Samantha's treating psychiatrist. I had full access to the police reports."

"Dr. Flint, would Reardon be capable of subjecting other women to the torture she experienced in order to frame my client?"

"A good question. Not many women could go through torture, then subject another woman to that same experience, but Samantha Reardon was in no way normal. We all have personalities that are thoroughly ingrained. Our personalities are usually very difficult, if not impossible, to change. People with personality disorders have maladaptive personalities. The signs they present vary with the disorder.

"Prior to her horrible victimization, Samantha Reardon had what we call a borderline personality, which lies between a neurosis and a psychosis. At times she would exhibit psychotic behavior, but generally she would be seen as neurotic. She demonstrated perverse sexual interests, antisocial behavior, such as passing bad checks or shoplifting, anxiety, and strong self-centeredness. Her relationship with her ex-husband typifies this kind of behavior. There were periods of intense sexuality, frequent instability, and he found her impossible to reason with and totally self-centered. When she was caught stealing, she showed no interest in the charges, no remorse. She used sex to distract Dr. Reardon and gain favors from him. She destroyed his finances without regard to the long-term consequences for both of them. When Samantha was kidnapped and tortured she became psychotic. She is probably still in that state.

"Samantha saw St. Jude's as an extension of her captivity. I was the only doctor to whom she related, probably because I was the only female on the staff. Samantha

Reardon hates and distrusts all men. She was convinced that the Hunter's Point mayor, the police chief, the governor, even, at times, the President of the United States —all men—were conspiring to protect the man who tortured her."

"So," Stewart interjected, "it's possible she would act on these fantasies if she located the man she believed was responsible for her captivity?"

"Most certainly. When she was here, she spoke of nothing but revenge. She saw herself as an avenging angel arrayed against the forces of darkness. She hated her captor, but she is a danger to any man, because she sees them all as oppressors."

"But the women? How could she bring herself to torture those women after what she went through?"

"Samantha would see any means that furthered her ends as acceptable means, Mr. Stewart. If she had to sacrifice some women in the process of attaining her goal, in her eyes that would be a small price to pay for her revenge."

2

Rick was sitting in the waiting room when Betsy arrived at work. He seemed subdued.

"I know I'm not expected, but I wanted to talk. Are you busy?"

"Come in," Betsy told him. She was still angry with him for telling Kathy that her career was to blame for their separation.

"How's Kathy?" Rick asked, as he followed her into her office.

"There's an easy way to find out."

"Don't be like that. Actually, one of the reasons I stopped by is to ask if she can sleep over. I just moved into a new apartment and it has a guest room."

Betsy wanted to say no, because it would hurt Rick, but she knew how much Kathy missed her father.

"Fine."

"Thanks. I'll pick her up tomorrow, after work."

"What else did you want to talk about?"

Rick was uncomfortable. He looked down at the desktop.

"I . . . Betsy, this is very hard for me. The partnership, my job . . ." Rick paused. "I'm not doing this very well." He took a deep breath. "What I'm trying to say is that my life is in turmoil right now. I'm under so much pressure that I'm not thinking straight. This time by myself, it's given me some distance, some perspective. I guess what I'm saying is, don't give up on me. Don't close me out. . . ."

"I never wanted to do that, Rick. You're the one who closed me out."

"When I left, I said some things about how I felt about you that I didn't mean."

"When you're certain how you feel, tell me, Rick. But I can't promise how I'm going to feel. You hurt me very badly."

"I know," he said quietly. "Look, this merger I'm working on, it's got me tied up night and day, but I think everything will be under control in a month. I've got some time off in December and Kathy has Christmas vacation, so she wouldn't miss school. I thought maybe the three of us could go somewhere where we could be by ourselves."

Betsy's breath caught in her chest. She didn't know what to say.

Rick stood up. "I know I sprang this on you without

any warning. You don't have to answer me right away. We have time. Just promise me you'll think about it."

"I will."

"Good. And thanks for letting me see Kathy."

"You're her father," Betsy said.

Betsy opened the office door before Rick could say anything else. Nora Sloane was standing next to Ann's desk.

"Do you have a minute?" Sloane asked.

"Rick was just leaving," Betsy answered.

Sloane stared at Rick for a second.

"Are you Mr. Tannenbaum?"

"Yes."

"This is Nora Sloane," Betsy said. "She's working on an article about women litigators for *Pacific West* magazine."

"Your wife has been a wonderful help."

Rick smiled politely. "I'll pick up Kathy around six and take her to dinner," he told Betsy. "Don't forget to pack her school things. Nice meeting you, Ms. Sloane."

"Wait," Betsy said. "I don't have the address and phone number at your new place."

Rick gave them to her and Betsy wrote them down. Then Rick left.

"The reason I dropped in is to see if we can schedule some time to discuss the Hammermill case and your strategy in the Darius case," Sloane said.

"I hope this won't upset your plans, Nora, but I'm getting off Martin's case."

"Why?"

"Personal reasons I can't discuss with you."

"I don't understand."

"There's a conflict. Ethical problems are involved. I can't put it any other way without violating the attorney-client privilege."

Nora rubbed her forehead. She looked distracted.

"I'm sorry if this affects the article," Betsy said. "There isn't anything I can do about what happened."

"That's all right," Nora replied, quickly regaining her composure. "The Darius case isn't essential to the article."

Betsy opened her appointment book. "As soon as I'm officially off Martin's case, I'll have plenty of free time. Why don't we tentatively schedule a meeting for lunch next Wednesday?"

"That sounds fine. See you then."

The door closed and Betsy looked at the work on her desk. They were cases she'd had to put off because of Martin Darius. Betsy pulled the top case off a pile, but she did not open the file. She thought about Rick. He seemed different. Less self-assured. If he wanted to come back, would she let him?

The buzzer rang. Reggie Stewart was calling from Hunter's Point.

"How's tricks?" Stewart asked.

"Not so good, Reg. I'm off the case."

"Did Darius fire you?"

"No, it's the other way around."

"Why?"

"I found out Darius did kill the women in Hunter's Point."

"How?"

"I can't tell you."

"Jesus, Betsy, you can trust me."

"I know I can, but I'm not going to explain this, so don't press me."

"Well, I'm a little concerned. There's a possibility Darius is being framed. It turns out Samantha Reardon is a very weird lady. I talked to Simon Reardon, her ex. He's a neurosurgeon and she was one of his surgical nurses. He became infatuated with her and the next thing he knows, they're married and he's on the verge of bankruptcy. She's shoplifting like crazy, running up his credit cards, and his lawyers are rushing around covering up the lady's indiscretions. Then Darius kidnaps and tortures her and she really goes over the edge. I met with Dr. Flint, her shrink at St. Jude's. That's where she was committed after she tried to kill Reardon."

"What?"

"She knifed him and a friend he brought home. They subdued her and she spent the next few years in a padded cell insisting that the man who kidnapped her was still at large and she was the victim of a conspiracy."

"She was, Reg. The authorities covered up for Darius. I can't fill you in on the details, but Samantha may not have been completely crazy."

"She may have been right about the cover-up *and* insane. Dr. Flint thought she was mad as a hatter. Reardon was an abused child. Her father ran away when she was two and her mother was a hopeless drunk. She learned morals from a street gang she ran with. She has a juvenile record for robbery and assault. That was a stabbing, too. She was smart enough to get through high school without doing any real work. Her I.Q.'s been tested at 146, which is a hell of a lot higher than mine, but her school performance was lousy.

"There was an early marriage to Max Felix, a manager at a department store where she was working. I called him and he tells the same story Dr. Reardon does. She must be a great lay. Her first husband says he couldn't see up from down while she was cleaning out his bank account and charging him into debt. The marriage only lasted a year.

"Next stop was a community college, then nursing school, then the good doctor. Dr. Flint says Reardon had a personality disorder—borderline personality—to begin with, and the stress from the torture and captivity made her psychotic. She was obsessed with avenging herself on her captor."

Betsy felt a queasy sensation in the pit of her stomach.

"Did you ask Dr. Flint if she would be capable of subjecting other women to the kind of torture she endured just to frame Darius?"

"According to Dr. Flint, it wouldn't bother her one bit to slice up those ladies, if that's what it took to accomplish her plan."

"It's so hard to believe, Reg. A woman doing those things to other women."

"It makes sense, though, Betsy. Think about it. Oberhurst interviews Reardon and shows her a photo of Darius; Reardon recognizes Darius and follows Oberhurst to Portland; she reads about the hassle Darius is having at the construction site and figures it's the ideal place to bury Oberhurst after she kills him; later, she adds the other bodies."

"I don't know, Reg. It still makes more sense for Darius to have killed them."

"What do you want me to do?"

"Try to get a picture of her. There weren't any in the newspaper accounts."

"I'm way ahead of you. I'm going to look at her college yearbook. She went to the State University in Hunter's Point, so that should be easy."

Stewart hung up, leaving Betsy very confused. Moments before, she was certain Darius had killed the Portland women. But if Reggie's suspicions were right, Darius was being framed, and everyone was being manipulated by a very intelligent and dangerous woman.

3

Randy Highsmith and Ross Barrow took I-84 down the Columbia River Gorge until they came to the turnoff for the scenic highway. Stark cliffs rose up on either side of the wide river. Waterfalls could occasionally be seen through breaks in the trees. The view was breathtaking, but Barrow was too busy trying to see through the slashing rain to enjoy it. The gusting winds that funneled down the gorge pushed the unmarked car sideways. Barrow fought the wheel and kept the car from skidding as he took the exit.

They were in country. National forest, farmland. The trees provided some protection from the rain, but Barrow still had to lean forward and squint to catch the occasional street signs.

"There," Randy Highsmith shouted, pointing to a mailbox with the address stuck on in cheap, iridescent numerals. Barrow turned the car sharply and the back wheels slid sideways on the gravel. The house Samuel Oberhurst was renting was supposed to be a quarter mile up this unpaved road. The rental agent had described it as a bungalow, but it was only a step up from a shack. Except for the privacy the surrounding countryside provided, Highsmith could not see a thing to recommend it. The house was square with a peaked roof. It may once have been painted red, but the weather had turned it rust-colored. A beat-up Pontiac was parked out front. No one had cut the grass in weeks. Cinder blocks served as front steps. There were two empty beer cans next to the steps and an empty pack of cigarettes wedged into a crack between two of the blocks.

Barrow pulled the car as close to the front door as he could and Highsmith jumped out, ducking his head, as if that would somehow protect him from the rain. He pounded on the door, waited, then pounded again.

"I'm going around the side," he yelled to Barrow. The detective cut the motor and followed him. The curtains on the front windows were closed. Highsmith and Barrow walked through the wet grass on the east side of the house and discovered that there were no windows on that side and the shades were down in the windows at the back. Barrow peered through a small window on the west side.

"Looks like a fucking sty in there," Barrow said.

"No one's home, that's for sure."

"What about the car?"

Highsmith shrugged. "Let's try the front door."

Water dripped off Highsmith's face and he could barely see through his glasses. The front door was not locked. Barrow let them in. Highsmith took off his glasses and dried the lenses with his handkerchief. Barrow turned on a light.

"Jesus!"

Highsmith put on his glasses. A television stood on a low stand under the front window. Across from it was a second-hand sofa. The upholstery was torn in spots, stuffing was coming out and it sagged. A full suit of men's clothes had been thrown on the sofa. Highsmith saw a jacket, underwear, a pair of pants. Next to the TV, fitted into the corner, was an old gray, stand-up filing cabinet. All the drawers were out and papers had been thrown around the room. Highsmith was suddenly distracted from the chaos in the front room. He sniffed the air.

"What's that smell?"

Barrow did not answer. He was concentrating on a heavy chair that lay on its side in the center of the room. As he edged around it, he could see bloodstains on the chair and the ground around it. Scraps of heavy tape that could have been used to secure a man's legs stuck out from the sides of the chair legs. On a table a few feet from the chair was a kitchen knife encrusted with blood.

"How's your stomach?" Barrow asked. "We've got a crime scene here and I don't want your breakfast all over it."

"I've been in crime scenes before, Ross. I was at the pit, remember?"

"I guess you were. Well, take a gander at this."

There was a plastic soup bowl next to the knife. Highsmith looked in it and turned green. The soup bowl contained three severed fingers.

"John Doe," Barrow said softly.

Highsmith walked around the chair so he could see the seat. It was covered with blood. He felt queasy. In addition to the three fingers, Doe's genitals had been missing and Randy did not want to be the one who found them.

"I'm not certain who has jurisdiction here," Barrow said as he walked around the chair. "Call the state police."

Highsmith nodded. He looked for a phone. There was none in the front room. There were two rooms in the back of the house. One was a bathroom. Highsmith opened the other slowly, afraid of what he might find. There was barely enough room in the bedroom for a single bed, a dresser and an end table. The phone was on the end table.

"Hey, Ross, look at this."

Barrow came into the room. Highsmith pointed to an answering machine that was connected to the phone. A red light was flashing, indicating there were messages on the machine. Highsmith skimmed through a few messages before stopping at one.

"Mr. Oberhurst, this is Betsy Tannenbaum. This is

the third time I've called and I'd appreciate it if you would call me at my office. The number is 555-1763. It's urgent that you contact me. I have a release from Lisa Darius giving you permission to discuss her case. Please call anytime. I have an answering service that can reach me at home, if you call after hours or on a weekend."

The machine beeped. Highsmith and Barrow looked at each other.

"Oberhurst is hired by Lisa Darius, then he's tortured and his body ends up in the pit at Darius's construction site," Barrow said.

"Why did Lisa Darius hire him?"

Barrow looked through the door at the open filing cabinet.

"I wonder if that was what Darius was looking for—his wife's file."

"Hold it, Ross. We don't know Darius did this."

"Randy, say Darius found out what was in his wife's file and it was something that could hurt him. I mean, if he did this, tortured Oberhurst, cut off his fingers and dick, it was because that file had something in it that was dynamite. Maybe something that could prove Darius is the rose killer."

"What are you getting . . . Oh, shit. Lisa Darius. He couldn't get at her before, because he's been in jail since we discovered the bodies."

Barrow grabbed the phone and started dialing.

4

The Oregon Supreme Court sits in Salem, the state capital, fifty miles south of Portland. The hour commute was the only thing Victor Ryder disliked about being a Supreme Court justice. After all the years of seven-day work weeks and sixteen-hour days he had spent in private practice, the more leisurely pace of work at the court was a relief.

Justice Ryder was a widower who lived alone behind a high evergreen hedge in a three-story, brown and white Tudor house in the Portland Heights section of the West Hills. The view of Portland and Mount Hood from the brick patio in the rear of the house was spectacular.

Ryder unlocked the front door and called out for Lisa. The heat was on in the house. So were the lights. He heard voices coming from the living room. He called out to Lisa again, but she did not answer. The voices he heard came from the television, but no one was watching it. Ryder switched off the set.

At the bottom of the stairs, Ryder called out again. There was still no answer. If Lisa had gone out, why was the set on? He headed down the hall to the kitchen. Lisa knew her father always snacked as soon as he got in the door, so she left notes on the refrigerator. The refrigerator door was covered with recipes and cartoons, affixed to the smooth surface with magnets, but there was no note. There were two coffee cups on the kitchen table, and the remains of a piece of coffee cake on a cake dish.

"Must have gone off with a friend," Ryder said to himself, but he was still bothered by the TV. He cut a piece of coffee cake and took a bite, then he walked to Lisa's room. There was nothing out of place, nothing that aroused his suspicion. Still, Justice Ryder felt very uneasy. He was about to go to his room to change when he heard the doorbell. Two men were huddled under an umbrella on the front steps.

"Justice Ryder? I'm Randy Highsmith with the Multnomah County district attorney's office. This is

Detective Ross Barrow, Portland Police. Is your daughter in?"

"Is this about Martin?"

"Yes, sir."

"Lisa's been staying with me, but she's not here now."

"When did you see her last?"

"At breakfast. Why?"

"We have some questions we wanted to ask her. Do you know where she can be reached?"

"I'm afraid not. She didn't leave a note and I just got in."

"Could she be with a friend?" Highsmith asked casually, so Ryder would not see his concern.

"I really don't know."

Ryder remembered the TV and frowned.

"Is something wrong, sir?" Barrow asked, keeping his tone neutral.

"No. Not really. It's just that there were two coffee cups on the kitchen table, so I thought she was entertaining a friend. They'd been eating a piece of coffee cake, too. But the TV was on."

"I don't understand," Barrow said.

"It was on when I came home. I couldn't figure out why she'd leave it running if she was talking with a friend in the kitchen or leaving the house."

"Is it normal for her to go out without leaving a note?" Barrow asked.

"She hasn't lived at home for some time and she's been staying in the house at night since Martin got out. But she knows I worry about her."

"Is there something you're not telling us, sir?"

Justice Ryder hesitated.

"Lisa's been very frightened since Martin was released. She talked about leaving the state until he's back behind bars."

"Wouldn't she have told you where she was going?"

"I assume so." Ryder paused, as if he just remembered something. "Martin called Lisa the night he was released. He said there was nowhere in Portland she would be safe. Maybe he called again and she panicked."

"Was he threatening her?" Barrow asked.

"I thought so, but Lisa wasn't certain. It was an odd conversation. I only heard Lisa's end of it and what she told me he said."

Highsmith handed the judge his business card. "Please ask Mrs. Darius to give me a ring the minute you hear from her. It's important."

"Certainly."

Barrow and Highsmith shook hands with the judge and left.

"I don't like this," Barrow said as soon as the front door closed. "It's too much like the other crime scenes. Especially the TV. She'd have turned that off if she was going out with a friend."

"There was no note or rose."

"Yeah, but Darius isn't stupid. If he's got his wife, he's not going to broadcast the fact. He could have changed his m.o. to put us off the track. Any suggestions?"

"None at all, unless you think we've got enough to pick up Darius."

"We don't."

"Then we wait, and hope Lisa Darius is out with a friend."

Part Seven

GONE, BUT NOT FORGOTTEN

Chapter Twenty-three

I

Betsy heard a car pull into the carport and looked out the kitchen window.

"It's Daddy!" Kathy yelled. She had been waiting in the living room all afternoon, giving only half-hearted attention to the television, since Betsy told her she was going to Rick's for the weekend.

"Get your things," Betsy told Kathy as she opened the door.

"They're all here, Mom," Kathy said, pointing to her backpack, book bag, small valise and Oliver, the stuffed skunk.

The door opened and Kathy jumped into Rick's arms.

"How you doin', Tiger?" Rick asked with a laugh.

"I packed myself," Kathy said, pointing at her things.

"Did you pack your toothbrush?" Betsy asked suddenly.

"Uh oh," Kathy said.

"I thought so. Run and get it right now, young lady."

Rick put Kathy down and she raced down the hall for the bathroom.

"She's very excited," Betsy told Rick. He looked uncomfortable.

"I thought I'd take her to the Spaghetti Factory."

"She likes that."

They stood without talking for a moment.

"You look good, Bets."

"You should see how I look when I haven't had to spend the day in Judge Spencer's court," Betsy joked self-consciously, sidestepping the compliment. Rick started to say something, but Kathy was back with her toothbrush and the moment passed.

"See you Monday," Betsy said, giving Kathy a big hug and kiss. Rick gathered up everything but Oliver. Betsy watched from the doorway until they drove away.

2

Alan Page looked up from his desk. Randy Highsmith and Ross Barrow were standing in the doorway. He glanced at his watch. It was six twenty-five.

"I just got off the phone with Justice Ryder. She's still missing," Barrow said.

Page put down his pen.

"What can we do? There's not a shred of evidence pointing toward Darius," Page said. He looked pale and sounded exhausted and defeated.

"We have a motive, Al," Barrow said. "Lisa Darius is the only person who can connect Martin to Sam Oberhurst. He couldn't get to her when he was in jail. I say we have at least probable cause. No sooner is he out than she's missing."

"And there was that phone call," Highsmith added.

"Ryder can't be certain there was a threat. The call can even be interpreted as a warning to Lisa to be careful of someone else." Page shook his head. "I'm not making the same mistake twice. Unless I'm certain we have probable cause, I'm not asking for a search warrant."

"Don't get gun-shy, Al," Highsmith warned. "We're talking about a life here."

"I know that," Page answered angrily. "But where do we search? His house? He's not going to be stupid enough to keep her there. Some property he owns? Which one? I'm as frustrated as you are, but we have to be patient."

Highsmith was about to say something when the intercom buzzed.

"I know you didn't want to be disturbed," his secretary said, "but Nancy Gordon is on the line."

Page felt cold. Highsmith and Barrow straightened. Page put the call on the speaker phone.

"Detective Gordon?"

"I'm sorry I disappeared on you, Mr. Page," a woman said. Page tried to remember what Gordon sounded like. He remembered a throaty quality to her voice, but their connection was bad and the woman's voice was distorted.

"Where are you?"

"I can't tell you that now," Gordon said. Page thought she sounded sluggish and uncertain.

"Have you read the news? Do you know Darius is out, because we didn't have your testimony at his bail hearing?"

"It couldn't be helped. You'll understand everything in a while."

"I'd like to understand it now, Detective. We have a situation here. Darius's wife has disappeared."

"I know. That's why I'm calling. I know where she is and you have to act quickly."

3

Darius Construction was in trouble. When Darius was arrested, the company was on the verge of bringing in two lucrative projects. Both jobs were now with other construction companies and no new projects would appear while Darius was under indictment. Darius had been counting on the income the projects would generate to help him with the company's financial problems. Without the new income, bankruptcy was a real possibility.

Darius spent the day closeted with his accountant, his attorney and his vice presidents working on a plan to save the company, but he had trouble keeping his mind on business. He needed Betsy Tannenbaum, and she had dropped him. At first he'd wanted her to represent him simply because he thought a feminist attorney would give him an edge with the jury. Then Betsy won the bail hearing and convinced him that she had the skills to save him. Their recent meeting had increased his respect. Tannenbaum was tough. Most women would have been too frightened to confront him alone. They would have brought a man for protection. Darius believed Betsy would never break under the pressure of a trial and he knew she would fight to the end for a client in whom she believed.

When the meeting ended at six p.m. Darius drove home. He punched in the alarm code for his gate and it swung open with a metallic creak. Darius glanced in the rearview mirror. He saw the gleam of headlights as a car drove past the gate, then the driveway turned and he lost his angle.

Darius entered the house through the garage and deactivated the alarm. The house was cool and quiet. While Lisa was living with him, there was always an undercurrent of noise in the background. Darius was learning to live without the murmur of kitchen appliances, the muted chatter from the television and the sounds Lisa made passing from room to room.

The living room looked sterile when he turned on the light. Darius took off his jacket and tie and poured himself a scotch. He wondered if there was a way to talk Betsy into coming back. Her anger was evident, but anger could cool. It was her fear that was keeping Betsy from him. He could not blame her for thinking him a monster after what she learned from Colby. Normally a woman's fear would excite Darius, but Betsy's fear was driving her from him and he could not think of a way to allay it.

Darius draped his tie and jacket over his arm and walked upstairs to his bedroom. He had barely eaten all day and his stomach growled. He switched on the bedroom light and set his glass on his dresser. As he turned toward the closet, a flash of color caught his eye. There was a black rose on his pillow. Beneath the rose was a sheet of stationery. Darius stared at the note. His stomach turned. He spun toward the doorway, but there was no one there. He strained for the slightest noise but heard only the normal house sounds.

Darius kept a gun in his dresser. He took it out. His heart was beating wildly. How could someone get into his house without setting off the alarm? Only he and Lisa knew the alarm code and . . . Darius froze. His mind made the logical jump and he headed for the basement, switching on the house lights as he went.

Darius paused at the top of the cellar stairs, knowing what he would see when he turned on the light. He heard the first siren when he was halfway down. He thought about going back, but he had to know. A police car skidded to a halt in front of the house as Darius reached the bottom of the stairs. He put his gun down, because he did not want to risk being shot. Besides, he would not need it. There was no one in the house with him. He knew that when he saw the way the body was arranged.

Lisa Darius lay on her back in the center of the basement. She was naked. Her stomach had been sliced open and her entrails poked through a gaping, blood-soaked hole. The body of Patricia Cross had been left in Henry Waters's basement in exactly this way.

4

As soon as Rick and Kathy drove away, Betsy went back to the kitchen and fixed herself something to eat. She had toyed with the idea of going out for dinner or calling a friend, but the idea of spending a quiet night alone was too appealing.

When she was finished with dinner, Betsy went into the living room and glanced at the television listings. Nothing looked interesting, so she settled into an easy chair with an Updike novel. She was just starting to get into it when the phone rang. Betsy sighed and ran into the kitchen to answer it.

"Mrs. Tannenbaum?"

"Yes."

"This is Alan Page." He sounded angry. "I'm at Martin Darius's estate. We've rearrested him."

"On what grounds?"

"He just murdered his wife."

"My God! What happened?"

"Your client gutted Lisa Darius in his basement."

"Oh, no."

"You did her a real favor when you convinced Norwood to release Darius on bail," Page said bitterly. "Your client wants to talk to you."

"Do you believe me now, Tannenbaum?" Darius asked. "Do you see what's going on?"

"Don't say anything. The police are listening, Martin. I'll see you in the morning."

"Then you're sticking with me?"

"I didn't say that."

"You've got to. Ask yourself how the police found out about Lisa and you'll know I'm innocent."

Was Darius really innocent? It didn't make sense that he would kill his wife and leave her body to decompose in his own basement. Betsy thought over what she knew about the Hunter's Point case. Betsy imagined Henry Waters answering the door, Nancy Gordon walking down the steps to Waters's basement, the shocked look on Waters's face when he saw Patricia Cross sprawled in her own blood, disemboweled. It was Patricia Cross all over again. Darius had asked her to find out how the police knew Lisa Darius was in his basement. She tried to remember how the police had found out about Patricia Cross.

"Put Page back on," she told Darius.

"I don't want anyone talking to Darius," she told the district attorney.

"I wouldn't think of it," Page replied rudely.

"You're wasting your anger on me, Alan. I knew Lisa Darius better than you did. This hurts, believe me."

Page was silent for a moment. He sounded subdued when he spoke.

"You're right. I had no business biting your head off. I'm as mad at myself for screwing up at the bail hearing as I am at you for doing such a good job. But he's staying in this time. Norwood won't make another mistake."

"Alan, how did you know you'd find Lisa's body in the basement?"

Betsy held her breath while Page decided if he would answer.

"Ah, you'll find out anyway. It was a tip."

"Who told you?"

"I can't tell you that, now."

A tip, just like the anonymous tip that led the Hunter's Point police to Henry Waters's basement. Betsy hung up the phone. Her doubts about Darius's guilt were starting to grow. Martin Darius had murdered the women in Hunter's Point, but was he innocent of the Portland murders?

Chapter Twenty-four

I

The door to the jail interview room opened and Darius walked in. He was dressed in the shirt and suit pants he had been wearing when he was arrested. His eyes were bloodshot and he seemed less self-assured than he looked during their other meetings.

"I knew you'd be here, Tannenbaum," Darius said, trying to appear calm but sounding a little desperate.

"I don't want to be. I'm required to represent you until another attorney relieves me of my obligation."

"You can't leave me in the lurch."

"I haven't changed my mind, Martin. I meant everything I said the other day."

"Even though you know I'm innocent?"

"I don't know that for certain. And even if you are innocent, it doesn't change what you did in Hunter's Point."

Darius leaned forward slightly and locked his eyes on hers.

"You do know I'm innocent, unless you think I'm

335

stupid enough to murder my wife in my basement, then call Alan Page and tell him where to find the corpse."

Darius was right, of course. The case against him was too pat and the timing of this new killing too opportune. Doubts had kept Betsy up for most of the night, but they had not changed the way she felt about Darius.

"We'll be going up to court in a few minutes. Page will arraign you on a complaint charging you with Lisa's murder. He'll ask for a no-bail hold and ask Norwood to revoke your bail on the other charges. I can't see any way of convincing the judge to let you out on bail."

"Tell the judge what we know about Gordon. Tell him I'm being framed."

"We have no proof of that."

"So this is how it's going to be. I guess I figured you wrong, Tannenbaum. What happened to your high-blown sense of ethics? Your oath as an attorney? You're going to throw this one, aren't you, because you can't stand me?"

Betsy flushed with anger. "I'm not throwing a goddamn thing. I shouldn't even be here. What I am doing is letting you know the facts of life. Judge Norwood took a big chance letting you out. When he sees the pictures of Lisa spread-eagled in your basement with her guts pulled through her abdominal wall, he is not going to feel like letting you out again."

"The State calls Victor Ryder, Your Honor," Alan Page said, turning toward the rear of the room to watch the courtly justice walk past the spectators and through the bar of the court. Ryder was six feet three with a full head of snow-white hair. He walked with a slight limp from a wound he had received in World War Two. Ryder kept his back rigid, scrupulously avoiding eye contact with

Martin Darius, as if he was afraid of the rage that might overpower him if he set eyes on the man.

"For the record," Page said as soon as Ryder was sworn, "you are a justice of the Oregon Supreme Court and the father of Lisa Darius?"

"Yes," Ryder answered, his voice cracking slightly.

"Your daughter was married to the defendant, was she not?"

"Yes, sir."

"When Mr. Darius was arrested, did your daughter move in with you?"

"She did."

"While Lisa was staying at your home, did her husband phone her?"

"Repeatedly, Mr. Page. He phoned from jail several times each evening."

"Is it true that inmates can only make collect calls?"

"Yes. All his calls were collect."

"Did your daughter accept the calls?"

"She instructed me to refuse them."

"To the best of your knowledge, did your daughter speak to the defendant while he was incarcerated?"

"She may have, once or twice immediately after his arrest. Once she moved in with me, she stopped."

"What was your daughter's attitude toward her husband?"

"She was scared to death of him."

"Did this fear increase or decrease when Mr. Darius was released on bail?"

"It increased. She was terrified he would come for her."

"Did the defendant phone Lisa Darius after his release on bail?"

"Yes, sir. The first evening."

"Did you hear the conversation?"

"Snatches of it."

"Did you hear the defendant make any threats?"

"I believe he told her she would not be safe in Portland."

"When you say you believe he said this, what do you mean?"

"Lisa told me he said it. I was standing at Lisa's shoulder and could hear some of what he said."

"Do you know if Mrs. Darius believed the defendant meant this as a threat?"

"She was confused. She told me she wasn't certain what he meant. He seemed to be implying Lisa was in danger from someone else, but that didn't make sense. I took it that he was threatening her indirectly, so no blame could be placed on him."

"Justice Ryder, when was the last time you saw your daughter alive?"

For a brief moment the judge lost his composure. He sipped from a cup of water before answering.

"We had breakfast together between seven and seven-thirty a.m. Then I drove to Salem."

"When did you return home?"

"Around six in the evening."

"Was your daughter home?"

"No."

"Did you see anything in the house that alarmed you?"

"The television was on, but no one was home. The sound was high enough so Lisa should have heard it and turned it off before she left."

"Was there evidence that she'd had a visitor?"

"There were two coffee cups in the kitchen and some coffee cake was out, as if she'd been talking to someone."

"Did your daughter leave a note telling where she was going?"

"No."

"Nothing further."

"Your witness, Mrs. Tannenbaum," Judge Norwood said.

"He's lying," Darius whispered. "I never threatened Lisa. I was warning her."

"He's not lying, Martin. He's saying what he honestly believes happened. If I push him, he'll just harden his position."

"Bullshit. I've seen you take witnesses apart. Ryder is a pompous asshole. You can make him look like a fool."

Betsy took a deep breath, because she did not want to lose her temper. Then she leaned over to Darius and spoke quietly.

"Do you want me to push Justice Ryder until he breaks down, Martin? Do you really think it will help you get bail if I cause one of the most respected judges in the state, and the father of a young woman who has been brutally murdered, to crack up in open court in front of one of his colleagues?"

Darius started to say something, then shut up and turned away from Betsy.

"No questions, Your Honor," Betsy said.

"Our next witness is Detective Richard Kassel," Page told the judge.

Richard Kassel sauntered down the aisle. He was dressed in a brown tweed sports coat, tan slacks, a white shirt and a bright yellow print tie. His shoes were polished and his black hair was styled. He had the smug look of a person who took himself too seriously.

"Detective Kassel, how are you employed?"

"I'm a detective with the Portland Police Bureau."

"Did you arrest the defendant yesterday evening?"

"Yes, sir."

"Tell the judge how that came about."

Kassel swiveled toward the judge.

"Detective Rittner and I received a call over the police radio. Based on that communication, I entered the grounds. The door to the defendant's house was locked. We identified ourselves as police and demanded that the defendant open the door. He complied. Detective Rittner and I secured the defendant and waited for the other cars to arrive, as we had been ordered to do."

"Did other officers arrive soon after?"

Kassel nodded. "About fifteen minutes after we arrived, you and Detective Barrow arrived, followed by several others."

Betsy's brow furrowed. She checked something she had written during Justice Ryder's testimony. Then she made some notes on her pad.

"Did you discover the body?" Page asked.

"No, sir. Our instructions were to stay with the defendant. The body was discovered by other officers."

"Did you give Mr. Darius his *Miranda* warnings?"

"Yes, sir."

"Did Mr. Darius make any statements?"

"Other than to ask to call his lawyer, no."

"Your witness, Mrs. Tannenbaum."

Betsy looked unsure of herself. She asked the judge for a minute and pretended to look through a police report while she worked through her thoughts.

"Detective Kassel," Betsy asked cautiously, "who told you to enter the Darius estate and arrest Mr. Darius?"

"Detective Barrow."

"Did he say why you were to arrest Mr. Darius?"

"Yes, ma'am. He said there was a tip that the defendant had killed his wife and her body was in his basement."

"Did Detective Barrow tell you who gave him the tip?"

"I didn't ask."

"How was Mr. Darius dressed when he opened the door for you?"

"He was wearing a white shirt and pants."

"Mr. Darius, please stand up."

Darius stood.

"Are these the pants?"

Detective Kassel took a second to look at Darius. "Yeah. Those are the ones we arrested him in."

"And this is the white shirt?"

"Yes."

"It's in the same condition as when you arrested him?"

"Yes."

"There's no blood on this shirt, is there?"

Kassel paused, then answered, "No, ma'am."

"Did you view the body of Lisa Darius at any point?"

"Yes."

"When it was still in the basement?"

"Yes."

"Mrs. Darius was disemboweled, was she not?"

"Yes."

"There was blood all over that basement, wasn't there?"

"Yes," Kassel answered grudgingly.

"The gate to the Darius estate is locked. How did you get in?"

"Detective Barrow had the combination."

"How is it that you arrived at the Darius estate so far ahead of Detective Barrow, Mr. Page and the other officers?" Betsy asked with an easy smile that disguised the tension she was feeling. She would know if her suspicions were correct after a few more questions.

"We were parked outside it."

"Was that by chance?"

"No, ma'am. We had the defendant under surveillance."

"How long had you had him under surveillance?"

"We've been surveilling him for quite a while. Back before his first arrest."

"Just you and Detective Rittner?"

"Oh, no. There were three teams. We switched off. You can't do that twenty-four hours."

"Of course not. When did your shift start on the day you arrested Mr. Darius?"

"Around three in the afternoon."

"Where did you start?"

"Outside his office."

"I assume you took over for another surveillance team?"

"Right. Detectives Padovici and Kristol."

"When had they started?"

"Around five in the morning."

"Where did they start?"

"The defendant's house."

"Why did the other team start so early?"

"The defendant gets up around five-thirty and leaves for work around six-thirty. By getting there at five, we kept him covered when he left his place."

"Is that what Kristol and Padovici did?"

"Yeah."

"I suppose they followed Mr. Darius to work?"

"That's what they said."

"Anything unusual happen that day, according to the detectives?"

"No. He went right to work. I don't think he ever left his office. Detective Padovici said it looked like he sent out for sandwiches at lunchtime. Around six a bunch of guys in suits left. I think they were having a meeting."

"When Mr. Darius left, you followed him home?"

"Right."

"Was he ever out of your sight?"

"No, ma'am."

"How long after Mr. Darius arrived home did you receive the instructions from Detective Barrow to enter the Darius estate and arrest Mr. Darius?"

"Not long."

"Give me your best guess."

"Uh, about fifteen, twenty minutes."

Betsy paused. She felt sick about asking the next series of questions, but her sense of duty, and the possibility that the answers could prove her client innocent, overcame her revulsion at the prospect of Martin Darius walking free.

"Did you ever see Mr. Darius with Lisa Darius that day?"

"No, ma'am."

"What about Padovici and Kristol? Did they say they saw Mr. Darius with his wife?"

Kassel frowned, as if he suddenly realized where Betsy's questions were leading. Betsy looked to her left and saw Alan Page in an animated discussion with Randy Highsmith.

"I can't recall," he answered hesitantly.

"I assume you wrote a daily surveillance log listing any unusual occurrences?"

"Yes."

"And the other members of the surveillance team also kept logs?"

"Yes."

"Where are the logs?"

"Detective Barrow has them."

Betsy stood. "Your Honor, I would like the logs produced and Detectives Kristol and Padovici made available for questioning. Justice Ryder testified that he last saw his daughter at seven-thirty a.m. Detective Kassel says Padovici and Kristol reported that Mr. Darius left his estate at six-thirty and went directly to work. If neither team saw Mr. Darius with his wife during the day, when did he kill her? We can produce the people who were with Mr. Darius yesterday. They'll say he was in his office from about seven a.m. until a little after six p.m."

Judge Norwood looked troubled. Alan Page leaped to his feet.

"This is nonsense, Judge. The surveillance was on Darius, not his wife. The body was in the basement. Mr. Darius was with the body."

"Your Honor," Betsy said, "Mr. Darius could not have killed his wife before he got home, and he was only home for a short time when Detective Kassel arrived. The person who disemboweled Lisa Darius would have blood all over him. There was no blood on my client. Look at his white shirt and his pants.

"I suggest that Mr. Darius is being set up. Someone was at Justice Ryder's house having coffee with Lisa Darius during the day. It wasn't the defendant. Lisa Darius left the house without turning off the television. That's because she was forced to leave. That person took her to the estate and murdered her in the basement, then phoned in the anonymous tip that led the police to the body."

"That's absurd," Page said. "Who is this mysterious person? I suppose you'll suggest the mystery man also butchered the four people we found at your client's construction site."

"Your Honor," Betsy said, "ask yourself who knew the body of Lisa Darius was in Mr. Darius's basement. Only the killer or someone who saw the murder. Is Mr. Page suggesting that Mr. Darius found his wife alive in his home, butchered her in the fifteen minutes or so between the time Detective Kassel lost sight of him and the time Detective Kassel arrested him, got no blood on his white shirt while disemboweling her and was such a good citizen that he reported himself to the police so they could arrest him for murder?"

Judge Norwood looked troubled. Betsy and Alan Page watched him intently.

"Mrs. Tannenbaum," the judge said, "your theory depends on Mr. Darius leaving his estate at six-thirty and being in his office all day."

"Yes, Your Honor."

The judge turned to Alan Page. "I'm keeping Mr. Darius in jail over the weekend. I want you to give copies of the logs to Mrs. Tannenbaum and I want the detectives here Monday morning. I'll tell you, Mr. Page, this business has me seriously concerned. You better have a good explanation for me. Right now, I can't see how this man killed his wife."

2

"Goddamn it, Ross, how did this slip by you?"

"I'm sorry, Al. I don't review the log entries every day."

"If Darius didn't go near Justice Ryder's house, we have trouble, Al," Randy Highsmith said.

"The surveillance teams must have screwed up," Page insisted. "She was there. She got into the basement somehow. Didn't you tell me there were paths through the woods? The surveillance teams weren't watching Lisa. She could have used the paths to sneak onto the estate while the teams were tailing Darius."

"Why would she go to the estate if she was terrified of Darius?" Highsmith asked.

"He could have sweet-talked her over the phone," Page said. "They were man and wife."

"Then why sneak in?" Highsmith asked. "Why not drive through the front gate and up to the front door? It's her house. It makes no sense for her to sneak in if she was going back willingly."

"Maybe the press has been hounding her and she wanted to avoid reporters."

"I don't buy that."

"There's got to be a logical explanation," Page answered, frustrated by the seeming impossibility of the situation.

"There are a few other things that are nagging at me, Al," Highsmith told his boss.

"Let's hear them," Page said.

"How did Nancy Gordon know where to find the body? Tannenbaum's right. Darius couldn't have killed Lisa at night, because she was alive in the morning. He couldn't have killed her off the estate. We had him under surveillance every minute during the day. If Darius did it, he killed her in the house. There aren't windows in the basement. How would anyone else know what was going on? There are problems with the case, Al. We have to face them."

3

"How was the meeting?"

"Don't ask," Raymond Colby told his wife. "My head's like putty. Help me with this tie. I'm all thumbs."

"Here. Let me," Ellen said, untying the Windsor knot.

"Can you fix me a drink? I'll be in the den. I want to watch the late news."

Ellen pecked her husband on the cheek and walked toward the liquor cabinet. "Why don't you just go to bed?"

"Bruce Smith made some dumb comment on the highway bill. Wayne insists I hear it. It should be on toward the top of the news. Besides, I'm too wound up to go right to sleep."

Colby went into the den and turned on the news. Ellen came in and handed the senator his drink.

"If this doesn't relax you, we'll think of something that will," she said mischievously.

Colby smiled. "What makes you think I have the energy for that kind of hanky-panky?"

"A man who can't rise to the occasion shouldn't be on the Supreme Court."

Colby laughed. "You've become a pervert in your old age."

"And about time, too."

They both laughed, then Colby suddenly sobered. He pointed the remote control at the screen and turned up the volume.

". . . a startling new development in the case against millionaire builder Martin Darius, who is accused of the torture-murder of three women and one man in Portland, Oregon. A week ago Darius was released on bail when trial judge Patrick Norwood ruled that there was insufficient evidence to hold him. Yesterday evening, Darius was rearrested when police found the body of his wife, Lisa Darius, in the basement of the Darius mansion. A police spokesman said she had been tortured and killed in a manner similar to the other victims.

"Today, in a court hearing, Betsy Tannenbaum, Darius's attorney, argued that Darius was the victim of a frame-up after it was revealed that police surveillance teams followed Darius all day on the day his wife was murdered and never saw him with his wife. The hearing will resume Monday.

"On a less serious note, Mayor Clinton Vance is reported to have . . ."

Colby turned off the set and closed his eyes.

"What's wrong?" Ellen asked.

"How would you feel if I was not confirmed by the Senate?"

"That's not possible."

Colby heard the uncertainty in his wife's voice. He was so tired. "I have to make a decision. It concerns something I did when I was governor of New York. A secret that I thought would stay buried forever."

"What kind of secret?" Ellen asked hesitantly.

Colby opened his eyes. He saw his wife's concern and took her hand.

"Not a secret about us, love. It concerns something I did ten years ago. A decision I had to make. A decision I would make again."

"I don't understand."

"I'll explain everything, then you tell me what I should do."

Chapter Twenty-five

I

Alan Page looked at the illuminated digital display on his alarm clock as he groped for the phone in the dark. It was four-fifteen.

"Is this Alan Page, the district attorney for Multnomah County?" a man asked.

"It is, and I'll still be d.a. when the sun's up."

"Sorry about that, but we have a three-hour time difference here and my flight leaves in thirty minutes."

"Who is this?" Page asked, awake enough to be annoyed.

"My name is Wayne Turner. I'm Senator Raymond Colby's administrative assistant. I used to be a detective with the Hunter's Point Police Department. Nancy Gordon and I are good friends."

Page swung his legs over the side of the bed and sat up.

"You've got my attention. What's this about?"

"I'll be at the Sheraton Airport Hotel by ten, your time. Senator Colby wants me to brief you."

"This concerns Darius?"

"We knew him as Peter Lake. The senator wants you fully informed about certain matters you may not know."

"Such as?"

"Not over the phone, Mr. Page."

"Is this going to help my case against Darius?"

"My information will make a conviction certain."

"Can you give me a clue about what you're going to say?"

"Not over the phone," Turner repeated, "and not to anyone but you."

"Randy Highsmith is my chief criminal deputy. You talked to him. Can I bring him along?"

"Let me make myself clear, Mr. Page. Senator Colby is going as far out on a limb for you as someone in public life can go. My job is to see that the limb doesn't get sawed off. When Mr. Highsmith called, I gave him the runaround. You're going to hear the things I did not want Mr. Highsmith to know. This is not by my choosing. It's the senator who insisted I fly to Portland. It's my job to do what he wants, but I'm going to protect him as much as I am able. So there will be no witnesses, no notes and you can expect to be patted down for a wire. You can also be assured that what you hear will be worth any inconvenience you suffered by being awakened before dawn. Now, I've got to make my flight, if you still want me to."

"Come on down, Mr. Turner. I'll respect your wishes. See you at ten."

Page hung up and sat in the dark, wide-awake. What would Turner tell him? What possible connection was there between the President's nominee to the United States Supreme Court and Martin Darius? Whatever it was, Turner thought it would guarantee Darius's conviction, and that was what mattered. Darius would pay. Since the first bail hearing, the case seemed to be slipping away from him. Not even Lisa Darius's tragic death had given the prosecution substance. Maybe Turner's information would save him.

Wayne Turner opened the door and let Alan Page into his hotel room. Turner was impeccably dressed in a three-piece suit. Page's suit was wrinkled, his shoes unpolished. If anyone looked like he had just flown three thousand miles, it was Page.

"Let's get the striptease out of the way," Turner said when the door was closed. Page took off his jacket. Turner patted him down expertly.

"Satisfied?" Page asked.

"Not one bit, Mr. Page. If I had my druthers, I'd be back in D.C. You want some coffee?"

"Coffee would be nice."

There was a thermos on a coffee table and the remains of a sandwich. Turner poured for both of them.

"Before I tell you a damn thing, we have to have some ground rules. There is an excellent chance that Senator Colby will not be confirmed if what I tell you is made public. I want your word that you will not call the senator or me as a witness in any court proceeding or make what I tell you available to anyone else—even members of your staff—unless it is absolutely necessary to secure the conviction of Martin Darius."

"Mr. Turner, I respect the senator. I want to see him on the Court. The fact that he's willing to risk his nomination to give me this information reinforces the feelings I've had about his worth to this country. Believe me, I will do nothing to jeopardize his chances, if I can help it. But I want you to know, up front, this prosecution is in a lot of trouble. If I had to bet, I'd pick Martin Darius to walk, based on what I've got now."

2

Kathy insisted on eating at the Spaghetti Factory again. There was the usual forty-five-minute wait and the service was slow. They were not back in Rick's apartment until after nine. Kathy was pooped, but she was so excited she did not want to go to bed. Rick spent half an hour reading to her. He was surprised how much he enjoyed reading to his daughter. That was something Betsy usually did. He enjoyed dinner too. In fact, he had enjoyed all the time they spent together.

The doorbell rang. Rick checked his watch. Who would be calling at nine forty-five? Rick looked through the peephole. It took him a moment to remember the woman who was standing in the hall.

"Miss Sloane, isn't it?" Rick asked, when the door was open.

"You have a good memory."

"What can I do for you?"

Sloane looked embarrassed. "I really shouldn't intrude like this, but I remembered your address. You told Betsy before you left the office. I was in the neighborhood. I know it's late, but I was going to arrange a meeting with you for background for my article, anyway, so I thought I'd take a chance. If you're busy, I can come some other time."

"Actually, that would be best. I've got Kathy with me and she just went to sleep. I don't want to disturb her, and I'm pretty beat myself."

"Say no more, Mr. Tannenbaum. Could we meet later in the week?"

"Do you really want to talk to me? Betsy and I are separated, you know."

"I do know, but I would like to talk to you about her.

She's a remarkable woman and your view of her would be very informative."

"I'm not sure I want to discuss our marriage for publication."

"Will you think it over?"

Rick hesitated, then said, "Sure. Call me at the office."

"Thank you, Mr. Tannenbaum. Do you have a card?"

Rick patted his pockets and remembered his wallet was in the bedroom.

"Step in for a minute. I'll get you one."

Rick turned his back on Nora Sloane and started into the apartment. Nora was taller than Rick. She glided behind him and looped her left arm around his neck while she drew the knife out of her deep coat pocket with her right hand. Rick felt himself jerked up on his toes when Sloane leaned back and tilted his chin up. He did not feel anything when the knife slashed across his throat, because his body went into shock. There was a jolt when the knife slid into his back, then another jolt. Rick tried to struggle, but he lost control of his body. Blood spurted from his neck. He viewed the red fountain like a tourist staring at a landmark. The room wavered. Rick felt his energy drain out of him along with the blood that drenched the floor. Nora Sloane released her hold and Rick slid to the carpet. She closed the apartment door quietly and looked around. There was a living room at the end of the hall. Sloane walked through it, down another hall and stopped at the first door. She pushed it open gently and stared at Kathy. The darling little girl was asleep. She looked lovely.

Chapter Twenty-six

Betsy was finishing breakfast when the doorbell rang. A light rain had been falling all morning and it was hard to see Nora Sloane through the streaked pane in the kitchen window. She was standing on the welcome mat holding an umbrella in one hand and a large shopping bag in the other. Betsy carried her coffee cup to the front door. Nora smiled when it opened.

"Can I come in?" Sloane asked.

"Sure," Betsy said, stepping aside. Sloane leaned her umbrella against the wall in the entryway and unbuttoned her raincoat. She was wearing tight-fitting jeans, a light blue work shirt and a dark blue sweater.

"Can we sit down?" Nora asked, gesturing toward the living room. Betsy was confused by this morning visit, but she sat down on the couch. Nora sat in an armchair across from her and took a gun out of the shopping bag. The coffee cup slipped from Betsy's fingers and shattered when it struck the marble tabletop. A dark brown puddle formed around the shards.

"I'm sorry I frightened you," Sloane said calmly.

Betsy stared at the gun.

"Don't let this bother you," Sloane said. "I wouldn't hurt you. I like you. I'm just not certain how you'll react when I explain why I'm here, and I want to be certain you don't do anything foolish. You won't do anything rash, will you?"

"No."

"Good. Now, listen carefully to me. Martin Darius must not be freed. On Monday, before the hearing starts, you will ask to use Judge Norwood's jury room to speak in private with your client. There's a door that opens into the corridor. When I knock on the door, you'll let me in."

"Then what?"

"That's none of your concern."

"Why should I do this for you?"

Nora reached into the shopping bag and pulled out Oliver. She handed the stuffed animal to Betsy.

"I have Kathy. She's a sweet child. She'll be fine, if you do what I tell you."

"How . . . how did you get Kathy? Rick didn't call me."

"Rick's dead." Betsy gaped at Nora, not certain she had heard her correctly. "He hurt you. Men are like that. Martin is the worst example. Making us act like dogs, forcing us to fuck each other, mounting us as if we were inanimate objects, cartoon women, so he could live out his fantasies. But other men do the same thing in different ways. Like Rick. He used you, then discarded you."

"Oh, God!" Betsy wept, stunned and only half-believing what Sloane said. "He's not dead."

"I did it for you, Betsy."

"No, Nora. He didn't deserve this."

Sloane's features hardened. "They all deserve to die, Betsy. All of them."

"You're Samantha Reardon, aren't you?"

Reardon nodded.

"I don't understand. After what you went through, how could you kill those women?"

"That was hard, Betsy. I made certain they didn't suffer. I only marked them when they were anesthetized. If there was another way, I would have chosen it."

Of course, Betsy thought, if Reardon kidnapped the women to frame Martin Darius, it would be easier to deal with them if they were unconscious. A nurse who assisted in surgery would know all about anesthetics like pentobarbital.

Reardon smiled warmly, reversed the gun and held it out to Betsy.

"Don't be afraid. I said I wouldn't hurt you. Take it. I want you to see how much I trust you."

Betsy half-reached, then stopped.

"Go on," Reardon urged her. "Do as I say. I know you won't shoot me. I'm the only one who knows where Kathy is. If I was killed, no one would be able to find her. She'd starve to death. That's a cruel and horrible way to die. I know. I almost died from starvation."

Betsy took the gun. It was cold to the touch and heavy. She had the power to kill Reardon, but she felt utterly helpless.

"If I do what you say, you'll give me Kathy unharmed?"

"Kathy is my insurance policy, just as I was Peter Lake's. Nancy Gordon told me all about the governor's pardon. I've learned so much from Martin Darius. I can't wait to thank him, in person."

Reardon sat quietly for a while. She did not move. Betsy tried to stay just as still, but it was impossible. She shifted on the couch. The seconds passed. Reardon looked as if she was having trouble framing her thoughts. When she spoke, she looked into Betsy's eyes with an expression of deep concern and addressed Betsy the way a teacher addresses a prize pupil when she wants to make certain that the student understands a key point.

"You have to see Darius for what he is to understand what I'm doing. He is the Devil. Not just a bad person, but pure evil. Ordinary measures wouldn't have worked. Who would believe me? I've been committed twice. When I tried to tell people in Hunter's Point, no one would listen. Now I know why. I always suspected there were others working with Martin. Nancy Gordon confirmed that. She told me all about the conspiracy to free Martin and blame Henry Waters. Only the Devil would have so much power. Think of it. The governor, the mayor, policemen. Only Gordon resisted. And she was the only woman."

Reardon watched Betsy intently. "I'll bet you'll be tempted to call the police as soon as I leave. You mustn't do that. They might catch me. I'll never tell where Kathy is if I'm caught. You must be especially strong when the police tell you Rick is dead and Kathy has been kidnapped. Don't weaken and give me away."

Reardon smiled coldly.

"You must not put your faith in the police. You must not believe that they can break me. I can assure you that nothing the police can do to me compares to what Martin did, and Martin never broke me. Oh, he thought he did. He thought I was submitting, but only my body submitted. My mind stayed strong and focused.

"At night I could hear the others whimpering. I never whimpered. I folded my hate inside me and kept it safe and warm. Then I waited. When they told me Waters was the one, I knew they were lying. I knew Martin had done something to them to make them lie. The Devil can do that—twist people, change them around like clay figures—but he didn't change me."

"Is Kathy warm?" Betsy asked. "She can get sick if she's in a damp place."

"Kathy is warm, Betsy. I'm not a monster like Darius. I'm not inhuman or insensitive. I need Kathy to be safe. I don't want to harm her."

Betsy did not hate Reardon. Reardon was insane. It was Darius she hated. Darius knew exactly what he was doing in Hunter's Point when he created Reardon by stripping her of her humanity. Betsy handed the gun to Reardon.

"Take it. I don't want it."

"Thank you, Betsy. I'm pleased to see you trust me as much as I trust you."

"What you're doing is wrong. Kathy is a baby. She never did anything to you."

"I know. I feel badly about taking her, but I couldn't think of any other way to force you to help me. You have such high principles. I was upset when you told me you were dropping Darius as a client. I counted on you to get me close to him. But I admired you for refusing to represent him. So many lawyers would have continued for the money. I helped you with your marital problems so you'd see how much I respect you."

Reardon stood up. "I've got to go. Please don't worry. Kathy's safe and warm. Do what I told you and she'll be back with you soon."

"Can you have Kathy call me? She'll be frightened. It would help her if she heard my voice."

"I'm sure you're sincere, Betsy, but you might try to have my calls traced. I can't take that chance."

"Then give this to her," Betsy said, handing Oliver to Reardon. "It will make her feel safe."

Reardon took the stuffed animal. Tears streaked down Betsy's face.

"She's all I have. Please don't hurt her."

Reardon closed the door without answering. Betsy ran into the kitchen and watched her walk up the driveway, back straight, unwavering. At that moment, Betsy suddenly knew how the husbands felt when they came home to find only notes that read "Gone, But Not Forgotten."

Betsy wandered back to the living room. It was still dark, though a sliver of light was starting to show on the fringe of the hills. Betsy slumped on the couch, exhausted by the effort it took to keep her emotions at bay, unable to think and in shock. She wanted to mourn Rick, but all she could think about was Kathy. Until Kathy was safe, her heart would have no time to ache for Rick.

Betsy tried not to think of the women in the autopsy photographs, she tried to block her memory of the picture Darius had painted of his dehumanized prisoners, but she could not stop herself from seeing Kathy, her little girl, frantic and defenseless, curled up in the dark, terrified of every sound.

Time passed in a blur. The rain stopped and the sky changed from dark to light without her noticing. The pool of cold coffee had spread between the fragments of the broken cup and across the top of the coffee table. Betsy walked into the kitchen. There was a roll of paper towels under the sink. She tore some off the roll, found a small paper bag and grabbed a large sponge. Doing something helped. Moving helped.

Betsy picked up the pieces of the cup and put them in the paper bag. She sponged off the tabletop and used the paper towels to wipe it down. As she worked, she thought about help. The police were out. She could not control them. Betsy believed Samantha Reardon. If Reardon thought Betsy betrayed her, she would kill Kathy. If the police arrested her, she would never tell where she was holding Kathy.

Betsy put the wet towels into the bag, carried the bag into the kitchen and put it in the garbage. Finding Kathy was the only thing she cared about. Reggie Stewart was an expert at finding people and she could control him, because Reggie worked for her. More important, he was sensitive. He would put finding Kathy ahead of arresting Samantha Reardon. Betsy would have to act quickly. It was only a matter of time before someone discovered Rick's body and the police investigation started.

Reggie Stewart's flight from Hunter's Point landed in Portland after midnight, and Betsy's call aroused him from a sound sleep. He had wanted to go back to bed, but Betsy sounded so upset and cryptic on the phone, he was concerned. Stewart smiled when Betsy opened the door, but his smile faded as soon as he saw Betsy's face.

"What's up, Chief?"

Betsy did not answer Stewart until they were seated in the living room. She looked like she was barely under control.

"You were right. Samantha Reardon killed the people at the construction site."

"How do you know that?"

"She told me, this morning. She . . ."

Betsy closed her eyes and took a deep breath. Her shoulders started to shake. She put a hand over her eyes. Betsy did not want to cry. Stewart knelt next to her. He touched her, gently.

"What's happening, Betsy? Tell me. I'm your friend. If I can help you, I will."

"She killed Rick," Betsy sobbed, collapsing into Reggie's arms.

Stewart held her close and let her cry.

"Have you told the police?"

"I can't, Reggie. She has Kathy hidden somewhere. The police don't know Rick is dead. If they arrest Samantha, she won't tell where she has Kathy hidden and she'll starve to death. That's why I need you. You have to find Kathy."

"You don't want me, Betsy. You want the cops and the FBI. They're much better equipped to find Kathy than I am. They have computers, manpower . . ."

"I believe Samantha when she says Kathy will die if she learns I went to the police. Reardon has already murdered the four people at the site, Lisa Darius and Rick."

"How do you know Reardon so well?"

"The day after Darius hired me, a woman calling herself Nora Sloane phoned me. She said she wanted to meet me for lunch to discuss an article she was writing about women defense attorneys. She wanted to use my cases as the centerpiece. I was flattered. When Darius was arrested, she was already my friend. When she asked if she could tag along while I worked up Martin's case, I agreed."

"Reardon?"

"Yes."

"Why did she kill Rick?"

"She said she killed Rick because he left me."

"If she killed Rick because he hurt you, why hurt you more by kidnapping Kathy?"

Betsy decided not to tell Stewart about Reardon's instructions. She trusted her investigator, but she was afraid Stewart would warn the police if he learned of Reardon's plan to get into the jury room with Darius.

"After I found out Martin killed the women in Hunter's Point, I told him I wouldn't represent him, and I told Reardon I was dropping Martin as a client. She was very upset. I think she wants to be able to control the case. With Kathy as a prisoner, she can force me to do things that will ensure Martin's conviction. If you don't find Kathy, I'll have to do what she says."

Stewart walked back and forth, thinking. Betsy wiped her eyes. Talking to someone helped.

"What do you know about Reardon?" Stewart asked. "Have you seen her car? Has she mentioned anything about where she lives? When you met for lunch did she pay with a credit card?"

"I've been trying to think about those things, but I really don't know anything about her. I've never seen her drive, but I'm certain she has a car. She had to transport the bodies to the construction site, my house is out of the way and she's attended all of Darius's court appearances."

"What about where she's living? Has she mentioned a long ride to town, how beautiful the view is in the country? Do you have her phone number?"

"She's never talked much about herself, now that I think about it. We've always talked about me or Darius or the battered women cases and never about her. I don't think I ever asked her where she lives. The one time I asked for her phone number, she said she would call me, and I didn't press her. I do remember that she paid for the lunch with cash. I don't think I've ever seen a piece of i.d."

"Okay. Let's hit this from another angle. Darius chose an isolated farmhouse so no one would see him bringing the women there and to cut the chances that anyone would stumble onto the women while he was away. Sloane doesn't have the problem of a wife and job, she could stay with the women most of the time, but she came to court when Darius had appearances and she met with you a number of times. I'm betting she's living in a rural area that's near enough to Portland so she can come to town, then get back, easily. The house probably has a basement so she can keep her prisoners out of sight. She'd also have to have electricity . . ."

"I asked if she'd let Kathy phone me. She said she wouldn't because she was worried I might trace her calls. She must have a phone," Betsy said.

"Good. That's the way to think. Utilities, a phone, garbage service. And she's a single woman. I have contacts at Portland General Electric and the phone company who can check to see if a Nora Sloane or Samantha Reardon started phone service or electricity around the time Reardon came to Portland. I've got a buddy at the Motor Vehicle Division who can run her names to see if we can get her address off a license application.

"She probably rented the house. I bet she set everything up the first time she was in Portland, so it would be ready when she moved back, but she probably didn't start the services until she came here the second time.

"I'll call Reardon's landlady in Hunter's Point and try to get the exact date she followed Oberhurst and the date she returned to Portland. Then I'll check real estate listings for rural houses with basements for rent in the tri-county area for the first time she was in Portland. I'll see how many were rented by a single woman . . ."

"Why not purchased? It would be safer. She wouldn't have to worry about the owner coming to the house to collect the rent or check on its condition."

"Yeah. She'd think of that. But I had the impression she didn't have a lot of money. She was renting in Hunter's Point and she had a low-paying job. I'm guessing she's renting. I'll cross-check what we find about the utilities with the rentals."

"How long will that take?"

The look of excitement on Stewart's face faded.

"That's the problem with using me instead of the police, Betsy. It's going to take a while. We can hire people to do some of the work, like checking the real estate ads, then I can follow up, but this is all very time-consuming and we could miss her altogether. She may have said she was married and her husband was coming later. She may have found a house in the city that suited her purposes. She may have rented under one name and taken the phone and utilities under another. Fake i.d. is pretty easy to come by.

"Even if I've doped this out correctly, it's a weekend. I don't know how many of my contacts I can get through to and when they can get into their offices to do the work."

Betsy looked defeated. "We don't have a lot of time. I don't know how well she's taking care of Kathy or what Reardon will do to her, if she decides she doesn't need me."

"Maybe you should reconsider. The police and the FBI can be discreet."

"No," Betsy said emphatically. "She said Kathy would die if I told them. There would be too many people involved. There's no way I could be certain she wouldn't learn about the investigation. Besides, in her twisted way, I think Reardon likes me. As long as she doesn't see me as an enemy, there's always the hope she won't harm Kathy."

The rest of the day was so bad, Betsy had no idea how she would get through a second one. It was hard to believe that only a few hours had passed since Samantha Reardon's visit. Betsy wandered into Kathy's room and sat on her bed. *The Wizard of Oz* lay on its side on Kathy's bookshelf. They had four more chapters to read.

Was it possible that Kathy would never learn about Dorothy's safe return home? Betsy curled up on the bed, her cheek on Kathy's pillow, and hugged herself. She could smell Kathy's freshness on the pillow, she remembered the softness of her skin. Kathy, who was so precious, so good, was now in a place as distant as Oz where Betsy could not protect her.

The house was chilly. Betsy had forgotten to turn on the heat. Eventually the cold made her uncomfortable. Betsy sat up. She felt old and wasted, chilled to the bone by the icy air, as if her blood had been drained from her, leaving her too weak to cope with the horror that had invaded her life.

The thermostat was in the hall. Betsy adjusted it and listened to the rumble of the furnace starting up. She drifted aimlessly from room to room. The silence overwhelmed her. It was rare for her to be completely alone. Since Kathy's birth, she had always been surrounded by sound. Now she could hear every raindrop fall, the creak of timbers, water dripping in the kitchen sink, the wind. So much silence, so many signs of loneliness.

Betsy saw the liquor cabinet, but rejected the idea of numbing herself. She had to think, even if each thought was painful. Liquor was a trap. There was going to be a lot of pain in her future and she had to get used to it.

Betsy brewed a cup of tea and turned on the television for company. She had no idea what show she was watching, but the sound of laughter and applause made her feel less alone. How was she going to get through the night, if getting through the day was so unbearable?

Betsy thought about calling her mother but rejected the idea. Rick's body would be discovered soon and Rita would learn that Kathy was missing. She decided to spare her mother suffering for as long as possible.

Stewart called at four to check on Betsy. He had

talked to his contacts at the utility companies and the phone companies and had hired several investigators he trusted to scour the real estate ads for the relevant time period. Stewart insisted on coming by with Chinese take-out. Betsy knew he was doing it so she would not be alone. She was too tired to tell him not to come and she appreciated the company when he arrived.

Stewart left at six-thirty. An hour later, Betsy heard a car pull into her carport. She hurried to the door, hoping, irrationally, that her visitor was Samantha Reardon bringing Kathy home. A police car was parked in one side of the carport. A uniformed officer was driving. Ross Barrow got out of the passenger side. He looked troubled. Betsy's heart beat wildly, certain he was here to tell her about Rick's murder.

"Hello, Detective," she said, trying to sound nonchalant.

"Can we step inside, Ms. Tannenbaum?" Barrow asked.

"Is this about Martin's case?"

Barrow sighed. He had been breaking the news of violent death to relatives for longer than he cared to remember. There was no easy way to do it.

"Why don't we go inside?"

Betsy led Barrow into the house. The other officer followed.

"This is Greg Saunders," Barrow said. Saunders nodded.

"Do you want some coffee?"

"Not right now, thank you. Can we sit down?"

Betsy walked into the living room. When they were seated, Barrow asked, "Where were you last night and today?"

"Why do you want to know?"

"I have an important reason for asking."

"I was home."

"You didn't go out? No one visited you?"

"No," Betsy answered, afraid to mention Reggie Stewart.

"You're married, aren't you?"

Betsy looked at Barrow for a moment, then looked down at her lap.

"My husband and I are separated. Kathy, our daughter, is staying with him for a few days. I've been taking advantage of the peace and quiet to sleep late, catch up on some reading. What's this all about?"

"Where are Mr. Tannenbaum and your daughter staying?" Barrow asked, ignoring her question.

"Rick just rented a new apartment. I have the address written down. But why are you asking?"

Betsy looked back and forth between Barrow and Saunders. Saunders would not meet her eye.

"Has something happened to Rick and Kathy?"

"Ms. Tannenbaum, this isn't easy for me. Especially since I know you. The door to your husband's apartment was open. A neighbor found him."

"Found Rick? How? What are you talking about?"

Barrow looked Betsy over carefully.

"Do you want some brandy or something? Are you gonna be okay."

"Oh, God," Betsy said, letting her head drop into her hands, so her face was covered.

"The neighbor has already identified Mr. Tannenbaum, so you'll be spared that."

"How did he . . . ?"

"He was murdered. We need you to come to the apartment. There are some questions only you can answer. You don't have to worry, the body's been removed."

Betsy suddenly jerked upright. "Where's Kathy?"

"We don't know, Ms. Tannenbaum. That's why we need you to come with us."

Most of the lab technicians were gone by the time Betsy arrived at Rick's apartment. Two officers were smoking in the hall outside his door. Betsy heard them laughing when the elevator doors opened. They looked guilty when they saw her step out. One of them held his cigarette at his side as if he was trying to hide evidence.

The door to Rick's apartment opened into a narrow hall. At the end of the hall, the apartment fanned out into a large living room with high windows. The lights were on in the hall. Betsy saw the blood immediately. It had dried into a large brown stain. Rick had died there. She looked up quickly and followed Barrow as he stepped over the spot.

"In here," he said, gesturing toward the guest room. Betsy walked into the room. She saw Kathy's book bag. Dirty jeans and a green, striped long-sleeve shirt lay crumpled on the floor in a corner. On the ride over, Betsy wondered if she could fake crying when the time came. She need not have worried.

"They're Kathy's," she managed. "She was so proud, because she packed everything herself."

There was a commotion at the front door. Alan Page tore into the apartment and went directly to Betsy.

"I just heard. Are you okay?"

Betsy nodded. Gone was the self-confidence Page had seen in court. Betsy looked like she could break into a million pieces at any moment. He took her hands and gave them a gentle squeeze.

"We'll get your daughter back. I'm putting everything we've got into this. I'll call in the FBI. We'll find out who has her."

"Thank you, Alan," Betsy answered dully.

"Are you through with her, Ross?"

Barrow nodded.

Page led Betsy out of the room and into a small den. He made Betsy sit down and he sat opposite her.

"Can I do anything for you, Betsy?"

Page was concerned by Betsy's pallor. Betsy took a deep breath and shut her eyes. She was used to thinking of Alan Page as a stone-hard adversary. Page's show of concern disarmed her.

"I'm sorry," Betsy said. "I just can't seem to focus."

"Don't apologize. You're not made of iron. Do you want to rest? We can talk about this later."

"No. Go ahead."

"Okay. Has anyone contacted you about Kathy?"

Betsy shook her head. Page looked troubled. It didn't make sense. Rick Tannenbaum had probably been killed the day before. If the person who took Kathy was after ransom he'd have called Betsy by now.

"This wasn't a robbery, Betsy. Rick's wallet was full of money. He had on a valuable watch. Can you think of anyone with a reason to hurt Rick?"

Betsy shook her head. It was hard lying to Alan, but she had to do it.

"He had no enemies?" Page asked. "Personal, business, someone in his firm, someone he bested in court?"

"No one comes to mind. Rick didn't get into court. He does contracts, mergers. I never heard him say anything about personal problems with anyone in his firm."

"I don't want to hurt you," Page said, "but Ross told me you and Rick were separated. What happened? Was he drinking, using drugs, was there another woman?"

"It was nothing like that, Alan. It was . . . He . . . he desperately wanted to be a partner at Donovan, Chastain and Mills and it looked like they weren't going to let him. And . . . and he was terribly jealous of my success." Tears welled up in Betsy's eyes. "Making partner meant so much to him. He couldn't see that I didn't care. That I loved him."

Betsy could not go on. Her shoulders shook with each sob. It all sounded so stupid. To break up a marriage over something like that. To leave your wife and daughter for a name on a letterhead.

"I'll be sending you home with an officer," Page said quietly. "I want to set up a command post in your house. Until we learn otherwise, we're treating Kathy's disappearance as a kidnapping. I want your permission to put a tap on your home and office phones, in case the person who has Kathy calls. We'll cut off any call from a client as soon as we know it's not the kidnapper. I'll have the office tapes erased."

"Okay."

"We haven't released Rick's identity yet and we aren't going to let the media know Kathy's missing until we have to, but we'll probably have to give out Rick's name in the morning. You're going to be hounded by the press."

"I understand."

"Do you want me to call someone to stay with you?"

There was no longer a reason to keep Kathy's disappearance from Rita. Betsy needed her more than ever.

"I'd like my mother to stay with me."

"Of course. I can have an officer drive her to your house."

"That won't be necessary. May I use the phone?"

Page nodded. "One other thing. I'll explain what happened to Judge Norwood. He'll set over the Darius hearing."

Betsy's heart leaped. She had forgotten about the hearing. How would Reardon react, if it was set over?

Reardon was holding Kathy because of the hearing. The longer it was put off, the greater was the danger that Reardon would harm Kathy.

"I'm going to work, Alan. I'll go crazy if I just sit at home."

Page looked at her oddly. "You won't want to tackle anything as complex as Darius's case now. You'll be too distracted to do a competent job. I want Darius more than I've ever wanted anyone, but I'd never take advantage of a situation like this. Believe me, Betsy. We'll talk about his case after the funeral."

The funeral. Betsy hadn't even thought about a funeral. Her brother had taken care of her father's funeral. What did you do? Whom did you contact?

Page saw how confused Betsy looked and took her hand. She had never noticed his eyes before. Everything else about the district attorney, from his lean build to the angles that made up his face, were so hard, but his eyes were soft blue.

"You look like you're about to fold up," Page said. "I'm going to send you home. Try to get some sleep, even if you have to take something. You'll need all your strength. And don't give up hope. You have my word. I'll do everything in my power to get back your little girl."

Chapter Twenty-seven

─────────

I

"Tannenbaum was killed Friday evening," Ross Barrow said as he uncapped a Styrofoam cup filled with black coffee. Randy Highsmith pulled a jelly doughnut out of a bag Barrow had placed on Alan Page's desk. It was still dark. Through the window behind Page, a river of headlights flowed across the bridges spanning the Willamette River as the Monday morning commuters drove into downtown Portland.

"Three days without a call," Page muttered to himself, fully aware of the implications. "Anything last night at Betsy's house?" he asked Barrow.

"A lot of condolence calls, but no kidnapper."

"How do you figure it?" Page asked Highsmith.

"First possibility, it's a kidnapping, but the kidnapper hasn't gotten in touch with Betsy for some reason known only to him."

"The kid could be dead," Barrow offered. "He wants to hold her for ransom, but fucks up and kills her."

"Yeah," Highsmith said. "Or, possibility number two, he has Kathy and he's not interested in ransom."

"That's the possibility I don't even want to consider," Page said.

"Do we have anything new, Ross?" Highsmith asked.

Barrow shook his head. "No one saw anyone leaving the apartment house with a little girl. The murder weapon is missing. We're still waiting on results from the lab."

Page sighed. He'd had very little sleep in the past few days and he was exhausted.

"The only good thing to come out of this mess is the extra time it's bought with Darius," Page said. "What was in the surveillance logs?"

"Nothing that helps us," Barrow answered. "Padovici and Kristol were on Darius from the moment he left his estate at six forty-three a.m. I talked to Justice Ryder again. He's positive he was eating breakfast with Lisa Darius at seven-thirty. The teams were on Darius constantly. Besides, Darius met with people all day, in his office. I've had every member of his staff and visitors interviewed twice. If they're covering for him, they're doing a great job."

"There has to be an answer," Page said. "Has the team we've got searching for Gordon turned up anything?"

"Nada, Al," Barrow answered. "No one's seen her since she checked into that motel."

"We know she's alive," Page said, his tone echoing his frustration. "She made that damn call. Why won't she show herself?"

"We have to start facing the fact that Gordon may have lied to you," Highsmith said. "Darius may have been a victim in Hunter's Point. Waters may have been the killer."

Page wished he could let Highsmith and Barrow

know what Wayne Turner had told him. Then they would know Gordon was telling the truth.

"Remember I suggested Gordon might be our killer, Al," Highsmith continued. "I think we'd better start considering her very seriously. I can't see any way she could have known we would find Lisa Darius in the basement, unless she put her there.

"What if she visited Lisa and convinced her to help her break into Martin's house to find evidence to convict him. They go through the woods. Lisa knows how to turn off the alarms. Martin Darius is at work all day and the house is deserted. She kills Lisa to frame Darius, waits until she sees him come home, then calls you. The only flaw in the plan is that Gordon doesn't know about the surveillance teams."

"Nancy Gordon did not kill those women," Page insisted. "Darius killed them, and he's not beating this case."

"I'm not saying Darius isn't guilty. I'm saying this case makes less and less sense every time I look at it."

Alan Page checked his watch. It was ten-thirty in Washington, D.C.

"This is going nowhere. I want to attend Rick Tannenbaum's funeral, and, believe it or not, I have some work to do that has nothing to do with Martin Darius or Rick Tannenbaum's murder. Let me know about any developments immediately."

"You want me to leave a doughnut?" Barrow asked.

"Sure. Why not? I should have at least one good thing happen to me today. Now get out and let me work."

Ross Barrow handed Alan a maple bar and followed Highsmith into the hall. As soon as the office door closed, Page dialed Senator Colby's office and asked for Wayne Turner.

"Mr. Page, what can I do for you?" Turner asked. Page could hear the tension in the administrative assistant's voice.

"I've been thinking about the senator's information all weekend. My situation is desperate. Even my own staff is starting to doubt Darius's guilt. We know Darius killed three women in Hunter's Point, including his wife and daughter, but the judge is starting to see him as an innocent victim and me as his persecutor. If Darius is released, I have no doubt he'll kill again. I don't see I have any choice but to ask the senator to testify about the pardon."

The line was silent for a moment. When Wayne Turner spoke, he sounded resigned.

"I was expecting your call. I'd do the same thing in your shoes. Darius has to be stopped. But I think there might be a way to protect the senator. Betsy Tannenbaum seems like a responsible person."

"She is, but I wouldn't count on her staying on the Darius case. Someone murdered her husband on Friday and kidnapped her little girl."

"My God! Is she okay?"

"She's trying to keep herself together. The husband's funeral is this afternoon."

"That might complicate matters. I was hoping we could convince her to tell Judge Norwood about the pardon in camera. That way he could use the information to deny bail without the public finding out about it."

"I don't know," Page said hesitantly. "You run into all sorts of constitutional problems if you try to bar the press. Besides, Darius would have to give his okay. I can't imagine him not trying to pull down Senator Colby with him."

"Take a shot at it, will you? The senator and I have

been talking this out. We might be able to weather the storm, but we don't want to, if we don't have to."

2

Storm clouds cast somber shadows over the mourners as the graveside service began. Then a light rain started to fall. Rick's father opened an umbrella over Betsy. Cold drops blew under it. Betsy did not feel them. She tried to pay attention to the eulogies, but her mind kept wandering to Kathy. She was grateful for the concern everyone had shown for her daughter, but every mention of Kathy drove a knife into her heart. When the rabbi closed his prayer book and the mourners began to drift away, Betsy stayed by the grave.

"Let her have some private time with him," Betsy heard Rita tell Rick's parents. Rick's father pressed the umbrella into her hand.

The cemetery spread across low, rolling hills. The headstones near Rick's grave were weathered, but well cared for. An oak tree would provide shade in the summer. Betsy stared at Rick's grave. What was left of her husband's body was covered by the earth. His spirit had flown. The future they might have had together would be a mystery forever. The finality terrified her.

"Betsy."

She looked up. Samantha Reardon was standing beside her. She wore a black raincoat and a wide-brimmed hat that left her face in shadow. Betsy looked around for help. Most of the mourners were walking quickly toward their cars to get out of the rain. Her brother was walking with the rabbi. Rita was talking to two of her friends.

Rick's family was huddled together, looking away from the grave.

"The hearing was supposed to be today."

"It's the funeral. I couldn't . . ."

"There will be no stalling, Betsy. I was counting on you and you let me down. I went to the courthouse and you weren't there."

"It's Rick's funeral."

"Your husband is dead, Betsy. Your daughter is still alive."

Betsy saw it would be useless to try and reason with Reardon. Her face was void of compassion. Her eyes were dead.

"I can call the judge," Betsy said. "I'll do it."

"You'd better, Betsy. I was so upset when I heard the hearing was delayed that I forgot to feed Kathy."

"Oh, please," Betsy pleaded.

"You've upset me, Betsy. When you upset me, I will punish Kathy. One meal a day is all she'll get until you've done as I say. There will be just enough water and just enough food so she can last. The same diet I received in Hunter's Point. Kathy will suffer because you disobeyed me. Every tear she sheds will be shed because of you. I'll be checking with the court. I better hear that a date has been set for the hearing."

Reardon walked away. Betsy took a few steps after her, then stopped.

"You forgot your umbrella," Alan Page said.

Betsy turned and stared at him blankly. The umbrella had slipped from her hand while Reardon was talking to her. Page held it over them.

"How are you holding up?" Page asked.

Betsy shook her head, not trusting herself to talk.

"You'll get through this. You're tough, Betsy."

"Thank you, Alan. I appreciate everything you've done for me."

It was hard dealing with grief in a house full of strangers. The FBI agents and the police tried to be unobtrusive, but there was no way to be alone without hiding in her bedroom. Page had been wonderful. He had arrived with the first invasion on Saturday night and stayed until dawn. On Sunday, Page returned with sandwiches. The simple, humanitarian gesture made her cry.

"Why don't you go home. Get out of this rain," Page suggested.

They turned away from the grave. Page covered them with the umbrella as they walked up the hill toward Rita Cohen.

"Alan," Betsy said, stopping suddenly, "can we hold the hearing for Darius tomorrow?"

Page looked surprised by the request. "I don't know Judge Norwood's calendar, but why do you want to go to court tomorrow?"

Betsy scrambled for a rational explanation for her request.

"I can't stand sitting in the house. I don't think the kidnapper will call, if he hasn't called by now. If . . . if this is a kidnapping for ransom, we have to give the kidnapper a chance to contact me. He may have guessed you'd tap the phones. If I'm at the courthouse, in a crowd, he might try to approach me."

Page tried to think of a reason to dissuade Betsy, but she made sense. There had been no attempt to phone or write Betsy at her home or office. He was beginning to accept the possibility that Kathy was dead, but he did not want to tell Betsy. Going along with her would give Betsy some hope. Right now, that was all he could do for her.

"Okay. I'll set it up as soon as I can. Tomorrow, if the judge can do it."

Betsy looked down at the grass. If Judge Norwood scheduled the hearing, Kathy might be home tomorrow. Page laid his hand on her shoulder. He handed the umbrella to Rita, who had walked down the hill to meet them.

"Let's go home," Rita said. Rick's family closed around her and followed her to the car. Page watched her walk away. The rain pelted down on him.

Chapter Twenty-eight

―――――――

I

Reggie Stewart sat in his modest apartment staring at the lists spread across the kitchen table. Stewart did not feel good about what he was doing. He was an excellent investigator, but cross-checking hundreds of names on dozens of lists required manpower, and could be done a thousand times more efficiently by the FBI or the police.

Stewart was also concerned that he was obstructing justice. He knew the name of Kathy's kidnapper and he was concealing this information. If Kathy died, he would always wonder if the police could have saved her. Stewart liked and respected Betsy, but she was not thinking straight. He understood her concerns about the way the police and FBI might act, but he did not agree with her. He had half-decided to go to Alan Page if he did not come up with something quickly.

Stewart took a sip of coffee and started through the lists again. They were from real estate offices, utilities companies, phone companies. Some of them had cost him, but he had not considered the price. So far, there were no listings for a Samantha Reardon or a Nora Sloane, but Stewart knew it wouldn't be that easy.

On his second trip through a list of new Washington County phone subscribers Stewart stopped at Dr. Samuel Felix. Samantha Reardon's first husband was named Max Felix. Stewart cross-checked the other lists and found that a Mrs. Samuel Felix had rented a Washington County home the week Oberhurst returned to Portland from Hunter's Point. Stewart called Pangborn Realty as soon as their office opened. The saleswoman who handled the deal remembered Mrs. Felix. She was a tall, athletic woman with short brown hair. A friendly lady who confided that she was not completely happy with moving from upstate New York, where her husband practiced neurosurgery.

Stewart called Betsy, but Ann told him she was on her way to court on the Darius case. Stewart realized the opportunity this presented. Reardon attended all the court hearings in the Darius case. She would probably attend this one and leave Kathy alone.

The house was at the end of a dirt road. It was white, with a porch and a weather vane, a happy house that was the least likely suspect to conceal suffering inside. Reggie Stewart circled around the house through the woods. He saw tire tracks in the front yard but no car. The door to the small, unattached garage was open and the garage was empty. The curtains were closed on most of the windows, but were open on the front window. There were no lights on inside. Stewart spent twenty minutes watching for any movement in the front room and saw none. If Samantha Reardon lived in this house, she was not there now.

Stewart darted across the yard and ducked into a

concrete well at the side of the house. Six steps led down to a basement door. The basement windows were blacked out with paint. If Reardon was duplicating Darius, Kathy would be in the basement. The painted windows reinforced that belief.

Stewart tried the basement door. It was locked. The lock did not look sturdy, and Stewart thought he could kick in the door. He backed up two steps and braced his arms against the sides of the concrete well, then reared back and snapped his foot against the door. The wood broke and the door gave a little. Stewart braced himself again and swung his leg against the damaged part of the door. It gave with a loud crack.

The basement was cloaked in darkness and Stewart could see inside only as far as the sunlight penetrated. He edged inside and was greeted by stale air and a foul odor. Stewart pulled a flashlight out of his coat pocket and played the beam around the room. Against the wall on his right were homemade shelves of unpainted wood holding a coil of hose, some cracked orange pots and miscellaneous gardening tools. A child's sled, some broken furniture and several lawn chairs were piled in the middle of the floor in front of the furnace. The odor seemed to emanate from the corner across from the door where the darkness was thickest. Stewart crossed the basement cautiously, maneuvering around objects, alert for any noise.

The flashlight beam found an open sleeping bag. Stewart knelt next to it. He saw encrusted blood where a head would lie and smelled a faint odor of urine and feces. Another open bag lay a few feet farther into the darkness. Stewart was moving toward it when he saw the third bag and the body sprawled across it.

2

The night before the hearing, Betsy was so preoccupied with Kathy that she forgot about Martin Darius. Now he was all she could think about. Samantha Reardon was forcing Betsy to choose between Kathy's life and the life of a man who did not deserve to live. The choice was simple, but it was not easy. As sick and twisted as he was, Darius was still a human being. When Betsy let Samantha Reardon into the jury room, she had no illusions about what would happen. If Martin Darius died, she would be an accomplice to murder.

Newspaper reporters surrounded Betsy as soon as she stepped off the elevator. She turned her head to avoid the glaring lights of the television cameras and the microphones as she hurried down the corridor toward Judge Norwood's courtroom. The reporters asked the same questions about Rick's murder and Kathy's disappearance over and over. Betsy answered none of them.

Betsy spotted Samantha Reardon as soon as she entered the packed courtroom. She walked past her quickly and hurried down the aisle to her seat. Darius was already at the counsel table. Two guards sat directly behind him and several others were spread through the courtroom.

Alan Page was just putting his file on the table when Betsy walked through the spectators. He caught Betsy as she entered the bar of the court.

"Are you certain you want to go through with this?"

Betsy nodded.

"Okay. Then there's something we have to discuss with Judge Norwood. I told him we would want to meet in his chambers before court started."

Betsy looked puzzled. "Should Darius be there?"

"No. This is between you, me and Norwood. I'm not letting Randy come in with us."

"I don't understand."

Page leaned close to Betsy and whispered, "I know Senator Colby pardoned Darius. The senator sent his a.a. to see me."

"Wayne Turner?"

Page nodded. "You know how the senator's confirmation hearing will be affected if news of the pardon is made public. Will you meet with the judge in chambers or are you going to insist we do this in open court?"

Betsy considered the situation quickly. Darius was watching her.

"I'm going to have to tell Darius. I can't agree to anything unless he consents."

"Can you wait until we meet with the judge?"

"All right."

Page went back to his table and Betsy sat next to Darius.

"What was that about?"

"Page wants us to meet with the judge in chambers."

"About what?"

"He's being mysterious."

"I don't want anything going on behind my back."

"Let me handle this, Martin."

Darius looked like he was going to balk for a moment. Then he said, "Okay. I trust you. You haven't let me down, so far."

Betsy started to stand up. Darius put a hand on her forearm.

"I heard about your husband and daughter. I'm sorry."

"Thank you, Martin," Betsy answered coldly.

"I mean it. I know what you think of me, but I do have feelings and I respect you."

Betsy did not know what to say. Before the hour was up, she would cause the death of the man who was trying to console her.

"Look, if the kidnapper wants money, I can help," Darius said. "Whatever he wants, I'll cover it."

Betsy felt her heart contract. She managed to thank Darius, then pulled away.

Judge Norwood stood when Betsy walked into his chambers. He looked concerned.

"Sit down, Mrs. Tannenbaum. Can I get you anything?"

"I'm fine, Judge."

"Do they have any news about Mrs. Tannenbaum's daughter, Al?"

"Nothing new, Judge."

Norwood shook his head. "I'm terribly sorry. Al, you tell your people to interrupt if they have to talk to you."

"I will."

The judge turned to Betsy.

"And, if you want to stop the hearing, if you aren't feeling well, anything at all, just tell me. I'll set over the hearing on my own motion, so your client won't be prejudiced."

"Thank you, Judge. Everyone is being so kind. But I want to go through with the hearing. Mr. Darius has been in jail for several days and he needs to know if he is going to be released."

"Very well. Now tell me why you wanted this meeting, Al."

"Betsy and I are aware of information about the Hunter's Point incident that is known to very few people. One of those people is Senator Raymond Colby."

"The President's nominee to the Court?" Norwood asked incredulously.

Page nodded. "He was the governor of New York

when the murders occurred in Hunter's Point. His information could affect your decision on bail, but it would badly damage Senator Colby's chances of being nominated."

"I'm confused. Are you saying Senator Colby is mixed up in the Hunter's Point murders?"

"Yes, sir," Page answered.

"And you agree, Mrs. Tannenbaum?"

"Yes."

"What is this information?"

"Before Mr. Page tells you," Betsy said, "I want to object to you hearing any of this testimony. If this information is used against Mr. Darius in any way, it will violate the due process guarantees of the United States Constitution and an agreement between Mr. Darius, the State of New York and the federal government. I think we need to hash this out in much greater detail before you call your witness."

"An agreement Darius made with those parties can't bind Oregon," Page said.

"I think it would."

"You two are getting way ahead of me. What type of agreement are we dealing with here?"

"A pardon, Judge," Page said. "Colby pardoned Darius when he was governor of New York."

"For what?"

"I'd prefer the contents of the pardon were not revealed until you decide the threshold question of admissibility," Betsy said.

"This is getting extremely complicated," Judge Norwood said. "Mrs. Tannenbaum, why don't we have the guards take Mr. Darius back to jail. It's obvious to me that this is going to take some time."

Betsy's stomach churned. She felt like she might collapse.

"I'd like to confer with Mr. Darius in private. Can I use your jury room?"

"Certainly."

Betsy walked out of the judge's chambers. She felt light-headed as she told the guards that Judge Norwood was letting her confer with Darius in the jury room. One of the guards went into the judge's chambers to check with Norwood. He came out a minute later and the guards escorted Darius into the room. Betsy looked toward the rear of the courtroom, just as Reardon walked into the hall.

A guard stationed himself outside the door to the courtroom. Another guard was in front of the door that opened into the hall. Betsy shut the door to the jury room behind them and turned the lock. A table long enough to accommodate twelve chairs filled the center of the large room. There was a narrow rest room in one corner and a sink, countertop and cabinet filled with plastic coffee cups and dishes against one wall. The other wall held a bulletin board covered with announcements and cartoons about judges and jurors.

Darius sat down at one end of the table. He was still dressed in the clothes he was wearing when he was arrested. The pants were rumpled and his shirt was wrinkled. He was not wearing a tie and he had jail-issue sandals on his feet.

Betsy stood at the edge of the table trying not to look at the door to the corridor.

"What's going on?" Darius asked.

"Page knows about the pardon. Colby told him."

"That son-of-a-bitch."

"Page wants to have the judge take Colby's testimony in secret, so the senator's chances of being confirmed won't be affected."

"Fuck him. If he tries to screw me, I'll take him down. They can't use that pardon anyway, can they?"

"I don't know. It's a very complicated legal issue."

There was a knock on the hall door. Darius noticed the way Betsy jerked her head around.

"Are you expecting someone?" he asked suspiciously.

Betsy opened the door without answering. Reardon was standing behind a guard. She was holding a black Gladstone bag.

"This lady says you're expecting her," the guard said.

"That's true," Betsy answered.

Darius stood up. He stared at Reardon. His eyes widened. Reardon looked into those eyes.

"Don't . . ." Darius started. Reardon shot the guard in the temple. His head exploded, spraying flesh and bone over her raincoat. Betsy stared. The guard crumpled to the floor. Reardon pushed Betsy aside, dropped the bag and locked the hallway door.

"Sit down," she commanded, pointing the gun at Darius. Darius backed away and sat in the chair at the end of the table. Reardon turned to Betsy.

"Take a chair on the other side from me, away from Darius, and fold your hands on the table. If you move, Kathy dies."

Darius stared at Betsy. "You planned this?"

"Shut up, Martin," Reardon said. Her eyes were wide. She looked manic. "Dogs don't talk. If you utter a sound without my asking, you'll suffer pain like you've never known."

Darius kept his mouth shut and his eyes riveted on Reardon.

"You made me an expert on pain, Martin. Soon you'll see how well I learned. My only regret is that I won't have those private moments with you that you shared with me. Those days alone together when you made me plead for pain. I remember each minute we shared. If we had time, I would make you relive every one of them."

Reardon picked up the black bag and placed it on the table.

"I have a question for you, Martin. It's a simple question. One you should have no trouble answering. I give you permission to answer it, if you can. Considering the time we spent together, it should be a breeze. What's my name?"

Someone pounded on the hall door. "Open up! Police."

Reardon half-turned toward the door, but kept her eyes on Darius.

"Get away or I'll kill everyone in here. I've got Betsy Tannenbaum and Martin Darius. If I hear anyone at the door, they die. You know I mean it."

There was a scraping at the door to the courtroom. Reardon fired a shot through the top of the door. Betsy heard several screams.

"Get away from the doors or everyone dies," Reardon yelled.

"We've backed off!" someone shouted from the hall.

Reardon pointed her gun at Betsy. "Talk to them. Tell them about Kathy. Tell them she'll die if they try to come in here. Tell them you'll be safe if they do as I say."

Betsy was shaking.

"Can I stand up?" she managed.

Reardon nodded. Betsy walked to the courtroom door.

"Alan!" she shouted, fighting to keep her voice from breaking.

"Are you okay?" Page shouted back.

"Please keep everyone away. The woman in here was one of the women Darius kidnapped in Hunter's

Point. She's hidden Kathy and she's not feeding her. If you capture her, she won't tell me where she's holding Kathy and she'll starve to death. Please keep everyone away."

"All right. Don't worry."

"In the hall, too," Reardon commanded.

"She wants everyone away from the hall door, too. Please. Do as she says. She won't hesitate to kill us."

Reardon turned her attention back to Darius. "You've had time to think. Answer the question, if you can. What's my name?"

Darius shook his head and Reardon smiled in a way that made Betsy feel cold.

"I knew you wouldn't know, Martin. We were never people to you. We were meat. Fantasy figures."

Betsy could hear people moving around in the courtroom and the corridor. Reardon opened the bag. She took out a hypodermic. Betsy could see surgical implements lying on trays.

"My name is Samantha Reardon, Martin. You're going to remember it when I'm through. I want you to know something else about me. Before you kidnapped me and ruined my life, I was a surgical nurse. Surgical nurses learn how to mend broken bodies. They see parts of the body maimed and twisted and they see what a surgeon has to do to relieve the pain injuries cause. Can you see how that information might be useful to a person who wanted to cause pain?"

Darius knew better than to answer. Reardon smiled.

"Very good, Martin. You're a fast learner. You didn't speak. Of course, you invented this game. I remember what happened the first time you asked me a question after telling me that dogs don't speak and I was foolish enough to answer. I'm sorry I don't have a cattle prod handy, Martin. The pain is exquisite."

Reardon laid a scalpel on the tabletop. Betsy felt sick. She sucked air. Reardon ignored her. She moved down the table closer to Darius.

"I have to get to work. I can't expect those fools to wait forever. After a while, they'll decide to try something stupid.

"You probably think I'm going to kill you. You're wrong. Death is a gift, Martin. It is an end to suffering. I want you to suffer as long as possible. I want you to suffer for the rest of your life.

"The first thing I'm going to do is shoot you in both kneecaps. The pain from this injury will be excruciating and it will cripple you sufficiently to prevent you from being a physical threat to me. I will then ease your pain by administering an anesthetic."

Reardon held up the hypodermic.

"Once you're unconscious, I'm going to operate on you. I'm going to work on your spinal cord, the tendons and ligaments that enable you to move your arms and legs. When you wake up, you'll be totally paralyzed. But that won't be all, Martin. That won't be the worst part."

A glow suffused Reardon's features. She looked enraptured.

"I'm also going to put out your eyes, so you won't be able to see. I'm going to cut out your tongue, so you won't be able to talk. I'm going to make you deaf. The only thing I'm going to leave intact will be your mind.

"Think about your future, Martin. You're relatively young. You're in good shape. A healthy specimen. With life support, you'll stay alive thirty, forty years, locked in the perpetual darkness of your mind.

"Do you know why they call prisons penitentiaries?" Darius did not respond. Reardon chuckled.

"Can't fool you, can I. It's a place for penitence. A place for those who have wronged others to think about their sins. Your mind will become your penitentiary and you'll be locked in it, unable to escape, for the rest of your life."

Reardon positioned herself in front of Darius and aimed at his right knee.

"You in there. This is William Tobias, the police chief. I'd like to talk to you."

Reardon turned her head and Darius moved with uncanny speed. His left foot shot up, catching Reardon's wrist. The gun flew across the table. Betsy watched it skid toward her as Reardon staggered backward.

Betsy's hand closed on the gun as Darius grabbed Reardon's wrist to shake loose the hypodermic. Reardon lashed out with her foot and kicked Darius in the shin. She jabbed the fingers of her free hand at his eyes. Darius moved his head and the blow caught him on the cheek. Reardon leaped forward and sank her teeth into Darius's throat. He screamed. They smashed against the wall. Darius held tight to the hand holding the needle. He grabbed Reardon's hair with his free hand and tried to pull her off. Betsy saw Darius turn white from pain. Reardon struggled to free the hypodermic. Darius let go of Reardon's hair and smashed his fist into her head several times. Reardon's grip loosened and Darius pulled away. The flesh around his throat was ragged and covered with blood. Darius grabbed Reardon's hair, held her head away from him and smashed his forehead against her nose, stunning her. Reardon's legs gave way. Darius snapped her wrist and the syringe fell to the floor. He moved behind Reardon, wrapping an arm around her neck.

"No!" Betsy screamed. "Don't kill her. She's the only one who knows where Kathy is."

Darius paused. Reardon was limp. He was holding

her off the ground so only her toes were touching. His choke hold was cutting off her air.

"Please, Martin," Betsy begged.

"Why should I help you?" Darius yelled. "You set me up."

"I had to. She would have killed Kathy."

"Then Kathy's death will be a fitting punishment."

"Please, Martin," Betsy begged. "She's my little girl."

"You should have thought of that when you decided to fuck me over," Darius said, tightening his hold.

Betsy raised the gun and aimed it at Darius.

"Martin, I will shoot you dead if you don't put her down. I swear it. I'll keep shooting you until the gun is empty."

Darius looked across Reardon's shoulder. Betsy locked eyes with him. He calculated the odds, then he relaxed his grip and Reardon collapsed on the floor. Darius moved away from Reardon. Betsy reached behind her.

"I'm opening the door. Don't shoot. Everything is all right."

Betsy opened the door to the courtroom. Darius sat down at the table with his hands in plain view. Two armed policemen entered first. She gave one of them the gun. The other officer handcuffed Reardon. Betsy collapsed on one of the chairs. Several policemen entered from the hall. The jury room was suddenly filled with people. Two officers lifted Reardon off the floor and sat her in a chair opposite Betsy. She was still struggling for air. Alan Page sat next to Betsy.

"Are you all right?" he asked.

Betsy nodded mechanically. Her attention was riveted on Reardon.

"Samantha, where is Kathy?"

Reardon lifted her head slowly. "Kathy is dead."

Betsy turned pale. Her lips trembled as she tried to hold herself together. Reardon looked at Alan Page.

"Unless you do exactly what I say."

"I'm listening."

"I want what Peter Lake got. I want a pardon for everything. The cop in the hall, the women, the kidnappings. I want the United States attorney to guarantee no federal prosecution. I want the governor here personally. We'll videotape the signing. I'll walk. Just like Lake. Complete freedom."

"If you get your pardon will you tell us where you're holding Kathy Tannenbaum?"

Reardon nodded. "And Nancy Gordon."

"She's alive?" Page asked.

"Of course. Nancy is the only one who continued to track Martin. She's the only one who believed me. I wouldn't kill her. And there's something else."

"I'm listening."

"I can give you the proof to convict Martin Darius of murder."

Darius sat rigidly at the far end of the table.

"What proof is that?" Page asked.

Reardon turned toward Darius. She smiled.

"You think you've won, Martin. You think no one will believe me. A jury will believe a crazy woman if she has proof to back up her testimony. If she has photographs."

Darius shifted a little in his seat.

"Photographs of what?" Page asked.

Reardon spoke to Page, but she stared at Darius.

"He wore a mask. A leather mask. He made us wear masks too. Leather masks that covered our eyes. But there was one time, for a brief moment, when I saw his face. Just a moment, but long enough.

"Last summer, a private investigator named Samuel

Oberhurst showed me pictures of Martin. As soon as I saw the pictures I knew he was the one. There was the beard, the dark hair, he was older, but I knew. I flew to Portland and I began to follow Martin. I was with him everywhere and I kept a photographic record of what I saw.

"The week I arrived, Martin threw a party to celebrate the opening of a new mall. I mixed with the guests and selected several women to use as evidence against Martin. One of the women was his mistress, Victoria Miller. I sent a picture of Martin leaving their room at the Hacienda Motel to Nancy Gordon to lure her to Portland.

"The evening after I gathered Victoria, I followed Martin. He drove into the country to Oberhurst's house. I watched for hours while Martin tortured Oberhurst. When Martin took his body to the construction site, I was there. I took pictures. Most of them did not come out, because it was night and there was a lot of rain, but there's one excellent photograph of Martin lifting the body out of the trunk of his car. The trunk light illuminated everything."

Page looked across the table at Darius. Darius met Page's stare without blinking. Page turned back to Reardon.

"You'll get your pardon. We'll go to my office. It will take a while to firm up everything. Will Kathy and Nancy Gordon be all right?"

Sloane nodded. Then she smiled at Betsy.

"You didn't have to worry. I lied about starving Kathy. I fed her before I came here, then I put her to sleep. I gave Kathy her stuffed animal, too, and made certain she was nice and warm. I like you, Betsy. You know I wouldn't hurt you, if I didn't have to."

Page was about to tell two of the officers to take

Reardon to his office when Ross Barrow rushed into the
room.

"We know where the girl is. She's all right. Tannenbaum's investigator found her in Washington County."

3

The woman the medics carried out of the dark basement
looked nothing like the athletic woman who told Alan
Page about Hunter's Point. Nancy Gordon was emaci-
ated, her cheeks sunken, her hair unkempt. Kathy, on the
other hand, looked like an angel. When Stewart found
her, she was in a drugged sleep, lying on a sleeping bag,
hugging Oliver. The doctors let Betsy touch Kathy's forehead and kiss her cheek, then they rushed her to the
hospital.

In the living room, Ross Barrow took a statement
from an excited Reggie Stewart while Randy Highsmith
looked at photographs of Martin Darius that had been
found during a search of the house. In one of the photos,
the trunk light clearly showed Darius lifting the dead
body of Samuel Oberhurst out of the trunk of Martin Darius's car.

Alan Page stepped out onto the porch. Betsy Tannenbaum was standing by the railing. It was cold. Page
could see the mist formed by her breath.

"Are you feeling better, now that Kathy's safe?" Page
asked.

"The doctors think Kathy will be fine physically, but
I'm worried about psychological damage. She must have
been terrified. And I'm frightened of what Reardon will
do if she's ever released."

"You don't have to worry about that. She's going to be locked up forever."

"How can you be sure of that?"

"I'm having her civilly committed. I would have done that even if I was forced to give her a pardon. The pardon wouldn't have prevented me from committing her to a mental hospital if she's mentally ill and dangerous. Reardon has a documented history of mental illness and hospital commitments. I spoke to the people at the State Hospital. There will have to be a hearing, of course. She'll have a lawyer. I'm certain there will be some tricky legal issues. But the bottom line is that Samantha Reardon is insane and she will never see the light of day again."

"And Darius?"

"I'm dismissing all of the counts except the one for killing John Doe. With the picture of Darius with Oberhurst's body and the evidence about the murders in Hunter's Point, I think I can get the death penalty."

Betsy stared at the front yard. The ambulances were gone, but there were still several police cars. Betsy wrapped her arms around herself and shivered.

"A part of me doesn't believe you'll get Darius. Reardon swears he's the Devil. Maybe he is."

"Even the Devil would need a great lawyer with the case we have."

"Darius will get the best, Al. He's got enough money to hire anyone he wants."

"Not anyone," Page said, looking at her, "and not the best."

Betsy blushed.

"It's too cold to stand out here," Page said. "Do you want me to drive you to the hospital?"

Betsy followed Page off the porch. Page held open the door for her. She got in. He started the engine. Betsy looked back toward Kathy's prison. Such a charming place. To look at it, no one would ever guess what went on in the basement. No one would guess about Reardon, either. Or Darius. The real monsters did not look like monsters, and they were out there, stalking.

Epilogue

At eleven-thirty on a sultry summer morning, Raymond Francis Colby placed his left hand on a Bible held by the chief deputy clerk of the United States Supreme Court, raised his right hand and repeated this oath, after Associate Justice Laura Healy:

"I, Raymond Francis Colby, do solemnly swear that I will administer justice without respect to persons, and do equal right to the poor and to the rich, and that I will faithfully and impartially discharge and perform all the duties incumbent on me as Chief Justice of the United States according to the best of my abilities and understanding, agreeably to the Constitution and laws of the United States. So help me God."

"Is she a judge too, Mommy?" Kathy Tannenbaum asked.

"Yes," Betsy whispered.

Kathy turned back to the ceremony. She was wearing a new, blue dress Betsy bought for their trip to Washington. Her hair smelled of flowers and sunshine, as only the freshly shampooed hair of a little girl can smell. No one looking at Kathy would guess the ordeal she had undergone.

The invitation to Senator Colby's investiture arrived

a week after the Senate confirmed his appointment to the Court. The Lake pardon had been the nation's hottest news story for weeks. Speculation ran rampant that Colby would not withstand the revelation that he had set free the rose killer. Then Gloria Escalante publicly praised Colby for saving her life and Alan Page commended the senator's bravery in making the pardon public while still unconfirmed. The final vote for confirmation had been wider than anticipated.

"I think he's going to make a good justice," Alan Page said, as they left the Court's chambers and headed toward the conference room, where the reception for the justices and their guests was being held.

"I don't like Colby's politics," Betsy answered, "but I like the man."

"What's wrong with his politics?" Page deadpanned. Betsy smiled.

A buffet had been set up at one end of the room. There was a courtyard with a fountain outside a set of French windows. Betsy filled a plate for Kathy and found a chair for her to sit on near the fountain, then Betsy went back inside for her own food.

"She looks great," Page told her.

"Kathy's a trouper," Betsy answered proudly. "The investiture came at a good time, too. Kathy's therapist thought a change of scenery would be beneficial. And we're going home by way of Disneyland. Ever since I told her, she's been on cloud nine."

"Good. She's lucky. You too."

Betsy stacked some cold cuts and fresh fruit on her plate and followed Page back toward the courtyard.

"How are you doing with Darius?" Betsy asked.

"Don't worry. Oscar Montoya is making a lot of noise about the pardon, but we'll get it into evidence."

"What's your theory?"

"We believe Oberhurst was blackmailing Darius about the Hunter's Point murders. The pardon is relevant to prove Darius committed them."

"If you don't get the death penalty, you have to lock him up forever, Alan. You have no idea what Darius is like."

"Oh, I think I do," Alan answered smugly.

"No, you don't. You only think you do. I know things about Darius—things he told me in confidence—that would change you forever. Take my word for it: Martin Darius must never leave prison. Never."

"Okay, Betsy. Take it easy. I'm not underestimating him."

Betsy had been so intense that she did not notice Justice Colby until he spoke. Wayne Turner was standing beside the new Chief Justice.

"I'm glad you came," Colby told Betsy.

"I was flattered you invited me."

"You're Alan Page," Colby said.

"Yes, sir."

"For you and Betsy, I will always be Ray. You have no idea how much your statement meant to my confirmation. I hope you can come to the party I'm throwing tonight at my home. It will give us a chance to talk. I'd like to get to know you two better."

Colby and Turner walked off and Betsy led Page into the courtyard, where they found Kathy talking to a woman with crutches.

"Nancy," Alan Page said. "I didn't know you'd be here."

"I wouldn't have missed the senator's swearing-in," she said with a smile.

"Have you met Betsy Tannenbaum, Kathy's mother?"

"No," Gordon said, extending her hand. "It's a pleasure. This is one tough kid," she added, ruffling Kathy's hair.

"I'm so pleased to meet you," Betsy said. "I tried to see you at the hospital, but the doctors wouldn't let me. Then you flew back to Hunter's Point. Did you get my note?"

"Yeah. I'm sorry I didn't write back. I've always been a lousy correspondent. Kathy tells me you're going to Disneyland after you leave Washington. I'm jealous."

"You can come too," Kathy said.

Gordon laughed. "I'd love to, but I have to work. Will you write me and tell me all about your trip?"

"Sure," Kathy said earnestly. "Mom, can I have more cake?"

"Certainly. Alan, will you show Kathy where the cake is?"

Alan and Kathy walked off and Betsy sat down beside Gordon.

"Kathy looks great," Gordon said. "How's she doing?"

"The doctors say she's fine physically and the psychiatrist she's seeing says she's going to be okay."

"I'm glad to hear that. I was worried about how she'd come out of it. Reardon treated her pretty well most of the time, but there were some grim moments."

"Kathy told me how you kept up her spirits. The psychiatrist thinks that having you there really helped."

Gordon smiled. "The truth is, she's the one who kept up my spirits. She's one brave little girl."

"How are you feeling?"

"Better each day. I can't wait to get rid of these," Gordon said, pointing at her crutches. Then she stopped smiling. "You're Martin Darius's attorney, aren't you?"

"Was. Oscar Montoya is representing him now."

"How did that happen?"

"After I spoke to Senator Colby and learned what he did to the Hunter's Point women I didn't want him as a client, and he didn't want me as his lawyer when he realized I helped Samantha Reardon get to him."

"What's going to happen to Darius?"

"He tortured Oberhurst. I saw the autopsy photographs. They turned my stomach. Alan Page is certain he'll get the death penalty when the jury sees the photos and hears what happened in Hunter's Point."

"What do you think will happen?"

Betsy recalled the smug look on Alan's face when he talked about how certain he was that he could convict Darius, and she felt uneasy.

"I'm not as certain as Alan. He doesn't know Martin like we do."

"Except for Gloria Escalante and Samantha Reardon, no one knows Darius like we do."

Darius had told Betsy, "The experiment brought me the most exquisite pleasure," when he described his kingdom of darkness. There was no sign of remorse or compassion for the pain his victims had suffered. Betsy knew Darius would repeat his experiment if he thought he could get away with it, and she wondered if Darius had any plans for her now that he knew Betsy had betrayed him.

"You're worried he'll get out, aren't you?" Gordon asked.

"Yes."

"Worried about what he might do to you and Kathy?"

Betsy nodded. Gordon looked directly into Betsy's eyes.

"Senator Colby has contacts at the FBI. They're monitoring the case and they'll keep a close watch on

Darius. I'll be told if there's even a possibility that Darius will leave prison."

"What would you do if that happened?" Betsy asked.

When Gordon spoke, her voice was low and firm and Betsy knew she could trust anything Gordon promised.

"You don't have to worry about Martin Darius, Betsy. He'll never hurt you or Kathy. If Darius sets one foot out of prison, I'll make certain he never hurts anyone again."

Kathy ran up with a plate piled high with cake.

"Alan said I could have as much as I wanted," she told Betsy.

"Alan is as bad as Granny," Betsy answered.

"Give the kid a break." Page laughed and sat next to Betsy. Then he asked her, "Do you ever daydream about arguing here?"

"Every lawyer does."

"What about you, Kathy?" Page asked. "Would you like to come here as a lawyer and argue in front of the United States Supreme Court?"

Kathy looked over at Nancy Gordon, her features composed and very serious.

"I don't want to be a lawyer," she said. "I want to be a detective."

Washington, DC

Vanessa Kohler had not chosen to conduct the interview with Terry Warmouth at the Cruise On Inn because Terry claimed she had been abducted from its parking lot. Vanessa had chosen to speak to the thirty-six-year-old shipping clerk at the tavern because she could smoke in it without getting dirty looks from her politically correct colleagues and because it served cheap scotch.

Vanessa was a hard-drinking, rail-thin, chain smoker with snarled blond hair and pale blue eyes. The forty-five-year-old reporter paid no attention to her looks and favored baggy jeans and bulky sweaters, unless she was on assignment. Tonight, she'd cleaned up a little and was wearing a black leather jacket over a T-shirt and tight-fitting jeans.

Vanessa looked at her watch. It was almost nine and Terry said she'd be at the tavern at eight-thirty. Vanessa decided to give her another scotch's worth of time before heading home. Sam Cutler, her boyfriend, was out on an assignment at some rock concert anyway, and there was nothing on the tube. She could think of worse ways to spend her time than drinking in the smoky ambience created by loud country music and raucous pool players.

A sudden cold draft told Vanessa that someone had opened the door. She shifted her gaze from the scarred tabletop to the front of the tavern. A heavy-set, big-haired woman wearing too much makeup was bathed in the red-green light of the jukebox. She cast anxious glances around the bar until Vanessa raised her hand. The woman hurried over.

"Vanessa Kohler from *Exposed*," she said as she handed Terry Warmouth her card. The woman's hand shook when she took it.

"Sorry I'm late," Terry apologized. She sat down and laid Vanessa's card on the table next to a puddle of beer. "This is Larry's bowling night, but his car wouldn't start. He had to wait for a ride."

"Perfectly understandable," Vanessa said.

"I couldn't let him know I was going out. He'd want to know where I was going and who I was meeting. I just hope he doesn't call from the alley. I'll be up all night getting grilled."

She flashed a weak smile, looking for sympathy. It took Vanessa a moment to catch on. She flashed back a smile that reeked of feminine solidarity.

"Can I buy you a beer?" the reporter asked.

"That sounds good."

Vanessa signaled for the waitress and ordered a pitcher.

"So, Terry, you ready to tell your story?" Vanessa asked when the waitress left.

"Yeah, sure," she said, though she didn't sound so sure.

Vanessa placed a tape recorder on the table between them. "Do you mind if I record this so I can report what you tell me accurately?" she asked, omitting the part about the recording being primo evidence whenever a fruitcake decided to sue.

Terry hesitated then said, "Sure, okay."

Vanessa pressed RECORD.

"This is gonna be in the paper, right? With my real name and everything?" Terry asked.

"You bet."

"Because it's the only way Larry will believe it, if it's in *Exposed*. He reads it like the Bible, every week. He says it's the only paper he can trust."

"It's good to know we have such loyal readers."

"That's why I called you, on account of Larry being such a loyal reader."

"Right. So, as I understand it, you're pregnant?"

Terry looked down at the table and nodded.

"You've got to speak up for the recorder, Terry," Vanessa reminded her.

"Oh, right. Yeah, I'm . . . I got. . ."

"Pregnant."

"Right."

"And this was a surprise?"

Terry reddened. "Yeah. I'll say." She looked up, her eyes begging for understanding. "Larry's gonna know it's not his. We tried like crazy after we was married." She hesitated. "You ain't gonna put this part in the paper, are you?"

"Not if you don't want me to."

"Well, don't. It would embarrass him something awful."

"What would?"

"The doctor told us I'm okay, but Larry's sperm don't swim real fast. I don't understand all of it, but it made him feel terrible, unmanly, you know. So, he'll know it weren't his kid."

"And whose kid will it be?" Vanessa prodded.

"The aliens."

"The ones who abducted you from the parking lot of the Cruise On Inn?"

"Yes," Terry answered in a little voice Vanessa could barely hear over the noise in the bar.

"Tell me how it happened."

"I was here . . ."

"What night was this?"

"Same as tonight. Larry's bowling night."

"So, Larry didn't know you were out on the town?"

"Uh, no."

"Were you alone?" Vanessa asked, watching Terry carefully when she answered. Her interviewee ducked her head and turned a deep red.

"Yeah, just me," she said.

"How come you came here? The Cruise On is pretty far from your house."

"It ain't so far from work."

"Been here with some of your pals from work, have you?"

"Some of my girlfriends," she answered too quickly.

"But that night you were on your own?"

"Yes. And it got late, so I knew I'd have to go so I'd be home when Larry got home. He doesn't like me going off on my own."

"Larry's the jealous type?"

"I'll say. He's always going on about how guys are staring at me and accusing me of staring back, when I'm not. It's sort of flattering, but it can get on your nerves, if you know what I mean."

"You bet," Vanessa answered with a nod. "So, tell me about the aliens."

"Yeah, okay. So I went out to my car, which was over at the end of the lot, and I was just about to open the door when I heard this like humming sound, and I looked up and there it was."

"There what was?"

"The ship. It was big and spinning and it looked like a saucer, but with lights."

"Any special color lights?"

"Uh, green, I think. I don't remember real well.

I was pretty shook. But it did look like a lot of those alien ships you write about in your paper. So it was probably from the same planet."

"Which planet is that?"

"They never said, but some of the other ones who got abducted knew the name of the planet and I bet it was one of those since the ship was so similar."

"What happened after you saw the ship?"

"Well, that's where it gets hazy. I do recall a beam of light coming down. But after that it's like you get when you have an operation and they give you drugs."

"Some of our abductees have said it's like a good high."

"Yeah, sort of like that. You know how you sort of float? Well that's what I was doing. But I do remember I was strapped down on this table and I didn't have any clothes on. And this tall one was on top of me."

"Having sex?"

"I don't know what they do. I didn't really feel anything. And then I was back in the parking lot."

"Naked?"

"Uh, no, the aliens must have put my clothes on."

"And the ship was nowhere to be seen?"

"No, they must have left after they beamed me back down."

"Made their getaway before anyone could see them?"

"Yeah, made their getaway," Terry echoed softly.

Terry was crying. Vanessa switched off the tape recorder. She reached across the table and took Terry's hand.

"Larry's not going to buy this, Terry. I know you're hoping he will because he likes my paper, but he's going to know."

Terry's shoulders were shaking and the tears were pouring.

"Who is it? Someone from work?"

Terry's head bobbed up and down for a second. When she lifted her tear-streaked face Vanessa tried to remember if she'd ever seen anyone who looked so miserable.

"But he says it isn't his," Terry said between gulps for air. "He . . . He says I must have been sleeping around or it's Larry's."

"Sounds like a real nice guy," Vanessa observed.

Terry wiped her eyes. "I sure thought he was."

"So you can't count on this guy and you can't tell your husband."

Terry's head bobbed a yes.

"What about an abortion?"

"How would I pay for it? Larry has all the money. If I asked him for some I'd have to explain why I wanted it. He'd ask for receipts if I said I was buying something. He watches money like a hawk."

Vanessa made a decision. She reached across the table and picked up the business card she'd handed Terry Warmouth. Then she wrote a name and phone number on the back of it.

"You call this doctor, Terry. You tell her I told you to call. I'll clear it with her first thing in the morning, so call from work around ten. She'll take care of you."

"But, the money . . . ?"

Vanessa squeezed Terry's hand. "Don't worry about the money. Just get this taken care of."

"I really want a baby," Terry sobbed. "I don't know if I can do it."

"That's up to you. You don't have to. Think about it. I know it's a hard choice."

Vanessa paused. "You could leave Larry, you know. Leave him and have the baby."

Terry looked stricken. "I couldn't leave Larry. I love him."

"Would he accept a child that wasn't his?"

"No, never! He'd kill me. Being a man, it's real important to him. If he knew I cheated . . . and I love him. I don't want to leave him." She looked like she was in agony.

Vanessa stood up. "I'm going to call my friend in the morning. Then it's up to you." She dropped some money on the table and slipped the tape recorder back into her purse. "Come on. Let's get out of here." Vanessa smiled. "I'll walk you to your car. Make sure the aliens don't get you."

Terry Warmouth didn't smile back. "I wish they would," she said.

* * *

Vanessa drove from the tavern to the offices of *Exposed* to finish a story about a giant rat that was stealing slum babies. The rat was supposed to be as big as a German Shepherd. Patrick Gorman, Vanessa's boss, had made up the story at the weekly staff meeting and assigned Vanessa to write it. Vanessa thought it was disgusting and had protested, finally getting Gorman to agree that she could substitute Terry Warmouth's alien abduction tale if it panned out. But it hadn't.

When Vanessa checked in with the security guard, he told her that no one else was around. That was fine with Vanessa. After her meeting with Terry Warmouth she craved solitude. Terry had exhausted her. Needy people always made Vanessa uncomfortable, which was odd considering her line of work. Supermarket tabloids lived off the exotic and psychotic tales told by people who had a tough time fitting into the real world. The people she interviewed talked themselves into believing in another Earth where the strange and wonderful occurred with enough frequency to let them escape from the demands of their drab existence.

Vanessa fixed herself a cup of coffee and toiled alone in the third-floor newsroom, accompanied only by the night noises that haunted the moldy old building where the minions of *Exposed* worked for low wages and no prestige. Vanessa's salary at *Exposed* was ridiculous, but she didn't need the money. What she did need was access to press credentials and data banks so she could proceed with her research.

Vanessa lived in a red brick row house in Adams Morgan. The area off 18th Northwest was funky and crowded with Ethiopian restaurants, jazz night clubs, bars and pizza parlors. Most nights, a rowdy college crowd packed the streets. Vanessa enjoyed the chaotic scene and her apartment was far enough from 18th to muffle the noise.

It was well after midnight when Vanessa opened the door to her fourth-floor apartment. She could afford better but had lived in Adams Morgan for years. Her neighbors kept to themselves and there was plenty of room for her research materials, which were mostly in the spare bedroom but had started to spill out into the living room. They consisted of the Warren Commission Report and books critical of it, tomes on the Roswell cover-up, and magazines with stories about CIA covert operations and the like. If a book or article alleged a government conspiracy Vanessa had it or had read it.

Vanessa flipped on the lights. The sight of a parcel with a return address from New York made her heart sink. The package was sitting on a small table in the foyer where Sam had stacked the mail. Vanessa carried it into the living room. She switched on the lamp beside the sofa and sat down to the groan of aged springs, placing the

package on top of the magazines and days' old
newspapers that littered her coffee table. She
stared at the package for a minute before ripping
off the brown paper wrapper. A letter lay on top
of her manuscript, covering the title and her
assertion of authorship. Vanessa stared at the letter before lifting it up. It was signed by an editor
at Parthenon Press who was supposed to be open
to new ideas and not afraid to challenge the
establishment. He had published a number of
controversial exposés of government cover-ups.
A book of his about a Marine who'd blown the
whistle on a training maneuver that had left two
recruits dead had just fallen off the bestseller list.

> *Dear Ms. Kohler:*
>
> *I read* Phantoms *with great interest. Unfor-
> tunately, I have decided that your book is
> not right for Parthenon Press. I wish you the
> best of luck placing your manuscript.*
>
> > *Yours Truly,*
> > *Walter Randolph*

Vanessa squeezed her eyes shut. She wanted to
fling the manuscript across the room and break
things. She fought to keep her rage in check and
tried to dissipate her bad energy by pacing the
worn carpet that covered her hardwood floor.
Something was going on here. It could be as simple as the fact that her press credentials were
from *Exposed* instead of *The New York Times*.

Of course, that level of credibility was closed to her. No reputable paper was going to hire someone with her history. But Vanessa was certain that something darker was at work.

Vanessa was a superb researcher and she had ferreted out Walter Randolph's unlisted home phone number as part of her background check on the editor when she was deciding to whom she would send her book. Vanessa dialed a Connecticut number and waited while the phone rang several times.

"Hello," answered a voice groggy with sleep.

"Walter Randolph?"

"Who is this?"

"Vanessa Kohler."

"Who?"

"*Phantoms*. You just rejected it."

"It's one-thirty in the morning, Ms. Kohler," Randolph answered, fighting to sound civil. "Would you please call me at work?"

"Who got to you?"

"I will not continue this discussion at this time."

"Was it my father? Did someone from the government visit you? Did they threaten you or buy you off?"

"I rejected your book because of insufficient documentation, Ms. Kohler. There was nothing sinister about the decision."

"You don't expect me to believe that?"

Vanessa heard a sigh on the other end of the line. "I don't know how you got this number, but a call at this hour is a violation of my privacy. I am going to end it in a moment, but, since you insist on knowing, not only have you failed to verify your rather dramatic claims, but your past makes it highly unlikely that any publishing house would give them any credence."

"My past?"

"Your mental history, Ms. Kohler. And now I must hang up. I have a hard day tomorrow and I need my sleep."

"Who told you I was hospitalized, who told you that?"

But Vanessa found herself talking to a dead line. She slammed down the phone, redialed and got a busy signal for her efforts. She was about to throw the phone at the wall when the front door opened and Sam Cutler walked in.

Vanessa was five-ten. Sam was a hair shorter but solid where Vanessa verged on anorexic. He wore a tight black T-shirt under a windbreaker and jeans. He was carrying his camera equipment. Sam's brown hair was receding up front but he had the eyesight of a bird of prey and was one of the few men Vanessa knew who'd never worn glasses.

Sam stopped in his tracks and Vanessa froze, arm cocked, the phone a moment away from destruction. Sam saw the manuscript on the coffee table.

"A rejection, huh? I was going to hide it until I came home. Then I got a call and forgot."

The arm holding the phone dropped to

Vanessa's side. "Someone got to the editor. I'm sure of it."

"How do you know that?" Sam asked, keeping his voice neutral because he knew the slightest sign of doubt where this subject was concerned could push Vanessa into an uncontrollable rage.

"He knew I was hospitalized. How did he find out about the sanatorium if someone didn't tell him?"

Sam crossed the room. He knew better than to try for physical contact now. He hoped that standing close would calm her.

"Maybe there was something in the papers," he suggested. "Your father is big news right now. There might have been a sidebar about the family."

Vanessa shook her head vehemently. "They want to discredit me. There's no way they're going to let this get out."

"Who is 'they'?" Sam asked, knowing he was treading on thin ice.

"My father, the military, the CIA. You don't think they were all involved? Once the truth gets out, Watergate will look like a tea party. They can't afford to let the public get even I hint of what I know."

Sam had been down this road before. "If that's true, why hasn't anyone tried to kill you?" he asked calmly. "Why haven't they stolen your manuscript? You haven't made a secret of what you're doing. Everyone knows about your book. You even tried to interview that guy at the CIA, and nothing happened."

Vanessa glared at Sam. "You don't understand how they work. They could steal my manuscript, but they know I'd just write the book again. And killing me would let everyone know that I was telling the truth."

"Everyone who? Come on, Vanessa. I respect what you're trying to do. I know you think you're right, but most people who know about this . . . Well, they don't believe it. And the CIA could make your death look like an accident, if they wanted to. You know that. No one would think you were killed to suppress your book. They'd think you were the victim of a hit and run or had a heart attack or something like that."

Vanessa slumped down on the couch. "You're right," she said. She sounded very tired. "Randolph is right." She closed her eyes and laid her head back. "I'm an ex-mental patient and I don't have a shred of evidence that proves that the Phantoms ever existed. They're all dead. There never was much evidence, anyway—just a few sheets of paper, and they're gone."

"You look all in, babe. Let's get to bed. You'll think better in the morning. You'll figure out what to do when your mind is clear."

Vanessa's hands curled into fists and her eyes snapped open. There was a vivid anger sizzling in them.

"He's going to win, Sam. He always wins and he's going to win again. I can't stop him, I never could."

"Ah, Van," Sam said, dropping onto the couch

beside her and wrapping an arm around her shoulder.

Vanessa's rage disappeared as quickly as it had appeared. She laid her head on Sam's shoulder and started to cry.

New York Times bestselling author

PHILLIP MARGOLIN

LOST LAKE

0-06-073502-3 | $25.95 US | $36.95 Can

Vanessa Kohler is a tabloid reporter in Washington, D.C. who writes fantastic stories about a vast government conspiracy that involves General Wingate, a popular presidential candidate. Most dismiss her as a crackpot paranoid, but Kohler knows that Wingate may not be the man he appears to be.

On sale 3/1/05
www.phillipmargolin.com

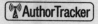
AuthorTracker